The

LONG
PATH
HOME

OTHER BOOKS BY THE AUTHOR

A GIRL DIVIDED

The
LONG
PATH
HOME

ELLEN LINDSETH

LAKE UNION
PUBLISHING

Text copyright © 2020 by Ellen Lindseth
All rights reserved.

Published by Lake Union Publishing, Seattle

www.apub.com

Amazon, the Amazon logo, and Lake Union Publishing are trademarks of Amazon.com, Inc., or its affiliates.

ISBN-13: 9781542004763
ISBN-10: 1542004764

Cover design by Faceout Studio, Tim Green

Printed in the United States of America

To D—
Keep reaching for those stars;
someday they'll be yours to hold.

Chapter 1

Snow-white feathers, delicate as moths, fluttered around her in the spotlight. The inevitable castoffs from her fans tickled her as they fell, whisper soft. A few lingered long enough to become stuck to Violet's sweaty skin. While the band's clarinet player wailed the melody, the large plumed fans in Violet's hands covered and uncovered her body in a practiced tease of fantasy and suggestion as she spun. Out in the dark house, the pulse of the audience's hearts pounded with expectation, urging her onward, driving her faster and faster. Perspiration trickled down her back as she let the audience's breath become her own. Her blood tingled, the heated gazes caressing her bare skin like an invisible lover's.

Exhilaration sang through her veins. Gone were the nagging exhaustion and pain of the past few weeks. Gone was all worry about the war that seemed no closer to ending than it had three years ago. Self-recrimination, regret, loneliness . . . all gone. She was—in this moment—loved, adored . . . accepted.

The percussionist picked up the pace, cuing the climax. One breath. Two. She sucked in the smoky blue air, even though it made her lungs burn. Then all at once she stopped her spin, her hands dropping to her sides, baring all. Right on cue, a stagehand cut the lights, leaving her enveloped in a steamy, sultry darkness. The audience roared to life, as they always did. The storm of masculine voices, catcalls and whistles, and the clapping and stomping of large, heavy feet both awed and thrilled her.

Reveling in the moment, she closed her eyes and soaked in the sounds of all that love and appreciation, let it fill every crack of her battered soul. Let it reverberate in her bones.

She savored the high, knowing it would fade all too soon.

Sal would be annoyed, of course, by her delay in clearing the stage, but he would also forgive her. He always did. Or he would once he finished counting the night's take. She was one of the revue's most dependable draws.

On the other hand, based on what she could hear out in the dark house, the crowd was smaller tonight than it had been even a month ago. There was just no getting around the fact that more and more boys were being called up on account of the war.

Her elation faded as reality shouldered its way back in. The audience continued to stomp and whistle, but she could almost feel the silence of the empty seats. The adoration of dwindling numbers—no matter how heartfelt—wouldn't keep the lights on. At some point the well would run dry. And then, no matter how much Sal loved her, the show would close and she would be let go. And be back on the streets, without a dime to her name. Again.

Not thinking about that tonight, Vi.

Lifting her chin, she called up her performer's high again and sauntered off the stage as if she didn't have a care in the world. A teenage stagehand waited behind the heavy velvet curtain to take her fans. His gaze never made it above her breasts, which were naked, save for the glittery, star-shaped patches glued to her nipples. He seemed mesmerized by the way they swayed with each step.

Once, years ago, walking around basically naked, exposed to the ogling of unfamiliar men, would have distressed her. Now she could barely remember why it had bothered her. Strange what a girl could get used to when her survival depended on it.

Sal glared briefly over his spectacles at her as she walked by, making sure she knew he was displeased by her tardy departure. Then his attention returned to the trio of female jugglers who had taken the stage. Relieved that he didn't seem too upset, she grabbed her threadbare silk robe off a painted wooden moon and headed toward the dressing room. Despite the crush of backstage workers, she carried the garment over her arm, reluctant to put it on. The air was so stiflingly hot and humid, she couldn't bear the idea of fabric on her skin, no matter how light or silky.

August in Chicago was always beastly hot, but this past week had been particularly bad. Sal had finally broken down and installed two big electric fans backstage yesterday to keep the performers from passing out before they even reached the stage. Still, rumors had been circulating that he was considering temporarily halting performances until the heat wave broke. Not only was the sweltering heat hard on the performers but it kept customers away, too.

Vi hoped it wouldn't come to that. She had bills to pay, and with the recent uptick in prices thanks to everything a girl might want—like shoes, fabric, coffee, and even bacon—being rationed, she couldn't afford to miss a single night of work.

A cadre of sequined, giggling dancers careened into her, enveloping her in a cloud of stale sweat and cheap perfume. Vi let them pass, too exhausted and drained by the heat to insist on the courtesy of letting her go first, which was due to her as one of the show's stars. She huffed a bitter laugh at the thought. *Star? Sure* . . . Star of a two-bit vaudeville whose claim to fame was naked chorus girls. *Oh, how the mighty have fallen.* Her younger, more idealistic self would've been incensed if she could see Violet now.

Chasing the thought away and wanting nothing more than to get back to the boardinghouse so she could soak her aching feet in Epsom salts, she pulled back the drape to her dressing room and then stopped in alarm.

A burly figure stood by her vanity, idly turning a fedora in his hands. He stared at the scarred surface as if the secret to immortality were scrawled there. Then he glanced up, and Vi's skin goose pimpled at the lust in his dark eyes.

She swallowed hard, her near nakedness no longer feeling so benign. "Tony, long time no see. What are you doing here? I thought you were working in California these days, keeping those Hollywood director types in line."

In her more naive days, before she had started working at the Palace, she had thought the repeal of Prohibition some twenty years ago had rendered the Mob irrelevant. She had been wrong. Like a veritable cockroach, it had merely moved on to more hospitable surroundings, namely the entertainment business. And not just the more adult types of entertainment, such as striptease and prostitution. She had soon learned that there was hardly a movie palace or cinema left in America that didn't answer to the Mob in some fashion or another. Hollywood itself had been forced to fall in line, often paying significant amounts for the "privilege" of having their films screened before a paying public, with an additional fee being collected by the Mob for each ticket bought.

With the war on and citizens desperate for an escape from reality, the venture had turned out far more profitable than bootlegging had ever been.

"I was, but I had some business to attend to here in town, so I thought I'd stop by and see my old friend Lily Lamour." A slow smile spread across Tony Vecchione's thick lips as the fedora stilled in his hands. "Look at you, Lil. An angel come down to earth." His black gaze glittered dangerously as it slid over her body. She barely repressed a shudder. He was dressed flawlessly as always, the starch in his collar points heavy enough to withstand the terrible humidity. But in the incandescent glow of her dressing lights, his olive skin glistened with sweat from the heat. She also noted that, despite the late hour, his jaw lacked its usual dark shadow of beard stubble, which meant he had recently shaved, and likely for her. Nausea built in her stomach at the implication of that.

She forced herself to move forward. "Such pretty words, Tony, but I'm afraid you're wasting your time if you're hoping for sex. I only have time for my career these days."

"So Sal said."

"Then why are you here?" It took all her acting chops to walk nonchalantly past the Mob hit man, but she managed to pull it off and reach her vanity before her knees gave way. She collapsed onto the small stool and turned toward the mirror.

He laughed. "Who said I was only lookin' for sex?"

"That's what you wanted the last time we chatted." Her fingers trembled as she wiped off her stage makeup.

"Ah, Lily," he said with another low laugh, using her stage name like everyone else in Chicago. She glanced at him in the mirror, not wanting to make eye contact but also afraid not to. He was the very definition of terrifying. "Is that why you invented that jealous boyfriend to keep me at arm's length? And yes, I know he was made up. I checked around after I left."

"It seemed the prudent thing to do."

"It was also unnecessary, because you misunderstood my intent."

He leaned down so his face was close to hers in the mirror, his ear brushing against her peroxide-blonde hair. His dark, predatory gaze met her wide green one in the silvered glass. "I had a more permanent arrangement in mind. One where a pretty doll like you gets a much better deal outta life than anything Sal can offer. Come with me tonight. Let me show you a good time. Listen to my proposal. I think you'll find it worth your while."

"I see." She leaned away and pulled a facial tissue from the box on her vanity, all the while keeping him in her peripheral view, much as she would a copperhead snake. Despite his easy smile, his body practically vibrated with energy, as if his blood were already well up. Which it likely was, given that she was sitting basically naked in front of him; that didn't bode well should she try to reject him.

She decided to try deflection first. "Should you even be here? I thought the reason you left Chicago was to get the Feds off your tail."

He shrugged, his gaze dropping to the reflection of her admittedly bountiful breasts. "I got a loose end I need to clean up. You know, business. But not tonight. Tonight"—he exhaled an invisible stream of air down her neck, and she fought the urge to bolt—"I got other plans."

He straightened abruptly and then ran a surprisingly gentle fingertip up her spine. Her body shivered, confused about whether to respond.

At first glance a gal might think, given Tony's expensive pinstriped suit, his stylish silk tie and pocket handkerchief that added just the right dash of color, and the impossibly white shirt, that he was a real catch. He also smelled good, if one liked spicy aftershaves, and paid meticulous attention to the details of male grooming, right down to the slicked-back gloss of his Brylcreemed hair.

But Vi wasn't swayed by any of that. She could never get past the reptilian coldness lurking in his nearly black eyes.

Nor could she get past what he did for a living. While usually not one to throw stones at other people's choice of work, Vi did have a problem with Tony's.

And yes, she was completely aware that as someone who took her clothes off for money, she was hardly the model of virtue. But killing people just because your boss told you to, people you had no personal beef with? That was flat-out wrong. At least in her book. Even if your boss was the head of the Outfit, Chicago's branch of the Mob.

He lowered his head again and nuzzled her temple. "So what's it gonna be, Miss Lily Lamour? My place or yours?"

For a moment she couldn't even respond, she was so paralyzed by the sight of their faces together, pale and dark, bleached blonde stark against midnight black, her bright green eyes wide next to his fathomless black. It was like a pictorial representation of good and evil, except that neither one of them was on the right side of morality.

He licked the top edge of her ear. The awful, unwelcome feel of his tongue on her skin broke her paralysis. She jumped to her feet and then hurried to the garment rack by the door. "I don't do permanent arrangements, either."

He stalked her, his voice silky, soft . . . deadly. "Lily, are you rejecting me?"

Ice swept through her blood. "Not necessarily," she said, placatingly. "But I'm of no use to you tonight. It's—it's the wrong time of the month, if you catch my meaning." Her tongue almost tripped on the lie. She prayed he wouldn't ask for proof.

He huffed in amusement. "Lily, you should know better than to think a little blood would repulse me."

Swallowing a surge of panic, she tried a different tack. "I'm also so exhausted from the performance, I can hardly stay awake. Perhaps we could postpone until the next time you're in town?"

"Sweetheart," he said softly, the lethal edge in his voice chilling her. "You know patience isn't my strong suit."

"Yes, I mean, I know. But I want to be sure I'm in the proper state of mind to hear you out. You deserve a girl's full attention."

The muscle twitching in his jaw told her he wasn't buying it.

She tried again. "How about tomorrow night after the show? I'll take a nap in the afternoon so I'm not so tired, and perhaps it will be cooler . . . What do you say? We can have a couple of drinks, get to know one another a bit. If I'm to discuss creating a mutually satisfactory arrangement, I feel like I should know you better."

She knew she was babbling but couldn't make herself stop.

"A couple of drinks." He gave her a long, considering look.

"Yes. You know, liquid courage and all that."

Another heart-stopping moment passed in silence. Then he nodded slowly. "All right, if that's what you want. But I'm not in the mood to be alone tonight, so we're gonna have those drinks now."

"I'm not exactly dressed," Vi pointed out, hoping any delay would give her time to think of a way out of her predicament. "Give a girl fifteen minutes?"

His soulless gaze ran down her body, a dull flush of excitement darkening his cheeks. Vi repressed a shudder. "As much as I prefer you this way, I'll allow you five minutes. But that's it. As I said, I'm not a patient man."

"Five minutes, perfect. And if you wouldn't mind, I don't want to hold our discussion in public; nor do I want to disturb my landlady so late at night. Perhaps we could go to your place? I'm fine with taking a taxi home afterward."

Not that his place was an oasis of safety, but at least it would offer them a little privacy. She didn't care to become known as Tony's moll. Her reputation was questionable enough.

Appreciation briefly warmed his obsidian eyes. "That's what I like about you, Lily—all sensibility, yet with the morals of an alley cat."

She twisted her lips into what she hoped was a smile. "Such sweet talk, Tony. So romantic! Now if you'll excuse me, somebody gave me only five minutes, and you're delaying me."

Tony chuckled but got the hint and left.

The moment the curtain fell closed behind him, Vi ran back to her vanity and yanked open the bottom drawer. Frantically, she dug through the assorted G-strings and nipple patches until she found a small amber glass bottle. Thank heavens she hadn't accidentally thrown it out. A gift from her landlady, who had also taught her how to make a decent Mickey Finn with it, the knockout drops had saved her from being raped more than once.

Some fellows just refused to believe she had no interest in selling her body on the side, especially given her line of work. They would accost her backstage, or follow her home, or shadow her around town. Rather than risk being injured by a rejected suitor, which could endanger her career, she would politely agree to a drink, preferably at a hotel or at their place, and then slip them a Mickey Finn at some point in the evening. The next time they met, she always thanked them for a lovely time and then regretfully mentioned she had a policy of no repeat business. It only created attachments that couldn't go anywhere, as they could well imagine, yes?

Of course, she had turned tricks back at the beginning, when she had been broke and starving. A lot of girls did when they first started out. Food didn't come cheap in Chicago. But once she had started moving up the ranks from chorus girl to solo stripper to headliner, she had also started earning enough dough to be choosy about her lovers. Very choosy. As in she slept only with fellows for whom cash inducements weren't needed and whose careers didn't morally repel her.

Tony failed in both categories.

She held the fragile bottle up to the light. Relief flooded her as she saw there was still a bit of liquid left inside. With any luck it would be enough, though Tony wasn't exactly a small man.

The trick would be finding a way to hide the bottle somewhere on her person until she was ready for it.

She eyed her garment rack, assessing and discarding dresses in rapid succession. The jade green silk had a lovely low neckline that would make it easy to stash the bottle between her breasts but would also draw Tony's eyes to her cleavage, which would be problematic if the bottle left a bump.

The black satin, on the other hand . . . was a backless sheath that would guarantee his attention stayed firmly on her derriere. The problem was the bodice was a single piece of fabric from neck to waist, leaving no easy way to access the bottle once hidden, since the whole dress was held up by the thin strap around her neck. But if she tied a sash around her waist, she could discreetly tuck the bottle in it. Or perhaps it would be safer in her clutch.

Hurriedly, she ripped the fabric patches off her nipples. The sharp sting as the glue let go made her eyes water as always. Blinking to clear her vision, she slipped the black dress off its hanger and threw it over her head. She didn't bother with a foundation garment, her stomach sufficiently flat from a persistent lack of food. Nor did she even take time to exchange her G-string for regular panties. The risk of Tony coming to collect her before she was ready pulsed like acid through her veins.

She quickly tied a red silk sash around her waist, though it honestly ruined the lines of the dress, slipped on a pair of black wedges, and tucked the amber bottle along with a tube of lipstick into her gold sequined clutch. With thirty seconds to spare, she whirled to the mirror and checked her appearance. She tucked a platinum-blonde curl back in place and inspected her bright-red lipstick as she worked to slow her panicked breathing. Thank the stars she hadn't had a chance to remove her false eyelashes. Even though they made her eyes itch and were often the first thing she took off after a performance, men seemed utterly enchanted by them. And she was all about enchanting Tony into downing his doctored drink without complaint.

The dressing curtain jerked open, and she jumped. Pasting a smile on her lips, she smoothed her dress as Tony gave her a thorough once-over, her heart ready to beat right out of her chest.

He scowled. "Lose the sash."

Praying she wasn't signing her death warrant, she straightened her spine like a queen and looked him right in the eye. "No."

Chapter 2

"It's all the rage now, and I either keep it or the date is off," Vi continued into the shocked silence that had followed her small act of rebellion.

For a long moment he stared at her as the muffled music of the show continued on the other side of the curtain. She hardly dared breathe, terrified that each passing second might prove her last. Then, as she had hoped, his libido won out over his offended sartorial senses, and the tension left his shoulders.

"Fine, but for the record, I don't like mouthy dolls who tell me no."

Her pulse skittered at the warning, but she managed to keep her expression smooth as she stepped forward. "Then we're in agreement, because I don't like being told no, either."

He was still scowling as he gestured for her to lead the way, but at least her death no longer seemed imminent. She batted her eyelashes at him as she passed, hoping to further ease the tension between them. Behind her she heard him chuckle, and her spirits dared to lift a little.

"God, I love bold women." His fingers grabbed her right butt cheek and gave it a hard squeeze. She bit back on a tart response even as her eyes watered. Her plan would work best if he didn't expect any resistance on her part. As long as she could play it cool for the first part of the night, she would be home free.

And cool was exactly how she played it for the next thirty minutes, right up to when Tony escorted her through a tidy, fenced-in yard to the freshly painted door of an attractive if small brick house. While he unlocked it, Vi looked around at the shadowy environs. Illuminated by only moonlight, with the crickets in full song, the quiet residential street seemed an unlikely place for a Mob hit man. But then again, maybe not. She supposed even the worst of humanity longed for a bit of peace now and then. Just as he might long to show off his ill-gotten wealth through nice clothes or a shiny black sedan like the one currently parked by the curb.

"After you, sweetheart." Tony held the screen door out of the way.

Trying not to feel like she was being invited to her execution, Vi glided past him and into the dark house. Behind her, Tony flicked on a switch, and light filled the living room. Surprise nicked her again. Somebody with obvious taste had decorated the room in cocoa brown and reddish orange with soft ivory accents. White lilies, artfully arranged in a Lalique-style vase, filled the room with their exotic fragrance. She somehow doubted Tony had put them there.

"If you don't like the furniture, I can return it," Tony said, coming to stand behind her. "I just had it delivered yesterday, but I'm sure the store won't mind taking it back if I tell 'em to."

"Pardon?" She couldn't have heard him correctly.

"All this." He gestured toward the interior. "It's yours, Lily. I've wanted to buy it for you since the first moment I saw you onstage six months ago, and Sal warned me you wouldn't come cheap. But to my mind, a doll as fine as you is worth the expense."

She was already shaking her head before he even had a chance to finish. "No, wait . . . you've got me all wrong. I'm not looking for a sugar daddy—"

"You live in a rented room on the South Side, Lil, whereas this whole house could be yours, rent-free. Which you're gonna need, unless you've got a stash of dough squirreled away somewhere that I don't know about. Because I've looked into your finances and you won't last long on your own after the show closes—"

"After it what?" Her ears buzzed slightly, as if she might faint. "What in heaven's name are you talking about?"

"The show, Lil. It's closing next week, when the month is up. The bosses want to stage something more family friendly so as to bring in more revenue. And to take some of the heat off the club, too."

"Who told you this?"

He stripped off his suit coat and tossed it over a cream-and-brown-striped armchair. "Frank. I talked to him yesterday, and he said it's a done deal."

And Frank, being the head of the Outfit's accounting and finances, would know.

Violet sank onto the floral couch, her thoughts spinning. "That's fine. Shows open and close all the time. There's always somebody hiring." Though the venues likely wouldn't be as nice as the Palace. "I can check with Bobby Lee over at the Heights. He likes my work."

Tony crossed to the polished walnut sideboard and started to pour himself a drink. "You're assuming I'll let you continue working. Which I won't."

She jerked her head up. "I wasn't aware I had given you a say in what I do."

He glanced at her, his expression smooth. "That's what we're here to discuss tonight."

"Excuse me? I thought I was here for a drink and maybe a discussion about future get-togethers. Because the only person who gets to run my life is me, and only me."

He dismissed her words with a wave. "You and I both know if I say you don't work, there's not a venue in town that'll dare hire you. Not even if you decide to go legit."

"Then I'll get a job doing something else. I can waitress or sell perfume."

"The family doesn't only handle entertainment, Lil. You know that. Its reach is wide."

"Not that wide. Not all of Chicago is in the Outfit's hands," she said hotly, even as she wondered if that were true. "And there are still other cities where I could work."

He snorted derisively. "Sure. You and I both know you won't leave. Your son is here. And yeah, I know all about little Jimmy, so don't bother denying it."

Shock stole her breath. It was her deepest fear come true. She had worked so hard to keep the Tonys of the world away from Jimmy, hoping the taint of her sins would never touch him. She had never breathed a word of his existence to anyone but Sal, who had helped her during those dark months. But never to the other dancers, nor to her landlady, nor to even her family . . .

Except she had told the bank, where she had set up a savings account in his name. Her heart sank at her unwitting mistake.

"You won't hurt him?" she asked finally.

"Don't worry. He's fine and he'll stay that way, assuming we reach an acceptable agreement."

She closed her eyes, despair bitter on her tongue. "Which is?"

"I should think it would be obvious to a bright doll like you."

She opened her eyes to find him standing right in front of her. "You want me to marry you?"

"Lily," he said disapprovingly. "You know better than to think I'd marry a showgirl."

"Right. Silly me." She huffed a pained laugh. *Oh, the irony of being considered too sullied to make a suitable wife to a Mob hit man.* It was like spoiled icing on the cake ruins of her life. "I forgot I'm not the sort of girl a fellow takes home to Mama."

"No, you're not," he said, not unkindly, as he caressed her cheek. She barely repressed her flinch. "*You* are the kind of girl that makes wise men foolish. The kind every fellow dreams of having in his bed all day and all night. Ready and willing to do whatever he asks, things no wife would dream of doing."

Nausea twisted her gut. "Gee, I'm flattered you think so highly of me."

"You have no idea," he said, totally missing her sarcasm. "The fact that other men stare at you night after night makes my blood boil. You were meant to be mine, Lil. Mine and mine alone."

She shuddered and leaned away, rubbing her arms. "Yes, well . . . mind if I make myself a drink?"

He blinked. "Forgive me. Where are my manners? Let me fix you one so we can toast our future."

She jumped to her feet as he turned toward the sideboard. "No! No, let me. Please. I'm very . . . particular about my spirits."

His gaze burned on her skin as she brushed past him.

"I didn't know you were a booze connoisseur," he said, surprise clear in his voice.

"Oh yes. I learned as a little girl at my father's knee," she said, keeping her back to him. A cold sweat prickled between her shoulder blades as she turned over one of the clean glasses. Her heart beat so hard and fast she was sure he must hear it. "How 'bout I make you one, too? I'm told I make a swell drink. Just the kind of libation a big, strong man like you might appreciate."

"Your dad some kind of bootlegger?"

"Not exactly." She reached for a crystal decanter and removed the stopper. A delicate sniff revealed it contained gin. Gin that was as dry as the desert. Perfect.

"Then what was he?" His husky voice was laced with suspicion, something she needed to allay as fast as possible.

She tossed a careless smile over her shoulder and winked. "A banker who knew how to keep his best customers happy even as they lost money. Now am I making you that drink or not?"

Her father would have been horrified if he'd heard her. He was one of the most honest, caring, generous people she knew. And a teetotaler. Or at least he had been last time she'd been home. With her luck, her disappearance may have led him to abuse the bottle. Another sin on a long list of them for which she would someday have to atone.

Tony relaxed and drained his glass. He chuckled as he placed his now empty glass on the sideboard next to her. "Your *papà* sounds like my kinda guy. Tell me, what does he think of his little girl stripping for a living?"

"Oh, he doesn't know," she said as airily as she could as she moved the glass closer. *And with any luck he never will,* she added silently. Just like he would never learn she'd gotten knocked up by her sister's boyfriend. If she hadn't been able to face his disappointment over that, there was no way she'd be able to tell him she now strutted buck naked onstage.

That development would die with her and never sully her father's ears.

She poured each of them two generous shots of gin and then a splash of dry vermouth. *Now for the finishing touch . . .*

"Do you have any ice, Tony? On a hot night like this, it would be just the thing."

"Absolutely, sweetheart. Anything you want." He pinched her ass, and she jumped, almost spilling vermouth onto the polished wood. He made an approving sound. "So responsive. Sure you want that drink?"

"Do bees like honey?" she said sweetly, despite the revulsion clogging her throat. "Ice, please."

She held her breath as he slunk off toward what she assumed was the kitchen. The second he disappeared, she opened her clutch and pulled out the amber bottle. Experience had taught her it was a fine line between adding enough to knock someone out and making the drink unpalatable. Unfortunately, Tony was larger than most, which meant she might have to increase the dosage more than she liked. But it was either take the risk of having him taste the drug or else face the prospect of having to have sex with the man. Bile crawled up her throat in horror at the thought of having such a soulless killer inside her body.

She would rather throw herself in front of a train.

Leather soles squeaked nearby. Out of time, Vi hurriedly added what she hoped was the correct number of drops, then stuffed the vial into her sash. Thank goodness she had thought to wear it, as he had given her no time to return the bottle to her clutch.

"Here you are, sweetheart."

"Thanks." She swizzled the ice thoroughly into each glass, letting the cold further dampen the taste. She took care to do Tony's drink last, so as not to cross-contaminate. No use blurring her senses when she needed them most. Picking up the now-sweating glasses, she turned to offer one to Tony. A smile curved her lips. "To us."

He lifted his glass to hers in silent toast. "Bottoms up. The night isn't getting any younger, and I, unfortunately, have an appointment early tomorrow."

Her fingers tightened on the delicate crystal glass as her stomach twisted in distress for whomever was on the other end of that appointment. It likely wasn't going to go well for them. She took a large sip of her drink. The icy bite of the cocktail soothed and refreshed her, and it took a real effort not to gulp it down, which wouldn't help matters at all.

If she wanted to survive the night, she was going to need a clear head.

Tony, following her lead, took a large swallow of his own drink and then grimaced. "What the hell did you put in this?"

"Oh, I'm sorry. Did I make it too strong?" she asked, rounding her eyes in mock concern. As she'd hoped, his fragile male ego defended itself immediately.

"No. I just prefer my drinks to be like my women: sweet, not bitter." He laughed at his joke, and Vi tried to do the same. Then her smile became genuine as he proceeded to down the rest of the drink in a single go. He smacked his lips. "Ah, not so bad after all."

"It's an acquired taste," she agreed, her mood steadily improving. Combined with the effects of his first drink, the knockout drops would overtake him any minute now. She was almost free. There was still tomorrow for her to worry about, but that was tomorrow.

After taking a healthy swallow of her own drink for courage, she set the glass aside and gazed at her target with sultry intent. She sauntered over, exaggerating the swish of her hips to capture his attention. The heat and the alcohol swirled in her stomach uneasily as she ran her fingers lightly down his shirtfront, but she didn't retreat. She had a job to do. A stage to set.

"Shall we sit? I feel like there's so much we should discuss."

He caught her hand. "How 'bout we save the talk for later?"

"Tsk, tsk." She forced herself to smile. "Business before pleasure. After all, a gal has to look out for her best interests. Same as you."

"Fine. But let's skip the niceties. Anything you want, within reason, is yours in exchange for me getting what I want."

"Except no ring," she said sarcastically, even though there was no way in hell she would marry someone like Tony Vecchione. She would rather die a shriveled-up old maid.

"If it comes with a leg shackle, no. Otherwise, you can have all the rings you want. Hell, put rings on your toes. I don't care." He dropped his head and nuzzled her neck. "Jesus, Lily—you smell so good."

"That's nice." She wedged her arm between them. "There's still something else I want to discuss."

"You talk." He licked her skin, leaving a damp, slimy trail. Vi's stomach lurched. "I'll listen."

"I'm serious," she said, giving him a little push. To her surprise, he stumbled slightly. Her mood skyrocketed. Hallelujah—the drug was starting to take effect.

Tony lifted his head, his eyes narrowing with suspicion. Apparently, she wasn't the only one who had noticed his rapidly eroding coordination. "What's going on?"

She widened her eyes. "Whatever do you mean?"

"I mean I wasn't this damn exhausted when I got here. What did you do to me?"

"Nothing. I swear," she answered, alarmed and concerned. Or she hoped that's how he would read her act. *Lord above, let him buy it,* she prayed, holding her breath. Because if he didn't, she was dead.

He shook his head as if to clear it and swayed.

She looped his arm around her shoulders to support him and then nearly staggered under his weight as he leaned into her. "Couch, Tony. Now."

The fear in her voice now wasn't faked. If he fell onto the floor, there was no way she would be able to move him. And Tony waking up on the floor tomorrow morning would severely diminish any chance of him believing they had spent a passionate night together.

"Damn you, Lily. I'll get you for thish," he said, his words slurring. "Don't think I won't."

"It wasn't me. It's the heat, like you said. You sit here, and I'll go get a cool cloth. You'll be fine in two shakes of a lamb's tail. Just wait and see." She did her best to angle him correctly as he collapsed like a sack of wet cement onto the sofa cushions. Not a moment too soon, either.

His head lolled back, his eyes rolling up into his head as she heaved him into a proper seated position. Panting with exertion, she eyed the now-unconscious Tony. Except for the faint rise and fall of his chest, he didn't move.

Lord above, she had done it!

Time for the next step of the plan. Cautiously, as if she were working with a rabid animal, she loosened his tie and unbuttoned his starched white shirt. She watched his eyelids for any fluttering signs of awareness as she switched to unfastening his pants. Nothing. Emboldened but still wary, she spread the waistband open and undid his suspenders. All she had left to do was to pull the shirttail free and then slide his pants and underwear down to his ankles.

While the first task required a bit of man wrangling, the last one was like wrestling with a rock slab. A rock slab with soft, squishy parts that she didn't want to touch but would have to.

Once she had finished rearranging his clothing, she blew a stray strand of hair out of her face and mentally prepared herself for the final and key part of the faux performance. Normally she took a certain perverse pleasure in fooling a would-be Casanova into thinking he had been victorious. This time, all she felt was revulsion. Aware of every minute passing, she retrieved the tube of lipstick from her clutch, then painted her lips and then the inside of her thumb and forefinger.

She turned back to the disheveled form of Tony and hesitated.

Don't think, just do. Come on, Vi.

Sucking in a deep breath, she reached down and smeared what she hoped would be enough lipstick on his exposed anatomy to suggest a certain sex act, one she was supremely glad she hadn't had to perform tonight. A shudder of disgust racked her as she worked. When she was done, she spread his legs wider, into a vee, truly tempted to add injury to insult. Except she had learned a few things while living on her own, and the wisdom of avoiding unnecessary risks was near the top of the list.

On the other hand, he had threatened not only her but Jimmy, and for that the risk was almost worth it. Almost.

With a sigh of regret, she leaned forward and whispered in his ear. "Fair warning: if you so much as touch a single hair on my son, I'll castrate you, Antonio Vecchione. *Capisci?*"

He didn't respond; nor had she expected him to.

She pressed an angry kiss on his mouth to stain it red with lipstick and then trailed red lip prints across his cheeks, chin, neck, and even the collar of his shirt. Tony snored softly but was otherwise as limp as a discarded bar towel.

Satisfied that there was now enough evidence to make Tony believe he'd had a good time, even if he couldn't remember any of it, she picked up his glass and carried it to the kitchen. After dumping the ice into the sink and giving the glass a thorough rinse with water, she took it back to the living room and poured half of her unadulterated drink into it. Now there were two glasses of an innocent, if very alcoholic, drink, one with lipstick prints that matched those on his collar and elsewhere.

Not wanting to stick around, she made a quick phone call, and within minutes a taxi arrived. As she pulled the front door shut behind her, she worried a little that it would remain unlocked through the night. Then she dismissed her concern. No one would dare rob a Mob assassin, not unless they had a death wish. And it wasn't like the house was in a bad part of town. Quite the opposite, in fact.

After getting into the back of the cab, she settled wearily onto the fabric seat and sorted through the worries all clamoring for attention. What Tony might do next in his pursuit of her could wait, since he'd likely be leaving town in the next few days. That he knew about Jimmy was a concern that could also wait, for the same reason. What she really needed to focus on was that the club might be closing soon. No club meant no job. And then there was Tony's threat to blackball her, effectively ending her dance career. Surely Sal would have some advice on that.

Whatever Sal suggested she do, she would, since she trusted him like no one else. Sal was the one who had taken her under his wing, calling her the daughter he'd never had but always wanted. Likely because she was ambitious, like him, better educated than the other girls, and keener on learning the business end of vaudeville.

Stripping paid only while one was young and beautiful, which meant she had another five years left, maybe ten at best. Then she would have to find a different line of employment if she wanted to eat, though she'd be damned if she'd ever stoop to selling her body again. Not that she judged those girls who still did. The cash had been nice, no doubt about it.

The problem was that fellows could get rough, or possessive. She'd had enough close calls during those first few years that, once she was able to pay rent on her dance wages alone, she had made the decision to only "lighten the spirits" of men she actually liked and found desirable. And if they gifted her with presents or cash in return—well, where was the harm in that? It wasn't like she had to safeguard her virginity for a husband. Anyone willing to marry a burlesque star would hardly expect an intact hymen.

There was definitely something to be said for having complete control over who she shared her body with. She wanted to live to a ripe old age, which meant minimizing risks where she could. No, her days of turning tricks were over. She would put herself through secretarial school first, entombing herself in a windowless office if she couldn't find some kind of stage work.

But those were worries for tomorrow. For now, she let herself relax into a daydream about getting back to her apartment and into pajamas and then soaking her feet in a bath of Epsom salts. A moment of bliss put off too long already tonight, and one she couldn't wait to attain.

Then maybe later, before bed, she would pull out her secret stash of photographs and newspaper clippings of her career pre-Jimmy and reminisce about the past. She needed to return the bankbook to the pile, in any case. It would also help keep her from worrying about Tony's reaction when he woke up and found himself alone. There was nothing she could do about it tonight, so she might as well leave it for tomorrow.

After all, tomorrow was another day.

Chapter 3

"Steamy" and "sultry" were usually considered good things in Vi's world. However, when the words were being applied to the current atmospheric conditions, not her performance, and it was only nine in the morning? Not so much.

Vi shifted on the wooden park bench and fanned herself, hoping to create even an illusion of a breeze. Her skin was as wet as if she had fallen in the Chicago River. Thank heaven she had been able to snag a seat beneath a huge elm tree. The shade from the broad, leafy canopy was the only thing keeping her from melting into a puddle of sweat.

The view made up for it, though. In front of her, seemingly unbothered by the heat, a gleeful, noisy band of little girls in dresses and boys in short pants played on the swings and teeter-totters while their nannies, mothers, or grandmothers wilted nearby. Not as many adults as there had been when Vi had first started coming to the park three years ago. The war had pulled so many parents into its machinery, children often came by themselves these days.

Vi thanked her lucky stars that her own son hadn't been similarly abandoned. Of course, she didn't know the family situation in detail, but the familiar presence of the nanny, dressed as always in a plain, drab dress, reassured her that he was still being well taken care of.

She hadn't always been so sure. At first, she had taken the orphanage's advice to forget about her baby. The first year had been lost to grief and survival anyway. But the second year had given rise to a deep and unquenchable fear that she had made a mistake. She had begged Sal to find her a way to see her baby again. Not so she could steal him away and raise him herself, though she had become more financially stable. Rather, to reassure herself she had done the right thing, to quiet the horrible, aching sense of loss that occasionally gripped her.

Against Sal's better judgment, he had given in to her repeated appeals for assistance and helped her to get the name and address of Jimmy's family by paying off the right people at the adoption agency. His caveat had been she could never contact the family or Jimmy. She had agreed, but with her fingers crossed behind her back. She had no intention of directly interfering with the family. But someday she would like to anonymously give him something, a small endowment, as proof of her undying love for him, her baby, the one person she valued above everything else in this world.

In the meantime, she had spent her mornings off shadowing the building where her son lived, learning the family's habits. When the nanny had begun taking her little charge to the nearby park every Tuesday and Thursday morning, Vi's schedule became cemented. Faithfully, every week for the past year, she had come to quietly watch the small miracle she had created grow and flourish.

As Jimmy ran by, his high-pitched voice filled with the innocent joyousness of youth, Vi's heart melted. The dappled sunlight brought out the red highlights in his russet hair that was so like her own—at least when hers wasn't bleached. The brown eyes were his father's, but she would never hold that against her son. Jimmy was nothing short of a marvel, a glimmer of perfection in her otherwise screwed-up life.

The familiar, bittersweet dream gripped her, of Jimmy running up to her instead of the nanny, his eyes bright with intelligence and wonder as he proudly showed her whatever treasure he had found in the grass—or grabbing her hand and towing her over to the swings so she could push him.

Oh, how she loved him. She would do anything for him. Absolutely anything. Even tear herself in two so he would have the chance to live a life far above what she had to offer. So far above that her sins would never touch him.

"He's a handsome boy."

Startled, she stiffened as Sal sank wearily onto the bench beside her. "Sal? What are you doing here?"

She couldn't remember the last time she had seen him outside the shadowy confines of the club.

"A better question would be what are you doing here?" he rasped, his voice rough from a lifetime of cigarettes. He leaned forward and placed his elbows on his knees, his hands loosely steepled as he watched the children. "You do know the police are out looking for you, yes?"

"I beg your pardon?" The stifling heat of the morning disappeared beneath a wash of ice. "Sal, that's nothing to joke about!"

His sad, dark eyes gave her a sidelong glance from behind his wire-rimmed spectacles. "Would I joke about something like that? To you, who I love like my own flesh and blood?"

"Yes, actually. If you thought it would get you something." She raised an eyebrow at him. "Remember when you said they'd caught the snake that had escaped during Howie's act, and I found it later, curled up in my red costume?"

He shrugged. "You were upset, and I needed you onstage."

"Exactly. So what's the angle this time? You want me to tame down my act?" Though she couldn't imagine why or what statute she had broken. Everything that needed covering had been.

Sal didn't answer. Instead, he studied the children on the playground, his lips set in a grim line. Her heart pounded as the seconds passed, her dread building with the realization he might not have been kidding.

"Rumor has it you were with Tony Vecchione last night," he said, "a rumor I find hard to believe since I know how you feel about his . . . business."

"We did go to his house to discuss my . . . my future, I suppose you could say. So, yes. I was with him for a while, but not long." Fear pooled in her stomach like lead. "Don't tell me the Feds saw us? God damn it. Now they think I'm his moll, don't they?"

"Was anyone else there with you?" Sal's expression was unusually grave.

"No, why?" she asked, confused now. She could have sworn Tony would be knocked out for several hours, but had he recovered enough to do someone in after she had left?

Her stomach cramped at the thought, and she swallowed hard.

Sal sighed and slumped forward again to rest his elbows on his knees. "I might as well tell you, though it pains me to be the bearer of bad news—he was found dead this morning. Shot at point-blank range between the eyes, with his trousers around his ankles and his revolver still holstered.

"And as cagey as Tony was, the cops are theorizing the person who got the drop on him must've been someone he trusted. Someone he didn't suspect wished him harm. Someone like the pretty dame who was seen leaving on his arm last night from the club."

Shock knocked her speechless for a moment. "It wasn't me, Sal. I swear it! He was completely fine when I left."

"Was he?" Sal's knowing gaze met hers. Sweat began trickling down her back, but it had little to do with the heat.

"He might have been a little . . . tired," she admitted. "But definitely alive."

"And a sitting duck for anyone who might have wandered by. Now we both know Tony had a lot of enemies, but the cops . . . they've got bigger problems. The fine citizens of that neighborhood are justifiably upset and are calling the mayor as we speak. They don't like having people murdered on their block, and they want someone held account-able. Unfortunately, without the cops having any other suspects, that someone is you."

"I don't believe this." She closed her eyes and worked to slow her racing heart. "Tony was the one breaking all the laws. Not me." And yet, unless the real murderer suddenly made an appearance, she would be the one going to jail.

Her eyes flew open. "Wait. He mentioned a loose end last night, something connected to Outfit business. That's why he was back in town."

Sal's eyebrows rose. "You think the loose end got to Tony before he could get to it?"

"It's either that . . . or, as you said, one of his many enemies caught up to him."

"True, but unless Tony mentioned any names, it's unlikely to help you much." Then Sal shrugged. "Still, I'll pass along the tip."

"Please do. And even if it doesn't help, I've gotta believe that whoever offed him will eventually start boasting about it, proving my innocence." Her brain worked feverishly on this sudden avenue of escape. "If I can stay out of sight long enough for the real killer to start blabbing . . ."

"Assuming he would do such a thing. And that you could suc-cessfully hide from the police. Their reach is wide." A statement that echoed Tony's one from last night about the Mob a little too closely for comfort.

"Nor would it be just the police you'd be hiding from," Sal con-tinued. "Truth is, the family is currently divided on what to do about you. Everyone agrees they want the cops' noses out of family business, but otherwise . . . ? I mean, who cares if some no-account showgirl takes the heat?"

"I would care!" Real fear gripped her. "I'm not going to jail, Sal."

"Nor would I let you. You're like my own child, Lil. Have a little faith."

"But you said the police are looking for me."

"Yes, but as a person of interest. There's no arrest warrant . . . yet."

She rubbed at the dull ache forming behind her eyes. "I'm confused. What is it you want me to do?"

"Not run. Not only would it end badly for you but also possibly for your little boy over there."

She stilled. "How do you mean?"

"Lily . . ." The disappointment was back in his voice. "You are out here twice a week, rain or shine. You think certain people haven't noticed, people who might be interested in finding a way to keep you in line?"

Vi's gaze flicked back to her son, and a crushing pain stole her breath. *No, no! This couldn't be happening. Not to Jimmy.* She had given him up for adoption precisely to avoid this, to keep the stain of her mistakes from touching him. As if that were even possible given her propensity for disastrous decisions.

Her vision blurred as she watched Jimmy come down the slide. No longer chunky with baby fat, he was becoming stronger and more slender every day. Someday he would no longer be a child, but a man . . . if he lived that long. "I didn't do it, Sal. I swear it."

"It wouldn't matter if you had." Sal turned to face her more fully. "As I said, the family is divided. There are some who see Tony's untimely demise as the perfect opportunity to undermine one of our rivals. In which case, it might be useful if you skipped town for a while, until an alternate, more advantageous fall guy is handed over to the commissioner."

"But you just said Jimmy would be in danger if I ran."

"Who said anything about running? I'm talking about taking a job elsewhere, until the heat is off. I made some calls this morning. Called in a few favors to see what I could do for you. Turns out someone important, someone connected to another branch of the family, has a problem that needs taking care of."

A dozen possibilities for what might be asked of her raced through her mind, each more damning than the last. She shook her head. "I won't kill anyone, Sal."

"Lily." Sal gave her another disapproving look, his third of the morning. "You should know better than to think I would ask that of you."

Vi knew no such thing but decided it was in her best interest not to say so.

Sal continued, "As I was saying, I have a friend who needs a song and dance gal, someone who is available immediately but also one with a squeaky-clean past. One that even the most persnickety of society matrons wouldn't turn up her nose at."

Vi huffed in disbelief. "You do realize my being a stripper who used to turn tricks is hardly the definition of squeaky clean."

"On the surface, sure. But don't sell yourself short. While you might have had a couple of bad breaks recently, at your core you're a good kid. You got heart. You got class. If you put your mind to it, and a new name, no one would guess you're anything but an all-American sweetheart."

"Maybe no one except all the men who have seen me perform."

Sal waved his hand dismissively. "Men have short memories. Trust me."

She plucked at her damp blouse and took a deep breath. "All right. Since I seem to be low on options, might as well tell me the rest."

"The good news? You'll be performing with the USO, onstage, as part of a legitimate Broadway-style musical—all on the up-and-up, with no nudity. And it's scheduled to go on tour shortly, out of New York."

She laughed without humor. "And your friend couldn't find someone on his own to take the part? That makes no sense. I would think there'd be a thousand girls willing to sell their soul for a traveling Broadway show."

"Maybe, but there's another part to the job. And this is where the rub lies: there is a very important person—actually the daughter of this very important person—also in the show. You would be expected to keep an eye on her *without* letting her know."

"So, I'm to babysit a Mob princess on the sly." Her head started to throb again.

"No, no. The daughter is no baby. She's eighteen. And apparently very headstrong. Willing to disregard the express wishes of her father, to the point of putting herself in mortal danger. This, of course, he cannot allow, but finds himself helpless to stop her."

Vi frowned. "I'm not wild about that 'mortal danger' part, and I don't know what you expect me to do about it. I'm a dancer, not a bodyguard."

"Which is exactly why you would be perfect. Having had no experience with traveling overseas, or even being away from home, the daughter will need a confidante, a friend to guide her. Someone to keep her away from handsome GIs and out of minefields."

"While I can probably do the former, assuming the girl will listen, war zones are outside of my area of expertise."

"Which is why you'd be only responsible for keeping her with the others and away from amorous soldiers."

"For how long?" She couldn't believe she was actually considering such a ludicrous assignment.

"Three months."

"Not a chance." She held up her hand to stop Sal's protest. "Even if I could deceive the USO into thinking I was some kind of Snow White, I can't be away from Jimmy that long."

"Actually, I think the correct verb is *won't*, since you're not actually caring for him. But consider this: If you go to jail, how long will that keep you away from your son?"

She glanced back at the playground, at Jimmy, her headache turning into a migraine. "What if I dye my hair and change my name again?"

Sal sighed. "Be reasonable, Lily."

"And why can't a powerful Mob boss rein in his own daughter?"

A wry smile twisted his lips. "She might or might not have uncovered the existence of an unfortunate relationship that would land her father in very deep water should his wife find out about it."

"She's blackmailing her own father?" Vi could almost admire the girl for that.

"Don't dissemble, Lily. Are you going to help my associate help you, or are you going to wait around here to be arrested?"

Good questions, both. As much as she hated the thought of leaving Jimmy, she might at least have the chance of seeing him grow up if she left town, something sticking around didn't leave as an option. She had no illusions that being female would keep her safe if the police brought her up on murder charges.

"When would I have to leave?" she managed despite the closing of her throat.

"I suggest immediately. There are still a few cops not in the family's pocket who are likely out looking for you right now."

Vi sucked in a deep breath and closed her eyes. Her ears buzzed faintly, warning her of an imminent faint. She bent forward and hung her head between her knees, all the while focusing on the flow of air in and out of her lungs.

Damn, damn, damn.

Tony's death had put her in a real bind. Even if Jimmy didn't know her from Eve, he was the center of her world. All those nights working the audience, strutting half-naked across the stage, skipping multiple meals to save up money—she had done it with the vain hope that she might yet be able to give him something of importance, something beyond just giving birth to him. But if she was arrested for murder, perhaps even convicted, she would have to stay away from him forever. Because who would want a murderer for a mother?

"Lily, we're running out of time here. Are you in or out?"

She lifted her head, and a tear slid down her cheek. "Sal, promise me you'll keep an eye on Jimmy for me, please?"

Sal's dark eyes were solemn. "Upon my life. And I'll send updates to my friend so you'll know how he's doing."

She swallowed and got shakily to her feet. "All right. Give me thirty minutes to go home and pack—"

Sal grabbed her arm, his grip almost painful. "You can't go home. You do that and you'll be picked up the second you step through the door. Think, Lily! With no one else to pin the murder on, the cops aren't going to just let you go once they have you."

"You can't expect me to show up in New York without even a toothbrush," she said in disbelief.

"You don't have a choice." He let go of her arm and reached into his coat pocket. He pulled out a folded piece of paper and handed it to her. "This is the address of the theater where the production is rehearsing, as well as the name of the director and the name of your charge. I'll make sure everything is arranged for you by the time you arrive."

She shook her head. "This is madness!"

His hand paused, the paper still between his fingers. "You got a better idea?"

The truth was she didn't. She took the paper from him, her heart in her stomach. "Fine. But I'll need this week's pay to afford the ticket."

"Of course." He shifted and pulled a wallet from his trouser pocket. After opening it, he selected several bills and folded them in half before handing them to her. "There's a bus that leaves for Indianapolis in an hour. From there you can catch one to New York."

"All right." She took the wad of bills from him. To her surprise, he started to take them back.

"Lily . . . listen to me. Even if the family manages to smooth things over with the police, you're still going to have to let this unhealthy obsession you have with your son go. You know that, right?"

She bit the inside of her cheek to keep from protesting and nodded.

He released his hold. "Then go, *ahuva*. My little one. All will be well."

Chapter 4

Exhausted and filthy after three days of nonstop travel from Chicago to New York, Vi sneaked into the darkened theater auditorium, praying no one would notice. As luck would have it, rehearsal was in full swing, so every eye was on the stage. Relieved, she blinked to adjust to the low light. Onstage, beneath a gorgeous scrolled, gold leaf proscenium, two male actors and a female one paused as light cues were called out and adjusted.

Silently, wanting to get the lay of the land before announcing her presence, she chose a seat so as to watch. The chair mechanism stuck at first and then released. She winced as the metal hinges scraped open, but no one looked back.

Sinking onto the soft velvet cushion, she almost groaned with pleasure. She had forgotten how tiring travel could be. It had been more than five years since she had completed that final leg of her journey and arrived at the Chicago Greyhound station, nervous as heck and yet so full of hope. She'd had it all planned out in her fifteen-year-old head: She'd get a job as an actress or work as a costumer for one of the Windy City's many theaters; then she and her baby would find a room with a friendly widow, just like in the movies. She would work and bring home her paycheck while the kindly widow babysat and prepared home-cooked meals.

It had all seemed so simple and straightforward, until reality had hit her like a bucket of ice water. Turned out no one wanted to hire an underage runaway. And the kindly widow she had hoped to meet in church? The woman never materialized. Soon the little money she had brought with her, which had constituted every penny stored in her ceramic bunny bank, had run out.

Finding herself in dire straits, she had then stumbled upon her most useful ability to date—becoming someone else. She became the counter clerk who'd had her purse stolen and needed a quarter for the ride home or the newlywed who had gotten lost downtown and needed a dime to call her husband at work. Or an experienced stripper who needed a new gig because her boyfriend manager had knocked her up and then fired her.

Sal had readily seen through that lie but had at least given her points for trying. On the other hand, the ticket seller at the bus station three days ago had fallen for her latest act, hook, line, and sinker. At first the troublesome fellow had tried to tell her everything was sold out until next month, on account of America's fighting men getting first priority. Then they had gotten to talking about the heat and how his live-in mother-in-law was getting on his nerves. On a pure whim, Vi created a cantankerous mother-in-law of her own, one that she was so desperate to escape she was going home to New York City to see her own family for a while, and oh—did he want to park his mother-in-law in her apartment while she was away?

Her "husband" wouldn't need it, since he was in the army—something she relayed with a tragic catch in her voice—and it wouldn't do for it to go to waste. In the pause while his gaze narrowed in possibilities, she had pulled out the key to her "second floor" apartment that "occasionally catches a breeze off the lake," and offered to sublet it to him for a couple of months. She had even offered to write a quick letter to her landlady, who was herself a crotchety old woman, so the two women would get along famously . . .

And just like that, a seat had appeared on the next bus out of town. And not one just to Indianapolis, like Sal had recommended, but one that went all the way to Philadelphia. Of course, the long stretch of unbroken travel also meant next to no sleep, since she hadn't dared let her guard down. Not when the Chicago police might have already noted her absence and called in the FBI for help.

Securing a second ticket to New York had been just as touch and go, requiring another sob story, convincingly delivered, to an elderly gentleman with the last seat. She hadn't liked lying to such a nice old man, but Angelina Maggio's father was counting on her to get to New York City as soon as possible, so her motives hadn't been entirely selfish. And, to be honest, the elderly fellow had seemed rather eager to give her the ticket. Of course, the attractive older lady making eyes at him from across the waiting area may have had something to do with that.

In any case, all that was behind her. She was here with nothing to do for the moment but soak in the heady smells and sounds of a legitimate production underway: the tang of varnish and paint and freshly sawed wood; the familiar mustiness of upholstered seats; the hollow, unamplified voices echoing in the empty auditorium; the pounding of a hammer backstage; and the occasional shout of a crew member. Her heart thumped unevenly under an unexpected barrage of emotions.

Her happiest memories had always involved being onstage, part of a dance performance or theatrical production, sweating under the hot blaze of footlights. Ever since her first dance recital at the age of six, she had known there was no place she wanted to be except on a stage. Her whole existence had soon centered on reaching that glorious day when she would escape dreary old Iowa and ascend to the dizzying heights of Broadway performer. How she had worked, and trained, and practiced to make that dream a reality . . .

Only to have it all come crashing down because of a stupid girlhood crush. It made Vi sick to remember how her younger self had misread

Robert's interest in her. Robert, one of her older sister's many suitors, who had been so kind and attentive whenever she and Fern had run across him at church—who had taken Violet aside after Fern had given him the brush and had told her she was the one he actually loved, never Fern. Her singing had entranced him, made him blind to any other girl's charms. He'd thought her beautiful and as graceful as a swan.

Looking back, she could hardly believe she had been taken in by such uninspired prose. But she had been, and soon they were meeting on the sly every chance they could get because her parents hadn't considered fifteen old enough to date. She had fancied herself Juliet to Robert's Romeo, one-half of a star-crossed pair that would defy the odds and become a love match immortal. Never mind that he had always managed to slip in a question about what Fern was doing or who she was seeing. Nor had it bothered her that, when they still had run across him at church, he would all but stare at Fern.

Well, okay, that was a lie. It had bothered her. A lot. But when she had accused him of liking her sister better, he had said he was showing concern for Fern because she was part of Vi's family, which would someday also be his.

Such naivete. It defied explanation now.

Yet, despite all her missteps and self-sabotage, here she was . . . in New York, in a Broadway theater, and about to join a new production. It was a miracle, and one she didn't wholly deserve. But too much of her old dreams remained for her to throw the chance away. Her only regret was that it had required her to leave Chicago, and Jimmy.

With the lighting situation resolved, the two male actors—an older man with silver hair and a younger, dark-haired man—began reading from their scripts again. Near as she could tell by their gestures, they were arguing about the blonde lying on the couch with her arm over her eyes, as if asleep. Or drunk, given the snippets of dialogue she caught.

Whichever it was didn't matter. What did was finding the man whose name was written on her paper right above Angelina Maggio's. Tuning the actors out, she scanned the front row of seats. One of those shadowy figures had to be the director she sought. At least she hoped so. It would do her no good to find Miss Maggio if she only ended up being left behind, waving *bon voyage* from the dock, because she had failed to first secure her spot in the play.

Vi chewed on her lip nervously. Despite Sal's assurance that the director would welcome her with open arms, she had enough stage experience to see this was no small-time production. The director had to be nervous about adding her sight unseen.

So how to reassure him, thus putting herself on firmer footing with the show?

Not by interrupting the rehearsal—that was for sure.

Nor by stinking, figuratively as well as literally, she thought as she gave her blouse a sniff. Bad first impressions were the very devil to overcome, and she owed it to Sal to at least smell one rung above a hobo.

Quietly she eased to her feet. Her tired muscles protested, but there was no time to lose if she wanted to avoid meeting the director looking—and smelling—like a pigsty. Still, she couldn't resist watching the actors a few more seconds. The men arguing while the blonde stirred made for some terrific staging. It also meant the scene was rapidly coming to a close. She needed to beat feet. Later, if all went well, she would have plenty of chances to watch.

Not fifteen minutes later she was back in the theater lobby, smelling and looking much more professional, even though the underarms of her blouse were still damp from being rinsed. Drawing a deep breath, she nervously smoothed her newly pinned hair, checking for stray ends. The recent dye job, hastily undertaken in Philly to further alter her appearance, had left her hair slicker and harder to style, if also closer to her natural deep sable color.

She would miss the attention that came with being blonde, of course, but moon-kissed locks were Lily Lamour's trademark. And then there was that small tug of pleasure at seeing the old Vi reemerge in the mirror. It was like meeting an old friend after a long break.

She hurried back into the auditorium, and her heart nearly stopped when she realized the house lights were up. Frantically she ran her gaze over the small groups of people gathered in the aisles, chatting, the rehearsal clearly finished for the day. A stoop-shouldered, balding man was talking to the blonde actress, and the way the woman listened to him caught Vi's attention.

One, that the actress was scowling meant she was likely receiving bad news. Two, that she also maintained steady eye contact with the fellow, despite her displeasure, suggested he was Gerald Stuart, the man Vi sought. Any actor or actress worth his or her salt would give the director his or her full attention when getting stage directions if they wanted to keep a part. Mistakes might be forgiven the first time, but not the second, and there was always another person waiting in the wings to grab your spot.

"Can I help you?"

Pressing a hand to her chest, Vi whirled to face two young women, one with wavy, light-brown hair and wide gray eyes, and the other a brunette whose green eyes were narrowed with suspicion. Mentally, Vi kicked herself for letting someone sneak up on her like that, let alone two people. If she had still been in Chicago, she would be in jail by now.

The gray-eyed girl studied her with a worried look. "Did I startle you? I'm sorry. It's just that the theater is closed to visitors during rehearsal."

"Oh, I'm not a visitor. I'm here to talk to Mr. Stuart," Vi said, wondering if this was the rebellious Angelina Maggio. She considered asking but then decided against it. No need to tip anyone off that she was there to do anything but dance. She continued in a more confident tone, "He's expecting me."

The gray-eyed girl's expression relaxed into a friendly smile. "In that case, I'll walk you over."

"Gertie," the brunette hissed. "Are you nuts? What if she's another snoop?"

Gertie's eyes widened. "Oh gosh! You aren't, are you?"

"No," Vi said firmly, wanting to nip any concerns about her presence in the bud. While she now knew the gray-eyed girl wasn't Angelina Maggio, there was still the brunette to consider. "But I don't want to delay you two. Just point him out, and I'll take it from here."

"Are you sure?" Worry clouded Gertie's pretty face. "It might help if someone goes with you; he's been a perfect grouch all day."

"A state not that uncommon in directors," Vi said with a sympathetic laugh. "Thanks for the warning, though."

The brunette grabbed Vi's arm. "Not so fast. If you're here to rat another one of us out, you can leave right now. The whole troupe is already steamed about losing Janet, including Mr. Stuart."

"Ow! Do you mind?" Vi shook the girl's hand off her arm. "I'm only here to talk to Mr. Stuart about joining his USO show."

The brunette's eyes narrowed. "Really? If you think you're good enough for a Stuart production, how is it that I've never seen you before? I know most of the dancers in the area."

"I'm not from around here. I was sent here from Ch—Iowa," Vi corrected quickly, "as a favor."

"Shy-owa?" the girl repeated suspiciously. Vi could've kicked herself for the slip.

"I was about to say Chariton, which is where I grew up, about two hours south of Des Moines, but then changed my mind since most people have never heard of it." Vi worked to keep her expression open, innocent.

"Why would an Iowa farm girl be sent to our production? We're not growing corn here."

With an effort, Vi kept her irritation in check. "Considering I've starred on the stages of Des Moines and Chicago as both an actress and a dancer and worked as a choreographer for both solo and ensemble performances these past three years, I'd say this show is lucky to have me."

The brunette's lips tightened. "Well then, don't let little ol' me get in your way, Miss Hotshot from Iowa. I'm sure Mr. Stuart would love to hear all about it." She turned away, snagging the other girl's elbow. "Come on, Gertie. We'd better leave before that pile of hooey stinks up the place."

"Hooey?" Vi spat as furious retorts gathered on her tongue. Then abruptly she remembered that not only was she supposed to be a squeaky-clean ingenue—not Lily Lamour, queen of the Chicago burlesque stage—this girl might also be Miss Maggio, her purported new best friend. "Wait . . ."

She might as well have been talking to the empty seats.

Lord above, she needed to keep her head in the game. Until Tony's killer was arrested, her safety and freedom depended on her doing two things: landing the spot in the USO show and befriending Miss Maggio—and not getting kicked out of the USO for moral deficiency. Okay, so that was three things. But the latter was key, which meant she needed to remember she was the girl she had invented on the way to New York City: Virginia Heart, a talented but virginal hoofer from the Midwest and all-American sweetheart, looking to do her patriotic duty by entertaining the boys overseas.

Pure as the driven snow, Vi. Come on, you can do this.

Exhaling the last vestiges of Lily and breathing in Virginia, she turned to see Mr. Stuart disappearing through one of the side doors next to the stage.

Oh no you don't. Ignoring the screaming of her sore feet, she sprinted down the aisle. "Mr. Stuart. Excuse me, sir . . ."

To her immense relief, the man turned around.

She slid to a stop in front of him and pasted on a bright smile. Never mind that it was met with a fierce scowl on his part. She was made of sterner stuff. One had to be to survive in the theater business.

"Sorry to bother you," she said, trying not to sound too obsequious. Virginia might be sweet, but she also had to demonstrate a certain level of confidence. "But I was told to contact you the minute I got to New York. Sal Fleischmann sent me?"

He snorted. "Well, it's about time. Do you realize how close we are to shipping out? I've half a mind to send you home and just be short a dancer. To hell with what Sue wanted."

Vi's heart stuttered in alarm, and she forgot all about playing someone else. He couldn't be serious, could he? Her future literally depended on getting this part!

"I'm so sorry. I got here as quick as I could. Please, give me a chance. I'm a fast study."

"That's what they all say." He started to turn away.

Visions of being bundled into a police car, never to see Jimmy again, had her grabbing the director's arm. "Wait, please. I really want this part. I *need* this part, and I'll do whatever it takes for me to get it."

"Oh?" He paused, and his gaze took on a speculative air as he looked at her. Her stomach sank as she realized what she had just said and how it could be interpreted. *Please, don't take that wrong. Please, please don't suggest I sleep with you . . .*

She, as herself, was desperate enough to do it, but her new persona? Virginia would be shocked and have to refuse, or else she would be behaving entirely out of character.

"Will you show up on time and keep your knees together, unlike your predecessor?"

Vi released her breath. Talk about an easy request!

"Of . . . of course." She made an X over her heart, even as she wondered if he was referring to the missing Janet. "Scout's honor!"

He snorted again. "That's *not* the scout sign, but fine. You can have the part, but only because I don't want Sue bitching about having to rechoreograph everything." He retreated a step, clearly impatient to be on his way. "Now be a good girl and go find my assistant. If she likes you, she'll talk to you about rehearsals and scripts. She'll also bring you up to speed on USO requirements."

"Do you mean Sue?" she called after him, but he was already out the door. She swore softly under her breath as she glanced around the auditorium.

Voices drifted from backstage, giving her an idea. Nothing of note ever escaped the stage crew, whether it be clandestine love affairs, actor rivalries, drinking problems, or even the current location of a missing directorial assistant. She hurried up the apron steps, mentally promising herself that she would find a place to rest as soon as she had Virginia's part in her pocket.

Once onstage—a location that never failed to exhilarate her as she looked out over the audience seats—she headed toward a handful of workmen gathered on the working side. Dressed casually in loose trousers and open-collared shirts, they appeared to be in the process of disassembling furniture and packing the pieces into wooden crates.

"Hiya, fellas." Assuming the role of Virginia, she smiled and tucked a strand of hair behind her ear as if shy. "Sorry to bother you, but Mr. Stuart told me to find his assistant. Is she around?"

One of the men straightened. He was lanky and tall. Over six feet, easily. His sandy-brown hair was turning silver at the temples, and something about the ease with which he moved told her he was the man in charge. He didn't bother returning her smile, though there was nothing unfriendly about him.

Shrewd brown eyes studied her for a moment. "Sue's gone for the day. Had some last-minute errands to run before we head out tomorrow."

She blinked, not quite sure she had heard him correctly. "Head out?"

"That's right. Just found out today that the whole production has to be boxed up and ready to ship overseas ASAP." He gestured toward the crates with his screwdriver. "As you can see, we were only halfway done with the construction when the orders came through, so things are a little crazy at the moment. But that's the army for you."

"We're leaving tomorrow?" The implications of that careened about her brain like a panicked mouse spotting a cat. All she had with her was lipstick, soap, a hairbrush, and the outfit she'd been wearing for the last three days.

The man's eyes narrowed. "We?"

Vi snapped back to the present quandary. "I'm the replacement dancer, which is why I'm looking for Sue. But now I'm wondering if I should be out shopping for the tour instead."

"Once Sue gets you sized, everything you'll need onstage will be provided, except for the shoes, which you can pay us back for, out of your earnings. As for basic sundries and a uniform, that'll be issued by the army. The only things you'll be on the hook for will be gal-type things, like makeup and stockings."

"Right." She pressed her hand to her chest to calm her still-racing heart. She had a couple of fins left from Sal. And if they shipped out tomorrow, that left only one night of room and board to cover, if she even bothered eating. She had gone to bed hungry before.

"What about food and lodging while on tour?" she asked to double-check.

"The USO pays for all that." He hesitated, the furrow between his eyebrows deepening. "Forgive me, miss, but you seem rather uninformed about the particulars of this tour. You do know that our show will be headed overseas working the Foxhole Circuit? And that we may be performing quite close to the front lines?"

"Not too close, I hope." Vi smiled weakly even as her stomach twisted.

"If we are, would it matter?" the man asked with a lift of an eyebrow. "Because if it does, now's the time to back out. The USO's mission is to lift the spirits of US servicemen, no matter where they're stationed. That means we could land in Europe, or the South Seas, or even North Africa. Due to national security they haven't told us what to expect, except that we'll be playing outside of the States. And they only told us that because we need passports."

A new worry stabbed her. Sal hadn't mentioned anything about a passport. She wasn't even sure how to get one, let alone with an assumed name and in less than a day.

It was on the tip of her tongue to say that, upon reflection, she wouldn't be joining them after all. Then her son's sweet face appeared in her mind. If she bailed now, she might never get to see him grow up. Of course, if she died overseas, she wouldn't, either, but how often did the USO actually lose one of their performers? Plus, this was the second chance she had been dreaming of—performing in legitimate theater with a Broadway director. Did she really want to throw it away in a fit of cowardice?

Swallowing her anxiety, she forced her lips into a smile. "Sounds like a grand adventure. I can't wait!"

Both his eyebrows rose at that, but then he wiped his hand on his overalls and held it out to her. "Then welcome to the unit. I'm Wyatt. Wyatt Miller. Technical director for the show."

Her hand was totally engulfed by Mr. Miller's much larger, stronger one. "Virginia. Virginia Heart, but everyone calls me Vi."

"Not Ginny? I thought that was the usual nickname for Virginia."

"Yes, well, I prefer Vi."

"Then Vi it is. Welcome to *One Fine Mess*—an original musical comedy by Gerald Stuart." His hand swept grandly toward the stacked crates. "Music, dancing, and mayhem in two acts, guaranteed to please the pickiest of GIs."

"Sounds wonderful." She tucked the loose strand of hair behind her ear again. This time her nervousness was real. "Um . . . Mr. Miller . . . since Sue is gone, could you tell me what time I should show up tomorrow and where?"

"Grand Central Terminal at two p.m. with all your luggage. Track eleven."

She frowned. "But that's a train station. I thought we were shipping out?"

Mr. Miller laughed. "We have to be inducted first and go through basic training first, like any other soldier headed toward the front. You're in the army now, sister."

She blinked, her sense of having fallen into a bad dream increasing by the second. "They're sending us to boot camp?"

"Bingo." He started to turn away and then stopped. "Anything else I can do for you?"

She caught the impatience in his voice and was reminded of time passing. They both had a lot to do before tomorrow—finding an inexpensive suitcase being at the top of her list. "No. Thank you."

"Wait, Miss Heart, is it?"

She glanced up into his concerned face. "Yes?"

"You got somewhere to stay tonight?"

A frisson of alarm ran through her. Even though he seemed like a decent enough guy, he was still a man, and men liked sex . . . "Yes. Why?"

"You wouldn't be the first would-be starlet to spend her last dime getting here," he said not unkindly. "And Lord knows you won't be the last."

"Yes, well. I'll be fine, so don't worry about me." And she would be fine, as long as she stayed wary of those who would take advantage of her. Like older men who might want to recapture their youth with a younger woman.

"I see." Mr. Miller paused and then turned to the other fellow. "Hey, Hank. You okay finishing up?"

Hank, who was almost done taking apart a coffee table, nodded without looking up.

Mr. Miller headed over to an open toolbox, leaving Vi standing alone. She shifted on her feet uncertainly. Was he through talking to her? She didn't want to offend a senior member of the production staff by leaving midconversation. On the other hand, she didn't want to stick around if it meant giving the wrong impression. In her experience, men often mistook hesitation on a woman's part as an invitation.

Before she could decide, Mr. Miller returned with a lunch pail in hand.

"Good, you're still here. If you're game for it, I have a friend that might be willing to put you up. I'm thinking her sofa would be a sight more comfortable than spending the night in some back alley."

"I can take care of myself," she said with a mental roll of her eyes. Back alley, indeed. All-night diners or train station restrooms were much better choices.

"Glad to hear it." The skepticism in the tone of his voice told her he wasn't buying it. Clearly he took her as some fresh-off-the-farm rube, though that wouldn't be far off the mark if she really were Virginia—so maybe that was good?

To her surprise, he started walking toward one of the exits without another word.

Distrust warred with pragmatism. Was he really going to leave her to fend for herself? And did she really want to spend the night on the floor somewhere, in questionable safety, wondering if she would be robbed in her sleep?

Deciding a good night's rest was definitely worth groveling for, especially after traveling for the last three days and then having to travel again tomorrow, she sprinted after him. Pride was all well and good, but it had its practical limits. Sal had taught her that when he had all but pulled her out of the Chicago River.

She had been eight months pregnant, unable to find work as a dancer because of her condition, and literally starving. Depressed and tired of struggling just to survive, she had stopped on her long trek back to the room she shared with two other girls and stared down from the Adams Street Bridge into the cold, swirling waters. Her life had nearly ended that afternoon, but for Sal. By some miracle his taxi was taking him over the bridge at the same instant, and he had recognized her from an audition earlier in the week. Sensing something was direly wrong, he had ordered the driver to stop and then jumped out to grab her just as she was leaning over the edge.

After listening to her troubles over dinner, he had offered her bus fare home, but she'd refused. She hadn't wanted to endure her parents' disapproval, couldn't bear to see Robert again or face the horrible task of telling her sister who the baby's father was. Her pride wouldn't let her. Nor would her dreams for her future, because if she had come clean about the pregnancy, she knew her parents would've made Robert marry her. And yes, fifteen-year-old Vi had wanted to get married. Someday. But not until she'd had her chance to be a Broadway star.

Sal hadn't shamed her for those dreams, but he had made her face the hard realities of them. He could give her work as a costumer for his dancers so she could eat. He would give her a loan to cover the hospital expense when the time came, with the proviso that she had to work for him until she paid it off. And she had to put the baby up for adoption.

On this he had been resolute. Economic conditions were still depressed in the US, and he didn't see them improving anytime soon. He knew of a good agency, one that catered to wealthy parents. Vi was a beautiful girl, and smart. If the baby's father was those things, too, it would be easy to find the baby a good family. One that could give the little tyke all he needed, or at least a lot more than a fifteen-year-old stripper could.

"Pride goeth before a fall," Sal had told her solemnly as he'd waited for her decision on that chilly March evening.

And she had already fallen so far . . . Learning to swallow her pride had been a hard lesson, but she had done it, and survived. And if that's what was needed now, that's exactly what she would do.

Chapter 5

"Don't take this wrong, dear," Mrs. Wittman said over breakfast the next morning. "But I don't think you're getting enough sleep."

Vi glanced up at the widow, her mouth too full of hastily consumed toast and jam to respond. Not that she could disagree with the woman's conclusion, given the bruised appearance of her eyes. If she weren't running so late from oversleeping, she would reassure the sweet old lady that she was fine and her exhaustion only temporary from being on the road for three—no, four days now.

Except she didn't have time to say all that. Not after Mr. Stuart's crack yesterday about showing up on time. The only reason she was risking his wrath by eating breakfast was that she was starving. That, and she couldn't bear disappointing Mrs. Wittman, who had gone out of her way to make a huge breakfast for her unexpected couch guest. The woman had even washed and pressed Vi's clothes last night, while Vi had slept.

Such kindness couldn't be ignored.

"Wyatt doesn't, either," Mrs. Wittman went on, her expression becoming wistful. "But he never listens to me, even though I tell him he's always welcome to at least nap here."

Vi suspected the older woman would love Wyatt to do more than just nap. From the longing in her eyes last night when Mr. Miller had dropped Vi off to stay, the widow was clearly sweet on the technical director. Vi had actually felt a little awkward about accepting Mrs. Wittman's hospitality when it was so obviously offered with the hopes of securing Wyatt's affection.

"But listen to me go on and on, when you've got a train to catch." Mrs. Wittman pushed another plate toward her, one with sliced peaches and some cheese. "Here, help yourself, dear. I've got some ham, if you'd rather. How about a few soda crackers to take with you? Train rides can be so long."

Vi gulped down her glass of milk—she hadn't drunk it for years, but Mrs. Wittman had insisted. Scooting her chair back, she wiped her lips on the frayed but spotlessly clean napkin. "Thanks for everything, Mrs. Wittman. Breakfast was delicious. And would you have any clue on how to get a passport on short notice?"

The question had been worrying her all morning.

Mrs. Wittman pursed her lips thoughtfully while Vi stood and collected her dishes. She didn't want to burden the woman any more than she already had.

"Can't say that I do. But I bet Wyatt would. I'm always amazed at how much that man knows about everything. I tease him that someday his head is going to explode with all that knowledge."

Vi weighed the idea as she sprinted to the bathroom to brush her teeth. He had helped her enough already. If she asked another favor, would it be the one that would push their relationship into a sexual one? Turning men down, particularly ones who held power over whether she got a part or not, was tricky.

On the other hand, she wouldn't need a passport if she missed her train. Deciding to worry about it later, Vi gathered her things, thanked Mrs. Wittman profusely—yes, she would take the crackers if that would make her feel better—and then bolted for the nearest subway stop.

It was a near thing. With only two minutes to spare, Vi slid into the vast central plaza of Grand Central Terminal, her lungs burning with exertion. *Please, please let the troupe be here somewhere.*

A brief parting in the crowd exposed a large group of well-dressed people drifting toward where the regional trains boarded. Among all the wool coats and brightly colored ladies' hats, Vi caught a glimpse of a tall, lanky man who looked a lot like Wyatt chatting with a stoop-shouldered gentleman who could easily be Mr. Stuart, the director. But what sealed the deal was when a smartly dressed blonde turned to speak to someone behind her, the comment punctuated with a dramatic flourish of a gloved hand. *Bingo.*

The tightness in her shoulders dissipated. She waved to get the group's attention. "Mr. Miller, Mr. Stuart. Hello!"

Mr. Miller glanced her way and then pulled Mr. Stuart to a stop. "Miss Heart, you made it. And in the nick of time."

"Mr. Miller, I'm so glad I found you all!" Smiling brightly as she hurried over, she held out her hand. "Mr. Stuart, hello again. I'm Virginia Heart. We met yesterday at the rehearsal."

Mr. Stuart ignored her outstretched fingers. "I remember. You're replacing that irresponsible child that ran afoul of the USO, the one in the chorus . . ." He turned to the fortyish blonde woman next to him expectantly.

"You mean Janet," the woman said. "Janet Robinson." Intelligent, pale-blue eyes set in an attractive face examined Vi from head to toe. After a beat, the woman extended her hand. "Nice to meet you, Miss Heart. I'm Sue Daldakis, the stage manager."

Ah. So more than just an elusive assistant. Vi turned up the wattage on her smile, as stage managers were often the real power behind the throne. "I'm so excited to meet you. I can't even believe my luck. I've always dreamed of being in a Gerald Stuart show. And to be in the USO, too!"

That last part might have been pouring it on a bit thick, since Sue's eyes narrowed. "Yes, well, you're not officially in until I see how you perform. Remind me again of your theater experience?"

Vi tucked a stray hair behind her ear as she quickly curated the list of her performances into something Virginia might have done. "Um, a few community productions. I know how to tap-dance, have taken ballet. Worked in a few musicals." The most thrilling being a starring role in the Des Moines stage production of *Broadway Melody of 1936*. The *Des Moines Register* had called her an "up-and-coming talent," a "girl protégé," and "absolutely stunning in the role of Irene Foster."

It had been her last big role before the disaster with Robert.

"Do you sing?"

"No," Vi said as the warm bubble of remembered past successes popped.

The answer clearly disappointed the stage manager, but it was an issue on which Vi wouldn't budge. It wasn't that she couldn't sing, because she could. Quite well, in fact, or she never would've landed the role of Irene. The truth was she *wouldn't* sing, because she could no longer bear the awe she saw in people's faces when they heard her. The same awe she had seen in Robert's face when her singing had first captured his attention. The awe that had fueled her youthful desires and then torn her family apart.

"Well, I suppose you could just mouth the words," Sue said with a frown. Then she turned to the gaggle of young women behind her. "Miss May? Come and meet your new travel partner."

Sue turned back to Vi. "I've created a buddy system for all the girls, to ensure safety and morality. You and Miss May will be traveling and rooming together for the duration of the tour, except when the army has alternate accommodations for the performers. Marcie can also teach you the dances so you can get up to speed as soon as possible."

Before Vi could respond, a young, slightly plump brunette joined them. Her dark-brown eyes reminded Vi of a cocker spaniel's—large and lovely, but without a lot of thought going on behind them.

"Hiya," the girl said, holding out her hand. "I'm Marcie May."

Marcie's smile was so sweet and genuine, the cocker spaniel comparison seemed even more apt. Vi decided right then and there that she liked the girl.

"Virginia Heart," she said, shaking the girl's hand with enthusiasm. "But call me Vi."

"Lovely," Sue said, her attention already sliding away. "If you'll take over the introductions, Marcie, I've got to make sure Mr. Stuart's luggage and all the props make it onto the train."

"Yes, ma'am," Marcie said obediently, but Sue was already off.

"She seems nice," Vi observed.

"She is. I sometimes think this production would fall apart if not for her. Well, and for Wyatt, too. He's the tech director."

"I met him yesterday." Vi eyed the tall man, who was listening attentively to Mr. Stuart. "He seems very nice. A real gentleman."

Marcie laughed. "Got your weather eye out already, do you? Well, don't get your hopes up. Love entanglements of any kind—that's what our USO recruiter called them—are right out. We girls are supposed to represent all that's good and wholesome. So no canoodling with the soldiers, officers, other actors, or even stagehands." Marcie ticked off the prohibited items on her fingers as she listed them.

"Is that all?" Vi said with a lift of her eyebrows. Apparently there were going to be a lot of rules on this tour, and she personally disliked rules. "Seems with five fingers, the USO could have picked one more category of verboten."

"Oh, there's a fifth one." Marcie rolled her eyes. "No canoodling with foreigners, either. Though honestly, I can't imagine why anyone would. Everyone knows American men are the finest in the world."

Vi wasn't sure she entirely agreed, having met some pretty rotten examples of American manhood. Still, Virginia Heart wouldn't have had the same experiences as Lily Lamour, so she let it go.

"What about the rest of the troupe? Anything I need to know? Professional jealousies, tensions . . . forbidden love entanglements?" In her experience, every production had its fair share of backstage dramas. Better to find out about them up front than accidentally have one blow up on her later.

Forewarned was forearmed.

To her surprise, Marcie's smile dropped. Almost furtively, the girl looked around and then leaned toward Vi. "You didn't hear this from me, but I think something funny is going on between Mr. Miller and Luciana. They're always huddling up backstage, whispering." She straightened, her eyes rounding with concern. "But don't get me wrong. I'm not going to turn them in or anything. Luciana can associate with whomever she likes. And Mr. Miller, well, he's well respected and almost universally liked. Mr. Stuart says he's an absolute genius backstage! There's nothing he can't make or fix."

"Don't worry," Vi reassured her new travel buddy, even as she stored the tidbit away for later. "It won't change my good opinion of either one. I've been in theater long enough to know those kinds of things happen."

His being involved with someone might also explain why he hadn't bothered to ask for any favors in return for helping her last night.

Marcie's expression smoothed. "I probably shouldn't have said anything. Loose lips sink ships and all that, but"—she giggled—"that's so me. My mother always did say I couldn't keep a secret to save my soul."

Good to know, Vi thought. She would have to be that much more careful around her travel buddy, lest the whole unit find out her secrets.

Marcie continued. "I don't know if you got to meet anyone else yesterday, but the three fellas over there ahead of Wyatt—Charles, Matt, and Victor—are the male leads. And the two women with them are Ann and Luciana, the female leads."

Vi's ears perked up at "Ann," which could be a shortened, more anglicized version of Angelina. Her gaze immediately sought out the actress with the darker complexion. The woman certainly looked the part of a Mob princess with her slashing black eyebrows; glossy, dark hair; and full, sensual lips. Perhaps her nose was too bold to be strictly beautiful, but the woman was still striking. Traffic-stoppingly so.

Or was that Luciana? Vi frowned. The name was more typically Italian, which would match her appearance. But if so, that would make the blonde Ann, and she didn't look Italian in the least.

"Don't count on becoming friends with them, though." Marcie cast a disparaging look at the actors and actresses. "They ignore us chorus girls as much as possible. They treat us as if we're bringing the quality of the production down, but I disagree. They should be danged happy to have us. I mean, let's be honest, soldiers like dancing girls!"

"Professional snobbery isn't uncommon," Vi said mildly, her attention on the two actresses as she wondered if she should press Marcie for more information. She would likely find out on her own soon enough, so why risk making her travel buddy suspicious?

Marcie sighed. "You're probably right, and I try not to let it get to me. But it seems so . . . unfair."

Vi worked to keep her expression sympathetic, but honestly, had the girl never worked in theater before? "What about the rest of the cast?" She flicked a glance toward Gertie and the rude brunette, her stomach filling with dread. *Please don't be Angelina.*

"Those are the other two dancers." Marcie's voice dropped to a whisper again. "Gertie, the one on the right, is a real sweetheart. You'll like her. But Frances . . ." Marcie let her voice trail off, leaving Vi to supply her own ending.

Vi nearly sighed with relief that the girl who had accosted her in the theater yesterday wasn't going to be her responsibility. At least fate wasn't *that* cruel. "Is there anyone else in the show? Anyone who isn't here today?"

Marcie looked puzzled for a moment. Then her expression cleared. "Oh, you mean Janet?"

"Sure," Vi said, recognizing the name from yesterday, though the chances of that being Miss Maggio were slim to none. "Frances said she was ratted out?"

"Well, no one knows for sure, but a representative from the USO showed up at rehearsal on Monday, pulled Janet aside, told her she was out and that she needed to leave immediately. So she did."

"And no one protested?" Vi asked, momentarily distracted from the problem of the missing Mob princess.

Marcie shrugged. "Everyone knows that the USO is a stickler for moral values, and Janet was a little on the loose side. The bigger problem was that it left us with only three dancers and that we'd have to change all the choreography."

"Well, I'm here now," Vi reassured her as Sue started handing out train tickets to the assembled cast. "So your worries are over."

"And I am so glad," Marcie said fervently as the troupe started heading toward the platform. Vi smiled, though in truth she was feeling a bit ill. While she might have solved all her travel buddy's problems, her travel buddy had not solved hers.

Had Sal misheard the daughter's name or gotten the show wrong? At this point it seemed likely, but with the conductor calling all aboard, she didn't have time to call him and check. All she could hope was that if there had indeed been some kind of mistake, she would find out in time to fix things. Her future pretty much depended on it.

Chapter 6

US Army Camp Kilmer turned out to be nothing like what Hollywood matinees had led Vi to expect. It was more of a small city than a rustic Boy Scout camp. And while there were indeed white-painted wooden barracks and American flags flying proudly in the breeze, there was also a score of very large, very permanent buildings that wouldn't look out of place in her hometown, including what appeared to be a multistoried modern hospital.

The traffic was very urban-like as well, with a steady stream of cars, trucks, motorcycles, and jeeps buzzing by. And there were the signs, which were posted everywhere. Besides the expected ones indicating street names or pointing the way to "ORDNANCE" or "ARTILLERY" or the "PX," there were more surprising ones, like "SOFTBALL DIAMONDS"— plural, she noted—"CINEMA," "THEATER," and even "BILLIARDS." Everything a GI could want while he waited for the orders that might possibly mean his death.

Unsettled by that thought, Vi turned her gaze to the other thing Hollywood had gotten wrong. The young men, the proud fighting men of the United States Army, weren't all uniformly good looking with aw-shucks smiles, either. As far as she could tell, the whole gamut of American male society was represented in the crowded streets, from the scrawny to the roughneck, the truly handsome to the downright homely, from the palest white to the darkest brown. It was a bit over-whelming to be around so much testosterone. Even for her.

Marcie gave a low whistle of astonishment as she joined Vi on the sidewalk. Overhead, a low growling lifted Vi's gaze to the blue, blue sky. A quartet of fighter planes passed off in the distance, perhaps on their way to Europe. Vi shivered. All too soon, she might be joining them on that trek.

As the rest of the cast spilled out of the bus to claim their lug-gage from the driver, Vi self-consciously wiped her damp palms on her travel-worn skirt. While the drab brown of an army uniform would never be her first choice of colors, she was really looking forward to having a clean change of clothes. Maybe she could even get permission to add a few sequins here and there to liven up the khaki.

"Mr. Stuart, sir?" A clipboard-carrying soldier not much older than her strode up to Wyatt.

"I'm just the lowly tech director." Wyatt pointed good-naturedly to where Mr. Stuart stood talking to Sue. "That's the gentleman you're looking for."

Without missing a beat, the soldier headed over to the older man. "Mr. Stuart, sir, as soon as your group has its things, I've been assigned to get you all kitted out. After that, you'll be given your bunk assign-ments, and then the captain has a welcome ceremony all planned out for you."

"Sounds wonderful." A thin smile momentarily lightened Mr. Stuart's stern countenance. Then he turned and looked at Sue, who immediately sprang into action.

Sue clapped her hands to catch everyone's attention. "All right, cast, grab your bags, and fall in by this gentleman here."

The pandemonium that followed was no less than Vi expected given the characters she had met so far. As one, the troupe surged forward with no attempt at forming a line, all while throwing out a thousand questions at the soldier. Not wanting to be trampled, Vi hung back with Mr. Miller and Mr. Stuart, where it seemed safer.

The soldier held up his clipboard like a shield and took a nervous step back. "Ladies and gentlemen, please. If you will follow me, I'll take you to the quartermaster. So if you'll save your concerns for him."

"Quartermaster?" Frances echoed sarcastically and just loud enough to be overheard. "You hear that, Gertie? Wonder what you gotta do around here to rate a *full* one."

Sue shushed Frances with a scowl and then profusely apologized to the soldier, who turned out to be a corporal, not a sergeant like Vi had first guessed. One would think she would be better at identifying ranks given her line of business—well, her old line—but she had never cared who had bought her drinks. It wasn't like she was going to marry them, so what would be the point of her knowing a captain from a major from a lowly private?

His composure restored, Corporal Somebody-or-other glanced at his clipboard again. "Also, is there a Miss Virginia Heart present?"

Vi hesitated and then raised her hand. "Here."

He rechecked the clipboard. "It looks like we're missing your induction papers, so if you'll come with me after I drop off the rest of the troupe with the quartermaster? And bring your passport."

"Pardon?" A cold sweat beaded on her skin. She had known this moment was coming, but she hadn't planned on it being so soon. She'd hoped for a few more days to figure things out.

"Don't worry," Marcie said with a little laugh as she came to stand beside Vi. "I know 'induction' sounds scary, but the army isn't drafting you. It's mostly so they'll have next of kin information if something happens to us. We all had to fill them out."

Vi forced herself to laugh, too. "Well, that's all right, then. I was starting to wonder what I'd gotten myself into."

As she followed the others toward a low wooden building, she tried to distract herself with this new question of who she should name as next of kin. It actually wasn't all that obvious. One choice would be her parents, given they would likely be the ones tasked with burying her, should the occasion arise. She hoped not, though. Returning to Iowa in a box was not the kind of homecoming celebration her parents deserved. Though maybe they would prefer it that way; who knew?

She hadn't talked to them in five years, too afraid of what they might say. She had never actually said goodbye, either, taking the cowardly route of leaving a note instead. That both acts had hurt her parents was a given. Nor had it likely helped that she had blamed her running away on wanting to be a star and on her growing impatience with all their rules.

She had no doubt they'd believed her note, because some of it was true. All the best lies contained grains of truth. She had been tired of all the restrictions, and she really had wanted to spend more time in the spotlight, not merely exist in the shadow of her older sister.

And yet . . . she missed her family. She missed Fern's eye rolls when she asked to tag along on dates. She missed her mother's hugs and quiet words of wisdom, even if Vi hadn't always listened. She even missed her father's corny jokes, the ones he trotted out whenever she or Fern were in a bad mood over one thing or another.

But as the days away from home turned into weeks, and then into years, going back seemed even more impossible than ever. How did one tell her parents that not only had she had sex without being married but she had gotten pregnant, given the baby up for adoption, resorted to prostitution for a year to pay the rent, and now worked as a stripper, a job she was not only good at but actually enjoyed? In truth, she was proud of how she had overcome so many obstacles and yet also very aware of how far she had landed from her parents' dreams for her.

And that made her think of Jimmy and the small savings account she had set up for him. If she died, her parents wouldn't know to forward it to his family, but Sal would, having helped her with the paperwork. So perhaps she should use Sal as her next of kin? He, at least, could be counted on to say a prayer for her as he settled her affairs in Chicago. But then her parents wouldn't know, unless they drew their own conclusions after her semiannual letters, the ones where she regaled them with carefully constructed lies about her theatrical successes all over the country, stopped. Assuming they actually still got them. For all she knew they might have moved.

On that depressing note, she accompanied the corporal to a small one-story building wedged between two much larger ones, all painted white. There he handed her off to a different fellow, one with wire-rimmed spectacles, who was busy typing on a typewriter. Vi waited while he painfully hunted-and-pecked his way to the end of the form.

When he looked up, a harried expression on his thin, clean-shaven face, Vi was shocked at how young he appeared. As in he might be clean shaven because he didn't need to shave. Yes, the draft age had been lowered to eighteen. But she would be surprised if he was even that old.

Feeling positively ancient at the ripe old age of twenty-one, she managed a slight smile. "Hiya, soldier. I'm here with the USO and was told you have some forms for me to fill out?"

He glanced up and then blinked owlishly. A dull flush crept up his neck. "Uh, hi."

Flattered by his response, she winked at him. "'Uh, hi' yourself, handsome. My missing induction papers? The name is Heart. Virginia Heart."

"Um, yes . . ." His flush deepened, pleasing her even more, as he sprang into action. Drawers opened and shut as he hunted through file folders. "Hang on a moment, miss. I have them right here . . ."

She kept her smile as she waited, trying for a nonchalant air even though her heart was beating way too fast. Finally he found the correct folder and pulled out a blank sheet. After briefly fumbling with a pen, he managed to hang on to one long enough to hand it to her along with a personal information form.

"If you could fill this out for me, miss? Once you're done, I can make your dog tags and get you on your way to the quartermaster."

She hesitated as she ran her gaze over the questions, hardly daring to hope. "Is this everything?"

"There's still the physical, but the medical officer will take care of that. And the loyalty oath that needs to be signed. And the form for getting paid, and then another for requisition of supplies—"

She held up her hand to stem the flow of information. Goodness, the army had a lot of forms! "But for the moment, this is all you need?"

"Yes, miss. Name, date of birth, address, religion, any schooling, current occupation, and next of kin. Oh, and I'll need to see your passport."

"It's in my suitcase. May I bring it by later?" She smiled sweetly to disguise the lie.

He swallowed, his face turning pink. "Uh, sure. Just don't forget. The army can't send you overseas until we see it."

"Deal." She set the paper on his desk and quickly completed the form, trying not to overly worry about his warning. There was still time for her to ask Wyatt, or even Sue—who didn't want to be caught short a dancer—the best way to remedy the situation. With only a small pinch of trepidation she added her signature at the bottom, affirming that all the information given was verified and true.

As lies went, signing the form wasn't that big. The only false information on the form was her new name. She had also decided to list Sal as her next of kin, which still didn't feel quite right. On the other hand, as long as she sent her next missive home from overseas, maybe her family would guess they should contact the USO with any questions?

"There." She glanced up. The young man's gaze was glassy—dazed, even. Too late she realized she had given him a really swell view down the front of her blouse. For Lily the display was rather tame, but for her new persona? Staying in character, she clutched her collar together as she straightened, as if embarrassed. The soldier flushed a dark, guilty red.

Hastily, she handed him the form. As if she'd just given him a live hand grenade, he leaped out of his chair and vanished into the room behind him. The metal clacking of a machine mystified her for a moment, but then he reappeared with a thin metal-ball chain and two dog tags. With fumbling fingers, he managed to thread the tags and fasten the clasp of the chain.

"Here you go." He held the tags out, his gaze not quite meeting hers. "You're all official now."

As she took the tags, all her amusement faded. The warm metal in her palm burned with the enormity of what she was doing. There was no going back now. In for a penny, in for a pound, her grandmother always said. Unfortunately, she suspected she was in for a lot more than a pound.

Another soldier waited outside the office to escort her back to the quartermaster's. This one, a slightly older private with black hair cut so short it looked blue, wasn't quite as awestruck by her as the previous fellow. And, as luck would have it, he was also particularly chatty and well able to maintain the conversation all by himself.

Nodding pleasantly, as if following the discussion, she instead reflected on what had happened in the office moments ago. Would Virginia have flirted with the fellow? Was she giving herself away through unconscious behaviors like leaning over without thought to her cleavage?

The answers were likely no and yes, which meant she had to do a better job of staying in character or risk being kicked out of the USO before she even got signed up. It was so frustrating, really. Projecting an air of innocence around women was relatively easy, but around men? Not so much. For some reason, the Y chromosome always brought out the siren in her.

She was literally going to be her own worst enemy if she didn't get her act together.

By the end of the day, however, Vi was worried less about maintaining her disguise than not having a nervous breakdown. At every turn the army seemed determined to erase any hope of privacy. There were official photographs taken for army records. Fingerprints inked on numerous official-looking cards. A *very* thorough physical that had her, of all people, blushing with embarrassment, and a whole plethora of vaccinations that left her feeling like she'd been accosted by a rabid porcupine.

The ultimate trial, though, was having to sit through the mandatory lecture on avoiding venereal diseases. The doctor, an older man who looked just as uncomfortable discussing the topic as she felt hearing it, also advised her to stock up on feminine pads for her monthly periods, since the army didn't stock those items and supplies overseas would be sporadic at best. And, by the way, becoming pregnant would get her sent home immediately, and on her own dime, so it would be best if she "kept her knees together."

Vi didn't know whether to laugh or cry at that piece of advice. While she appreciated his concern, that horse had left the barn long ago. The only way she could get pregnant now would be through divine intervention.

Finally, the army decided it was through with the troupe for the day. No more briefings on codes of conduct or the importance of military discipline or the need to keep quiet about anything they might see or hear. A hot meal and a brief rehearsal afterward were all that she had left to endure. Then it would be sweet, sweet bedtime. Vi could hardly wait.

With thoughts of soft pillows and clean sheets dancing in her head, she followed the troupe into the mess hall. Her stomach immediately growled at the smell of fried chicken and buttery mashed potatoes. She

looked around to see where the line started, her frazzled nerves starting to relax, when she caught a soldier staring at her from across the
crowded hall. Not staring as if she were the prettiest thing he had ever
seen. No, *staring*. As if he thought he recognized her but couldn't quite
place the where and the why of it.

Her fingers suddenly numb, Vi tucked a strand of dyed hair behind
her ear. There was no way he could have recognized her. In her modest
garb, with no stage makeup, and hair recently returned almost to its
natural brunette color, she was as far from Lily Lamour as she could
make herself without surgery. She had to be imagining it.

Chapter 7

"Does that fellow know you?" Marcie asked, coming up beside Vi.

Vi's hopes that she had been imagining his stare crashed and burned into complete ash. "I don't think so."

She ran through all the faces of fellows she'd known growing up and desperately tried to place him while Marcie cocked her head and considered the soldier with naive curiosity.

"Maybe he thinks you're pretty. In any case, you should probably go talk to him. You know, to practice our new role of goodwill ambassador."

Vi gave a shaky laugh. "You can. I'm too exhausted, and I don't actually like talking face-to-face with strangers. I'm at my best when my audience is at least three feet away and speechless with awe."

Marcie frowned. "Truly? I always thought theater people would be a more social lot, given how gregarious they are in public."

"I think a lot of us are much shier than people give us credit for," Vi said, a bit surprised by the girl's use of "they," as if she didn't consider herself a theater person. "How many shows have you been in?"

Marcie gave a small shrug as she picked up a tray and joined the mess line. "Not many. I mean, probably nothing you've heard of."

"Try me." Not that Vi was familiar with New York theater, but there might be some overlap with the Chicago scene.

"It doesn't matter," Marcie said airily as one of the cooks put a scoop of mashed potatoes on her plate.

Again Vi was surprised. Most thespians loved to go on and on about their various roles. That her travel buddy kept demurring likely meant she had very little actual experience, which begged the question of how the girl had gotten a role in the show. Maybe the production wasn't quite as top tier as Vi had expected? True, Sal had gotten her a spot sight unseen, but she was also a seasoned performer, having worked up to nine shows a week for the last two years, so the risk to the show was small.

"What does matter," Marcie continued with more enthusiasm, "is that I'll have a chance to help cheer up our men fighting overseas." Then she added, with a rueful laugh, "And I'll get away from my parents for a while. They can be rather . . . strict. Especially my father. He tries to run my life, thinking he knows what's best for me. But he doesn't!"

Vi could empathize. Looking back, she could definitely say the smothering weight of all her family's rules had contributed to her recklessness with Robert. Of course, now she could see her parents had been trying to keep her safe, but at the time she had felt unjustly confined, which had only added fuel to the fire.

Her sister hadn't helped the situation by warning Vi that she was "too young" to understand things like adult love and real desire and should leave romancing to her elders.

"What you feel is just puppy love," her sister had said. "It's not real."

Vi had been incensed.

So of course you decided to prove her wrong, Vi thought in self-disgust. Never one to let a challenge pass unmet, she had redoubled her efforts to make Robert fall in love with her. She'd already had a crush on the fellow, and with Fern declaring she was no longer interested in dating someone "who only wanted to be an auto mechanic"—something that hadn't bothered Vi in the least, since she had planned on having a wildly successful career in theater—Vi had decided to pull out all the stops.

If only she had bothered to run that plan by someone, they might have pointed out how wrong it was for a twenty-two-year-old man to agree to meet a fifteen-year-old in private. Or agree to kiss her less than chastely. Or suggest they go even further in the back seat of his father's car. But she hadn't because she was so sure she could handle "adult" matters on her own.

Yep, and you handled it like a real pro, Vi . . . a professional fool.

Having reached the end of the chow line, her mouth watering at the delicious smells rising off her tray, Vi joined Marcie, who was looking around for a place to sit. To Vi's dismay, the soldier was still staring.

Victor, the older actor, stopped beside them. "Need help finding a table?"

"It is rather crowded," Vi said.

"I doubt we'll have trouble finding seats, though," Marcie said with a surprising hint of bitterness. "If you haven't noticed, Vi is attracting a lot of attention."

"You mean all us gals are," Vi corrected, because it was true.

Marcie rolled her eyes. "Yeah, right. A person would have to be blind not to see you've got all the curves. The rest of us look like chopped liver next to you."

"Hey," Vi said, stung, "there is absolutely nothing wrong with your figure. And I won't be blamed for how I look. You want others to love what you've got? Love it yourself first. Or at least pretend to."

"Ladies, ladies," Victor interjected smoothly, soothingly. "Remember: we're ambassadors for the United States now. Everything we say or do from here on out will be part of the public record. So sheathe those claws—everyone is tired and road weary—and eat. We have rehearsal in fifteen minutes."

Clamping down on her irritation—because the actor was right about being road weary—Vi followed Marcie to the closest table, which also happened to be where the staring soldier was sitting. Vi pasted on a smile for the men they passed, even though what she really wanted to do was bean her travel buddy over the head with her tray. Did she not hear Vi say she didn't want to talk with strangers tonight?

Why, oh why, couldn't her travel buddy have been a male?

A man would've listened to her. Men Vi knew how to talk to. Men she could charm with a smile or a flutter of lashes over her big green eyes. Her power over the male sex was so unconscious, so innate, she hadn't even realized she had it until she had entered fifth grade and the other girls began to hate her for no reason she could pinpoint. She truly hadn't understood the problem at first. Yes, all the boys hung around her, but it wasn't her fault. She wasn't the prettiest girl in town. That was her sister, Fern. Nor was she the smartest, though she studied hard. Or the most athletic, despite being naturally good at dance. Or the most anything—except maybe sought after.

What she did possess was a genuine affection for men, and she'd never had any qualms letting them know it. She liked the way they looked and smelled, the way they sounded, the texture of their skin, their beards . . . everything. Or rather she liked *most* men. Not the rude ones, or the ones who assumed her body was up for grabs, or the ones who tried to boss her around. Or those who dared threaten Jimmy.

Especially not those.

"Hiya," Marcie greeted the soldiers as she set her tray down on the table in the space that had magically appeared for her.

Calling on all her acting ability, Vi took the seat next to the soldier who had been staring at her, and smiled shyly. Tiny sparks of unease prickled her skin as she tucked her hair behind her ear. Lord above, she hoped she could pull off the innocent act this time and not let it slip like she had at the induction office. "I hope this seat wasn't taken?"

"It's n-not," he stammered, his brown eyes as round as dinner plates. About her age, with thick chestnut hair and an adorable chin dimple, he didn't look like someone who would deliberately want to ruin her life, but she had been wrong about such things before.

"Where are you from?" she asked, giving him her full attention. *Might as well get this over with.*

If she was going to be exposed for a fraud, it would happen in the next few seconds. And perhaps it would be better for it to happen here than overseas, since the army had just told them that disgraced USO performers would be responsible for their own tickets home.

She was painfully short on dough at the moment.

The soldier's Adam's apple bobbed. "Canton, Ohio, miss."

"Canton? I've never been there," she answered honestly, as a small spark of hope took hold. Maybe he hadn't recognized her. "Is it nice?"

"Nice? It's only the birthplace of the National Football League!" Marcie leaned over Vi and shot the soldier a mischievous smile. "Never mind my friend, here. I love football. It runs in the family. In fact my father nearly named me Cantonia to celebrate the Bulldogs winning the championship in '23."

The soldier laughed. "You're kidding."

"I wish." Marcie rolled her eyes. "I was born the day after the game, and he was still in a good mood, having won a ton of money on the point spread."

Vi stopped cutting her chicken and raised an eyebrow at her travel buddy in surprise. "Your father is a gambler?"

Most of the gamblers she knew were perpetually broke, and Marcie's wardrobe was anything but cheap. Not that Vi begrudged the girl her expensive duds. Once upon a time she had worn nice clothes, too, not just secondhand outfits from better-off friends or ones she had sewn by hand.

A startled expression flashed over Marcie's face, as if she had said something she hadn't meant to. Then the smile was back in full shine, the moment gone. "He's a businessman, actually. A kind of manager. If he places a bet, it's only when he's pretty sure he'll win."

"Nothing like a sure bet." The soldier grinned and stuck out his hand to Marcie, practically knocking over Vi in the process. "Harvey Wilson."

"Marcie May."

The two shook hands, and Vi felt, for the first time in what had been a long while, invisible. It was a rather queer sensation, even though invisibility was the whole point of becoming Miss Heart. Still, it was going to take some getting used to.

While Marcie and Harvey continued their conversation, Vi stirred the canned peas on her plate into the mashed potatoes so they would stop rolling off her fork. Even though her attention kept drifting with fatigue, she learned that Marcie had grown up in New York City, which Vi had already guessed from her accent. That the girl adored football as much as she detested baseball, which was "a real snooze." That she would love to ride on a motorcycle and, like Harvey, thought it would be fun to fly airplanes. But her father would never allow such dangerous activities.

When Marcie mentioned she had gone to an all-girl Catholic school, Vi wasn't at all surprised. Even though she herself had been raised Lutheran, she'd had Catholic friends growing up, and their families were even stricter about rules and morals than hers had been.

"If I'd had longer legs, I would have been a Radio City Music Hall Rockette," Marcie confided with a dramatic sigh to the soldier, who was all ears. "But Rockettes have to be at least five feet five inches, and I'm only five two."

Vi stifled a snort. She doubted Marcie had been any closer to a Rockette audition than the sidewalk, given all the edicts of her father. But she kept the thought to herself as she pulled the breading off the chicken leg, looking for any sign of actual meat.

"It's Radio City's loss," Soldier Wilson declared, looking outraged on Marcie's behalf. "You're prettier than all of them."

Marcie blushed. "Why, thank you, Harvey."

"Marcie, eat." Vi pointed a fork at her travel buddy's untouched tray. "Rehearsal is coming up fast. And remember the USO rules we just swore to uphold?" *As in don't treat any one soldier as more special than another.*

Marcie's face fell as she caught the hint. "Oh, that's right." Then she frowned in disgust. "Stupid rules. I finally find a nice fella and I'm not allowed to enjoy it."

"Don't worry, miss," Soldier Wilson said earnestly. "I'll understand if you can't write me until your tour is over. How 'bout I give you my parents' address, and soon as you get back to the States, you can contact them for my forwarding address."

Marcie batted her eyelashes and cooed, "You really want me to write you?"

"Would I ever!" The soldier practically had stars in his eyes.

Vi sat back and stared. Where had the shy little Marcie gone? And more important, what the heck did the girl think she was doing? Chatting with a fellow, stroking his ego was one thing, but leading him on with promises of more? That was quite another, which made Vi think Marcie might not know the difference between harmless flirtation and outright seduction. It was akin to not knowing the difference between lighting a sparkler and a stick of dynamite, and just as dangerous for a woman.

"Unit 2-9-1-8," Sue called out over the clamor of forks scraping and too many conversations. An instant hush followed, allowing her to continue. "Rehearsal in the rec hall in five minutes, so finish up. Late arrivers will be court-martialed."

Vi grabbed her tray and stood. "Come on, Marce. That's our cue to beat feet."

Neither Marcie nor Wilson seemed to hear her.

Irritated with the both of them, Vi wondered if Marcie *wanted* to get kicked out of the USO. If so, maybe, just maybe, Vi should let her. After all, she had enough to worry about on this trip without having to babysit an obstinate, naive, headstrong girl . . .

She paused midstep on her way over to where the others were dropping off their trays and scraping their plates.

Those same adjectives could also be applied to the missing Mafia princess. And Marcie certainly looked the part, with her dark hair and eyes. *Catholic?* Check. *Overprotected?* Check. *Impulsive and reckless enough to blackmail her own father?* Check and double check. True, the name didn't fit. But what if the girl was using a stage name, trying to hide her identity, much like Vi was?

If so, it would be both good and bad news: good because Vi rather liked the girl, despite her irritating moments, but also bad because, from what she had seen tonight, it might be harder to keep her charge out of trouble than she had expected.

"You could've waited," Marcie groused, coming up beside her. "Now I won't be able to get his address."

"Good," she said, relieved as much by that news as by no longer facing the possibility she might have to drag the girl to rehearsal kicking and screaming.

Marcie huffed in annoyance. "Are you always such a killjoy?"

"Only when I see someone doing something stupid." Vi handed her tray to a Negro soldier stacking them on a cart to be washed.

"Virginia"—Marcie stressed the name in a way that made Vi's hackles rise—"we're *supposed* to be warm and welcoming and supportive to the troops. Not prudish wallflowers."

"The name is Vi, and just because a fella wears a uniform doesn't mean he's a good guy. Uncle Sam is just as likely to call up a no-good rat as a decent man, so *you* need to be more careful."

Marcie scoffed as she handed her tray to the same dark-skinned soldier, who seemed to be following the conversation with interest. "You're just jealous."

Vi wanted to roll her eyes. Considering that just last week she'd had men literally eating out of the palm of her hand, she was hardly going to be jealous over some soldier wanting Marcie's address. But she couldn't tell Marcie that. Nor could she say she was also the voice of experience when it came to the dangers of flirting, so Vi merely shrugged. "If you say so."

Marcie narrowed her eyes, clearly unwilling to give up the fight. "You know what, farm girl? You wouldn't last a single day in my world, so stop trying to give me advice."

Stung, Vi finally lost patience with the girl. "Look here, princess. I'd be careful casting slurs while wearing those brand-new shoes even though there's a war going on. Just what kind of 'business' does your daddy conduct, anyway? He got some kind of in with the black market?"

Marcie paled. "He's just a manager, like I told you. That's it."

Before Vi could even respond, Marcie had spun away, all but running after the other actors exiting through the door of the mess hall.

"Good job, Vi," she muttered to herself. "Way to make friends."

"Bet you anything her daddy's tied in with the Mob," a male voice said from behind her. "I'd watch yo'self around her, if I were you."

Vi turned to look at the dark-skinned soldier, one of the kitchen crew, curiously. "What makes you say that?"

"Her attitude. Her accent. I've been around her type before. Waited on them, listened in when they thought no one was paying attention—because being colored is like being invisible sometimes, you know? Though I was never in New York. I mostly worked the clubs in Chicago."

Her pulse kicked. "Chicago . . ."

The soldier leaned forward and whispered conspiratorially, "Don't you worry, Miss Lily. I don't know why you're working undercover with the USO, but I won't rat you out. You were always real good to my uncle George, even if you never noticed me. But I was only there the one summer before I got called up."

Vi forced her lungs to expand, to take in air before she passed out. George was the Negro bartender at Sal's club, and Vi had never been one to limit her friendships based on a person's skin color. If someone was willing to be nice to a fallen woman, she couldn't help but be nice right back. And George had been a true gentleman, keeping an eye on her when she was mingling with customers, discreetly sending the bouncer over if a patron forgot his manners.

"Am I that easy to recognize?" she asked, dread squeezing her throat.

The fellow smiled reassuringly. "No, miss. I happen to have a keen eye for faces." A flush bloomed faintly under his brown skin. "And I'd be a liar if I said I didn't think you were the prettiest and best performer there."

Vi blinked again, having never been complimented by a Negro. Not that it bothered her. It was just she had never contemplated her attractiveness to anyone but white men. "Thank you," she said after a moment. "For the compliment, and not giving me away."

He winked at her, but his dark-brown eyes were serious. "Have a good evening, miss. And don't be late to your rehearsal! The stocks ain't no place for a woman."

Reminded of the time, Vi spun around and made a beeline for the rehearsal. On the way she considered and then discarded the soldier's reassurance that no one else would recognize her. It was a chance she just couldn't take. If Janet had been kicked out for morality violations, Vi didn't even want to ponder her chances as an unwed mother turned stripper.

She would have to try harder to be invisible.

And pray to a god she no longer trusted that her past sins wouldn't be exposed. At least not until she and Marcie were back home, safe in the States, once more.

Chapter 8

"Over to your left," Sue called out the next afternoon as Ann and the other actors scrambled down the cargo netting as part of their boot camp instruction. "No, your other left, Victor! For heaven's sake, pay attention. And don't you dare fall!"

Vi, having made the same descent earlier with the chorus girls, winced as Ann's foot got caught, pulling her knee in an awkward, painful direction.

"Ouch!" Marcie exclaimed, watching the action next to Vi. "That had to have hurt. Good thing she doesn't have to dance in the show. And why do we have to practice abandoning ship, anyway? Wouldn't terror alone give a person sufficient motivation to abandon ship as fast as possible?"

Vi didn't bother answering what was clearly a rhetorical question. In truth, she didn't see the logic in the troupe being here at all. Why did a bunch of thespians need to learn how to march in step or handle a rifle, anyway?

"You know what was the worst?" Marcie continued as the last of the actors made their way onto solid ground. "Testing out the gas masks. I couldn't believe they made us do that! What if the gas had leaked and ruined our throats? We'd be sunk as a show."

"It did leak on Luciana. Remember?" Vi suppressed a shudder as she recalled how the actress, her eyes red and streaming, had been bundled off posthaste to the first aid station. "So we still could be sunk, unless Mr. Stuart can pull another actress out of his hat at a moment's notice."

Marcie made an impatient sound. "He found you, didn't he? And besides, Mr. Miller is so infatuated with her, he'd find a way to keep her in the show even if she croaked like a frog."

Vi glanced at Marcie in surprise. "You think he's got it that bad?"

"Haven't you noticed how he stares at her during rehearsal?"

"Well, no. I've been too busy learning the dances."

"I have," Frances said. Then she arched her perfectly drawn and shaded eyebrows as she continued, "But I doubt they're a couple any-more, considering how hard he made her cry last night."

"What's that?" Marcie asked, suddenly all ears.

Nothing like the prospect of gossip to make friends out of enemies, Vi thought with a mental eye roll. And where had Frances found time to apply full makeup between reveille and roll call?

"Are you sure it was Mr. Miller who made her cry?" Doubt pinched Gertie's forehead as she joined the conversation. "That doesn't sound like him at all. He's so nice!"

"I think he was breaking things off," Frances speculated in a hushed voice. "Those two have been thick as thieves since day one. Perhaps things were getting too hot and heavy between them."

"You mean they were . . . ?" Gertie's gray eyes widened. "But that's against the rules!"

Frances burst into laughter. "Oh, Gertie. Lord love you. Luciana's a star! Remember? And when did stars ever have to follow rules?"

"Wait," Vi said, her attention caught. "Luciana is a star?"

Frances waved her hand dismissively. "Only if you count landing the role of an understudy in last year's premiere of *Oklahoma!* at the Saint James. Which is what she should have been in this show, too. Everyone knows she can't cut it as a lead."

Marcie snorted. "You're just jealous because you can't face the fact that Luciana has a better voice than you and has sung with some really famous bands."

"And you're just sore because I'm twice the dancer you are," Frances shot back.

"Stop it, both of you!" Gertie's sweet face crumpled as if about to cry. "Shouldn't we be pulling together as a family? That's what my acting coach always said."

"It's all right, Gertie," Vi said soothingly, her heart going out to the sensitive girl. "Even the closest of sisters snipe at each other once in a while. It doesn't mean we aren't all on the same team." She shot a meaningful glance at the other two dancers. "Right?"

Marcie came, somewhat surprisingly, to Vi's aid and hugged the slender girl. "That's right, Gertie. Don't worry. We'll be like one big, happy family soon, warts and all—which is why I didn't like it that Mr. Miller made Luciana cry."

Frances made a gagging face. Vi elbowed her and got a not-very-sisterly glare in return.

From across the field, Sue narrowed her eyes at Gertie and Marcie and then came over. "Is everyone all right?"

"Yes, ma'am," Frances said, stepping forward with a bright smile. "Gertie was just feeling a mite homesick, so we were cheering her up. Gotta take care of each other."

Vi rolled her eyes. Of course Frances would take credit for the idea. The other dancer was so obsequious around Sue it made Vi's teeth hurt. Still, she had to give the brunette credit for trying to butter Sue up. It's what she would've done if she had actually given a damn about advancing her alter ego's career. The truth of it was, she intended to ditch Miss Virginia Heart as soon as the tour was over and it was safe to return to Chicago.

The rest of the actors joined them.

Ann rubbed her injured knee and looked around. "Where's Luciana? Shouldn't she be back by now?"

"I'm sure she's fine," Victor said soothingly, while Sue counted heads to make sure everyone was there.

"Speak of the devil; here she comes." Matt pointed toward the dirt road, and everyone turned to look. "Lucky girl. I swear she was probably watching, waiting for the exercise to end."

"Do you blame her," Victor said, sounding amused, "considering how close our Ann came to losing her leg in that net?"

"It wasn't that bad," Ann said. She waved as the other actress got closer. "Luciana, thank God. I was afraid the army had done you in already, leaving the rest of us to figure out how to stage the show without a villain."

"You'd still have Victor." Luciana stopped at the edge of the group and smiled sheepishly. "Sorry that took so long, but apparently clearing me to return to 'action' required a lot of paperwork."

Sue turned to Vi. "Speaking of paperwork . . . Miss Heart, I had a message from the USO office saying your passport information is missing."

Vi worked to keep her expression smooth, unconcerned. "There was an error on my first one, so I had to turn it in to get fixed. But I should have it back in time to sail."

Sue didn't seem much appeased. "Let's hope so, though you should've told me before."

Vi bit the inside of her cheek and stayed silent, knowing she would only dig her hole deeper if she tried to defend herself. The truth was she hadn't applied for anything yet, a situation she knew she needed to remedy as soon as possible—or, as the army said, ASAP.

As Sue turned to the others and began explaining the schedule for the rest of the day, Marcie sidled up to Vi.

"Don't feel bad," the girl whispered. "It took forever to get my passport sorted out, too. The fellow at the courthouse wasn't too keen on taking just my parish priest's word that I'm over eighteen and wanted my parents' permission instead."

Vi glanced at her travel buddy in surprise. "Couldn't you have just shown him a birth certificate?"

Marcie shrugged. "I didn't have it with me."

"So why didn't you ask your parents to vouch for you?" Though Vi suspected she knew what the real problem was.

Marcie glanced uneasily at Sue and the others. "I didn't want to bother them."

I bet, Vi thought with a laugh. If Marcie was indeed the rebellious Mob daughter who wasn't supposed to be doing something as risky as touring the Foxhole Circuit with the USO, involving her parents would've been the last thing she wanted to do. "For future reference, I heard baptismal certificates work, too." At least she hoped so, having just forged a baptismal certificate for herself on borrowed letterhead.

Sue glared in their direction again, so Vi clammed up. The need to stay in Sue's good graces, at least until the troupe was safely overseas, trumped any further attempts to gain Marcie's confidence. At least for now.

Though it sure would be swell if she could confirm Marcie's identity as the missing Mob daughter. Perhaps if she called Sal to see if Angelina Maggio might be working under a stage name. She had noticed a pay phone earlier, outside the PX, so she would have the means, if not the moola. Not that she was too worried. Sal would likely spring for a collect call, as long as it was from her. And as long as she didn't make it a habit.

The problem was finding the time to call. Between Sue and the army, every minute of every day was accounted for, from reveille to lights out. And there was Sal's schedule to consider, too. Having been gone almost a week, she guessed the show had already closed. So would he be home or at the club working on a new lineup? Perhaps if she sneaked out and called late enough, she might be able to reach him at home—a place she knew existed in theory even if she had never been there.

She could also ask about Jimmy while she was at it. Her chest ached at the thought. Oh, how she missed seeing her little boy. He was all that was good in the world, all that was precious. The only good thing to have come out of her screwed-up life.

She gave herself a mental shake. What she should really be asking about was the status of the investigation into Tony's murder. She might be free and clear and able to return home on the next Greyhound, the USO be damned. The mere possibility made her fingers itch to dial Sal right now.

Then she remembered the deal that had been cut with Miss Maggio's father and silently cursed. Papa Maggio would not be happy if she reneged, and an angry Papa Maggio, with all his Mafia connections, would be a much bigger threat to her future happiness than a mere murder conviction.

Bottom line was she had to somehow locate Miss Maggio before the unit shipped out, or her goose would not only be cooked—it would be cooked, dressed, and served up on a gold platter with gravy on the side.

"Virginia, did you hear me?" Sue's voice interrupted her gloomy train of thought. "It's time for you and Miss May to show me what you've learned so far."

Chapter 9

"Well, that was a barrel of fun," Marcie groused as the door to the rec hall slammed behind them. She looked toward the fading sunset and sighed. "Do you think it's too late to back out?"

Vi rolled her neck, her muscles all knotted from the sting of Sue's critiques. "Nope, not if you don't mind being AWOL. We're part of the army now, sister."

"Well, that stinks."

"Not as badly as our dancing, at least according to Sue," Vi said dryly.

Marcie wrinkled her nose and then laughed ruefully. Linking her arm through Vi's, she gave her a sideways look. "Speaking of Sue, I heard her mention something about it being a shame you wouldn't be singing. Is that true?"

Tension threaded Vi's shoulders, though she kept her tone mild. "It is."

"Are you a terrible singer, as in tone deaf, or do you think you won't have time to learn the music? Because I'd be happy to help you with the latter."

Vi debated how to answer for a moment and then decided on the truth, since it would be simpler to remember going forward.

"Neither. I just made a decision several years ago to stop singing."

Marcie pulled them both to a halt and stared at her. "Why would you do that?"

"For the same reason we make any decision in life: personal preference."

Marcie shook her head. "I think you're nuts, because that's a serious handicap in this business. I mean, it's one thing if you can't sing, but to not do it just because you don't want to?"

"I didn't ask for a lecture."

"I just think you're being foolish. It's not like singing is a mortal sin. It's not even a venal one, unless you belong to one of those sects that think having fun of any sort is bad . . ." The dawning horror on Marcie's face made Vi laugh.

"Relax. You're not paired with a wet blanket. I have no problem with fun; exhibit one—I love to dance. And I even drink on occasion—"

"And kiss boys, too?" Marcie asked with a wink and a sly smile.

"When I'm not part of a USO tour, sure."

Marcie was shaking her head again. "Vi, Vi, Vi . . . what am I going to do with you?" She laughed and then pulled Vi's arm close. "Corrupt you, that's what!"

The impossibility of that had Vi wanting to both laugh and cry.

Perhaps after she had gotten over being chewed out by Sue for not being further along, she would be less emotional about things. Not that she blamed the stage manager for having such impossible expectations. It was an old director's trick to start out strict and then lighten up as the production progressed. To start gentle and then suddenly turn fierce when things refused to jell was much harder on everyone. The former method led to respect from the cast, the latter to frustration and worse.

"Hey, there's Gertie and Frances!" Marcie's steps hesitated. "And Ann and Luciana. Darn them."

"What's wrong?"

"I don't like how Ann is always looking down her nose at me, like I'm some kind of pond scum. And Luciana makes me uncomfortable."

"How so?" Vi glanced at the dark-haired actress and noticed nothing unusual. She was on the quiet side, sure. But a lot of theater folk were quiet offstage, all their energy having been expended in front of the footlights.

"She . . . I don't know, it's like she's trying to see into my head, and I don't like it."

Vi playfully elbowed the girl in the ribs. "Maybe it's all those secrets you're trying to keep."

Marcie didn't laugh. "Is it bad that I wish they weren't traveling with us?"

"Only if you go around saying so," Vi said seriously. "Productions are like families—you can't always pick who is part of it. But you can do your level best to make it work."

"I'll try." Marcie's lips tightened as she watched the two actresses head toward the mess hall. "But no promises."

"Speaking of families," Vi said, an idea forming, "any chance you could cover for me tonight after lights out? I promised my mother I would call once I got into the show, and I haven't had time."

"Won't you worry her by calling so late? Not to mention you'd be taking a real risk." Marcie shook her head discouragingly. "If I were you, I'd write her a letter. It'd not only be safer than breaking curfew but also would give her something she could reread while you're overseas."

It was a reasonable suggestion, or would be if time hadn't been of the essence, and reassuring her mother had been what Vi had actually planned.

"Perhaps, but what I really want is to hear my mom's voice."

Which was cross-her-heart, hope-to-die true, even if it wasn't in the cards anytime soon. Truth was, she was afraid to call her parents. Maybe if she had called during those first frantic months on her own, or anytime after that, things wouldn't have gotten to this point. But to not call once in five years? That was unforgivable. Her parents would likely hang up on her before she got past "hello." She would if her child did the same to her.

Of course, she would also turn around and immediately have the operator reconnect her, her worry and love overriding disappointment. But she had no idea if her parents felt the same way.

"Just cover for me, please?" Vi batted her eyes at her travel buddy. "I'll owe you one . . ."

Marcie threw her hands in the air. "Fine. But I'm not bailing you out if you get caught."

A few hours later, Vi prayed her travel buddy would remember the cover story they had agreed upon as she sneaked out the barracks window. A silent, inky blackness entombed the camp due to the strict blackout orders issued for all the cities and military encampments up and down the Eastern Seaboard. With barely enough light from the slivered moon to make out the different buildings along the road, she headed toward the PX.

She winced as her shoes crunched softly on the gravel path. Nerves jittered in her stomach as an engine growled somewhere in the distance. She had no idea what she would do if she ran across a sentry. They were around, she knew. She just hoped they would stick to the perimeters of the camp and not bother a harmless young woman trying to call her ex-boss.

Relief fluttered in her veins as the PX and the phone booth morphed out of the shadows. Thankfully, the area looked utterly deserted, but then maybe she was the only one foolish enough to be out after taps.

Slipping inside the phone booth, she glanced up to check if there was a light bulb that might go on if she closed the door to muffle the sound of her conversation. It didn't look like it. Easing the door shut, she was proven correct a moment later when no light illuminated. Breathing a silent prayer that her luck would continue to hold, she picked up the handset and clicked the cradle switch.

"Hello?" she called softly. "Long distance, please." Her heart raced as what felt like an eternity passed until the correct operator clicked on. "Yes, can you please place a collect call to Chicago? I'm trying to reach Mr. Sal Fleischmann of Albany Park."

Tears filled her eyes as Sal's familiar, hoarse voice came on the line. Due to the expense, she jumped right to her questions, and his answers were just as quick: yes, Jimmy was fine; no, she couldn't return yet as the police investigation had stalled, and she was still being sought; and no, he didn't think the baptismal certificate would be enough for a passport, at least not for an expedited one. For that, she would need a US citizen to vouch for her identity.

In better news, he did confirm that *One Fine Mess* was indeed the correct show. So Vi was where she was supposed to be.

"Tell me the names of the actresses again?" he asked after she told him that there wasn't an Angelina Maggio to be found.

"Well, there's Ann, which could be short for Angelina, except she's blonde and blue eyed, and Luciana, who looks more the part."

"Not all Italians are dark," Sal chided her. "Give me their last names."

Vi closed her eyes in dismay. "I don't know any of the last names, except for my travel buddy's, and hers is May."

"What was that?" Sal asked sharply. Vi repeated herself, and her old mentor began to laugh, a raspy, coughing sound. "Ah, I'll bet you anything she's the one."

"I was starting to think so, too," Vi said, thinking back to her conversation with the Negro soldier that first night. "But why are you so sure? I haven't even described her to you."

"No need to," Sal said with another amused wheeze. "Maggio is Italian for May, the month . . ."

A sharp rap on the glass door drowned Sal out and her heart stopped. She threw up her hand to block the sudden bright light in her eyes, and then it was gone again. A flashlight being switched off.

"Miss, I need you to step out here."

She pressed her hand against her chest, hoping to catch her breath, but couldn't. With eyes still partially blinded by the flashlight, she fumbled for the door handle. Then a white helmet and white gloves came into view. It was an MP. Military police.

Rats.

She opened the booth door.

"Do you have authorization to be out this late, miss?" the MP asked politely. From his size and the timbre of his voice, she guessed him to be in his forties, so a career army man. Not someone who would be wild about women running amok on his watch.

She licked her suddenly dry lips. *Come on, Vi, think!*

Older men often had a soft spot for helpless, crying females, right?

She gave a soft sniff and ran a finger under each eye as if wiping tears. "I-I'm so sorry." Her voice trembled convincingly, though from honest fear, not sorrow—not that he needed to know that. "I was s-so homesick, I had to call home. Am I in trouble?"

"I'm afraid you are. You can't go around willy-nilly after call to quarters without prior authorization. To whom do you report, miss?"

She started to say Sue, when a different name came to mind. Someone who might be more sympathetic to her plight, and someone who might be able to fix her passport problem by vouching for her. What had Marcie said? "There's nothing he can't make or fix."

Well, let's hope her travel buddy cum Mafia princess was right, because there was a lot about her situation right now that needed fixing.

Vi wiped her eyes again and tried to look contrite, though how much of her expression the fellow could see in the dark was hard to judge. "I-I suppose if you must turn me in, you'd better take me to Mr. Wyatt Miller. Though I would rather you didn't."

"Mr. Miller, you say?" The MP crossed his arms, and Vi hoped she was doing the right thing. "I think I can find him for you. Let's go."

Chapter 10

"Could this voyage be any longer?" Marcie plopped onto the deck next to Vi. She crossed her arms and scowled at her bare feet. The Atlantic Ocean splashed unimpressed against the hull of the troop carrier as the sun burned down, undimmed by a single cloud in the endless sky. "I'm tired of sitting around, cooped up either in our room or on deck, and want to be there already."

Vi inspected her own toes for signs of a sunburn and sighed. "I can't believe the army made me cough up five bucks to get a rushed passport. But that seems to be the way of things around here: hurry up and wait."

Actually, it had been Mr. Miller's five dollars, since Vi had only a dollar and five cents left to her name. The loan had come with a lecture, too, about being responsible and planning ahead. His criticism had stung, since she was responsible when not forced to do things on the fly thanks to dead hit men. Still, it had been exceedingly nice of him to drive her to the county courthouse, vouch for her identity, and otherwise make sure all the t's were crossed and i's dotted on her paperwork.

Someday, she would find a way to return the favor, because kindness like that shouldn't go unrewarded.

"At least the breeze is nice," Vi continued, tilting her face to catch the cooler air sweeping in off the ocean.

"Not nice enough to make up for being stuck on this boat for two straight weeks." Marcie sighed and collapsed back on the gray-painted deck. "I don't know how you can stand it with that fellow always shouting over the loudspeaker that it's time to get up, or time to eat, or time to drill, or time to whatever. And forget about finding any privacy!"

Vi hid a smile. Now that she knew who Marcie really was, it was no wonder her travel buddy was miffed by all the rules and regulations of army life. It had to be quite the change for her.

"They lied, Vi," Marcie proclaimed, throwing an arm out dramatically. "Join the USO; it'll be exciting, they said. Have the experience of a lifetime. Do your part to cheer up our troops. You'll never regret it." The girl snorted. "I should've thrown my passport away as soon as I got it. Saved myself a lot of grief."

Vi stifled a yawn. "I have a feeling things will be plenty exciting soon enough. Don't worry."

Her travel buddy sat up. "You know what would be grand? If we could practice our dances in front of the sailors. Except"—she collapsed back onto the deck—"fat chance of that. The captain won't even let us be on the same deck with them!"

"Which is for our own safety, Marce. There are several thousand of them, if you include the soldiers belowdecks, and only seven of us women, if you include Sue. The last thing he wants is a riot." Not to mention the no-fraternization edict also reduced the chances of someone recognizing her as Lily Lamour, something that still worried her, though the fear faded with each passing day.

"Luciana doesn't seem afraid," Marcie said a bit peevishly.

Vi frowned as she reached for the long-sleeved shirt she had borrowed from Gertie. She hoped that wherever they landed would have ready-made clothing for sale. She was so tired of wearing other people's things. "Why would you say that? And what's your beef with Luciana, anyway? You're always cuttin' her."

Marcie shoved a sweaty lock of hair out of her face. "Obviously you didn't see her yesterday morning, taking private shooting lessons from the captain himself. Bet that wasn't his only pistol she was looking to handle."

Vi let the dig at Luciana slide, more struck, and even a little impressed, that the dark-haired actress had thought to ask for shooting instruction. "You know, becoming more at ease with a gun, considering how we will be touring in a war zone, doesn't seem all that unreasonable. What we learned at Camp Kilmer was pretty rudimentary."

"It wasn't the lesson I object to but how it was conducted," Marcie said darkly. "The two of them all cozied up and smiling. Good thing she's through with Wyatt or there would've been trouble."

Vi gave her friend the side-eye. "You're jealous!"

"And why shouldn't I be?" Marcie gestured toward the sailors who were hanging over the railing on the upper deck, ogling them. "A whole ship full of men and I can't even smile at one without being reprimanded."

"You don't have to smile." Vi glanced up and winked at the men, earning a cheer. The flirtatious side of her preened a bit at the attention. "Just be yourself: sweet, innocent."

"Easy for you to say. Don't think I haven't noticed how men fall all over themselves when you're around. You and Luciana, both." Marcie plopped back onto the deck with a sigh. "I'm blaming my parents. They never left me unsupervised around anything male, so I never got a chance to practice . . . well, men-attracting things!"

"They probably wanted to protect you."

"Yeah, by making me so clumsy and awkward around men I will never find one on my own," Marcie said glumly.

Vi laughed. "Oh, come on."

"I'm not kidding! My parents are relics from the eighteenth century, I swear. In their eyes 'good girls' marry whomever the family picks out for them, love be damned." Marcie flung her hand out. "I'm nothing more than a pawn, someone to find an advantageous match for in order to bolster the family fortunes. I swear they all dream of becoming Rockefellers or Kennedys or Vanderbilts. Except they don't really approve of those families, either, because they aren't . . . well, not enough like us."

Vi made a sympathetic noise, having seen firsthand how cliquish the Mafia was. Nor was she surprised to learn that Marcie's parents had had a strict sense of what societal success meant. All parents did, as far as Vi could tell.

Growing up as the daughter of a respected, well-liked banker, as well as a veritable pillar of the community, had come with its own set of expectations around decorum and public behavior. Her parents had made it very clear that their girls should be well behaved, do well in school, and then find matrimonial happiness with a steady, responsible man. Working for a living wasn't expected or even encouraged, unless it was meant to be a hobby and didn't take away from time with the family.

Oddly, she had never questioned the mismatch between her parents' goals and her own of being a Broadway star. That Marcie had was one more thing to admire about the girl, even if it did sting to hear her complaints about having to get married when Vi likely no longer had that option. Not with her past.

And why was it that one didn't truly value an opportunity until it was taken away?

With a sigh, she looked up at the endless blue sky and wondered if it was sunny in Chicago. She thought of a small boy and sparkly sequins and all the other precious things she had left behind, perhaps forever.

"I wonder where we'll end up." Marcie scrunched her nose. "I hope not England. I hear the weather there is awful. Rainy, gloomy . . ."

"On the other hand, we'd at least speak the language."

"Ugh. I hadn't thought of that. I hope we don't land in North Africa, then. I don't know a word of African."

"I think French might work there, too. At least that's what I gathered from watching *Casablanca*."

"I didn't get to see that movie. Once Mama heard it was about a love triangle involving a married woman, that was that!"

"I think it was about more than just that," Vi said dryly.

"In any case, I don't speak French, either."

"Well, don't look at me." Vi stretched her arms over her head to ease the cramp in her back. "I only know German, and heaven forbid we ever end up playing for Nazis!"

"Unless we were spies." Excitement lit Marcie's eyes. "Do you think you could teach me? Then we could go undercover and smuggle out secrets. It'd be so much more glamorous than being a mere chorus girl."

"So much more dangerous, you mean."

"But think of the fun." Marcie sat up straighter, her eyes widening. "Ooh, can you imagine if we get sent to Italy?"

"Why?" Vi said dryly. "Neither one of us speaks Italian. Though, come to think of it, Luciana might."

"Bah! That *contadina* wouldn't fool anyone as a spy."

Vi blinked, startled by the unfamiliar word. "Canta deena? Is that some kind of female singer?" Her Latin was pretty rusty, but she was pretty sure "canta" had something to do with singing.

"Singer?" Marcie laughed in genuine amusement. "Well, I suppose in a way I can see how you got that. But it's not *canta*, but *conta*." She stressed the longer vowel. "Contadina, which is Italian for . . . well, farmer or peasant."

"Luciana is a farmer?" Vi asked casually, even as her pulse raced. In all the weeks they had known each other, this was the first time Marcie had given even a hint of her real identity—assuming Sal and she were right and Marcie really was Angelina Maggio. She decided to give her travel buddy a little push into disclosing more. "So how is it an Irish girl knows Italian?"

Marcie wrinkled her nose. "Irish? Whatever made you think that?"

"Well, your last name, for one. The Mays I've met were from Ireland."

"Really?" Marcie's gaze slid away. "I had no idea."

"So 'farmer,' eh?" Vi tucked the word into her memory, not buying Marcie's evasion about her ancestry.

"It's considered a bit of an insult, so be careful using it," Marcie warned.

"Why?" Vi asked, surprised. In Iowa, farming was a venerated profession.

Marcie shrugged. "It just is."

"You still haven't said how you learned the word," Vi reminded the girl. For someone who said she couldn't keep a secret, her travel buddy was proving remarkably cagey about her Italian roots.

Marcie rolled her eyes. "It wasn't hard. I mean, there's no way someone can grow up in Brooklyn without picking up a few words of Italian here and there. Particularly insults and swear words."

"Kind of like how I know all kinds of improper words in German thanks to growing up in a town chock-full of German immigrants," Vi said with a wry laugh.

"Just so!" Marcie laughed and grabbed Vi's hand, giving it a squeeze in her excitement. "I'm telling you, if the show flops, we should become some kind of spy duo."

Vi shook her hand free. "No thanks. The life of intrigue might appeal to you, but I want to get home again as soon as possible."

"Oh, I'm sorry. Did you leave a fellow behind?" Marcie's eyes rounded in sudden compassion, the mercurial mood shift so typical of the girl, Vi almost laughed, despite the ache in her chest.

"Yeah. I guess you could say that," she said, thinking of Jimmy and then trying *not* to think about how far she had traveled from him.

"I wish I had someone waiting for me to come home." Marcie looked out over the ocean, her expression wistful. "At least someone I liked."

Vi pulled herself back to the present. "Not just some fellow your parents picked out?"

Marcie nodded, and then she glanced back. "Is it so awful I want to marry for love?"

"Love is overrated," Vi said flatly, her memories of Robert less than romance inspiring. "And so is marriage, for that matter."

"But what about children? Don't you want any?"

For a moment, she couldn't speak as a familiar pain sliced through her, awful and inescapable. She closed her eyes, focused on the feel of the sun on her skin, the sound of the gulls overhead. *Breathe, Vi. She didn't know.* She opened her eyes. "Children aren't an option for me. I suffered an injury when I was fifteen that made it impossible."

As Marcie's eyes widened in shock, Vi forced herself to smile.

The news, when she learned it, had devastated her. It had come up as she was being discharged from the hospital after Jimmy's birth. She could still see the serves-you-right glint in the doctor's eyes as he explained how complications during the admittedly difficult delivery had irreparably damaged her. This after she had already given her baby up for adoption, so there was no chance of ever undoing the void that had opened in her soul.

"I'm sorry." Marcie laid her hand over Vi's and squeezed gently. "That really stinks."

Vi blinked back sudden tears. The utter inadequacy of "stinks," given the awful reality, struck her as both darkly funny and deeply sad. And yet there was nothing she could do to fix it, except go back in time and be someone else, to wit, someone more likely to think before jumping into the unknown with both feet.

"Well, I'll be . . ." Marcie let go and pointed down the deck. "Am I seeing things, or is Ann actually waving us over to talk to her and Luciana? And look, there's Sue, too."

Vi wiped her cheeks and looked where her travel buddy was pointing. Sure enough, Ann was waving them over. "I wonder what's up."

"Should we go find out?" Marcie asked.

"If it means no more talk of marriage, absolutely." Vi jumped to her feet.

By the time they had reached the small group, Gertie and Frances were there, too.

"News," Ann exclaimed in her perfect East Coast diction as everyone drew near. "Sue finally has some news for us."

Sue, not looking nearly as excited, frowned at Vi and Marcie. "Why aren't you two ladies in uniform?"

"Because we were working on our dances," Marcie said with an airy wave of her hand. "And it's difficult to get the moves right in army-regulation skirts."

"You're not kidding," Frances said, with a roll of her green eyes. "And the pants aren't much better; I have to roll them up so far to keep from tripping on them."

Sue scowled, clearly unimpressed.

"News?" Gertie prompted gently, ever the peacemaker, her worried gaze bouncing between all their faces.

Sue's expression lightened. "There's been no official word, but the scuttlebutt"—which was the army slang for gossip—"is that the voyage is almost over and we'll be landing in two days' time. So I want you all to get started packing up your things, in case we land earlier."

"Do we know where yet?" Frances asked, taking Gertie's arm as if to reassure her.

"Well, it'll either be North Africa or Italy," Sue said. "Because see that smudge over there, on the horizon?" Six gazes turned toward the starboard side of the ship. "That's the coast of Africa. We went through the Strait of Gibraltar last night."

"Truly?" Even Ann, who never seemed impressed by anything, looked awed by the information.

"Well, if it's Italy, Luciana here can help translate," Frances said. "Right, Luciana?"

Luciana didn't say anything, her gaze fastened on the opposite horizon.

Surprised by the actress's silence, Vi studied Luciana's expression for a clue to her thoughts. It wasn't like Luciana to ignore people. In Vi's experience, the actress was as kind as she was beautiful, and easy to talk to once one got past her slightly imperious manner. It had been Luciana who had explained Ann's dislike of the dancers, saying it wasn't their fault. Ann's fiancé had run off with a dancer the year before, breaking the blonde's heart, and she had yet to recover.

Having fallen victim to a man's lies herself, Vi had utterly forgiven Ann from that point on.

"Well, that's it, kiddos," Sue said. "Vi, Marcie—I don't want to catch either of you on deck out of uniform again."

And with that last bit of advice, she strode off toward the stairs leading to the upper decks.

"Time to be drab again," Marcie grumbled. "Think she'll soften up once we land?"

"Nope. We're with the army now." Vi watched the other women drift off on a wave of excited chatter. All except Luciana, who shivered and then glanced around the deck, looking a little lost.

Concern tugged at Vi's conscience, despite a hard-and-fast rule of not getting involved in other people's business. No good ever seemed to come of it. Jealous boyfriends, broken promises, troubled marriages? Not her problem. Through with some guy and no longer caring who he went out with? Not falling for it. She'd been burned believing Fern on that last one, which had resulted in the Robert fiasco. And her experience with mobsters had only cemented her belief that she was better off minding her own concerns.

Still, something about Luciana's sad, almost pensive expression gave Vi pause. It was as if the actress wanted to talk something over with a friend, but there was no one there. Except her.

Vi sighed. She really wasn't any good at the whole female-friend business. Men were all right because they were so straightforward about what they thought and liked. Women had always been more of an enigma to her.

On the other hand, if Luciana, who was much closer to the directors than Vi, was worried about something that might even tangentially affect Marcie's safety, Vi wanted to know about it.

"What's the holdup?" Marcie asked. "Aren't you going to change?"

Vi hesitated a moment more and then made her decision. "You go ahead and get started. There's something I want to talk to Luciana about. Nothing important. Just girl talk."

Marcie gave her an odd look. "Oh-kaaaay, but don't take too long. Sue was pretty steamed."

"Don't worry. I'll be along shortly."

Vi waited until Marcie was out of sight. Then she turned, screwed up her courage, and spoke. "Luciana?"

The actress glanced up with a startled, doe-like air.

"I—I wanted to tell you how much I like watching you perform. I'm learning a lot."

"Thank you," the actress said softly, her slight singsong accent more pronounced offstage. A ghost of a smile lifted the corners of her mouth. "That's so nice to hear. And may I return the compliment? You are a very talented dancer. I've been watching you rehearse with Miss May, and the show will be much stronger with you in it."

"Oh! Thank you." The unexpected praise almost threw Vi off track. Then she gave herself a mental shake. *Stay on task, Vi. Be a friend; gain information.* "I couldn't help but notice you seem rather down. Is it something to do with the show?"

Luciana blinked. "The show? No, not at all. Though I'll be glad when we can get back to full rehearsals. It's hard to perfect one's role when scenes are forever rehearsed out of order. But I doubt the soldiers will demand perfection."

"Unless they were former theater critics," Vi said. The remark earned a small laugh from Luciana. "It's not something Mr. Miller said, then? Frances said he made you cry the other day, when we were at Camp Kilmer."

Luciana's lips parted in surprise, but then she quickly composed herself. "I was unaware anyone saw us." She took a deep breath. "Please tell Frances not to worry. Mr. Miller was merely passing along some bad news."

"Nothing too bad, I hope," Vi said. "I know how hard it is to perform when your mind is elsewhere."

"Don't we all." Luciana smiled gently, and then sorrow filled her dark eyes again. "Since you were so kind as to ask: Mr. Miller brought me news of my relatives in northern Italy. Ones we had lost touch with after the Nazis took over. When the Allies landed, we hoped we would soon hear from them again. When we didn't, we made inquiries through . . . various channels. The embassy received a report while I was at the camp, and . . ." She blinked as if to hold back tears and looked out over the ocean again. "The news wasn't good. The Nazis have taken them away."

"They're not dead, then?" Vi asked, trying to get a better grip on the situation. "I mean, it probably isn't good the Nazis have them, but at least they're still alive."

"If they were only Italian, perhaps." The actress took another deep inhale. "But they are also Jews. And worse, my cousin apparently fell in with the Italian resistance. He was arrested by the Italian fascists, and now the Germans have rounded everyone up: his parents, grandparents, siblings, everyone."

Vi's breath left her as if she'd been hit. She could scarcely imagine how Luciana could stand it. If she had learned her family, even one of the more distant branches, had been captured by Nazis, the news would have brought her to her knees. "I'm so, so sorry."

"Thank you." Luciana's tremulous smile tore Vi's heart even more. "When I auditioned for the USO, I hoped we would go to Italy, since that's where I was born. But now that my family is gone, any homecoming will be bittersweet, to say the least."

"Is there anything I can do? Anything any of us can?"

"Defeat the Germans?" Luciana said with a wry laugh. Then her expression turned thoughtful. "You wouldn't happen to speak Italian?"

"Not a lick. German? Sure. And even a few words of Norwegian and Swedish."

"Really?" A curious expression crossed the actress's face and then was gone. "I suppose the person I should be asking is Miss May. Though Sicilian isn't all that useful once one leaves the island."

"I'm sorry, what?"

The actress shrugged. "I don't know for sure, but I suspect May is a stage name. She has that look of someone from *Sicilia*. And Maggio—that's May in Italian—is a common enough surname."

The latter part Vi already knew, but the first? "I meant your comment on Sicilian. Do they not speak Italian there?"

"Yes, and no." The actress's lips twisted slightly. "Millennia of trade have taught them our language, of course. But their dialect is their own and unlike any other in Italy, something they are quite proud of."

"Meaning if she teaches me Italian, no one in the rest of Italy will understand me?"

Luciana's amusement grew. "It's not that bad. Though honestly, no matter what accent you learn, you'll never be completely understood everywhere. Remember there was no 'Italy' a hundred years ago. So the concept of a unified language is new to us. Every region has its own dialect, its own history, its own customs."

"But Italy fights as a single nation." Vi was pretty sure of that fact.

"No." Luciana smiled sadly. "Not at the moment. Not as the Allies would wish. It all comes down to our history. If you were to ask an Italian who they are fighting for, it wouldn't be the Allies or the Germans. It would be for their hometown, for their friends and relatives. For what they know and love, because armies come and go. Kingdoms rise and fall. Political systems flourish and fail. What doesn't change is the Italian heart, which is strong and full of passion. But will the Italian people help us, you might ask? I suppose it will depend on who you talk to and who you mean by 'us.'"

Vi gave a half laugh. "Thanks for the heads-up."

"You're welcome. Now if you'll excuse me, I should probably go inside. I'm not so bold as to risk Sue's wrath," Luciana said with a smile. She started to turn away, then stopped. "Virginia . . . I meant what I said just now about your talent. If something should happen to me, I'd like—"

"Nothing will happen to you," Vi said quickly, shocked the actress would dare the Fates like that.

"Nevertheless," Luciana said, raising her finger to quiet Vi. "You might wish to learn my lines, just in case."

"Except that I don't sing," Vi told her, even as her mind reeled at the possibility.

Luciana's expression fell. "Ah. Then I guess not. I'm sorry."

"Don't be."

Vi stood on deck for another moment after Luciana went inside, torn between astonishment and dread. That Luciana had thought her good enough to be an understudy thrilled her to no end. But it also made her uneasy. Not that she was superstitious, but she wouldn't mind a lucky rabbit's foot about now. Particularly since Luciana's portrayal of Italy hadn't been all that reassuring.

Even though Luciana hadn't said anything directly, Vi worried Marcie's heritage could prove a problem. It made sense that there might still be regional jealousies and conflicts despite a central government. Rather like siblings under a shared roof, she imagined, each one trying to best the other, trying to stand out, wanting to feel superior if only for a moment.

That's the way it had been with her and Fern. They had stood together against outside threats, like when Artie Crandall had teased Vi in seventh grade about being so busty and Fern had given him a dressing down like no other—a rare show of sisterly love that had made Vi cry. And Vi had let the air out of Charlie Keller's tires after he had broken Fern's heart by standing her up on the night of a big dance.

Yet they had been competitive, too, both trying out for the same part and throwing fits if the other one got it. They had argued and fought and told the other they wished they had been born an only child. But only in private. Vi wished, now, that she had spent more time telling Fern how much she had admired her and that her jealousy had been fueled by thinking herself an inferior copy.

How clearly she could see that now.

"Virginia Heart, what are you doing out there?" Sue called from the deck stairs.

Vi jerked back to the present. "Sorry. I thought I lost an earring, but I found it!"

Hurrying inside, Vi resolved to write an additional letter home, and this one to Fern and Fern alone. She would apologize for being such a brat and say all the things she should have years ago.

It also made her think she should be more like a big sister to Marcie, rather than a babysitter. Someone like Fern. A confidante. Someone who would stand with Marcie against a common enemy. Someone who would also shore up Marcie's defenses where she was most vulnerable. Because that was what Vi had needed five years ago and didn't get. In her case, there hadn't been enough love in the world to make her feel whole, because she had always believed Fern was better, and that was what had left her vulnerable to Robert.

Vi suspected Marcie had a similar weak spot, in that she didn't see her own value. Which meant anyone who made her friend feel desirable would be "in like Flynn," and Vi would not—*could* not—let that happen.

Vi had promised Sal she would take care of Marcie, and so she would.

Because no one should have to go through what she had.

Chapter 11

"So that's Italy." Marcie sounded singularly unimpressed as the mountainous coast came closer.

"Not what you expected?" Vi asked, squinting to see if she could make out anything more than cliffs and peaks in the bright morning sunlight. Fortunately, it wasn't too hot yet, allowing the girls to stand along the rail and sightsee without wilting in their uniforms.

"I don't know." Marcie turned her back to the view and shrugged. "The way some people in Little Italy talk about it, one would think wine flowed in the rivers and citrus trees bloomed on every hillside while birds of paradise flitted in the breeze."

Vi shot her an amused look. "In other words, heaven on earth."

Marcie huffed a soft laugh. "Precisely."

Vi returned her attention to the rugged landscape, wishing she could remember more of Italy's geography. She knew the Alps were in the North and Venice had canals, but wasn't the rest of Italy flat, with lots of grapevines? "It doesn't look like heaven from here."

Marcie sighed and tilted her head back to catch the sun. "You know what's funny? Italy was never a place I dreamed of visiting, or even really thought about. London, maybe. Or Paris. But not Italy, and yet here I am."

"Not even Rome?" Vi was surprised. She had naively assumed every Catholic person wanted to go there, in particular to the Vatican, to meet the Pope.

Marcie shrugged. "I guess I was never bitten by the bug, despite my mother dragging me to Mass every chance she got."

"I wouldn't mind seeing the Sistine Chapel," Gertie said, sounding wistful. "But I doubt Frances would be up for it, and Sue said we couldn't go anywhere without our travel buddy."

"I'm sure Sue would make an exception as long as you're with someone in the cast," Vi said, giving the girl a brief squeeze.

"Assuming you could find someone else to stay with Frances," Marcie said, her face still to the sky. "Of course, we might not even make it to Rome. We could be stuck in the South, entertaining flyboys."

"Where did you hear that?" Gertie asked in surprise.

Marcie shrugged. "Here and there. And speaking of Fran, where is she?"

Vi looked around, surprised the girl wasn't with them. It wasn't every day one got to sail along the coast of Italy.

Gertie continued gazing longingly at the horizon. "She's around . . . somewhere."

Vi's eyebrows rose as she spotted a very flirty Frances entertaining a small group of sailors.

Poor Gertie, Vi thought. She didn't stand a chance trying to keep Frances in check, though that wasn't really her job. Unlike Vi, if Gertie's travel buddy ended up pregnant or kicked out for immoral behavior, no one would hold her accountable. Vi wasn't so lucky.

"It's so strange to think that this time last year, Italy was our enemy," Gertie continued in her soft, sweet voice.

"Italy was never our enemy," Marcie said sharply. "Mussolini, yes. And his fascist party, to be sure. But they are all *babbi*—" She said the word with a snarl. "The rest of Italy—the *real* Italy—had no interest in fighting anyone. Certainly not the Americans, who were our allies in the Great War."

Gertie turned to Marcie in surprise. "'Our allies'? Is your family Italian?"

Vi could have kissed the girl for asking. Even though she already knew the answer, having the knowledge out in the open would make her life so much easier.

"No!" Marcie said. Then she added a touch defensively, "And even if they were, would it matter? We all came to America from somewhere."

Not exactly a definitive answer. But perhaps close enough that if Vi accidentally let something slip, Marcie wouldn't be suspicious.

"I guess I never thought about it," Gertie said slowly. "But I suppose not, since we're all on the same side now."

Silence descended over the trio for a few minutes as the mountainous shoreline got closer. It looked deceptively peaceful and bucolic.

"Is there still any fighting going on in Italy?" Gertie asked. "I mean, we liberated Rome months ago, and since Rome is the capital city, the war is over for them, right?"

"We're on a ship full of soldiers, Gert," Vi pointed out dryly. "I doubt Uncle Sam is bringing them to Italy for a vacation."

"I know that," Gertie said with something approaching irritation. If she was even capable of such an emotion. "But Frances said the men were only here to join up with other units on their way to France."

"I heard that rumor, too," Marcie said before Vi could question the veracity of Frances's source. "But if you had read the papers before we left, you'd know our men are still fighting hard to push the Germans out of northern Italy."

"Really?" Gertie's eyes widened. "The front page only mentioned France and the Pacific. I guess I thought that meant Italy was conquered. Kind of like North Africa."

"No," Vi said gently, even as Marcie rolled her eyes. Vi understood her travel buddy's impatience with Gertie's ignorance, but not everyone had relatives in Italy, so not everyone paid attention to the situation over here.

And she also was sensitive to what would likely be Gertie's next thought.

Sure enough, the dancer started to pale. "Then we . . . I mean, I knew the USO sometimes went to the front lines . . . but I thought, when we passed Spain, that we would be going somewhere—"

"Safe?" Marcie interjected. "If you wanted to be safe, you shoulda stayed home."

"Marcie!" Vi shot her a hard look. "Be nice. Or did you forget we're all supposed to be a family? And to be honest, I'm not particularly keen on going into a war zone, either. *You* might be looking forward to some excitement, but *I*, for one, would really like to get back in one piece."

Marcie threw up her hands in disgust and turned away. Vi inwardly sighed. Sometimes she forgot how "young" her travel buddy was, despite their almost being the same age. Likely it was the hard lessons of the past five years that left Vi feeling at least a decade older. Living on the street could do that to a gal.

Frances drifted over. "Hiya, Gertie. What gives?"

Gertie attempted to smile. "Nothing. Vi and Marcie here were just telling me about the fighting in Italy."

"Oh, don't worry," her friend said. "We'll probably be stationed in Rome, where all the best theaters are, and get to sightsee on our days off. And think of all the soldiers just dying to see pretty American girls like us!"

"When they're not literally dying, fighting Nazis," Marcie said under her breath. Vi shot her another sharp look.

Providentially, Sue called to them at that moment, telling them to gather their things and to meet in the wardroom ASAP. Vi held her tongue while Frances and Marcie traded murderous looks. *Keep your head down, Vi. You don't have a dog in this fight.*

But that was wrong, she reminded herself. She was no longer Lily Lamour, looking out for only herself. She had Marcie's well-being to look out for, too. It was time for her to start being the sister she had never been for Fern.

And maybe, in the process, she could finally begin to balance the scales between herself and the universe . . . and her older sister.

Chapter 12

"Welcome to Naples!" Lieutenant Guilford said with a pearly-white smile and a sweep of his arm. "We were expecting you yesterday, but never mind. You're here now, and that's all that matters."

"He reminds me of a carnival barker," Marcie practically yelled in Vi's ear as a tank rumbled by, one of many being unloaded from the cargo hold of the ship next to theirs. The whole harbor was as busy as an anthill, with soldiers and sailors everywhere shouting to one another, directing traffic and platoons of fully kitted-out soldiers.

"Well, he is our publicity agent, which is almost the same thing," Vi said with a laugh. A passing soldier with a red beret grinned at them. Marcie gave him a little wave, and his grin got even bigger. Vi elbowed her travel buddy in the ribs, which earned her a scowl.

"We would have been here sooner," Wyatt said, stepping forward to shake Lieutenant Guilford's hand when Mr. Stuart didn't immediately respond. Vi eyed the latter man curiously, trying to decide if the director, who stood to the side, staring off into space, meant to be rude or was lost in artistic reverie. "But our ship had to detour a fair bit to avoid submarine activity."

Vi blinked and forgot about Mr. Stuart. This was the first she had heard of there being any actual danger on the voyage. Endless exhortations to be careful, yes. Repeated reminders to be alert, yes. But never a word from the captain that they were being actively hunted by submarines.

This new knowledge made her feel a bit lightheaded.

"We're also a bit rusty, having been cooped up on the ship for so long," Sue said as the lieutenant shook hands with her, too. "Any idea when we can get onto a stage and brush the cobwebs off?"

Lieutenant Guilford's sparkling smile disappeared. "Oh, I do apologize. I thought you might enjoy a little R and R after your long trip, so I didn't reserve a rehearsal space. I'll fix that. In the meantime, the army has you scheduled for some additional training."

The troupe groaned at this news, and Lieutenant Guilford held out his hands in supplication.

"I know, I know, but it won't be as bad as you all are thinking," he said. "It's only a few briefings on the country and its customs. There will be plenty of time to relax and swim; you'll find numerous pools available to officers and the USO. There are also a few shops I could recommend, though you ladies may find the selection a bit limited. The environs in this part of Italy are generally safe, so feel free to explore. Except the beaches. Don't go there. Those are strictly off-limits."

"Whatever for? The water looked lovely on the way in," Ann said with a faint frown.

"It's not the water, miss." Lieutenant Guilford's face became unexpectedly grim. "It's the mines. The Germans buried them everywhere along the coast."

A kind of pall settled over the group, and it was a much more subdued company that piled into the waiting jeeps, leaving the luggage and crates to be loaded onto a truck that would follow behind.

As the jeeps growled through the narrow streets of Naples, Vi's odd sensation of having been dropped onto an entirely different planet deepened. Vi felt as if she had landed on a different planet. Much was as she would've expected of a busy port town. Middle-aged women with bags over their arms perused the wares of the street vendors, while tired-looking farmers unloaded battered trucks or mule carts. Old men in baggy pants stood on street corners, hands in their pockets, watching the jousting of trucks, autos, pedestrians, and bicycles as they fought for equal rights to the road. The sidewalks and streets teemed with seemingly normal activity.

And yet, eerie, blackened, and hollowed-out buildings appeared and disappeared down every cross street, their cracked and jagged facades a silent reminder of battles recently fought. Soldiers of various countries, distinguishable by the different caps and trim on their uniforms, chatted among themselves, their rifles slung over their shoulders. Most disturbing of all, though, were the frightfully thin children weaving and darting between it all and laughing as if oblivious to the devastation around them.

But then, the war was nothing new to them. For some, it was all they had ever known. It struck her then that this—this ability of the children to play and the citizens of Naples to continue living their lives despite the devastation—was the true essence of what it meant to be human. That incredible gift to rise up from the ashes, no matter how awful the circumstances, to dust oneself off and move forward. That had to be mankind's greatest quality.

As the city blocks gave way to fields and farmhouses, the view changed but was no less disturbing. Even Ann and Marcie, who were wedged into the jeep's back seat next to Vi, fell into a shocked silence.

Scorched and twisted olive trees stood silent watch over fields marred by craters that were the work of shells and hand grenades. Abandoned farmhouses, roofs gone and doors torn off, spoke of lives lost. Dreams upended. Marcie pinched her nose against the stench of hemp rotting unharvested in the fields. What must the countryside have smelled like after the fighting had first moved on, and plants weren't the only casualties disintegrating in the heat and sun?

Finally the jeeps entered the town of Caserta, their destination according to their driver. A handful of bone-thin children stopped their play with a makeshift ball to watch them pass. Vi's heart twisted as she compared their gaunt visages to her last glimpse of Jimmy, his full cheeks rosy with health and vigor. Her chest ached for their parents. How different their dreams for their children's lives must have been from this.

"Looks like we're not in Kansas anymore," Ann said over the jeep engine's growl and gnashing of gears. "Take a gander at that!"

Vi glanced toward Ann's side of the street, steeling herself for some new awfulness, and then did a double take. An enormous, ornate, five-story building made of white and gold stone—a palace, really—rose up into the bright-blue sky in a surfeit of splendor. Large enough to cover several city blocks back home, with a vast lawn stretching out in front of it, crisscrossed by paths, it dominated its surroundings.

Beautiful stonework around the windows and along the roof gave it an air of elegance despite the damaged roof and broken glass panes. Three stately arches were embedded into the front facade, each one nearly three stories tall from ground to apex and wide enough to accommodate a horse-drawn carriage or even a small truck.

The number of military vehicles parked out front gave rise to that last thought and also suggested that, whatever it had been in the past, it now served at the pleasure of the Allied army.

Oh, how the mighty have fallen, she thought to herself in a black humor.

Ann tapped the driver on the shoulder. "What building is that?"

Vi leaned forward, curious, too.

Lieutenant Guilford shouted the answer over his shoulder. "The Reggia di Caserta. It was a royal residence in the 1700s, built to rival the Versailles in France. Now it's the headquarters for the British Armed Forces. Before that it housed the Italian Air Force Academy, which was why it was bombed. Luckily only one shell found its mark, so most of the building is still intact."

"I don't suppose we're staying there?" Vi asked hopefully, seduced by the idea of sleeping within such grandeur. Especially after the cramped conditions aboard the ship.

"No, miss," Lieutenant Guilford said. "Nor would you want to. There's no hot water, and all that missing glass means you'd be at the mercy of the mosquitoes. And that's not a good idea, believe me."

"Oh," Vi said, a little sorry to have the building's grandeur diminished.

"But it does have a gem of a theater," the lieutenant continued. "Several other units have already performed there and raved about the acoustics."

"Well, that's fine, then," Ann said, sharing a conspiratorial wink with Vi. Vi agreed. Imagine being able to boast once she got back to the States that she had graced the stage of European royalty! It'd be quite the feather in her cap. That is, assuming she did get back.

Her mood slipped.

Marcie nudged Vi in the ribs and gestured toward the other side of the jeep. "Is it just me, or do the natives seem less than happy to see us?"

Tearing her thoughts from Jimmy and Sal and the fate of the club, Vi looked where Marcie was pointing. Several pedestrians had stopped to watch them pass, their vacant, weary faces reminding Vi of her conversation with Luciana. The American jeeps weren't signs of liberation to these people but merely continuing occupation.

"I suspect they've seen things we can't even begin to imagine," Vi answered. "Still, I'm glad they aren't our intended audience."

"Amen to that," Marcie said, her tone light. Her expression, however, remained troubled. "I suspect they would be a tough crowd."

Vi couldn't disagree. An undertone of weariness and anger seemed to permeate the landscape. Emotions that didn't go well with a light musical comedy.

The jeeps soon rumbled to a stop in front of a modern two-story building. It looked rather like a motel, or perhaps an apartment building. Two wings of rooms with balconies on the second floor and cement patios on the first flanked a central lobby entrance. On the other hand, the architecture was so plain, the construction materials so utilitarian, it couldn't be anything but a military structure.

"Here we are," Lieutenant Guilford said cheerfully as the driver turned off the engine. "It's not the Ritz, but I hope you'll find it comfortable enough. Your luggage should be arriving shortly."

Ann, Marcie, and Vi jumped from the back of the jeep while the other cast members piled out of their respective transports. Sue, ever on top of things, began counting heads as everyone stretched and began chatting. The two middle-aged male actors, Charles and Matt, immediately paired off and headed toward Ann, eager to compare initial impressions of Italy. Victor hung back with Wyatt, who was talking to one of the jeep drivers. Luciana stood off to the side, alone, her gaze fastened on the technical director.

Vi wondered if the two were still involved. On board the ship, she hadn't seen any evidence of a marked preference for each other's company, though the close quarters might have made them more cautious.

Lieutenant Guilford, once again all smiles, gathered the troupe and ushered them inside, promising refreshments. That was welcome news to Vi. She had been too nervous in the last twenty-four hours to eat properly.

The building was basically laid out on a wheel-and-spoke plan, with a large communal space in the center and three wings—not two, as she had first thought—of semiprivate rooms.

"We're short on space at the moment, so I'm afraid you ladies will all be in one single room with bunk beds." The lieutenant gestured to the wing on his left.

"How delightful," Frances muttered.

"Unless you'd rather share beds, like the men will be doing," the lieutenant continued, giving her the side-eye. "On the upside, this building does have hot water, at least as of this morning. But please remember the plumbing in Italy is, well . . . rather delicate. Be mindful of what you flush or risk the ire of the entire building."

"Even better," Frances said with a roll of her eyes. Gertie giggled. Sue shot them both a hard look.

Dismissed to store their gear, everyone headed off in the appropriate direction. Vi's spirits sank when she walked into the women's room. What would have been spacious for two people was positively cramped with the seven of them. Sue claimed the luxury of the single cot, which was positioned near the door.

"Probably because she doesn't trust Frances not to sneak out at night," Marcie said sotto voce to Vi.

"More likely she doesn't trust any of us," Vi said dryly.

"At least I don't make goo-goo eyes at every passing officer." Marcie scowled in Frances's direction. "One might think she had just escaped a convent instead of a huge ship overloaded with men. And then there's her preference for silver and brass. It's disgusting."

"You'd excuse her if she targeted enlisted men instead?" Vi asked somewhat seriously, remembering how Marcie had all but thrown herself at the soldier in the Camp Kilmer mess hall.

"It would certainly be more fair. Officers get enough perks without stealing all the girls, too."

Vi shot her buddy a look. "You do remember that we were given officer status when we joined the USO."

"And then there's our room!" Marcie continued. "Clean, modern, with hot water . . . and yet on the way here, what did I see? Devastation, everywhere. And does anyone care? No, not really, except about the palace—everyone is glad *it* escaped the bombing. Because it is so magnificent. So grand. Never mind that the gaudy monstrosity was built on the backs of the peasantry."

"Wait, this from the person who mockingly called Luciana a contadina?" Vi massaged her head, which had started to ache from lack of food and sleep. "Forgive me, but I assumed you held a dim view of farmers, and here you are championing them."

"I hold an even dimmer view of dukes and kings who do nothing for their people but who are ever eager to use their labor and earnings."

Vi closed her eyes and struggled to muster the remains of her patience. "Marce, we are guests here. Remember? We're not supposed to insult them or their way of life."

"Porta rispettu a lu locu unni stai." Luciana's sweet, musical voice startled Vi into opening her eyes again.

Beside her, Marcie stiffened, color suffusing her cheeks. "You dare talk to me about respect after what your great-grandparents did in Sicily?"

The actress's dark, soulful gaze settled on Marcie. "You forget my people have suffered injustice, too. And yet I still love Italia and will do my best for her. Can you not do the same?"

Luciana's question was met with a taut silence.

Vi glanced from one to the other. "'Porta respetta' . . . what was the rest?"

The actress smiled a touch sadly. "It's an old Sicilian proverb, *'porta rispettu a lu locu unni stai'*: show respect for the place you are in." She glanced at Marcie. "Even if one isn't sure it deserves it."

"Well, you can keep your advice to yourself," Marcie said, with a haughty lift of her chin. "I'm an American, through and through."

"I understand mixed loyalties," Luciana said, her gaze steady. "But the blood remembers even if we wish to forget. So be careful. The camorra have no love for Sicilians . . . Marcella Maggio."

Vi groaned inwardly as all the color drained from Marcie's face. This was not going to end well.

"I knew it! My papa sent you to spy on me, didn't he?" Marcie's voice shook.

Vi looked at the actress curiously. She had never considered that Papa Maggio might have more than one person watching over his little girl.

Luciana's eyebrows rose. "Why would he? I have no ties to the Mafia. Those criminals give Italians a bad name."

Marcie's hands balled into fists. "My father is not a criminal!"

"Are you sure about that?"

Marcie growled and cocked her fist back.

Vi grabbed her travel buddy's arm. "Whoa! Easy, cowboy."

"She just insulted my papa!"

"She merely voiced an opinion shared by a lot of people," Vi said, and then lowered her voice. "And you've got an audience. So shut it, unless you want to get sent home."

"But—"

Wyatt popped his head through the door. "The luggage is here. Come on out and claim it before it gets stolen."

Vi could've kissed the man for his impeccable timing. Luciana, after shooting Vi an apologetic look, hurried out of the room after him. Marcie sank onto the bunk and crossed her arms, still clearly steamed.

"He's kidding, right?" Gertie asked from her bunk after Wyatt had disappeared. "No one would take our things, would they?"

Frances stretched and then headed for the door. "Better not wait around in case he wasn't."

Gertie hopped down. "You gals coming?"

"In a minute," Vi said. The opening Luciana had created was too valuable to pass up.

After they were alone, Marcie snorted and then said softly, "I bet you anything Luciana—that *buttana*—was the snoop who got Janet canned."

Vi suspected the cause was much closer to home—as in Papa Maggio had wanted a better travel partner for his progeny. Still, she didn't want to discount Marcie's instincts without giving them a proper hearing. Snoops, whether for the USO or anyone else, presented a very real threat to her, and ultimately her future. Yet Luciana seemed more the type to have secrets of her own. Secrets that might present a different kind of danger.

Perhaps it's time I do a little snooping myself . . .

Feeling a bit like Pandora, she sat next to Marcie on the bunk and opened the proverbial box. "So what really happened to Janet?"

Chapter 13

"Nothing." Marcie stood. "We'd better catch up with the others."

"You said Luciana ratted her out, which means she must have had something to hide," Vi said, refusing to move. "What was it?"

Marcie hesitated, her expression becoming troubled. "Does it matter? Janet was nice and a good dancer. She might have missed a few rehearsals, but not enough to fall behind. And she was so excited to be a part of the show. She couldn't wait to get to meet other USO performers, like the Andrews Sisters or Bob Hope."

"I wouldn't mind that, either," Vi said. "But if you think she was kicked out over missing rehearsals, wouldn't that point to Sue or Mr. Stuart?"

"Well, yes, but . . ." Marcie glanced around nervously as if to check that they were alone. "Between you and me, I don't think that was it. As I said, she was a good dancer. But she'd had an abortion not long before she tried out, and hadn't told anyone. Well, she told me, but only because her cramps were so bad one day, I'd wanted to call a doctor."

Vi's heart sank even as it went out to Janet. Unwanted pregnancies weren't always a sign of promiscuity—a girl could be in love and unlucky or could be the victim of forced sexual attention—but society didn't always see it that way.

She herself had known several dancers who, having found themselves unexpectedly knocked up, had taken the back-alley way out to keep their jobs. It always hurt her to think of a mother being forced into such a decision, but she was also aware that it would be entirely too easy to moralize when she would never again find herself in such a situation.

"And you think someone might have found out and tipped off the USO," Vi said.

"That's my theory, yes. You know what the USO is like."

"I do. But I'm curious: Why blame Luciana?"

Marcie crossed her arms and scowled. "Because there's something shady about her. First palling around with Mr. Miller, then the captain aboard ship. Breaking rules whenever it suits her. Knowing things she shouldn't."

"Like your real name is Marcella Maggio?" Vi asked, finally getting the opening she wanted.

Marcie cocked one dark eyebrow. "Does it matter?"

"It does if I can't trust you to be straight with me." Vi took a deep breath. "My point is, Luciana's shadiness aside, I'm not convinced she's the one who ratted Janet out."

"Then who did?"

"Have you considered the fact that you're the daughter of an uptight, traditional, *Catholic* father—your words—and how he might feel if he found out that his little girl was traveling with a woman who'd had an abortion? Especially when the two of you would be surrounded by young sex-starved soldiers while on tour. Men don't become angels just by adding a uniform."

Marcie's chin came up. "Who are you, my mother? And even if my father had found out about Janet, he wouldn't have interfered."

"Are you sure? Answer me this, then: Did Janet disappear before or after Sue assigned travel buddies?"

"Before. No, wait—after." Marcie's eyes widened. "You really think my father had something to do with it?"

"You tell me."

"But if my father knows . . ." Marcie glanced at the door and scowled. "I bet it's still Luciana's fault, the buttana. I bet she told him."

"Why?" If anything, Marcie should have deduced Vi was the spy, having taken Janet's place. "She just told us she doesn't like the Mafia."

"She could be lying. She quoted a Sicilian proverb, after all."

Vi frowned, confused. "Wait, what's wrong with that?"

"Pfft. Americans don't know anything. Sicilians are considered pigs by our 'countrymen,'" she said bitterly. "Even in America, where all men are supposedly equal, we get no respect from other Italians. It's been that way ever since the Italian peninsula was united—by force, mind you— and Sicily, along with Naples, was reduced to nothing by the fascists of the North." Marcie squared her shoulders. "But we are a proud people. We still remember that less than a century ago, Sicily was the capital of the Kingdom of the Two Sicilies. Rich. Powerful. The envy of Europe."

"I see," Vi said, and she did. After Marcie's impassioned rant and Luciana's veiled warning on board the ship, it was becoming clear there was more than a little bad blood between the different regions of Italy. It also gave Luciana's caution to "show respect for the place you are in" added weight. "You still haven't answered my question about your name."

Marcie's chin rose a notch. "Can't I have a stage name like everyone else?"

"What if something happens to you and the army needs to contact someone? Tell me you at least gave them your real address."

Some of the steel left Marcie's spine. "I didn't think about that." Then she straightened, and her eyes flashed. "It doesn't matter. My parents don't care about me, anyway."

Vi felt her headache returning. "Marcie, I don't care if you have a stage name. I don't care if you are Sicilian-not-Italian, or that your father might be Mafia. But I would like to know what name to give to the authorities if you are ever injured. Especially since I'm your travel buddy and responsible for your whereabouts."

Marcie regarded her solemnly for a long moment. "Do you promise not to tell anyone unless you absolutely have to?"

"Cross my heart, hope to die," Vi said wearily, making the sign of an X over her chest.

"Don't say that!" Marcie exclaimed, rapidly crossing herself. "May we both live long and happy lives."

Vi sighed mentally at the girl's mercurial mood shifts. "Of course."

Marcie leaned close and whispered dramatically, as if divulging state secrets, "My real name is Angelina Marcella Maggio. My parents are Antonio Maggio and Beatrice Vecchione Maggio, of Lower Manhattan. Got that?"

The rush of relief at finally having that secret out in the open, so she would no longer run the risk of tripping herself up, almost had Vi missing the last part. Her heart stopped. "Vecchione?"

Tony was a Vecchione. Was it possible he was related? The Fates wouldn't be that unkind, would they? If so, she had an even more pressing reason to make sure Marcie made it home in as pristine a condition as possible, given the war. Trading favors was the name of the game in the Mafia's world. If Vi safeguarded Marcie, perhaps Mama Maggio would be willing to forgive any part Vi had played in her relative's death.

Because the truth was, thanks to her, Tony had been particularly vulnerable that night he had died. And since the truth had a way of coming out whether one wanted it to or not, there was no way Vi was going to squander this chance of balancing the scales, even if it meant being glued to Marcie's hip twenty-four hours a day.

Marcie shrugged. "It's my mother's maiden name. She kept it because she has a cousin Beatrice and everyone kept getting them confused, which was a problem because the other Beatrice is a real witch!" She stopped and peered closely at Vi. "Is something wrong? You're pale."

"Nothing's wrong." Vi managed a smile even as her thoughts raced. "Beatrice Vecchione Maggio. Got it. Now let's go get our luggage."

Chapter 14

Three days later, Marcie dropped onto the cracked pavement of the Reggia di Caserta's courtyard next to Vi. Her face was beet red from exertion and the heat. "Sue is trying to kill us, I swear."

Too exhausted to answer, Vi fanned herself with a script. Thank heavens Sue had let them wear their dance outfits this morning instead of their wool uniforms.

To everyone's relief, Lieutenant Guilford, after much badgering from Sue, had finally managed to release them from further training and had even found them a place to rehearse. The troupe had whooped it up when he mentioned it would be at the palace. Unfortunately, the reality was quite different than they had expected.

The palace's jewel of a theater had already been booked by the Andrews Sisters, who were coming into town, along with a comedian whose name Vi didn't recognize. Outranked and outgunned, Vi's unit had been given one of the paved interior courtyards to rehearse in while the theater was readied for the bigger names.

To be fair, the courtyard, one of four identical ones, was spacious enough to fit the entire company. The beautifully carved stone and windowed walls also made for good acoustics, so it was easy to hear Sue's cues and corrections. On the flip side, the walls also allowed precious little airflow, despite one side opening up onto the rather windy central gallery that bisected the palace.

Longing for a breeze, Vi flicked her glance toward the gallery. Near as she could figure, the massive columns holding up the arches must be deflecting the flow of air from the courtyard, which was why they were all dying of heat. Clearly a design flaw on the part of the architect.

"Take fifteen, everyone," Sue called from where she sat next to a sweating and miserable-looking Mr. Stuart. "Then we'll run act one from the top one more time."

Vi groaned silently. Wrung out from the heat, all she wanted to do was nap.

"Do you think we'll get to use real props this time?" Gertie asked from where she and Frances were slumped on the other side of Vi. "I need to start practicing with a real tray in my hand if I want to make it look natural."

"Talk to Wyatt," Frances said dully, her head leaned back against the wall. "Maybe he'll uncrate them for you."

"No, that's all right. He's busy enough as it is. I can wait until we get to Rome."

Frances's eyes popped open, and she turned to stare at her partner. "Rome? Where did you hear that?"

Gertie shrugged. "I overheard Luciana on the phone in the common room last night. She was speaking Italian to the other person on the line. At least I think so. But anyway I heard her say 'Roma' several times, which is Italian for Rome, right? So I figured that's where we must be heading next."

Vi stared at the girl. "Luciana was on the telephone?"

"Yes, but I think she said she had family over here." Gertie frowned slightly. "Didn't she?"

A missing one, Vi thought. No reason to worry Gertie unnecessarily, though, by saying as much aloud. The girl was jittery enough about being in a war zone.

"Hmm." Frances tapped her lower lip thoughtfully. "I wonder if that means we'll be getting a new publicity officer."

"One that's unmarried this time?" Gertie teased. "Though I think it would be difficult to find anyone more swoon-worthy than Lieutenant Guilford."

Vi mentally rolled her eyes as both girls completely skipped the important part of Gertie's observation. Was she the only one who found Luciana calling someone within a week of landing curious? Someone who spoke Italian and had a conversation about Rome, even though she would swear Luciana had said her family was in northern Italy. Vi wasn't great with maps, but she was pretty sure Rome was near the middle of the "boot."

"If one goes for that kind of smarmy charm," Frances said with a sniff. "I prefer my men more manly. A little dangerous, even."

Vi snorted. Lord help Frances if she ever did manage to land a "dangerous" man. As far as Vi could tell, the girl didn't have the skills to deal with anything but the tamest of fellows.

"Shoot," Marcie muttered, drawing Vi's attention. Her travel buddy was holding her canteen upside down. A lone, lazy drop of water gathered on the rim, but nothing else.

Vi sighed and took the empty metal container from her. "Here, give that to me. I'll go find a place to refill it. Mine is empty, too."

"I can do it," Marcie said as Vi staggered to her feet on tired legs.

"That's all right. No need for both of us to get in trouble if I'm not back in time."

Marcie made a face. "You just want a chance to explore."

"There is that," Vi admitted with a laugh. "But tell you what—I'll let you go next time. Deal?"

"Deal." Marcie leaned back against the wall and closed her eyes. "But don't think I'll cover for you if you take too long."

"Liar," Vi said with a small laugh, knowing the opposite was likely true. Marcie, for all her tough talk, didn't have a spiteful bone in her body, which was one of the reasons Vi was becoming so fond of her.

As she entered the central gallery, a blessed breeze greeted her. Closing her eyes in pure bliss, she let the sweat on her skin dry for a moment as she soaked in the cool shade of the tall columned corridor.

The rumble of an engine warned her of the small truck coming up behind her. Stepping to the side, she let the canvas-covered vehicle pass, marveling at the sheer size of the palace, a building large enough to have traffic pass through the center. As the truck exited toward the driveway leading toward the busy street, she turned and looked at the much more pastoral tableau framed by the gallery arch behind her.

Silent landscaped lawns that seemed to go on forever slowly rose from the gravel turnabout toward a high hill in the far distance. Heat haze obscured the pools and fountains that ran up the center, not that there was much to see. The fountains had all been turned off, the fuel for the pumps needed elsewhere. Still, the view was impressive.

She couldn't even imagine the wealth it had taken to build this place. Or the passion that had been poured into its design and creation. That it was so battered and run-down now depressed her. Maybe when the war was over, the Italian government would restore it to its former glory. It would take a mint to do it, though.

A shout echoing down the enormous stone staircase leading to the grand hall broke the spell. She turned to hail whoever it was clattering down the steps. A spit-and-polish British officer with a harried air and a leather satchel tucked under one arm raised his hand as if greeting her.

She turned on a sunny smile. "Pardon me, sir, but where are—" Movement out of the corner of her eye caught her attention, and she stopped, ready to jump out of the way of another vehicle.

Instead, it was just a dirty and rumpled soldier striding briskly toward her, having just saluted the guards at the oversize front doors. Several days' growth of dark-blond beard obscured his lower face. He wore a US Army uniform and helmet. The rifle slung over his right shoulder seemed as much a part of him as the strong hand holding the strap. His skin, the scant bit she could see, was sunburned to a dark bronze.

Vi stared, fascinated by the sheer masculinity and grit radiating off him. If ever there was a soldier who looked fresh from the front, he was it. But the front was hundreds of miles away, at least as far as she knew. So what was he doing here? He looked as out of place as a dockworker in a Rockefeller dining room.

She would've felt self-conscious showing up here so disheveled. The soldier, on the other hand, didn't appear concerned. A weary pride emboldened his long, loose-limbed stride. He looked about, unabashed, a man on a mission. For a moment their gazes met, and a strange fluttering sensation filled her chest. Eyes as blue as a cloudless summer sky, all the more startling for the deeply tanned skin surrounding them, assessed her. Then his attention flicked up the stairs to where the British officer stood.

The soldier paused and gave a brief salute.

"I say, Sergeant, what's the meaning of showing up like this, looking like the very devil," the officer snapped in his crisp, formal accent. "I've half a mind to send you out again. We've ladies working here."

"Sorry, sir. I was ordered to rendezvous immediately with USO unit 2918. I was told they were here." The man's intense, direct gaze flicked to her again. Her breath caught as those blue eyes seared into her.

Lord, there was something about him. Something primal and alluring . . .

His attention abruptly returned to the British officer, as if dismissing her.

Unsettled, Vi crossed her arms. Yes, she was sweaty and flushed, but she didn't look *that* bad. Though maybe she could use a splash of water on her face after refilling the canteens.

"You'll find them at the end of the corridor, just there, on the left. In the courtyard," the officer said, his disgust barely concealed.

"Thank you." The sergeant's voice was a gravelly baritone that matched his gritty exterior.

"Damn Yanks," the officer muttered as the sergeant turned away. The man appeared not to have heard. Or more likely, he had heard and didn't care.

Having had to endure her own share of slurs being tossed at her, she couldn't help but respect him all the more.

"Excuse me," she called after the sergeant. "I can take you to them, if you'd like. Since I'm one of the performers."

He hesitated for the briefest second. "Are you Miss Rossi?"

"No, I'm Miss Heart, Virginia Heart."

"Then no, Miss Heart. Thank you, but I've got it in hand."

"But I could . . ." The rest of her offer trailed away as he strode off.

"May I help you, miss?" The British officer's tone was solicitous.

Her self-confidence shaken a bit by the sergeant's rejection, she turned to the fellow and smiled brightly. "Why, yes!"

As she asked for directions to the nearest water tap, she found herself arching her back, so that her crop top, tied in front, pulled a bit more tightly over her breasts. And maybe she shouldn't have batted her eyelashes quite so much, but the stunned, slightly glazed expression on the officer's face went a long way toward righting her off-kilter world.

After refilling the canteens, she smoothed her hair and splashed water on her face to cool it. Feeling refreshed, she hurried back to the courtyard. Even though she was in no hurry to see the sergeant again— getting the brush-off from him once had been quite enough—she was curious to know what he wanted with her unit.

Marcie accosted Vi as soon as she rounded the corner, her eyes round with excitement. "Oh, my goodness, I'm so glad you're back. A soldier just showed up, wanting to talk to the directors. A real Captain America. Take a look!"

"Is that so?"

The sergeant stood with Mr. Stuart, Sue, and Wyatt, with the same loose-limbed athleticism she'd remembered. To her relief, he had his back to her. Still, the solid breadth of his shoulders was a sight to behold.

Idly, she wondered if he danced. He had the build and looked as if he could easily lift her above his head in the most romantic of pas de deux.

"Isn't he dreamy? Frances is practically salivating over him. And I don't blame her."

"He's not a captain," Vi corrected as she turned and spotted Frances primping near Gertie. "He's a sergeant."

"Ooh, a noncom." Marcie's hungry gaze sized up the sergeant like a candy bar. "Even better. That means he's fair game as far as the USO is concerned."

"He's not a rabbit to be snared, Marce," Vi said, tamping down her irritation as she handed Marcie her canteen. "He's here to do a job. Just like us."

"Who is?" Frances said as she joined them. Her cat-green eyes were fastened on the sergeant, her look just as lascivious as Marcie's.

"Vi just told me he's a sergeant and not an officer," Marcie gushed. "Maybe we should go introduce ourselves?"

Vi wanted to smack both of them. "Do you not see Sue and Mr. Stuart standing right there? You'll get canned before our first performance!"

Frances shot her a smug look. "Oh, come on. All work and no play make Jane a very dull girl, and we wouldn't want to risk becoming dull! Besides, the USO wants us to entertain the GIs, and he looks like he could use a bit of entertaining."

"Fine, if you want to get sent home in disgrace, knock yourself out," Vi said, already starting to consider whether they could do the show with only three dancers. "But don't say I didn't warn you."

"Don't mind if I do." Frances fluffed her hair and then headed over.

Vi turned her back on the scene and uncapped her canteen. Still smarting from being cut by the dreamy sergeant, she had no desire to see Frances succeed where she had just failed.

Marcie hesitated, though—Lord love her—worry clouding her face. "Do you really think it's a bad idea, Vi?"

"I do. There's such a thing as timing, meaning you don't try to seduce a man while he's talking to your bosses."

"They're directors, not bosses, and oh my!" Marcie settled against the wall next to Vi, her gaze on the action unfolding in front of her. "I sure wish I could swish my hips like that."

Vi made a noncommittal sound as she put the canteen to her lips. As she drank, she tried to convince herself she was glad the sergeant had ignored her. It likely meant her disguise was working, which would be for the best.

Marcie's forehead wrinkled as if perplexed. "Do fellows really go for that? We were told in cotillion to walk as if we had a book on our head. That it was more attractive."

"It depends on what kind of attention you're trying to attract." Vi took another swig to keep from turning around. She didn't want or need to know if the sergeant was buying Frances's act . . . did she?

She hesitated and then turned her head in time to catch the brunette in full swing. Frances wasn't bad, she had to admit. But Vi was better. Much better.

Which was cold comfort as she watched the sergeant do a double take as Frances sauntered up.

Suppressing a twinge of irritation at how predictable men were, she turned away.

Invisibility is good, remember?

Sure. And so was being respected for one's talent and intelligence, but that didn't mean she had to like being dismissed.

Next to her Marcie gave a muffled snort. "Serves her right."

"What does?" Vi studied her nails in feigned disinterest.

"Sergeant Dreamboat just turned his back on her. Deliberately. You should see her face!"

Vi's lips quirked in unladylike schadenfreude. At least she wasn't the only one to get shot down by the fellow.

"Maybe we should call him Sergeant Disaster instead," Marcie said with a giggle. Then she abruptly turned toward the wall. "Here she comes. And, boy, does she ever look steamed."

"She shouldn't be. If anything, she should be glad." Vi stretched her back, wanting to stay limber for the dance. "She was taking a serious risk with Mr. Stuart and Sue right there."

"And don't forget Mr. Miller," Marcie added. "Though he might not have noticed. He only has eyes for Luciana."

A brief image of the sergeant's double take flashed in Vi's head. Two of the other three in the group had noticed Frances at the same time: Sue and Wyatt. Not Mr. Stuart, but then the director didn't seem aware of much. Sue had frowned in displeasure. And Wyatt . . . well, it had been hard to read his reaction, but it wasn't disinterest exactly.

"Are you sure about Mr. Miller and Luciana? I haven't seen them hanging around each other much."

Before Marcie could answer, Frances stalked up. She turned and leaned against the wall, her arms crossed, her expression cool.

"Sergeant Dangerous didn't want cheering up?" Marcie asked innocently. Vi snorted softly in amusement, the new moniker fitting him much more closely.

Frances shot her a venomous look. "Can it, Dorothy. Or better yet, click the heels of those expensive black market shoes of yours and go home."

"Ooh, it's the Wicked Witch of the West." Marcie threw up her hands in exaggerated self-protection, eyes wide in mock fear. "We'd better be careful, Vi."

"Considering how Dorothy does the witch in"—Vi's gaze drifted back to the directorial group and the sergeant—"I think it's Frances who should be careful."

"Why? You think I'm afraid of some wop and her sidekick?" Frances snorted. "Hardly."

Marcie went rigid. "What did you call me?"

Vi reached out and caught Marcie's fist. "Let it go. The only person being diminished here is Frances, by demonstrating how small her mind is."

"Easy for you to say." Marcie twisted, trying to break Vi's grip. "You weren't the one being insulted."

At that Vi gave her friend a little jerk, forcing the girl to look at her. "Actually, I've been insulted more times than I can count, by people of much higher consequence. And you want to know something? No good comes from letting it get to you. Especially with one's career on the line."

Marcie pulled her arm free, her dark eyes snapping. "Fine." She turned and bared her teeth at Frances. "But if she does it again, I'll claw her eyes out."

Frances made a rude gesture and then walked away. Marcie growled but stayed put by Vi's side.

Low male laughter echoed off the walls. Vi glanced back at the sergeant. The discussion appeared to be over, with Wyatt and the sergeant walking toward the central gallery. Wyatt's hand rested on the man's shoulder as if they were old friends, though nothing in the soldier's posture suggested the sentiment was returned. Everything about him was as alert and self-contained as when he'd walked in.

"I wonder why he was sent to find us," Vi said aloud.

Marcie shrugged. "Perhaps to request another stop to our tour?"

If so, Vi suspected that stop would be close to the front lines. He had that look about him. And the addition would make sense. Battle-weary soldiers would likely be more desperate than most for entertainment. Anything to take their minds off what they'd just lived through. Rather like the men back home in her club, hoping for a little escape after a hard day's work. Except dodging bullets had to be far more stressful and dangerous than even the worst factory job.

As she considered the role of the USO from that perspective, a sense of rightness stole over her. If there had ever been a role she had been born to do, making men forget their troubles was it. More, she wanted to do it as a way to atone for her sins, to make something admirable out of all those nights learning to entertain men onstage. A way to use her fall from grace for good.

Sue clapped her hands. "All right, everyone. Let's pick it up where we left off. Ann? Charles?"

As Vi and the rest of the company regrouped, with Ann and Charles taking up their position, arm in arm in the "wings," she remembered the USO briefing on how they would be paying visits to hospital wards and rest areas, where the troupe would be interacting one-on-one with the soldiers. As long as she managed to remember she was Virginia and not Lily, and thus not get canned, she could kill three birds with one stone: do a good turn for the family, stay clear of the Chicago police investigation, and perhaps find a way to redeem herself. All wonderful things in her book.

While it was one thing to make the boys back home forget their troubles for a night. It would be something altogether different, and nobler, to do it for the men fighting to free the world.

Lighter than she had felt in weeks as she took her place with the other dancers, she could almost see the soldiers' smiles, feel their adoration warming her skin. It would be like a return to heaven.

She couldn't wait.

Chapter 15

Two days later, Vi dragged her exhausted body into the common room seeking breakfast. Excitement hummed beneath the usual chitchat as Vi sought out a clean coffee cup. Bleary eyed from a restless night, she decided she wasn't up to hearing whatever news had everyone in a tizzy. Not yet. First things first. She poured herself a cup of coffee and snagged the last *sfogliatella*.

Her stomach rumbled in ravenous anticipation. A specialty of the region, the pastry was a flaky, multilayered slice of heaven with a delicate orange flavor and sweet cheese filling. She had never tasted anything so delicious in her life and would be perfectly happy if the troupe never left Caserta. It almost made up for the awful army-supplied coffee.

"Vi, over here." Marcie waved at her from the couch. Gertie, next to her, waved also. Thankfully there was no sign of Frances, which suited Vi just fine. She was too tired to deal with bad attitudes this morning.

"Did you hear the news?" Marcie asked as Vi collapsed into the chair across from her. "We're finally going to get a chance to perform in front of the troops! And we get to fly there, too. We're supposed to pack up right after breakfast."

Vi's stomach instantly lost interest in the pastry. "Fly? Like in an airplane?"

"Of course, silly. How else does one fly? Lieutenant Guilford pulled a few strings so we wouldn't have to ride in trucks the whole way. Wasn't that swell of him? And it means we can get to our first stop that much quicker."

"Marvelous." Vi set the coffee cup down before her trembling hand spilled the contents. "Where is our first stop, anyway?"

"It's all hush-hush for security reasons, but Lieutenant Guilford did say we were traveling north, so it should be cooler!"

"Well, that's a relief." Then Vi thought of Sergeant Dangerous, with his battle-roughened exterior. "I wonder if we're bypassing Rome and heading even farther north."

"Wherever we go, I hope it isn't to the front lines." Gertie's narrow shoulders were strung tight. "I don't want to die."

"You're not going to die," Marcie said, sounding exasperated.

"Al Jolson nearly did," Gertie pointed out.

"From malaria," Marcie said, "which he caught in the South Seas, not Europe."

"What about Jane Froman? She was on a USO tour in Europe when she almost lost her leg last year."

"Can we talk about something else?" Vi asked, feeling even more ill as she recalled exactly how the famous performer was injured . . . in a plane crash.

Marcie ignored her. "Bad luck can strike anywhere. Besides, you knew what you were signing up for before we left the States. The Foxhole Circuit by its very name suggests we're going close to the front."

"It didn't sound so scary at the time," Gertie said defensively. "I'd never seen a bombed-out city before. And no one told me everyone overseas would be armed."

"It's all right, Gertie." Vi rubbed her temples, struggling with her own bout of nerves. Cars she was okay with. Boats, too. Even pack mules. But airplanes? "I have to admit war zones look a lot different in color than they did in the black-and-white newsreels. Nor do they smell like popcorn and movie theaters."

Marcie rolled her eyes at that. Then her gaze flicked to somewhere behind Vi. Abruptly she straightened on the couch. "He's here again," she hissed.

Vi frowned and turned to look. "Who?"

It took a second, but then she recognized the soldier in the doorway as a cleaner, more respectable version of Sergeant Dangerous. Gone was the road dust and scruffy beard, leaving his angular, attractive jaw—with its paler skin—on full display. And wasn't it just her luck that he would choose this morning to make his reappearance, a morning when she looked like hell.

She didn't know whether to laugh or cry.

Perhaps if she could find some flaw in his manly perfection, so as to balance the playing field? She narrowed her gaze. His cheekbones were a bit too high, and his full, lushly curved lips a tad on the feminine side . . . or would be on someone else. Everything else about him was too hard edged and steely to be anything but male. And his deceptively lazy ease of movement that she'd noticed that first day was completely masculine.

And those eyes . . . such a piercing, unworldly blue. She could gaze into them for days.

Sue clapped her hands, startling Vi out of her inspection.

"Attention, everyone. Some of you have already heard, but we're moving out this morning. Sergeant Danger"—Vi choked on her coffee at his name—"here is our army liaison for the first leg of our journey. As he's in charge of our safety, if he tells you to do something, please do it posthaste and without argument. And yes, Matthew, I'm looking at you."

"Good luck to the sergeant with that," Marcie said in a whisper. "Matt doesn't listen to anyone except Mr. Stuart."

Vi cocked an eyebrow at the handsome actor who played Ann's love interest in the show. He lounged on the far side of the room, his shoulder against the wall, a small smile on his lips, looking anything but ashamed. "Well, if he wants to stay alive, he'll need to change his tune."

"Also," Sue continued, "I've just been advised that I mispronounced our new liaison's name. It's Sergeant Dang-er, like hanger." She gave the sergeant a small embarrassed smile. "So I do apologize."

"I don't care what his name is. I wish he wasn't our liaison." Gertie shivered. "He was so rude to Frances."

"Rudeness doesn't mean he's a bad soldier." Vi's attention returned to the sergeant, whose gaze was traveling around the room, touching on each inhabitant. Then for a brief instant his gaze met hers, and her lungs forgot how to work. Time stretched as he paused, focusing on her.

And then his perusal of the troupe continued, releasing her.

She exhaled shakily, once again ruing her haggard appearance. "In fact, my impression is that if anyone can keep us safe, it would be him."

"I agree. Rude or not, he makes me feel safer just by being in the same room." Marcie made a purring sound. "Imagine how it would feel to be in his arms."

Vi shot her travel buddy a sharp look. "Marcie . . ."

Marcie rolled her eyes and sighed. "I know, I know. But a gal can dream, can't she?"

"The trucks taking us to the airfield should be here in"—Wyatt looked at his watch—"twenty minutes. Finish your breakfast and pack up. And remember to be in uniform unless you plan to walk. Only military personnel get to fly."

Resigning herself to an aerial death, Vi tossed down the rest of her coffee and pastry. After busing her cup, she lingered for a moment, absorbing the ambiance of the room, trying to secure it in her memory.

Someday, God willing, she would want to look back on these days and reminisce.

"For I shall never pass this way again . . . ," she said softly, reciting one of her father's favorite sayings. Her father's beloved face materialized in her mind, compassionate and kind. Yet firm, too. Resolute. Lord, how she missed him.

"Our time here on earth is limited," he had told her and Fern, over and over. "So we must do as much good as we can, while we can."

He had taken that philosophy to the bank, literally, since he was the owner. And had become much beloved by the community because of it. It had also been the reason she had run away. After all those lectures on how one had but a single chance at life, and how one shouldn't ruin it with intemperance, how could she have possibly told him about the baby? If there was ever an unfortunate example of ruining one's life before it even got started, that had to be it.

How could she even think of bringing a baby into such an environment? One of disappointment and public shame? She couldn't do it. Not to the baby, not to herself, not to her family.

"The plane isn't waiting around for stragglers."

She looked up, startled to find herself alone with Sergeant Danger in the room.

"You look a bit lost," he said not unkindly. "Do you need help?"

"No." She drew a deep breath to gather her scattered thoughts. "I was . . . That is, it won't take me as long as the others to pack." Then she gave him a small smile. "So, no, thanks, I've got it in hand."

It was a deliberate echo of what he had told her two days ago. Not that she was holding a grudge or anything.

Sergeant Danger's lips twitched. "Sorry if I gave you the brush the other day. I wasn't in the best of moods. And that limey's disapproval didn't help."

"He *was* horrid, wasn't he?" Vi agreed with a laugh. "I doubt I would've shown the restraint you did."

"I've likely had more practice," he said simply.

A fragile connection stretched between them as they stood there, smiling. Perhaps he hadn't formed as awful an opinion of her as she had thought.

"Virginia!" Sue called from the hallway. "Get a move on."

Startled and dismayed by how easily the sergeant had distracted her, she darted toward her room, not bothering to excuse herself. Darn her woolgathering. If she hadn't been thinking about her dad, her mask wouldn't have slipped so completely with the sergeant. Because it hadn't been Virginia interacting with him. Nor had it been Lily. It had been utterly, frighteningly herself. Violet.

She couldn't let it happen again.

⁓

Thirty minutes later, firmly resolved to stay as far away from Sergeant Danger as humanly possible, she fetched her suitcase from the truck that had carried them to the airfield. The task wasn't as hard as she feared thanks to Charles and Matt following the sergeant around like schoolchildren, pestering him with questions.

Safe for the moment, her suitcase in hand, she drifted away from the others. To her surprise, the airfield hadn't been in Caserta, despite the palace having housed the Italian Air Force Academy, but several miles to the west, in another town altogether. Nervously, she gazed out over the tarmac toward the mountains hulking in the distance. A milky-blue heat haze filled the valley, blurring the peaks. The hills, what she could see, were raw and wild. Half volcanic rock, half green-and-gold vegetation, they were breathtakingly pretty. And also deadly if crashed into. She knew enough about airplanes to know that much.

With her attempts to calm herself incinerated by the thought, she turned her attention to all the crates and bags waiting to be loaded into the plane. She might not be a pilot, but she could only imagine all that weight might be an issue when it came to clearing mountain peaks. Perhaps they should leave some of those crates behind?

"Is there a problem?" Sergeant Danger's husky voice caught her off guard, and she jumped.

Placing a hand over her racing heart, she turned and then startled again. He was much closer than she had imagined him. An unexpected whiff of aftershave and warm, healthy male eddied around her, teasing and pleasant. Much more so than the heavier odors of oil and aviation fuel. She found herself leaning toward him despite her misgivings.

That this rough-and-ready man had bothered to slap on some aftershave this morning struck her as unexpected, though perhaps it shouldn't. The draft, after all, called up young men from all walks of life. For all she knew the sergeant could have been a banker, like her father, before being called up.

The irony of such a possibility made her want to laugh and cry at the same time. She had never thought about it, but most of the men here had likely never wanted to be soldiers, had never wanted to leave their homes and fight in a war. And yet here they were, carrying out their orders until killed, or wounded enough to return home. It wasn't right.

The whole situation wasn't right, but what could she do?

She blinked away the sudden rush of emotion. "It's nothing," she managed in answer to his question, glad he couldn't divine the real reason for her tears. "I've just never flown before."

"You'll be fine. Trust me, riding in a plane is a piece of cake compared to jumping out of one." He winked at her, a breath-stealing smile curving his utterly kissable lips.

Then her stomach dropped as his words soaked in. "Jump out? Oh, good Lord, not on your life! I'd rather go down in a flaming wreck. There's no way I would be able to make myself jump."

His smile vanished. "Don't say that. You'll jinx the flight, which would be highly unappreciated by the pilots."

"You're kidding." But he wasn't, she could see, and being a theater person, she understood jinxes and superstitions. "I'm sorry. Hopefully you were the only one who heard me."

"Apology accepted," he said, his expression grim. "But be careful what you say—cursing a man's luck, no matter how innocently, can be just as deadly to him and his unit as actual gunfire. A fellow who thinks his luck has run out tends to make bad choices, taking out his team as well."

"I wasn't thinking. I'm sorry."

"Yeah, well." He exhaled tightly. "I realize this is your first tour, but I gotta be straight with you: it might be your last if you don't start paying attention. It's why I don't like civilians mixing with GIs. You only make our lives more dangerous."

She opened her mouth to apologize again, but he was already striding away toward the men loading the plane.

Angry tears filled her eyes. How dare he chastise her over something she had no way of knowing? Whatever connection she had felt with him earlier crashed and burned. She had been right the first time. He was a jerk.

Chapter 16

The noise inside the airplane was deafening as the twin engines roared in an effort to lift the bumping and swaying plane over the peaks. Vi closed her eyes and prayed. Fear and nausea created an unholy combination in her stomach, one that made her glad she hadn't finished her breakfast. Her irritation at the sergeant had gotten her through the first fifteen minutes of the flight. Then the heart-stopping lurches and dips started, and any courage she'd had before fled.

Spending hours in the back of a truck would've been heaven compared to this. Who cared how long it took? Her chances of getting home to Chicago would be greater than they were at the moment.

She wasn't alone in her misery. Most of the troupe was either wide-eyed and pale or turning an unhealthy shade of green, like Matt. Not all, though. Charles read his book, though how he could concentrate she had no idea. Mr. Stuart appeared to be napping, and Luciana was deep in conversation with Sergeant Danger.

The noise kept Vi from overhearing, but from Luciana's hand gestures, Vi suspected they were talking about something important. The actress kept punctuating her speech by smacking the knife edge of one hand against the palm of the other, as if to make a point.

The sergeant, for his part, listened attentively, with his long legs stretched out, his body relaxed. Every once in a while he would grab the hanging strap above him for stability, but otherwise he might as well have been sitting on a bus for all the concern he showed. It was infuriating. Worse, he seemed so at ease with Luciana, answering her points with comments of his own, smiling briefly at something she said. A couple of times they even laughed together.

A stab of envy made her look away. So what if the sergeant didn't seem to mind Luciana "mixing with GIs"? The actress was welcome to him. Vi had far more important things to fret over than how not a single man had ever listened to her as if what she said actually mattered. Certainly not Robert, who had been more interested in the sound of his own voice. Not even her own father, kind and loving as he was. It had gotten only worse in recent years, as most men didn't really care what a burlesque dancer had to say, no matter how smart or well read she might be.

A sudden sway of the plane made her break out in a nauseated sweat. Desperate for a distraction, she turned her thoughts to her future—assuming she had one beyond this flight. As much as she loved dancing and creating her own acts, it would be nice to be valued for something more than a pair of big knockers. Perhaps an actress, though she would have to go back to school and get her high school diploma. Every Hollywood actress she had ever read about had at least gotten that far. And it shouldn't be that hard. She'd been an honor student up until she'd dropped out to have Jimmy.

Or maybe she should consider secretarial school. Actresses could become too old for work, the same as dancers, even legitimate ones.

Speaking of dancers . . . She glanced at her travel buddy and found her twisted around on the metal bench and staring out the round window at the countryside below. Frowning slightly, Vi reached over to check all Marcie's buckles and belts to make sure they were still fastened. Two weren't, so Vi cinched them up, forcing Marcie back onto the metal bench that passed for a seat.

Marcie slapped her hand away. "Stop that! What are you doing?" she shouted over the roar of the engines.

"Making sure you don't go bouncing around the cabin. Head injuries are hard to dance with."

"Yes, well, I'm going to throw up if I don't look out the window."

"I'll take my chances," Vi shouted back. "I'm not dancing by myself during the dinner party scene."

"I tell you, I'm f—" Marcie didn't finish as a loud bang came from outside the plane, the reverberation palpable through the seats.

All conversation in the cabin stopped as the plane's tail skidded to the left.

"The engine!" Gertie yelled, her white face pressed to a window. "It's on fire!"

Vi and Marcie immediately joined her. Flames were indeed shooting out of a hole in the metal and streaking back toward the wing. Vi's heart stopped. *Oh no, no, no.* This couldn't be happening. She had *not* jinxed the plane. She hadn't.

Abruptly the flames went out, but the relief was short lived as the propellers slowed almost to a stop, indicating the engine was dead. At the same time, the plane yawed even harder to the right. Then it fishtailed abruptly to the left. Both Ann and Frances screamed. Even Luciana paled, her hand gripping the sergeant's knee. Vi understood the actress's impulse, wishing she could do the same. Then, before she could catch her breath, the plane swooped back to the right and began to tilt toward the remaining engine.

As the floor tilt increased, sobs and prayers filled the cabin. The frantic pounding of her heart made it difficult to tell, but she was pretty sure the remaining engine was starting to stutter, too. Vi bit her lip to keep from crying. *Keep it together, Vi. Falling apart will lessen your chances of survival.*

"Don't panic," Sergeant Danger shouted over the roar of the remaining engine. His gaze, alert and focused, swept the cabin, reassuring everyone. "As long as we have one engine, we're still good."

Vi had no way to know if he was telling the truth, as the airplane continued to bounce through the air, one wing significantly lower than the other. But then, maybe it didn't matter. Not panicking was always good advice, and there was nothing any of them could do about the engines.

And if worse came to worst . . .

A spike of terror shot through her as she realized just what that would entail.

She glanced at the sergeant, his joking comment about jumping out of airplanes suddenly—terrifyingly—a real possibility. To her surprise, he was looking back at her. For a moment she imagined she saw blame in those cool blue eyes. After all, he had heard her jinx the flight.

The radioman popped his head into the cabin. "Okay, folks. Cap'n is going to be setting us down soon as he can. He says not to worry, you'll all get to Rome as planned. Just a bit later than expected. And . . . uh, don't worry." With that he ducked back into the cockpit.

Marcie grabbed Vi's arm, her fingers digging in hard. "What does that mean?"

Vi winced, the pain not helping settle her nerves at all. "That we should keep our seat belts on and hope for the best."

"But I don't want to die," Marcie wailed loudly enough to draw the attention of everyone in the cabin.

Aware of all the eyes on them, Vi patted her friend's hand and then tried to pry Marcie's fingers off. "We're not going to die."

"There's so much I still want t-t-to do with my life," Marcie sobbed. "It's not fair."

There was a lot Vi wanted to do, too. Watching her son grow up being at the top of the list. Tears filled her eyes.

"Come on, little one. You're only defeated if you give up." The memory of Sal's gruff words fought to be heard over the engines. *"Until that moment, you still have a fighting chance. Don't squander it being afraid."*

Sal . . . Her chest hurt as she thought about the man who had pulled her off that bridge that fateful day, when she had all but given up on life, and who had later become almost a surrogate father to her. Would he follow through on his promise to watch over Jimmy?

You're not going to die!

Pulling herself together, she looked to see how the others were doing. Everyone, save the sergeant, seemed terrified. Faces pale, hands gripped tightly in their laps or on the overhead straps, no one said a word. *Poor Gertie.* Silent tears streamed down the girl's face as her chin quivered. Luciana was now clinging to Sergeant Danger's arm as if her life depended on it. Even Mr. Stuart looked worried, his eyes wide and alert for what had to be the first time the entire trip.

Her gaze touched on Sergeant Danger again and then stayed. He was the one bastion of calm in the whole cabin. *When in doubt, imitate the ones who know.* It was an old dancer's trick, useful if one got lost in the choreography. And if anyone knew about military airplanes and their capability to fly with one engine, surely it would be Sergeant Danger.

Following his lead, she straightened in her seat and let herself roll with the bumps. She stroked Marcie's arm with her free hand and encouraged her travel buddy to talk about what she would do once they landed. She smiled encouragingly at Gertie and even Frances. Ann and Sue both had their eyes closed, as if in prayer, which seemed completely reasonable to her. Wyatt scowled at the floor, his arms crossed.

After what seemed an eternity later, though likely only ten or fifteen minutes, the radioman reappeared to tell everyone they were getting ready to land and to buckle up. Vi clung to the utter lack of concern on Sergeant Danger's face as she rechecked Marcie's seat belt and then her own. Despite her effort to remain cool and collected, her nerves jangled as if in the face of a five-alarm fire with no exit. Still, she wasn't an actress for nothing. She would be damned if she let her fear show now, especially when Marcie was finally starting to calm down.

The plane banked farther to the left, the floor taking on what felt like a sixty-degree slant. Vi's lungs constricted, and she looked over at the sergeant.

This time his gaze met hers and held. Time stopped as she fell into the intense blue of his stare. The snarl of the last engine faded into the background. Her heartbeat still raced, but for a different reason. Vaguely, she registered that the plane had leveled out and that someone yelled they could see the landing strip ahead. But like a rabbit caught in a snare, she could no more look away from the man across her than she could breathe.

What did he see when he looked at her like this, so intently? A fool for jinxing the flight? A silly dancer with no brains at all? Except he didn't look angry. He looked . . . proud? Then—in a surprise to top all surprises—he winked. At her.

She blinked, sure she had imagined it. But no, his full, sinful lips were actually curving into a slight smile—one that fueled a dangerous desire building inside her. And it scared her. She hadn't felt this drawn to a man since . . . well, since Robert. And what had that gotten her but disaster?

Swallowing hard, she tore her gaze away, as unsettled by his interest in her as she was by her reaction to it.

A hard bump and then the plane shuddered.

She closed her eyes and forgot everything but heartfelt thanks as the wheels found the ground again. Marcie clutched at Vi's arm as the plane rattled down the runway, and Vi squeezed the girl's hand reassuringly as they bumped off into the grass and then slowly rolled to a stop.

An eerie silence filled the cabin after the remaining engine shut down. Then excited and relieved chatter erupted around her. They had survived! The radioman was greeted with loud cheers and applause when he came back to open the door. Then there were calls for the pilot. Everyone wanted to congratulate the fellow on a job well done.

With a shaky exhale, Vi wiped her sweaty palms on her uniform trousers as her castmates rejoiced. She let Marcie seize her in a bear hug and then watched her bound away to embrace Gertie and then Sue. Vi didn't immediately join the celebration, her own emotions were running so high. Now that she had stared down death, never again would she take life for granted.

Another second chance. One she didn't deserve but would take with both hands. She wasn't sure what she would do with it yet, but it would be big, a tribute to her parents. Not that they would ever forgive her, but maybe, just maybe, she could become someone they could be proud of.

Chapter 17

"So I have some good news and some bad news," Sue said to the assembled troupe as they huddled next to the broken airplane, clutching their musette bags and suitcases. Behind her, the soldiers tasked with towing the aircraft off from the runway, so they could reopen the airstrip, shouted instructions to each other, nearly drowning out her words.

It was quite the production, involving ropes, a few chains, and a truck with a tow hitch. Wyatt looked fascinated by the whole thing. Vi found it hard not to watch, as well.

"The commander says we are stuck here for the night," Sue continued, fighting to regain everyone's attention. "They should be able to ferry another plane in tomorrow if the weather holds. Meanwhile, the good news is they would love for us to perform for them! So get ready for opening night, boys and girls. We're finally getting a chance to do what we came here for."

Vi cheered along with the rest of the company. This was good news indeed! It had been entirely too long since she had last walked a stage.

Gertie caught her in a hug. "Can you believe it? I can't wait!"

"Me either." Vi hugged her back. She turned to look for Marcie, only to catch Sergeant Danger scowling. His reaction surprised her. Did his dislike of civilians around soldiers include USO performances? If so, why on earth had someone assigned him to be their liaison?

"Come on." Marcie snagged her arm excitedly. "Let's go get settled in."

Still perplexed, and a bit vexed by his attitude, Vi barely noticed as Marcie tugged her along after the rest of the troupe. Their destination was a large Quonset hut just to the side of two enormous hangars. A sign proclaiming NETTUNO hung over its metal front door.

"Is that where we are?" Vi asked Victor as he came up alongside her and Marcie.

"It is. The pilot said we're about thirty miles south of Rome."

That surprised her. "If we're that close, why are we spending the night here? With a couple of trucks we could be in Rome within the hour."

"Perhaps if we were in the States. But we're not. I don't know if you looked out the window at all, but the roads here are in rough shape, thanks to the war. And even if they were smooth as glass, we still would have to wait on official transportation. All army personnel—including USO troops—move at the pleasure of NATOUSA. If they have no free planes to come get us, we wait until they do."

"I see."

Since the North African Theater of Operations, US Army, was paying her wages, she supposed she shouldn't complain. And performing tonight did a lot toward making up for not getting to Rome.

Wyatt was already at the door to the hut by the time the troupe got there. He held the Quonset door while everyone filed in. Everyone but the sergeant. He stopped at the door and said something to Wyatt, who nodded, and then Sergeant Danger disappeared. As Vi turned her attention away, she noted she hadn't been the only one watching the sergeant. Luciana had been, too, with an odd, almost distressed expression.

Vi frowned, unsettled. Luciana was usually the calm, seemingly unflappable one in the troupe. Had Sergeant Danger said or done something to shake her? If so, maybe Vi should find out what, so as to make sure there wasn't also a threat to Marcie's well-being.

"Welcome to Nettuno," the officer at the front of the hut drawled with an easy smile, as if theater folk crash-landed onto his airfield all the time. "Sorry y'all had to cut your flight short, but we're thrilled to see you. The USO passes us over most times, on account of our being such a small outfit. Do you have someone my fellows can work with to get your stage set up?"

"Wyatt; is he here?" Sue asked, looking around.

"He and Luciana stepped outside," Matt said from the back. "They said they'd just be a minute."

Sue's mouth tightened with displeasure. An almost audible tittering percolated through the group, along with a few raised eyebrows and shared knowing looks. Apparently Marcie hadn't been off base about the two of them, though this was the first time Vi had witnessed Luciana and Wyatt disappearing together.

"Well, will someone go and bring them back?" Sue asked, the words clipped with annoyance.

"I will," Vi chimed in before anyone else could.

"Thank you, Virginia," Sue said, still sounding peeved. "That would be lovely."

Vi leaped into action, hoping the quicker she was out of there, the less likely someone would volunteer to go with her. Though she still didn't think Luciana was involved with Janet's dismissal, she had to admit something wasn't quite on the up-and-up with the actress's behavior. No one else had made clandestine phone calls or issued not-so-subtle warnings to Marcie to watch her step. But as Sal would say: better to know than have an opinion.

Cracking the door open, she cautiously stuck her head out, in case the trio was close by.

A wind gust carried a whisper of voices to her, one of them clearly female. Vi followed the sound toward the back of the hut. Her skin tingled as the voices grew louder, more impassioned. Her steps slowed as she reached the corner. She peeked around and then instantly pulled her head back.

Luciana, Mr. Miller, and Sergeant Danger were there, not more than three feet away. Heart racing, she waited for someone to call out that they had seen her. When no one did, she leaned closer to listen.

Mr. Miller's furious voice reached her first. "I don't care what you want. It's not going to happen."

Sergeant Danger responded in a low, soothing rumble, but the words were too quiet for Vi to hear. She leaned even closer.

"I disagree," Mr. Miller said hotly. "It definitely is my business. Miss Rossi is key to our production, and anything that endangers her will endanger the entire show."

"Are you saying the show is more important than ending the war?" This from Luciana. Her voice was low, cold.

Vi frowned, surprised that Luciana would take that tone with Mr. Miller, lover or not.

"We were sent here to perform, not second-guess the generals in charge," Mr. Miller snapped. "So yes. And your 'friends' can go to hell."

Sergeant Danger said something, again too low to be deciphered, but this time his tone held a definite note of command.

"I don't care," Mr. Miller said, the words clipped, sharp. "As far as I'm concerned, this conversation is over."

Deciding that was her cue, since their discussion was unlikely to get any friendlier or more informative, Vi squared her shoulders and rounded the corner.

"There you guys are." She smiled, feigning relief. "Sue sent me looking for you."

The three started almost guiltily. Then Luciana pulled it together first.

"Oh, I'm sorry," the actress said with a gentle smile. "Tell her I'll be there directly. Thank you."

"Sure." Vi shrugged as if it didn't matter one way or the other to her, but inwardly she was impressed at Luciana's recovery. Talk about a real actress. She turned to Wyatt. "She particularly wanted to see you, Mr. Miller. About the stage requirements for tonight."

"Fine." Wyatt turned to the other two. "If you'll excuse me?"

"I've said everything I need to say," Sergeant Danger said.

"I have as well," Luciana said coolly. She turned a warmer smile on Vi. "Let's go."

Vi hung back, letting Mr. Miller and Luciana go ahead of her. "Is everything all right?" Vi asked Sergeant Danger when the other two were out of earshot.

The sergeant was silent so long, Vi wasn't sure he would answer. Then he said, "It is. So whatever you think you overheard, you didn't. Just forget about it, all right?"

"All right." What Vi really wanted to do was press for more details, but the sergeant's stony expression warned her otherwise.

Following him back into the Quonset hut, she knew there was no way she could "just forget" Luciana threatening to leave the show, nor the mention of ending the war sooner. And then there was Mr. Miller's reference to Luciana being endangered, along with the entire production. Perhaps she could worm something more out of the technical director after the performance tonight, when everyone was relaxed and happy.

Because if there was something besides the war out there that could potentially threaten Marcie's safety, Vi definitely needed to know about it.

❧

The rest of the day progressed much more smoothly than the blown engine might have suggested. The soldiers cleared out a barrack for the women. A suitable stage was assembled near the airfield. Cables materialized from seemingly nowhere so there could be lights and sound. The weather even looked as if it would cooperate, the dark clouds that had gathered on the horizon slowly dissipating as the day went on, going from gray to white to mere wisps.

While Wyatt and a few volunteer soldiers worked like madmen to get the lights strung and the speakers connected to overhead microphones, Sue made the cast run through their lines twice, once without the dancers and once with. It was difficult to keep the beat without the help of the recorded music. Victor did the best he could by banging two blocks of wood together. Matt, Charlie, and Luciana handled the vocals better than Vi would have expected, given their lack of rehearsal and a starting pitch. She hoped it would go better once Wyatt had the speakers hooked up.

Her head positively ached as she imagined all the things that could go wrong, both back of the stage and in front. Good ol' opening night jitters. She knew the feeling well: the heightened sense of risk, the prickling of electricity running through her veins, the deep-seated terror that made her want to throw up.

She knew the nausea was temporary and would vanish the moment she stepped onto the stage. Still, as the troupe broke for dinner, she doubted she would be able to eat more than a few bites.

Standing in the chow line with the others, the tin plate from her standard-issue army gear in her hands, Vi watched the enlisted men, who would soon be her audience, from the corner of her eye. They seemed well and truly excited for the night's impromptu entertainment, which she took as a good sign. If she were honest with herself, she would admit to being more nervous than usual. Regular theater work was so much harder on a performer's nerves, in a way, than burlesque.

Burlesque was so straightforward. The audience came knowing exactly what they wanted, and she knew exactly how to provide it. She imagined it was like slinging hash at a diner. A hungry soul coming through the diner's door wasn't looking for fancy food or a fine-dining experience. They wanted grease and salt and everything that tasted good, and they wanted it in quantity, and they wanted it fast.

But these men . . . these soldiers deserved something finer, something equal to their sacrifice. She wasn't sure she was good enough, and she was only in the chorus. She didn't envy the leads at all.

It wasn't that she was stage shy. At the Palace she had never hesitated. She had been the star, the headliner, often the sole presence on the stage, and it had thrilled her down to her soul. Now, though, after watching Ann and Luciana practice all day, she wondered if she had cheated her way into the spotlight. If she hadn't been willing to take her clothes off, to do what other more modest girls would not, would she have found such success?

Marcie nudged her. "Penny for your thoughts."

Vi blinked away her self-doubts and smiled at her travel buddy. "Just reassuring myself we won't get booed off the stage tonight."

Marcie's eyes widened. "Is that a possibility?"

Victor leaned forward and patted Marcie's hand. "Not even remotely. At least not you, my dear. We men could face a different reality, but you ladies will charm them all. Never fear. Your mere presence here is a boon to their soul. A reminder of all that is good and kind in the world. They will adore you!"

"Oh, well. That's good," Marcie said, a soft blush stealing across her cheeks. A new and speculative warmth lit her dark eyes as she glanced at the young men across the mess hall. A few of them openly grinned back. "I like being adored."

"As long as it's at arm's distance," Vi said coolly. "You know the rules, and it's a long swim back to New York Harbor."

Marcie sat back in a huff. "For heaven's sake, all I'm doing is looking. I swear you're worse than my aunt Maria Valentina."

"And you're like a kitten in a den full of wolves. You might be just looking, but I guarantee some of those boys are sizing you up for dinner."

"And you've got a suspicious mind."

"What I've got is experience."

"Really?" Marcie scoffed. "Just what kind of experience does a virginal corn princess like you have? Stealing kisses behind the barn? Holding hands while milking the cows? Oh please."

Vi opened her mouth to reply, a scathing set-down on her tongue. Then she remembered who she was. Or rather who she was supposed to be. She quickly closed her mouth and turned away. It wouldn't do for anyone to see the truth in her eyes. "You're right. You go ahead and do what you want. Sorry for worrying about you."

Victor sighed. "Ladies . . . save all that passion for the stage. Though Virginia does have a point. A lot of these men have been away from their wives and sweethearts for a long time and may not remember how to treat a lady. Not that I want to say anything against our men in uniform! But you might not want to trust them if they get you alone."

Marcie sat back and crossed her arms. "I wouldn't. I wasn't born yesterday."

"Of course not," the older actor said soothingly. "But you are extraordinarily beautiful."

Marcie blushed while Vi fought not to roll her eyes. Her travel buddy was pretty at best. Luciana was the real looker. And Ann wasn't far behind.

Still, Marcie had cheered up, which Vi took as a sign that it was time to get them both out of there. She pushed her chair back and grabbed her mess kit. "Only forty-five minutes to showtime. Ready to go, travel buddy?"

Marcie sighed. "If we must."

"You don't want the wrath of Sue for being late. And she wants us limbered up and in full costume twenty minutes before the curtain rises."

Marcie hesitated, her eyes turned once more to the soldiers who were all but preening for attention. Then to Vi's relief, she followed Vi's lead and picked up her kit.

Hungry, hopeful gazes followed the two of them as they left, but it no longer worried her. The men could look all they wanted, as long as they didn't touch. She was pretty sure Papa Maggio would be less than pleased if his daughter returned pregnant, and Vi didn't trust Marcie to take the necessary precautions to avoid such a disaster. Assuming Marcie even knew what to do. It wasn't something nuns or parents taught good Catholic girls.

After dropping off their mess kits at the barracks and brushing their teeth, Vi and Marcie headed over to where an open-air stage had been hastily erected. Scaffolding to hold the lights and backdrop had been pieced together with ladders and poles. The stage itself was little more than wood planking nailed to the top of crates. But at least it looked more or less level.

The sharp bang of hammers, interspersed with shouts, greeted them as they stopped to watch a crew of soldiers working on the stage. A last-ditch effort was being made to attach steps to either side. Wyatt was busy testing the sound system, which consisted of military-grade loudspeakers connected by loops of wire to a record player backstage, and the microphones dangling down in strategic places. Sue was checking the placement of props with the help of two grizzled mechanics.

"Well, it's not the Shubert," Ann said, coming up beside Vi and Marcie. "But—by God—it's a stage."

"That it is," Vi agreed, strangely moved by the sight.

It seemed only fitting and right for their first USO performance to be here, on this makeshift stage in the middle of the Italian countryside. Far better than a royal theater in Caserta or a posh one in Rome, though she would like to play somewhere ritzy eventually. But not tonight.

Tonight she would give the performance of her life. It no longer mattered that she had been forced into this role. Tonight she would seize the chance to prove herself. She would bare her soul, if not her body, to the audience with the hope of lightening their burdens if only for a moment.

Eager to get going, she carried her things toward the area designated as cast only. Dressing rooms had been created by draping sheets over head-high ropes. Two rags, one red and one blue, distinguished the women's room from the men's. Inside the roped-off area, a dozen or so shaving mirrors had been scrounged up to allow for makeup and hair checks. Flashlights were stacked in a pile to provide additional lighting once the sun set. There was even a small bouquet of flowers in a Coke bottle balanced on a crate in the corner.

Vi was touched by what had obviously been an all-out effort on the soldiers' part to make them feel welcome.

Sue echoed that thought when everyone gathered for the preshow briefing.

"No slacking," Sue admonished them. "These men have gone to great lengths to make sure we have everything we need."

"And if all that commotion coming from the front of the house is any indication, they're also going to be an enthusiastic audience," Victor added. "So, let's give 'em a show to remember!"

Vi bit her lip. Lord, she hoped the men wouldn't go away disappointed.

The field commander was up next. Stern faced, if a little soft around the waist, the fortyish commander met each and every one of their gazes with a direct, piercing one of his own.

"As this is your first performance as a USO unit, I want to reiterate what you've probably already been told. These men—not boys, mind you. Never boys. Not after what some of them have lived through— these men are not your usual audience. Many have never been to a theater performance before and may not behave as you might expect. The MPs will do their best to keep things under control, but you can assist by eliminating any provocative content. To be blunt, no kissing. No extended physical contact between men and women. And absolutely no mention of sex! Is that clear?"

The troupe nodded.

"Also be prepared for hoots and hollers, especially if you make any reference to Italy or any other cities here. And if things get out of hand, we may have to stop the performance. Any questions?"

Ann raised her hand. "Excuse me, sir, but you make it sound like we're performing in front of a bunch of animals."

"These men have been out of polite society for a while now, if they even knew what that was to begin with." The commander smiled grimly. "And what are we really anyway, under all our urbane sophistication, but a 'bunch of animals'?"

Vi snorted softly, his frank assessment of mankind echoing her own. She'd been on the receiving end of man's baser nature so many times in the past, she knew firsthand how thin the veneer of civilization really was.

The commander bade the company good luck and then disappeared around the curtain to join his men.

Sue drew a deep breath. "All right. You heard the commander. Tone down whatever you can. Particularly you dancers. And be prepared for anything." She turned to Mr. Stuart. "Anything you want to add, Gerry?"

The company all leaned in, curious to hear what he might say, after all these weeks of virtual silence.

His gaze traveled around the gathered players, and then, to Vi's shock, a slight smile erased his usual scowl. "I know I've had Sue push you hard these last few weeks, and I know some of you were starting to question why you had given up lucrative contracts and risked your personal safety to come here. I hope the next hour and a half answer that for you. And even if it doesn't, I want you to know that I am so proud of each and every one of you. You've not only met my expectations. You have exceeded them. So let's go do what we came here for. Let's entertain those troops. And break a leg."

"Three cheers for Mr. Stuart," Victor said. "For launching this production and bringing it to fruition."

"And to our indomitable Sue, and Wyatt, too," Ann added, her voice wobbling a bit. "We wouldn't have made it without you."

Tears filled Vi's eyes as she cheered with the others. Her heart swelled almost to bursting. In this moment, she didn't want to be anywhere else. Yes, she hated being away from Jimmy, but to feel a part of this wonderful ensemble, to be so accepted, it was the second chance she hadn't known she wanted. Standing here, it was almost as if Robert had never happened. Not that she would wish Jimmy unborn, but, oh—to feel like herself again! The her that had existed before her foolish mistake.

It was as if a mantle of lead weights had been lifted from her shoulders, letting her stand free and unencumbered by shame. Something Lily had never managed to do, for all her defiance and success.

An overall-clad soldier whistled from the stage to catch their attention and then gave a thumbs-up.

Sue glanced at her watch and grinned. "Right on time. Places, everyone!"

Chapter 18

The first act went off without a hitch. The audience ate up Ann's portrayal of the girl next door fresh off the farm, seeking fame and fortune in Hollywood. They tolerated Matt, her devoted high school sweetheart, who came next, their attention rapt when he begged her to come home and marry him. Her refusal had even been greeted with a smattering of boos and several hollers from the crowd of "What's the matter with you?" Then came Luciana's sultry entrance that, even though toned down, nearly had the stage rushed. The whole valley reverberated with an avalanche of wolf whistles and shouts of "Share a little of that with us, will ya?"

It was a bit unsettling, and Vi traded nervous glances with Marcie, who was positioned on the other side of the stage. The MPs soon had everyone settled down, and Victor, playing the part of movie director, handled the interruptions like the professional he was. Luciana, on the other hand, looked pale and a bit shaken, perhaps unused to such a boisterous audience. Lord knew it had thrown Vi, and she was used to being propositioned in the middle of her act.

Charles, as the faux movie's hero, in all his over-the-top smarminess, was the last to take the stage. The audience, fully engaged now, greeted him with sarcastic hoots. And then it was time for the first song and dance number. Vi held her breath as Ann took center stage, ready to sing about how terrifying it was to chase her dreams, how she was torn between love and fame, yet the siren call of the movies was all she could hear. Matt moved downstage left, his clear tenor picking up the countermelody as Victor and Luciana disappeared offstage so that there would be room for the dancers.

Vi's heart began beating so furiously it nearly choked her as she waited for her cue. Marcie, pale and determined, stood in the opposite wing, doing a last-minute back stretch right behind Frances. Gertie's breath fell warm and fast on Vi's skin. Vi hoped the girl wouldn't hyperventilate.

Sue, from her position just offstage, lifted her hand as she whispered cues into her headset. Her hand fell, and the lights changed. The dancers were on.

Vi threw her shoulders back and strutted proudly onto the stage, the footlights temporarily blinding her. She had to trust Marcie was doing the same from the other side. Gertie and Frances would follow two beats later. Not that Vi could hear their shoe taps, given the roaring wave of cheers and whistles that greeted them.

Elation, sweet and electric, lit up her veins, making her feet light as air. Unable to help herself, Vi winked at Marcie as they met in the middle. Marcie wobbled a smile back, and then all four of the chorus girls turned toward the audience.

Her heart skipped a beat.

She had seen plenty of audiences, from farmers in overalls to old women in their Sunday best, from young children to rough-edged workers fresh from the docks. She had gladly performed in front of them all. But never had she seen anything so moving as this: a veritable wall of khaki men, some sitting two to a chair, others standing, and still others clinging to the side of the packed bleachers.

Only experience kept her feet moving to the beat, her smile in place, as she drank the sight in.

She'd had no idea so many soldiers would attend. They must have come from miles around just to see this modest little musical that honestly would have never even made it off-Broadway—though she would never tell Mr. Stuart that. It humbled her. And inspired her. And suddenly she wanted to never do anything but dance her heart out for these boys, these *men* who were throwing so much love her way. She wanted to return it all in equal measure. She wanted to give them more.

The second act flew by as smooth as butterscotch. Vi had peeked around the curtain to watch the soldiers leaning forward in their seats. In the reflected stage light, their faces revealed their total absorption. They shouted their opinions with increasing enthusiasm to Ann when she sang about how she couldn't decide between Charlie or Matt, fame or family, success or true love. They hissed when Luciana, playing the part of the jealous diva, schemed to ruin Ann. And, of course, they cheered when Vi and the other chorus girls returned to the stage for their second dance number.

Mr. Stuart positively beamed as he took in the action onstage and the audience's reactions to it. Maybe the show would prove a hit, after all. Vi hoped so. She had nothing but love and respect for the man in this moment.

Everyone's spirits were running high backstage as the third act opened. Everything pointed to an unmitigated success as the play unspooled toward the climactic scene. And then disaster struck. As Luciana strode across the stage, her character gesturing wildly in a high dudgeon, her foot apparently caught on an uneven board. Her eyes widened as she tried to catch her balance. Victor noticed first and rushed toward her, but it was too late. Luciana landed in an ungraceful heap at Victor's feet.

A confused silence settled over the audience as Luciana's glassy, pain-filled eyes glanced up at Sue offstage, begging for help. Vi winced as Wyatt's voice came through Sue's headphones, loud enough for everyone around her to overhear. But mostly her heart went out to Luciana.

It was every actor's nightmare, to be caught onstage out of character.

Even Mr. Stuart paled as the action onstage froze, the actors unsure what to do. Vi thought fast. Luciana's next lines were the setup for Ann's character's decision to go home. Vi knew the lines, having heard them enough times to memorize them: "You want success, you've got to be willing to sell your soul . . ."

Improvising on the fly, Vi grabbed Sue's playbook, earning a shocked look from Sue, and dashed onto the stage. Portraying boundless enthusiasm, and still in her dance costume, she flourished the playbook as she ran toward the fallen Luciana.

"Miss Diablo, I'm so glad I found you! I read your memoir and wanted to tell you I'm so inspired! I'm ready for stardom. I'm ready to do whatever it takes, just like you advised. Even if it means selling a piece of my soul . . ." Vi glanced pointedly at Ann, willing her to take the cue.

Ann hesitated for what felt like an eternity, though it was likely no more than a second. Then, God love her, she picked up the tossed bone and declared that she wasn't prepared to make that same sacrifice. She would rather know true love than be famous.

Victor followed suit, smoothly delivering his lines like the old pro that he was while he knelt to help Luciana up. Charlie fell in line and, staying in character as the enterprising movie star, escorted both Vi and a limping Luciana off the stage with talk of fictional projects he could envision for all of them.

From there the play hurtled unimpeded toward its romantic ending, with Ann and Matt returning to their hometown, engaged and in love. To Vi's relief, the soldiers shouted only approving remarks at the departing couple, perhaps hoping for a similar happy ending when they got home.

With one last song-and-dance number before the curtain came down, Vi crossed her fingers that no further disasters would strike. Sue gave the cue and Vi strutted back onto the stage with the other chorus girls. As the soldiers whooped and stomped their feet in approval, a high more potent than any from a mere drug surged in her blood. All her worries vanished. Rough opening nights didn't necessarily mean the rest of the run was doomed. And likely Luciana had only turned her ankle and not broken it. Everything would be all right. Because, in that moment, with the lights in her eyes and the music in her ears, nothing less seemed possible.

The rousing cheer that greeted the fall of the curtain surely had been heard all the way in Rome. Practically dancing in ecstasy, the whole cast went out, a limping and yet smiling Luciana supported on either side by Charles and Matthew. Then, arm in arm, the unit bowed as one. Not just once but three times as the applause and whistles kept coming. Finally, Wyatt cut the lights, signaling all involved it was time to call it a night.

"Oh my! Can you believe it?" Marcie squealed as they came off the stage. She seized Vi in a bear hug, laughed excitedly, and then turned to give Frances the same treatment. Vi smiled at her friend's reaction, her own spirits soaring on a postperformance high. It was like celebrating Christmas, Thanksgiving, and her birthday all at once. The only thing dimming it was her concern for Luciana, whom Victor was seating on a crate.

No sooner had Sue knelt beside the actress to examine her injured leg than a white-helmeted MP appeared.

"Excuse me, ladies. Gentlemen," he said, nodding at them all and somehow managing to sound both bashful and authoritative. "Sorry to interrupt, but the men . . . they want to know if they can come back and thank the cast in person. We'll run them off, if you'd like. But . . . well, they're just so grateful for you all being here."

Sue and Mr. Stuart shared a surprised look, and then she spoke up. "I think that would be fine. We don't have anywhere to be." She glanced down at Luciana. "Are you up for it?"

Luciana hesitated and then nodded.

Sue turned to the rest of them. "Line up, everyone. Over here next to Luciana, so she won't have to stand. We've got some well-wishers to greet."

To Vi's astonishment, it wasn't only a few who wanted to meet them. Not by a long shot. When the MP hollered to his buddy to let them back, a whole line of men formed within seconds. In fact, near as she could tell, the whole audience must have stayed behind, waiting for the chance to see them, their caps in hand, their faces creased with shy grins.

She soon lost track of how many hands she had shaken, how many questions she had answered about where she was from and did she know so-and-so, and how many spur-of-the-moment marriage proposals she had to gently turn down. It broke her heart, really. These men were so desperate for reminders of home, for any scrap of reassurance that the American people hadn't forgotten about them.

"Not that I blame the folks back home," a tall, lanky soldier from Poughkeepsie confided. "Everyone is so keen on liberating France, we can't even get our HQ to pay attention to us. And the worst part is that the guys up front are starting to feel abandoned because we're not sending any planes to provide cover for them. But the truth is, miss? We don't have 'em. They've all been moved to cover the troops in France."

"That's terrible!" Vi said, sick at the thought of those brave men at the front lines not getting the support they needed. "Surely something can be done."

He laughed softly and without humor. "Well, if you think of something, miss, you let me know. Truth is, there's just not enough matériel to go around. So, some men gots to go without."

The injustice of that bugged Vi long after the man had moved on to shake someone else's hand. Like everyone else back home, she had saved up kitchen fat for bombs, hauled boxes of rinsed and crushed tin cans to the local collection center, and bought war bonds whenever she had an extra sawbuck—which wasn't often.

With all the reports of record production levels and of millions of dollars being spent by the US government, year after year, to support the war effort, how could it be that there still weren't enough airplanes to go around?

It made her mad enough she wanted to head right back to her bunk and write her congressman a sternly worded letter.

"I have to say that went better than I expected." The gravelly baritone identified the speaker as Sergeant Danger before she even turned around.

"That good, huh?" She cocked one eyebrow, still outraged on behalf of the soldiers and spoiling for a fight. "Does that mean you're in a better mood now?"

Sergeant Danger gave her an odd look. "Was I in a bad one?"

"You were scowling earlier, when we got off the plane. And then again when I told Mr. Miller and Luciana that Sue was looking for them."

"Oh, yeah." His attention strayed to where the other actors were celebrating with a bottle of wine. She got the impression he wanted to change the subject.

Unfortunately for him, she didn't. "I thought being able to perform tonight was a wonderful thing."

His jaw tightened, and his eyes were steely when they met hers. "Sure, if you don't mind your time wasted by being delayed a day."

She stared at him, stung. "You think performing for our troops is a waste of time?"

He released a tired sigh. "Look, it's nothing personal. But being attached to you all isn't what I signed up for. I belong up in the mountains, with my unit, hunting Nazis. Instead I'm here nannying a bunch of civilians until . . . well, until I'm not."

"I see." Anger burned her cheeks. Her fellow players may be a lot of things, but they weren't merely a "bunch of civilians." They were professional thespians, and what they'd brought tonight had been sorely needed by the men. That the sergeant couldn't see that truly offended her.

Needing to look anywhere but at him, she glanced around. "Have you seen Luciana? Now that the crowd has thinned out, I want to make sure she's okay."

"Hey." He touched her arm. "I said it's nothing personal."

"I heard you." She shifted away from him. "And I think I see Miss Rossi over there, with what looks like a medic."

He put his hands in his pockets. "Yeah, that fall she took looked painful."

"And definitely not scripted." She let her worry for the actress push everything else aside. "I hope the USO won't send her home because of it."

"Why would you think that?" His tone was unexpectedly sharp, earning a frown from her.

"Well, her ankle is twisted for sure, and she landed pretty hard on her wrist. It might be broken."

His shoulders relaxed. "If that's all you meant, the doc can fix her up in no time; tell her to rest a couple of days and she'll be fine."

"Maybe if you're you," Vi said, shocked by his attitude. "But Luciana, being both a civilian and a woman, should merit more consideration. Not to mention we artists can be a bit on the sensitive side."

He snorted. "Miss Rossi is tougher than you think. I've seen soldiers sent back into battle recovering from far worse than a sore ankle or wrist. And don't you acting types always insist 'the show must go on'? Which is a sentiment I completely respect, by the way."

"Oh." Vi didn't know what else to say as her ire faded under his unexpected compliment. Luckily Sue picked that moment to start gesturing for Vi to come over. Relief flooded her. "I've got to go. Sue—"

Her voice trailed off as she realized she was standing alone, the sergeant having already walked away without so much as a "bye." Irritated, she watched him disappear into the gathering dark. How could one person be so frustrating? One moment he was all charisma and the next a total jackass. Like his dismissal of Luciana's injuries. "Tougher than you think," indeed . . .

She suddenly remembered what she had overheard earlier. The nerves and excitement of the performance had pushed it from her mind, but now it was back in full force. Added to what he had said tonight, she now wondered if Luciana was somehow the reason the sergeant had been pulled "from the mountains" and attached to their unit. If so, with Luciana injured, he likely would be sent back posthaste, which would make the sergeant happy. And her, too, right?

Pushing aside a queer sense of loss, Vi went to see what Sue wanted.

Chapter 19

Gertie sank onto her cot, her face pale. "What do you mean, Luciana won't be coming with us? Aren't we supposed to stick together, like family?"

Marcie sat next to the girl and hugged her. "Don't worry, Gert. It's only for a few days. The doctor wants to be sure there's nothing worse with her ankle than a bad sprain. Then she'll be cleared to rejoin us in Rome, and everything will be back to normal. You'll see."

"I'm starting to wish I was the one with the bum leg," Frances groused from her cot as she fluffed her pillow. "She gets to be waited on hand and foot, with a room all to herself and a good night's sleep, unlike me if you gals keep flapping your gums."

"Frances is right," Ann said tiredly from her bunk. "Luciana is in good hands, which means we can all stop worrying and call it a night. Reveille is going to seem awfully early tomorrow morning. Or maybe I should say *this* morning, since it's after midnight."

"But what if the injury turns out worse than the doctor thinks and she can't rejoin the show?" Gertie bit her lip as tears filled her eyes. "Will the USO send us home?"

Vi was wondering the same thing but hadn't wanted to ask aloud.

"Would that be so bad?" Marcie said, rubbing Gertie's back reassuringly. Vi eyed her travel buddy curiously. She was both touched and a little astonished by Marce's compassionate behavior tonight. It was a side Vi hadn't seen a lot of on the trip so far. "If we get sent home, you'll never have to perform near the front lines."

"But now I want to," Gertie all but wailed. "All those brave men hoping for a taste of home—we can't let them down."

"We won't," Vi said firmly. "Luciana will only be sidelined for a couple of performances at the most. In the meantime, Mr. Stuart will likely promote one of us to take her place. Actresses are switched mid-production all the time with no problems."

"That's right," Marcie agreed. "Think how we lost Janet, but then Vi arrived, and everything turned out fine. Perhaps even better, since Vi is a much better dancer than ol' Janet ever was."

"Yes, well," Vi said, appreciating the compliment but not the timing. "Let's all hope Luciana's recovery is swift."

"Especially since we don't have anyone to take her place," Ann said glumly.

"Oh, I bet that won't be a problem." Frances rolled over and pinned Vi with a hard look. "I bet someone here has already rehearsed the whole role in her head, just waiting for such an opportunity."

Vi frowned at the girl. "What are you talking about?"

"I saw how you stole the scene tonight with your little impromptu performance."

"I was trying to keep the show moving, since everyone seemed paralyzed by Luciana's fall."

"Victor could have handled it. In fact, he did, once he got over his shock from having to work around you!"

"Actually, I was rather glad Virginia jumped in when she did," Ann said from her cot.

Frances ignored her. "And then there's the whole thing with Janet and how you just conveniently showed up almost the same moment she was canned, without even having to audition."

Vi took a steadying breath to keep from losing her temper. Everyone, including her, was emotionally wrung out from the performance. "I admit it may have looked a bit irregular, but I had nothing to do with Janet getting the boot. All I know is your stage manager talked to mine, and off I went."

At least she thought that's how it had gone. Sal had been rather cagey about who he had talked to.

Marcie stood and shot Frances a nasty look. "Don't pay any attention to her, Vi. Frances wouldn't recognize talent if she fell over it."

"Which, as long as you're around, will never happen," Frances shot back. "Too bad Virginia didn't replace you instead of Janet, since you're the one dragging the show down."

Marcie's hand balled into a fist. "Listen here, you buttana—"

Vi sighed and clapped her hands once, loudly. "Marcie! Frances! That's enough." She glared at both of them. "Now is not the time to be at each other's throats. I understand being competitive, because trust me—I am! And I understand wanting to be the best performer in the show, because ditto—I do, too. But we're also professionals, so dial it down."

"Hear, hear," Ann said from her cot.

"These snide comments and personal attacks," Vi continued, "have got to stop. They're not helping the show."

"And they're upsetting me," Gertie said, her voice trembling. But she had her chin up, and Vi flashed her an encouraging smile.

"Oh, you're one to talk." Frances's cheeks were flushed as she glared at Vi. "You've been just as rude to me as I've ever been to you. And your wop sidekick there has called me a whore multiple times. Don't think I don't know what 'buttana' means. I asked Luciana."

Marcie's dark eyes snapped. "It doesn't mean whore; it means cun—"

"I realize I haven't been as gracious on this tour as I could have," Vi said, cutting Marcie off while conceding Frances's point. "I have regrettably spent too many years fighting for stage time as a solo dancer, which is about as dog-eat-dog a world as one can get. I forgot what it takes to stage a good play. But it's come back to me over the past few weeks, and I apologize for anything hurtful I might have said."

Ann applauded softly. "Nicely said."

Frances snorted. "Words are cheap. And it's not like I heard Miss May say anything conciliatory."

"In your dr—" Marcie started, but Vi stomped on her foot. "Ow." She glanced at Vi, frowned, and then turned back to Frances. "Fine. For the good of the show, I will stop calling you a cunt."

Gertie gasped at the vulgarity. Vi rolled her eyes.

"And . . . ," she prompted her travel buddy when Marcie didn't continue.

Marcie sucked in a breath. "And I'll try not to say anything else rude."

Sue entered at that moment, a notebook in her hand, her face—recently washed free of makeup—lined with fatigue. "What are you gals still doing up? It should've been lights out ages ago."

"Tell me about it," Frances groused before falling back onto her cot, her mood clearly no better for the apologies. Vi wanted to smack her despite calling for a production-wide truce.

Sue glanced around, her brow furrowing as if becoming aware of the tension in the room. "Is there something going on I should know about?"

"Yes." Ann pushed up onto her elbows, and Vi winced, sure she was about to be called out. "Gertrude was wondering what will happen if Luciana can't continue with the tour. And I have to admit, the possibility has got me worried, too."

Vi felt her shoulders droop in relief. *God bless Ann.*

"Well, I wouldn't let it keep you up at night." Sue tossed her notebook onto her cot by the door. Vi suspected now that it was less about keeping the dancers from going out than it was not letting amorous soldiers sneak in. "Mr. Stuart and I were just talking about what to do in case misfortune falls upon anyone else."

"What about having the dancers as understudies?" Frances asked eagerly.

"We talked about it." Sue dug around in her suitcase. "But for now, let's all hope and pray for a speedy recovery for Miss Rossi."

"Yes," Gertie agreed fervently. "Let's all pray for that."

The rest assented with varying degrees of sincerity, but at least a semblance of peace settled over the room. Vi, wanting to escape the others for a while, pulled the covers over her head. She had never liked sharing bedrooms with people, not even with her sister when they had been forced to bunk together so that Vi's aunt and uncle could have Fern's bed. The desire for a separate bedroom had always mystified her parents, since Vi shadowed her older sister the rest of the time, all but forcibly inserting herself into Fern's life. But not at bedtime. That was Vi's time to be herself, free of the competitiveness that usually needled her.

No different now than she had been as a child, she snuggled down farther under the blanket and relaxed, turning over the night's events in her head.

The performance could be counted as a success. She might be reprimanded tomorrow for running onto the stage, but at the moment she was proud of herself. She liked to think she had helped Luciana feel a little better about the situation, since the show hadn't fallen apart due to her mishap.

Another small success of the night was Sergeant Danger's backhanded compliment about the show. Though it hadn't been what one might call a rave review. "Better than I expected," indeed. Ha! With praise like that, maybe he should consider being a theater critic after the war.

On the other hand, given how little he wanted to be here, maybe she should consider it high praise, indeed. But she still wouldn't forgive him for being so callous about Luciana's injury.

She flipped over restlessly. Darn it all, she should be on cloud nine right now. The performance had gone so well. Marcie was safe and sound on the cot next to hers, and Luciana was going to be fine. Tomorrow, barring any unseen disasters, she would get to see Rome, and there was the even more exciting news of more shows to look forward to.

So why couldn't she sleep?

Vi sighed in frustration and plumped the pillow again.

So what if the plane had almost crashed today? It hadn't. And so what if Sergeant Danger had unsettled her with compliments and insults. If she was right about him and Luciana, he'd be gone soon. Maybe it was Gertie's talk of being sent home prematurely, though that should please her, too. She would be able to see Jimmy again, and reclaim her things from the landlady, and start looking for a new job.

She could leave Marcie and all her drama behind, her task completed.

She could become Lily again.

Her heart squeezed at the thought, though not with anticipation but regret, which surprised her. Being here—in Italy with Marcie and Sue and the actors and crew, performing for American fighting men far from home—had fulfilled her in ways she hadn't expected.

Yes, performing in a Broadway-level musical had always been a dream of hers. Yet it was more than that. Traveling with the unit, having to depend on each other through good times and bad, was like having a family again. She hadn't realized how much she missed having someone "have her back," like Marcie had tonight. At the club, other dancers were just as likely to stick a knife in her as boost her up.

And she enjoyed the way men had looked at her backstage tonight: respectful, adoring, almost shy. As if her good opinion mattered. Though she was well aware that the person who had earned that respect had been Virginia, not Violet. She wasn't so much a fool as to think the adoration was real.

How ironic, though, that she had to pretend to be innocent and unsophisticated to earn male respect. In truth, Lily was far stronger and tougher, more capable of handling life. Virginia would be lost on the streets of Chicago, trying to fend for herself. She, herself, had been lost all those years ago.

But the demands of learning how to survive on her own had transformed her into a diamond, sparkling and beautiful. And just as hard. So did she really prefer being Virginia? Or Lily?

Chapter 20

"I'm so happy for you!" Vi said the next morning, hugging Marcie with genuine enthusiasm after Sue announced that Marcie and Gertie had been chosen as understudies for Luciana and Ann, respectively. "That's fantastic."

Marcie drew a shaky breath as she pushed back. "I still hope Luciana will recover quickly, but it makes sense that somebody has to start learning her lines. The show must go on, even if I'm not entirely sure I'm ready to play such a major part."

"Well, if you're not sure," Frances drawled icily from her seat at the breakfast table, "maybe you should tell Sue to give it to someone who is."

Marcie's eyebrows rose. "Are you disagreeing with Mr. Stuart's decision?"

"Not at all," Frances said with a sniff. "I'm merely pointing out that some of us have actual acting experience."

"Gertie was definitely the best choice for Ann's understudy," Vi mused aloud, ignoring the brewing catfight. Later she would remind Marcie to stop reacting to Frances's digs. "And it makes perfect sense to leave the two strongest dancers in the chorus."

"Wait, what?" Frances asked, clearly taken aback by the unexpected compliment.

"Though we're all really good," Vi hastily amended, not wanting Gertie or Marcie to feel insulted.

"No, I agree with you," Gertie said. "You and Frances could dance circles around me and Marce. I can't tell you how much I've learned from working with you two. And Vi is right. If worse comes to worst, the whole cast will benefit from having a knockout chorus like you and Vi to distract the audience from Marcie's and my performance. They might not even notice how awful we were."

"Hey! Speak for yourself," Marcie said with a mock growl.

"You won't be awful." Vi gave Gertie a hug. "Either of you. Sue won't let it happen, and you'll have Charles, Matt, and Victor helping you every step of the way."

Marcie put her spoon down and turned troubled eyes toward Vi, her oatmeal forgotten. "You're not upset that you didn't get the part, are you?"

Vi smiled reassuringly at her. "You've been in the show since the beginning. It's only fair you get first shot at being a star."

Gertie's forehead furrowed. "I still don't know why we can't wait another day. I don't like leaving Luciana behind."

"I'm sure she'll be fine," Frances said, sounding slightly exasperated. "The lucky girl is probably getting breakfast in bed as we speak, with over a dozen fellas at her beck and call."

Gertie's expression lightened. "Do you think so?"

"Not only that," Vi said more seriously. "She's likely safer here than going up in another airplane with the rest of us."

Marcie shivered. "Ugh. Don't remind me. Think Sue will let me walk to Rome?"

"Congratulations on your promotion, Miss May," Ann said, sauntering up with a cup of coffee in her hand and a cool smile on her lips.

Despite the sentiment's kind delivery, the actress's gaze held no warmth.

179

Marcie shot to her feet. "Thank you. Though to be honest, I'd trade it all for Luciana to be hale and hearty again."

Some of the ice melted in the older woman's eyes. "That's kind of you to say so. If you need help with your lines, let me know. I have notes from early rehearsals that might prove useful."

"I would love—" Marcie began, when a commotion at the door of the mess hall cut her off. A harried-looking corporal—Vi was getting better at identifying rank—glanced around impatiently as if seeking someone in particular and then strode over to where the directors sat.

A hush fell over the hall. As one, the whole company strained to listen in without being overly obvious about it. Holding her breath with the rest, Vi watched as Mr. Stuart nodded, asked a question while Wyatt and Sue paid close attention, and then nodded again at the answer. Her nerves jittered as she waited for some kind of sign whether the news was good or bad.

Mr. Stuart stood. "I've just been informed that we will have a transport plane at our disposal at eleven o'clock. Please plan accordingly. Anyone not packed and ready to go by ten thirty will be left to the tender mercies of the MPs. Is that clear?" Mr. Stuart met everyone's eyes one by one. "Excellent. That is all."

After he sat, conversations sprang up around Vi like daisies. If any were meant to include her, she didn't notice. Instead her attention was on Ann, who stood to the side, alone. The hard set to her jaw was meant to warn people off, but the slight tightening around her eyes and mouth spoke of a different emotion. Sadness. Vi felt a deep tug of empathy as she watched the actress. She utilized that same expression herself whenever she felt alone and vulnerable but would have been damned first before admitting it.

Before she could talk herself out of it, Vi picked up her tray and carried it over to where the dishes were being collected. On the way back, she didn't return to the table with the dancers but stopped in front of the blonde actress.

Ann pretended not to see her, but Vi wasn't about to let her off that easy.

She touched the actress's arm to catch her attention. "I wanted to thank you for supporting me last night. With Luciana injured, it seems more important than ever that we pull together to keep the show running smoothly."

Ann looked startled. "Of course. And you're welcome."

"I know it'll be hard for all of us," Vi rushed on. "Especially given some of our experiences in past productions."

Ann stilled. "How so?"

Vi screwed up her courage and went for broke. "Luciana told me about your fiancé and how he fell for a chorus girl. I can only guess how much that stung. And if I could apologize on behalf of all dancers for the awful behavior demonstrated by that one, I would."

"I see." Ann's expression hovered between amusement and annoyance.

"Since it looks like Luciana will be remaining here for a couple of days while we move on," Vi continued, though she was starting to wonder why she was even bothering, "you won't have a travel buddy, and so . . . I was going to say if you ever need someone to go with you somewhere or help you with something, I'd be glad to fill in until Luciana is back on her feet."

Ann considered Vi for a long moment. "That's very kind, but what's the angle?"

"Angle?" It was Vi's turn to be surprised. "There isn't one." Except the small niggling of guilt told her that might not be true. As the older woman continued to study her in suspicious silence, Vi tamped down her annoyance and considered the question honestly. The answer was not a comfortable one.

Having been betrayed by love herself, she had thought it was because she felt empathy for Ann. Now she realized her compulsion was less about easing Ann's loneliness than absolving herself of guilt, for she had also been part of a betrayal: her sister's. Somehow she had hoped that by restoring Ann's faith in humanity she might be forgiven for hurting Fern, no matter how unwittingly she had done it. The fact remained that Vi had slept with her sister's eventual fiancé, and it would forever be a breach of trust between the sisters.

Though how was I supposed to know Fern would change her mind? a part of her traitorous brain protested. *She told me she was tired of him, and I believed her.*

Which was why she no longer believed in the truth of mere words. She had been too badly burned, by Robert and Fern both.

Suddenly wanting to be somewhere . . . anywhere else, Vi backed up a step. "I should start packing. But the offer stands if you should ever need me."

A curious shadow passed behind Ann's eyes. "I will. Thank you."

Chapter 21

To her relief, both of the airplane's engines remained happy and healthy, purring like well-fed lions the entire trip. Even better, the flight was blessedly short, mere minutes in fact. By the time they landed in Rome and Vi had followed everyone out into the beatific sunshine of central Italy, her spirits had fully recovered. The only fly in the ointment was that there was no room at the inn, so to speak.

Their new liaison, one Lieutenant Holland, looked truly apologetic. "Another USO unit was dropped off unexpectedly last night, and since you were delayed, we gave your hotel rooms to them. But not to worry! It's just a little snafu I'll soon remedy. Maybe you'd like to see the theater while you wait?"

"That would be wonderful," Sue said with a strained smile, even as Vi was cheered by the news they would be staying in a hotel versus army barracks. Being around soldiers twenty-four hours a day was fine and all, but she wouldn't mind a bit more privacy.

"I hope we get a chance to rehearse," Marcie whispered as Lieutenant Holland left to make arrangements. "I'm terrified I won't be ready in time for our first performance."

"Marcie, darling," Ann called out from where the actors were standing. "We need you over here."

Vi's eyebrows rose at the request. After last night and this morning, she had hoped the artificial social gap between leads and dancers would become a thing of the past. Apparently not. Still, she found the actors' snobbery annoying and more than a little counterproductive. Shows lived or died on the whims of the audience, sure. But shows could also be self-sabotaged from within by a divided cast.

Quashing her irritation, and with nothing to do but wait while Lieutenant Holland made arrangements for them, Vi looked around the airfield. Even though she knew they were nowhere near the center of Rome, she was disappointed to have not even a glimpse of the ancient wonders, like the Colosseum. Everywhere she looked it was all new construction, military in nature. Rather a bust, in her opinion. Still, the bright Italian sunshine was nice.

She turned her face up, letting the warmth soak into her.

"Have to say it looks a lot different now than when we first liberated it," a familiar male voice said.

Startled, she opened her eyes to see Sergeant Danger. "You've been here before?"

"Yes." Shadows flickered in his eyes as he looked out over the fields.

Her heart squeezed. "I'm sorry."

He glanced at her, startled. "For what? It wasn't you who started this damn war."

"No, but I wish . . . I just wish you didn't have to be here. That none of this was necessary."

He laughed without much humor. "Might as well tell mankind to stop living, then. War is in our genetics."

"I don't believe that."

"Then you've never been on the front lines. You've never seen what men can and will do to each other."

"No, you're right." She bit her lip and looked away, unsure whether she wanted to continue this conversation. It had dimmed the sunshine for her.

"Hey." He touched her arm, and she glanced back. A small, crooked smile quirked his otherwise unfairly perfect lips, and a sudden urge to make him smile more fully tugged at her. His face had been designed to reflect joy, not sorrow. He continued, "Look at the bright side. If it weren't for a bunch of fascists, you—and I—might never have seen Rome."

Vi squashed the fluttering of nerves generated by his touch. "Speak for yourself, because I haven't actually seen Rome yet. Remember?"

He laughed, the rough, whiskey warmth of it curling low and unwanted in her stomach. "That's what I like about you. You don't hesitate to speak your mind."

She chanced a glance up at him and then immediately regretted it. If he was handsome when solemn, he was devastating when amused. "Don't you have somewhere else to be, Sergeant?"

"I'm sorry." His smile faded. "I'm not trying to make you uncomfortable. I guess I'm out of practice talking to decent women. There aren't that many near the front. Make that none, except for terrified locals or the occasional prostitute, and neither of them are much interested in conversation."

"I suppose not," she said, both shocked and appreciative of his candor.

He drew a deep breath. "I'll go away."

"No," she said quickly, surprised at how much she wanted him to stay. "I . . . I like your company. I just don't want to get kicked out of the USO."

"Ah." Understanding gleamed in his eyes. Then the killer half smile reappeared, sending her pulse racing.

Oh, for the love of everything. The man was too attractive by half.

Forget how handsome he is and focus on finding out if he's a threat to Marcie!

"I was surprised last night, when you seemed worried over the show being canceled," she said casually, trying to stay focused on reading his expression and not become distracted by the strikingly pale blue of his eyes. "I thought you couldn't wait to be free of us."

"A soldier follows his orders, miss. What I want or don't want doesn't play into it."

"And what are your orders, exactly?" she asked as nonchalantly as she could. "Lieutenant Holland is here to take care of us in Rome. And Lieutenant Guilford was in Naples handling our arrangements. Why do we have an infantryman attached to us as well?"

He shrugged. "Why not?"

"Because you have somewhere more important to be, like with your men?" She let her eyebrows climb in silent challenge.

He laughed softly. "Throwing my words back at me isn't nice."

"Neither is dodging an honest question."

"You know, some dolls would actually appreciate having extra protection around in the middle of a war."

"I'm not your typical doll," she pointed out.

His gaze took on an appreciative aspect as he glanced at her. "No, you're not, which is why I'm practicing my rusty conversational skills on you."

"Because I'm the kind of girl who won't take things the wrong way?" Her mood slipped as she said the words. "Not like Gertie or the others."

"Which is a compliment, by the way. I wouldn't know what to say to a gal like Gertrude. I'd live every moment in terror that I would do or say something wrong and terrify her. Life is too short for a man to live in such fear."

She laughed; she couldn't help it. "Wait, you, a battle-seasoned infantryman, are terrified of Gertie? You, who dodge bullets and defy death at every turn?"

His cheeks turned a dusky red. "I take back what I said about you being easy to talk to."

"I'm sorry." She tried to put on a serious face, which lasted all of a second before she sputtered into more laughter. With an effort she pulled herself together. "I'm sorry, truly. I think I just needed a good laugh after all the disasters of yesterday. And the stress of the flight today, even though it was—thank the Lord—uneventful!"

"Hmm." He looked unconvinced.

"No, I'm serious," she said, suddenly afraid she had insulted him. "I have nothing but respect for you and all the others over here, fighting the good fight, helping to free the world from the shackles of tyranny."

"You sound like a goddamned recruiting poster."

"Tsk, such language," she scolded, but she couldn't keep her lips from twitching.

A reluctant warmth came back in his eyes. "Sorry, miss."

"You're forgiven," she said as primly as she could. And then both of them began to laugh. "Fine, guilty as charged. My beauty is only for show. Underneath lurks the heart of an unrepentant tomboy."

"And I, for one, am heartily glad. Pretty girls are a dime a dozen. Give me the one who is smart and brave and loyal."

"In other words, a real dog," she teased.

"Stop that," he said, his mood shifting on a dime. "If someone gives you a compliment, don't go shooting it down."

"Is that what you're doing? Complimenting me?"

"Don't you like being considered those things?"

"Sure, if I thought they were true." She tried to flash him a smile but failed.

"Well, I know you're smart. Wyatt told me how you rescued the show last night with your quick thinking." He held up a finger when she opened her mouth to argue. "Wait. I also know you're brave, because you didn't panic on that flight out of Caserta."

She batted his finger away. "I was scared out of my mind, for your information."

"Which would make you also courageous. Congratulations."

She shook her head. "You're wrong. I'm neither brave nor courageous. I just act like I am."

"Which is literally in the definition of both words. Acting as if *not* afraid: bravery. Acting *in spite* of being afraid: courage."

"And cowardice?" she asked a touch bitterly as she looked back on her life. "Any room for that in your ideal girl?"

"Hey." His strong fingers lifted her chin, making her gaze meet his. "You are not a coward. Not from what I've seen."

She pulled back, away from his hand. Away from the temptation to turn her cheek into his palm and believe his mistaken words. "Then you don't know me very well."

"Or maybe you don't see yourself as you really are. It's not as uncommon as you think; I deal with it all the time with men under my command. And I'll tell you what I tell them." He caught her chin again. His earnest blue eyes bored into hers, willing her to pay attention. "You are more than you think you are. You can do more, survive more, and conquer more than you ever thought possible. But the key is up here." He tapped his temple. "You gotta believe it in order for it to happen."

Shaken, Vi pulled away. "Now who sounds like a recruitment poster?" Then she groaned as determined-looking Frances began striding toward them. "Oh no . . . what now?"

"I think I see Lieutenant Holland waving me over," Sergeant Danger muttered.

Vi huffed a laugh in spite of herself. "Coward."

But he was already striding off.

Vi slapped on a serene smile. "Hiya, Frances. Are we ready to move out?" She hoped she sounded less unsettled than she felt. Her skin still tingled from the touch of the sergeant's fingertips.

"What were you two talking about?" Frances snapped. "I saw you two over here being all cozy."

"We were talking about the war."

"Sure you were." The girl's cat eyes glittered maliciously. "But you're wasting your time, you know. It's me he can't keep his eyes off of."

Vi sighed and looked around for Marcie. "If you say so."

"Just because you landed Janet's spot doesn't mean you can come in here, snap your fingers, and get whatever you want."

"Whatever I . . . ?" Vi stopped as sudden understanding hit her. The angry and frightened look in Frances's eyes was one she had seen before. "Look, Fran, I have no interest in trying to upstage you. Or taking away any man you've claimed for yourself," she said quietly. "So put down your dukes. I'm just here to perform for the troops."

Frances narrowed her eyes, as if not sure she believed Vi.

"I'm serious. Truce?" Vi held out her hand. A beat of silence greeted her offer, long enough that Vi suspected the answer was no.

Sure enough, Frances crossed her arms over her chest and gave a dismissive sniff. "You didn't think I was going to fall for the false friend act, did you? Ha! I've met your type before. And I'll be keeping a close eye on you and the sergeant from now on. After all, there's no fraternization allowed between USO personnel and soldiers, as someone was so *kind* to point out to me in Caserta. None. At. All. So if I were you, I'd forget about him."

"I wish I could," Vi said under her breath as Frances flounced back toward Gertie. Unfortunately, the sergeant had an almost-palpable halo of energy, a restlessness that drew her like a moth to a flame.

And what to make of Frances's parting shot, *I've met your type before?* Hopefully it was only spiteful rhetoric and not Lily somehow slipping out between the seams. Though there was the fact that the sergeant was always seeking her out.

Except of all her positive attributes the sergeant had listed today, her appearance hadn't been among them, except in passing. *Pretty girls are a dime a dozen.* Nothing about her having a stunning figure or a mouth that made men dream of sinful things.

So maybe her Virginia act was holding just fine and she was worried for nothing.

Lieutenant Holland hollered for everyone to line up. Grabbing her things, Vi slipped into line behind Gertie. She relaxed as Marcie took the place next to her, the girl's familiar presence helping dispel Vi's nerves. God bless Marcie for never treating Vi as anything other than Virginia.

May the rest of the unit be as unobservant!

And as for Frances's threat? Vi would have to start avoiding the sergeant from now on, despite a curious reluctance to do so.

Which probably made the break all the more important.

Chapter 22

Lieutenant Holland dropped the troupe off a half hour later at a theater deep in the heart of old Rome, with promises that he would have rooms for them soon. As Vi sat in the darkened auditorium watching the actors onstage, she had to admit that the USO had really done all right by them. The acoustics were outstanding. The layout made for a cozy, intimate audience experience that suited their scaled-down production. Nor could she fault the aesthetics. Truly it was a little jewel of a theater.

She was still a tad envious that it wasn't her up on the stage being shown all the blocking for Luciana's part, but her day would come. Better to be part of the chorus than not have a part at all. Frances's words haunted her, though. The girl was right. In any other production Vi would've been gunning for the top role. So why was she oddly content about being passed over this time?

It was damned curious. A question that she had no answer for.

She smoothed her hand over the soft velvet of the upholstered seat, deriving pleasure from the kittenish texture. It occurred to her that the plush fabric, so lovely to touch, might not stand up to rough GI gear. Had anyone thought about that? Or did anyone even care? Rome was an occupied city, after all. Still, she had a soft spot for beautiful fabrics and hoped the chairs would survive.

Onstage, beneath a proscenium that glowed with gold leaf on opulent scrolls, Marcie looked ready to burst into tears as she received yet another line prompt. Vi sighed, wishing Marce would calm down. No one was expecting perfection right out of the gate.

Someone sank into the audience seat next to hers. It was Wyatt.

"It's too bad about Miss Rossi," he said softly, so as not to disturb the action onstage. "Do you think Miss May will be up to the task?"

"Absolutely," Vi whispered back, surprised Wyatt was asking her opinion. But then, maybe it did make sense, since she was Marcie's travel buddy and most likely to know the girl's state of mind. "She's extremely excited, and a little nervous. It's her first major role."

He nodded, indicating he'd heard her, his gaze fastened on the stage. After a moment he continued. "What about you? Do you wish you had gotten the part?"

Something about the dark, and the fact that it was Wyatt and not Sue or Mr. Stuart asking, had her answering honestly. "I think I would've done well, having had starring roles before. But I don't begrudge Marcie having a chance at the spotlight."

Wyatt gave her a curious look in the half light of the auditorium. "What roles have you played?"

Vi wanted to kick herself. Virginia was just a dancer. *Violet* was the one with stage experience. And Violet didn't exist in Italy. "Nothing you would recognize. Our community theater could only afford to produce locally written plays or else really obscure ones."

"Ah." Wyatt settled back in his seat to watch Marcie stumble through her lines. "By the way, I was wondering if you saw Miss Rossi fall last night?"

Vi turned to look at him. She couldn't help it—the question seemed so odd. "Yes. Why?"

He kept his attention on the stage, his expression smooth. "Did it look planned to you?"

"The fall?" She frowned in confusion. "Are you suggesting Luciana may have faked it?"

"No, no." He was silent a moment as he watched the action onstage. "I was just curious what you might have seen, because I checked the stage before the show and didn't see anything amiss. But that doesn't mean a board couldn't have come loose."

"It was toward the very end, after a lot of dance numbers."

"True."

Vi settled back into her seat, but the rehearsal no longer had her full attention. Could Luciana have faked her fall? Vi couldn't imagine why the actress would have. The pain she had seen in Luciana's dark eyes as she had looked out into the wings for help had been real, Vi was sure of it.

And yet, there had been that conversation before the performance. The one where Luciana had accused Wyatt of putting the welfare of the show above ending the war. Had the actress decided to take matters into her own hands?

Surely not.

Gertie tapped her on the shoulder. "Ready to go try the new choreography?"

"Sure." Vi jumped to her feet, then hesitated. "Was there anything else, Mr. Miller?"

Wyatt glanced up at her, his thoughts clearly elsewhere. "No. You answered my question."

Vi followed Gertie to a side room where the dance rehearsal would be held. It felt wrong not to have Marcie there beside her while she stretched out, waiting for Lieutenant Holland to decipher Sue's instructions on the new formations. Of no help at all were Gertie and Frances, who kept crowding him, peering over his shoulder. Vi kept a more respectful distance. She could tell, even if Gertie and Frances could not, that the poor lieutenant was becoming more and more nervous the closer they moved.

"Um . . ." Lieutenant Holland tugged on his tie and collar as if to loosen them. His cheeks were flushed. "It looks like she wants you to change all the diamond patterns to triangles, with each dancer rotating to different points so everyone has a chance to be in front."

"Is this a drawing of it?" Frances reached across his arm to point at something on the page. Vi didn't miss how the girl's move emphasized her cleavage.

"Um . . . maybe?" he squeaked as he edged away from her. The paper shook in his hands.

Vi inwardly rolled her eyes and snatched the notes before he dropped them. "Here, let me see."

A useless half hour followed while Frances shot down all Vi's ideas. Vi, in turn, put her foot down when all Frances's formations kept her in the front. Frances countered by putting Gertie in front half the time while continually relegating Vi to the back.

Sue finally arrived and took over from the hapless Lieutenant Holland. Frances tried to blame Vi for the lack of progress—something that was patently untrue and even had nonconfrontational Gertie on the verge of saying so. To her credit, Sue didn't buy the story, and soon the rehearsal was back on track.

Finally it was dinner break, and Vi sat, exhausted, against the wall of the small room where they had been working. Frances and Gert looked wrung out, too. When Gert asked if she wanted to join them for a quick drink, Vi waved them on.

"I'm going to hunt down Marcie and see how things went. Maybe we'll join you later."

"If we miss you, will we see you for dinner?" Gertie asked. "There's a really good Italian restaurant near Via Santamaura. It's where all the Americans go."

"All the restaurants are Italian here," Frances said sarcastically. "Maybe you should give them a bit more to go on."

Gertie's face fell, and Vi wished she had the energy to kick Frances for it. While she understood the brunette's bad mood, having played a major part in creating it, there was no reason to take it out on innocent bystanders. And Gert was about as innocent as they came.

"Do you mean La Fiorentina, the place Lieutenant Holland mentioned?" Vi asked.

Gertie brightened. "Yes! That was the name."

"I'll ask Marcie. Maybe we'll see you there."

The sour look on Frances's face suggested she hoped not.

Done with the girl's animosity, Vi leaned her head back against the wall and closed her eyes. She heard the two leave, and then blessed silence filled the room. Well, not quite silence. The hushed rumble of men's voices somewhere nearby caught her attention. Unless she was mistaken, one was Wyatt. The other sounded suspiciously like Sergeant Danger, and he didn't sound happy.

Wondering what they were arguing about this time, she quietly got to her feet. The voices were coming from the door opposite the one Frances and Gertie had gone out. This one, given what she knew of the building, connected to the hallway running behind the stage.

She crept closer, praying they didn't open the door and discover her listening.

"This decision came from the top," Sergeant Danger said in a low voice, barely audible through the heavy wood. "So it's no longer up for debate. We need her."

"So do I! We've got a performance in three days," Wyatt said.

Vi's eyes widened at the news. Three days? Holy cow, that didn't leave much time to straighten out the new choreography. Worse, did Marcie know how little time she had to get her lines learned? Or was she off the hook, since Wyatt and the sergeant seemed to be arguing over Luciana's return?

"Not my problem," Sergeant Danger replied coldly. "You have alternatives; we don't. Not with the time constraints we're under."

"Which is not *my* problem. We're under orders as much as you are, and the USO says we perform as a unit. You don't like it? Take it up with the army. The OSS can go hang themselves. I'll see her kicked out before I let her endanger herself."

"Damn it, Miller. We're talking about the possibility of the war being extended for months, if not years. Are you truly willing to have all those deaths, all those lives of good and decent men that could've been saved but were needlessly lost, on your conscience?"

Her breath caught as she waited for Wyatt's answer. Surely Sergeant Danger was exaggerating . . .

"My responsibility is for the health and welfare of this troupe," Wyatt said flatly. "Those are my orders, and I will follow them, period. If you don't like it, talk to Sue or Gerry."

"You know I can't. They don't have the proper clearance."

"Then I guess you'll just have to recruit someone else."

"You would extend the war on account of a show?" The sergeant sounded incredulous.

"She signed a contract like everyone else."

There was a moment of silence, the tension between the men so thick, the chill of it crackled through the door.

Boots squealed on the tiled floor as the sergeant, with a frustrated sound, turned away. Vi shrank back, frantically hunting for a place to hide. She didn't want to be discovered eavesdropping. Then a door slammed farther down the hall, which meant the sergeant, at least, wasn't coming this way.

Afraid to breathe, she waited in terror for Wyatt to come through her door. She heard him curse and then listened with growing relief as the softer taps of his loafers headed away from her. The door down the hall slammed shut for a second time, and she exhaled.

She had to be wrong about what she'd heard. Wyatt and the sergeant couldn't have been arguing over Luciana's involvement in a secret mission that might affect the length of the war.

Yet the conversation had eerily echoed the one she had overheard in Nettuno between Luciana, Wyatt, and the sergeant. Luciana had said something about the fate of the world versus a silly show. And then, not eight hours after Wyatt had put his foot down and said her "friends could go to hell," she had fallen and twisted her ankle, effectively taking her out of the show anyway.

So why the argument, unless Wyatt was right about the fall being faked, and he now was threatening to make a stink about it?

Then I guess you'll just have to recruit someone else . . .

Vi chewed on her lower lip. Did Wyatt have the power to force Luciana to come back? The answer was likely yes, which would leave the sergeant in the lurch. Surely Wyatt hadn't meant substituting someone else from the show, since he'd also been so adamant about the show's importance. But if Luciana resumed her lead role, and since the choreography had already been switched to accommodate a missing dancer . . .

You have alternatives; we don't. Not with the time constraints we're under . . .

Oh heavens! If the sergeant needed an actress on short notice who was adventurous and also spoke Italian, he absolutely had an alternative: Marcie.

Horror stole her breath. The sergeant wouldn't let the actress go without a fight. His belief in his mission was too strong and his loyalty to his men too deep. He would do anything to shorten the war, including agreeing to swap for a different girl if Wyatt offered and the sergeant thought it would work. And Marcie? Her friend would likely jump at the chance if the sergeant asked. She was just impulsive and fearless and patriotic enough to think of it as a grand adventure.

With a shaky hand, Vi reached down to grab her bag and then headed for the front door. She had to stop this, but how? Because she would be damned before she let her friend rush headlong into danger, even if it was the girl's choice. Sal had put her in charge of keeping Marcie safe. And while Sal and Papa Maggio may have been thinking only "safe from losing her virginity," Vi meant to keep her safe from impulsively risking her life, too.

Which meant there was only one path left. She had to talk to Sergeant Danger and somehow convince him that no matter what Wyatt might say, Marcie's life was also too important to risk.

More important than the lives of Allied soldiers?

The question made her sick.

Because the answer had to be no, which meant perhaps never going home to Chicago, never seeing Jimmy again, and, worse, perhaps taking on the crushing guilt of her travel buddy's death, someone she had been charged to protect and had grown to genuinely like.

Lord, what a mess. No longer sure what she wanted to say to the sergeant, she reversed directions and headed toward the stage, where Marcie was likely waiting for her. If there was any justice in the world, inspiration would find her quickly, before disaster struck. Otherwise she and Marcie were both doomed.

Chapter 23

La Fiorentina was crowded by the time Vi and Marcie got there. Soldiers and locals crowded the front waiting area, angling for a place to sit, while waiters carrying bread and wine pushed between them. Vi stood on tiptoe and scanned the restaurant for Gertie and Frances. Her stomach growled at the mouthwatering smells of ripe tomatoes and garlic and lemon. It had been a long day, and she was hungry despite the worries plaguing her.

"Well, shoot. It looks like we missed them," Marcie said about the time Vi had reached the same conclusion. Disappointment pulled her friend's full lips into a pout even though Vi was elated. After the conversation Vi had overheard between Wyatt and the sergeant, she needed a quiet moment to think without the added task of trying to keep Frances and Marcie from throttling each other. "And here I had wanted to ask them about the new dance configurations."

Vi snorted at the bald-faced lie. What Marcie really wanted to do was impress the girls with all the new gossip she had picked up. Not that Vi held that against her friend. Even the kindest of theater people weren't above showboating when it was deserved. And being promoted from chorus to the rarefied circle of leads was definitely worth boasting about.

"Since they're not here, let's go somewhere else." Vi took her friend's arm. "Somewhere with an actual place to sit."

"Wait." Marcie shook Vi's hand off. "I think I see two empty places at that table over there, with those soldiers."

"Marce, you know how I feel about eating with strangers," Vi said, a headache forming at the mere thought. "Especially when I'm tired."

"You also need to eat, and the food here smells too delicious to pass up." Marcie took Vi's hand and raised it to her chest. Her dark gaze was soulful. "Please, for me? I'm only thinking about your health and well-being."

Vi inwardly winced as she recalled Wyatt's similar declaration.

My responsibility is for the health and welfare of this troupe . . .

If only she could believe him. Trust that he would protect Marcie with the same ferocity as he did Luciana. Because if the powers at the top, perhaps even the mysterious OSS, decided that the sergeant's mission trumped USO contracts, Marcie would be in danger. Because Vi knew without a shadow of a doubt that the lure of saving lives and possibly shortening the war would be irresistible to her spirited, impulsive friend. Why stop at taking on a starring role in a mere USO musical when she could swap it for an even more exciting one?

Vi shook off the troubling thought. "We can come back—"

The maître d' appeared beside them. "*Signorine*, may I help you?"

"Yes!" Marcie said quickly, before Vi could refuse.

Then, to both the man's and Vi's surprise, Marcie launched a volley of questions in rapid Italian. His dark eyebrows rose toward his slicked-back hair as she chattered on, pointing this way and that. He responded with a question of his own, and soon they were deep in conversation. Vi couldn't follow any of it, the few words that Marcie had taught her having been exchanged at the beginning.

The maître d's surprise soon turned to pleasure, and the next thing Vi knew, she and Marcie were being escorted to an empty table in the corner that had a "reserved" card on it.

"Best table in the house," Marcie said smugly as the maître d' pocketed the card and then pulled a chair out for her. He did the same for Vi and then said something to Marcie, smiling, in Italian.

"*Grazie,*" Marcie said with a smile of her own. Vi stared at her friend after the man disappeared again.

"That was impressive, Marce." *And a little alarming, given the situation,* Vi thought. If the sergeant knew how fluent her friend was, he might trade Luciana for her without a second thought. With an effort, she shook the fear off. "What did you say?"

"Well, he was surprised that we were women in uniform and that we—that is, I—spoke Italian. I told him I grew up speaking with my grandmother in New York, and he said he had only the tiniest difficulty in understanding me." Marcie's grin widened. "Not bad for a girl from the Bronx."

Vi frowned. "I thought you said you were from Lower Manhattan?"

Marcie waved her hand. "Details, details."

"Says she who styles herself a spy," Vi said with a light laugh even though she wanted to shake the girl. *Please, God, don't let Sergeant Danger draw her into any kind of plot . . .* "Seems to me if you're going to have a cover story, you should at least know where you're from."

Marcie shrugged. "I suppose. But you already know who I am. And besides . . ." She struck a pose. "I'm a citizen of the world. I'm from everywhere and nowhere." Then she grinned and leaned forward. "That's one of my lines from the play. How'd I do?"

"Just fine," Vi said absently, her brain more concerned with how best to keep her friend out of the sergeant's clutches. Unless she was wrong about the whole situation, in which case she might be better off leaving well enough alone. But if she wasn't . . .

You have alternatives; we don't. Not with the time constraints we're under . . .

That was the key, Vi realized as a waiter set down two glasses on the table and began to fill them with red wine. That was how she could keep Marce out of this mess. She could stall for time by keeping the sergeant away from Marcie. Then she and Marcie would both be home free. Her spirits rose. Hallelujah!

Marcie's dark eyes sparkled as the waiter left. "You'll never guess what Sue said this afternoon! She told me that she was very impressed with my work ethic, and with yours, and if Gerry—that is, Mr. Stuart—decides to open on Broadway when we get back, she's going to push for us to be cast above everyone else."

Vi's heart skipped a beat, the sergeant forgotten. "You're kidding me."

To open on Broadway had always been one of her dearest dreams.

"Nope. As long as we don't ruin her good opinion of us, we could be starring on the Great White Way together." Marcie practically danced in her seat with excitement. "Can you imagine? Then, boy, oh boy, won't my pop feel foolish, after telling me I'd fall flat on my face if I tried to work onstage."

The mention of falling onstage reminded Vi. "Hey, Marce—speaking of directors—Wyatt asked me the strangest question today. He wanted to know if I thought Luciana faked her fall."

Marcie paused, her wine halfway to her mouth. "Would that even be possible? I mean, wouldn't the doc have noticed if she wasn't really hurt?"

"I would think so."

Marcie set her wine down untasted, her excitement gone. "He just wants Luciana back."

"Well, you did say they have a thing for each other."

"Had, as in past tense." She twirled her glass on the table, despondent. "If he wants her back now, it must mean I stink in her part."

"I doubt that's the reason," Vi said firmly. "I saw you up onstage today, and while it was a little rough, I thought you were making huge strides."

"Thanks." Marcie was quiet a moment, her gaze on the table. Then she abruptly scooted her chair back, her eyes suspiciously bright. "If you'll excuse me, I gotta find the ladies' room."

"Marce." Vi reached out to stop her, but Marcie was too fast. *Now you've done it,* she thought. Marcie was under enough pressure without adding the specter of Wyatt's disapproval.

"*Scusi,* Signorina?"

Vi looked up. A gaunt woman in her late twenties with coppery-red hair and brown eyes was studying her, her sharp gaze both haunted and hopeful.

"You are with the USO?" the woman asked in accented English.

"I am," Vi said, her curiosity piqued.

"You play the role of Lydia in *One Fine Mess?*"

Vi's eyebrows rose in surprise. "You've heard of us?"

The woman waved her hand impatiently. "Are you Lydia?"

"No." Vi stared at the woman, perplexed. "My friend has that role."

The woman dug a folded paper from the pocket of her worn wool dress. "This is for her. Only her."

"All right." As Vi took the note, unease prickled up her spine. It was too soon for fan mail. They hadn't even performed in Rome yet. "Wait—where did you hear—"

The woman was already turning away, her movements quick. Vi frowned as the woman cut through the crowd waiting for seats and then disappeared. Telling herself she was only watching out for Marcie's safety, Vi opened the note.

To her dismay, it was written in Italian.

"What's that?" Marcie said, rejoining Vi at the table.

Vi examined her friend's face. Except for a telltale redness around Marcie's dark eyes and a few deeper lines around her mouth, the girl looked as confident as ever. But then, her friend was also an actress and in possession of more talent than Vi had originally given her credit for. "A note." She handed it across the table. "Can you read it?"

"Who's it from?" Marcie asked, taking it.

Vi didn't answer as her friend scanned the contents and then frowned. Her hope was that she could get a translation without mentioning the odd circumstances that accompanied the note's delivery. Perhaps it wasn't entirely ethical, but under the circumstances, Marcie's safety took precedence.

"How odd." Marcie turned the paper over to look at the blank side, her brow furrowed. "It's a notice of a watch being ready for pickup, but it doesn't say whose."

Vi relaxed as the mystery around the note faded. "If it's not yours, I'm betting it's Luciana's. The courier said it was for the actress that plays Lydia in our play, but she didn't specify which actress."

Still frowning, Marcie refolded the note. "You're forgetting Luciana is still in Nettuno."

It was a good point. Vi's spine prickled again.

"Maybe she called ahead? Gertie said she overheard Luciana in Caserta talking to someone in Italian and that she said the word 'Rome' several times. Maybe she was making arrangements to pick it up."

"Seems pretty farfetched to me."

Vi plucked the note out of Marcie's hand. "Maybe, but it's the simplest explanation and therefore likely the correct one." She tucked the note into her uniform pocket. "I'll give it to Sue in the morning, and she can take it from there."

"You know what we could do?" Marcie asked with some of her former excitement lighting her eyes again. "We could stop by the store ourselves. The address is in the note. If Luciana does have something to pick up, we could do it for her. That way she would be sure to get it, even if she joins us later in the tour."

Vi hesitated, something about the situation not sitting quite right with her. She couldn't put her finger on it, though. Maybe it was how fast the woman had left, how unusual the delivery. How had the woman even known they would be at the restaurant tonight?

Yet there was nothing in the note itself that seemed threatening. Likely it was, indeed, an order to pick up.

"All right," she said as the waiter appeared with their food. "Next time we get a morning or afternoon off, we'll go pick up Luciana's watch."

Chapter 24

Vi had no sooner collapsed onto the plush auditorium seats, along with the rest of the cast, who were ready for their well-earned rehearsal break, than a thump came from the back of the house.

"Mail call," a bespectacled soldier shouted before ducking back out the door to the lobby.

I wonder if we got the right bag this time, Vi thought as one of the Italian stagehands ran up the aisle to retrieve the large canvas duffel bag. Yesterday they had gotten one addressed to an entirely different USO unit—there were several in Rome at the moment—and it had taken Wyatt several phone calls to get the snafu fixed.

The stagehand ran back down the aisle and handed the satchel to Sue, who, like everyone else, was lounging on break.

Sue checked the tag on the rope tie. "Unit 2918. That's us, at least. Do I dare open it now or wait until after rehearsal, in case there's any bad news in it?"

Mr. Stuart, who must have been napping, jerked in his seat and then straightened. "Open what?"

"I vote now," Victor said, coming to the rescue as he often did. It was a talent Vi had come to admire and wanted for herself. "If it's not our mail, better to find it out sooner than later. If it is, then better to get the good news right away. And if it's bad news, that's all right, too. We'll have time to process it before tonight's first call."

"Victor has a point," Ann said.

Mr. Stuart nodded absently, as if he had been following the discussion. Vi suspected he hadn't. To be honest, Sue and Wyatt had the show so well in hand, he probably could have stayed behind and spared himself the rigors of an overseas tour. But perhaps he wanted to see firsthand how audiences responded to the play so he would know what changes to make before opening on Broadway.

Sue began calling names and handing out envelopes. "Gertrude Johnson. Ann Thiessen. Frances Smith—well now, it looks like you have two, lucky girl!"

"You know, ladies don't always have to go first," Matt complained, and Vi rolled her eyes. People who assumed all divas were female had obviously never met Matt.

Sue shot him a quelling look. "I'm reading them in the order they were bundled. Here's another one for Ann. And one for Charles Cooper."

"I bet Sue will make Matt wait until the very end now, just on principle," Marcie whispered. Vi smirked in spite of her exhaustion.

"And one for me," Sue continued. Matt dropped his head into his hands and slumped.

Charlie punched him good-naturedly in the shoulder. "Sorry, ol' chap. Guess nobody loves you."

"Marcie, here's one for you," Sue said, holding out an envelope.

"Me?" Marcie stared at the letter as if it were a snake.

"Well, go on. Take it," Sue said, sounding amused. "It won't bite."

"It might," Marcie said under her breath, but stepped forward to take it.

"And Virginia Heart." Sue turned toward Vi and held out what looked like a telegram.

Vi's heart skipped a beat as she stood and stretched out her hand. It had to be from Sal. He was the only one who knew where she was.

Please let Jimmy be okay . . . Nervous anticipation almost made her drop the flimsy paper.

"And that's it," she heard Sue say as if from a long way off. "Except for this letter for Matthew . . . Dark? Surely that doesn't say Clark."

Vaguely, Vi heard the others teasing Matt. Not bothering to look up, she slit the end and pulled out the message. With her heart in her throat, she scanned the brief message, then reread the last part, unable to believe what she was seeing.

> Dear Virginia My friend says you are well Everyone is
> fine here too Keep up the good work PS Your father
> wants to know your address Please advise Uncle Sal

The edges of her vision turned gray as she refolded the paper. How had her father found Sal? Had he learned about her old career? Or Jimmy? Surely Sal wouldn't give away her secrets without asking her first.

An arm settled around her shoulders, supporting her. "Are you okay? Is everything all right at home?"

Vi took a deep breath and blinked. The worried frown on Marcie's face reminded Vi where—and who—she was. "Fine." A patent lie, but she couldn't quite find the words to explain how her carefully separated worlds were about to collide and how terrifying the prospect was. "How was your letter?"

Marcie gave a rueful laugh. "Well, it looks like my family knows where I am and apparently has the whole time, which is rather demoralizing. No more feeling proud of myself for pulling a fast one on my pop."

Vi turned to face her friend and noticed she was unusually pale. Her heart went out to Marcie. With her own parental reckoning looming on the horizon, she was particularly sensitive to how vulnerable the girl might feel. "Was he angry?"

"Very." Then Marcie laughed again, with more of an edge this time. "But not as angry as my mother, who made sure to tell me I have made a terrible, terrible choice, because Frankie doesn't want to marry me anymore and so I've utterly failed as a daughter."

"Frankie being the man your parents loved but you didn't."

"Bingo." Marcie sighed. "I mean, it's true I didn't want to marry him, but I also didn't want him to outright reject me. It kinda stings, you know?"

"Almost makes you wish he'd reject you for being too short or not blonde enough instead of because you actually wanted to be someone."

"Exactly." Marcie sharpened her gaze. "You're trying to distract me from what was in your letter, aren't you?"

"No." Vi glanced over at the others, closing off any more confidences. Her emotions were still too rattled by the news of her father being in contact with Sal.

How had he tracked her down? She had always been careful about the return addresses she had used over the years, to prevent just such a disaster. And why now, after so many years, and when she was touring another continent? Had something happened to Mom, or Fern? A slew of awful scenarios threatened, paralyzing her with terror. Life was so fragile.

Sue clapped her hands, drawing Vi's attention. "Okay, boys and girls. You all are free to go; just be back two hours before curtain time. Don't be late. And, Marcie—good job this afternoon. Your characterization of Lydia is improving."

"Good job, travel buddy." Vi gave her friend a playful punch in the shoulder. "Guess all your hard work is paying off."

"If you call panicking work." Marcie stood and pulled Vi to her feet. "I don't know how I'll survive these next few hours. Everyone else has already had their opening night and are cool as cucumbers, whereas I'm a nervous wreck."

"You'll do fine. Meanwhile, how about we take your mind off tonight by putting Operation Watch into action? We can look for post-cards, too, since I'm thinking we both owe one to our families."

Marcie made an exasperated sound as she threaded her arm through Vi's. "Fine, I'll write my parents. But *after* we get Luciana's watch."

Vi and Marcie changed into their USO uniforms as fast as they could, eager to escape the theater lest Sue change her mind about the break. Outside, surrounded by the ancient city, the sun bright on her face, Vi's mood lifted. Yes, she might be facing a disaster back home, but right now she was here, in Rome, with a performance to look forward to. Immersing herself in the joy of the moment, she let Marcie puzzle out the map the hotel clerk had drawn them. The clock shop was apparently near the Janiculum, the second tallest hill in Rome. The clerk had approved of the area, saying there were several shops over there, on the west side of the Tiber, not yet picked over by soldiers.

Forty minutes later, after a few wrong turns and some backtracking, Vi and Marcie finally found the correct bridge, Ponte Palatino, and crossed over the Tiber. After stopping briefly on the far side to admire the ruins of the ancient stone bridge that had once run parallel to it, they hunted for the shop referenced on the note. Even though the ornate script painted on the window was in Italian, the purpose of the shop was clear from the goods displayed in the window.

Marcie hesitated. "Are you sure we should go in?"

Vi had to admit, she was feeling a little apprehensive herself. "Well, the woman did say to give you the note, which said to come get the watch. So no one can fault you for doing what it said. But I'd check the name on the claim ticket to be sure it really is Luciana's."

Marcie slid her an offended look. "As if I wouldn't."

Together, they entered the store. A bell tinkled over the door as it closed behind them.

As Marcie headed toward the service counter at the back, the note in hand, Vi paused in astonishment. Dozens of ornately carved cuckoo clocks ticked on the walls, while smaller mantel clocks—some disguised as statues or lamps or pieces of art—tocked from the counters. Even the corners were crammed with more grandfather clocks than Vi had seen in her life, their silvered and gilded faces staring solemnly back at her.

It was as if someone had gathered all the timepieces in Italy and confined them to this one small space. Almost as if the proprietor had hoped to contain time itself. Or perhaps stop it. All those precious seconds. Had he or she hoped to protect them from sorrow and regret, only releasing them once the war was over and it was safe to let those minutes and hours unspool again?

Then an even more compelling sight caught Vi's attention. A boy, perhaps four or five, his blond hair tousled and sticking up at odd angles, sat on the floor near the door leading to the back room. With the focus of a surgeon, he dug his small fingers through the contents of a box that appeared to be filled with buttons. Whenever he found what he wanted, he would smile slightly and hold it up to the faint light coming through the front window. Utterly consumed with the process, he ignored Vi and Marcie as he carefully placed each treasure on the floor into the design he was creating.

Caught in the spell of the shop, and of the little boy—Jimmy was about his age—Vi jumped when a woman spoke from behind her.

"Buongiorno."

Vi turned to see an attractive young woman—one with dark-brown hair, not red—standing beside the display counter.

Her inquisitive blue eyes darted between Vi and Marcie. *"Come posso aiutarti?"*

Waving the note, Marcie answered her in Italian while Vi studied the woman's expression. If the woman was surprised to see them instead of Luciana, there was no sign in her serene face. As far as Vi could tell, the woman's polite interest in the note was genuine, as if women in uniform showed up in her shop looking for watches every day. Given the army's preoccupation with everything being timed almost down to the second, perhaps they did. A working watch wasn't just a luxury to a soldier but a necessity.

Marcie turned to Vi, her forehead puckered in a slight frown. "She says there's no watch waiting for pickup and knows nothing about the note you got. So what do we do now?"

"Ask her to check in back for something other than a watch? Maybe somebody else took the order and sent the note."

Marcie hesitated and then turned back to the woman. While Marcie interrogated the clerk in Italian, something Vi couldn't help with, she drifted around the shop as if looking at the merchandise. What really interested her, though, was the little boy in the corner. Something about him, and the way he bit his lip as he concentrated, tugged at her heart.

"Marcie," Vi asked, interrupting the women, "how do I ask 'what's your name' in Italian?"

"Come ti chiami," Marcie replied breezily, and then went back to the clocks.

Vi crouched near the little boy, close enough to see what he was working on but not so close as to alarm him. *"Come ti chiami?"*

Long-lashed hazel eyes lifted to meet hers. He hesitated, the solemnity in his little face heart wrenching. "Enzo."

His gaze dropped back to the box, and she watched him in silence as he selected a bone button set in a metal filigree—Vi couldn't even imagine what kind of garment might have once borne something so elegant—and placed it into his design.

Vi glanced down at it and then did a double take. Whereas she might have expected an abstract picture or perhaps something benign like a dog or a car, Enzo was creating what was clearly a tank. Worse, he was putting red and white buttons under its treads. Vi hoped it wasn't meant to represent crushed people, but after the destruction she had witnessed in the countryside, she suspected otherwise.

What did one say to a child creating such a monstrous image? Certainly not "wonderful" or "that's so pretty."

Enzo pointed to the red-and-white button layer and said something in Italian. His childish voice held no emotional inflection, giving her no clue how to react. Still, she needed to acknowledge whatever he had said, so she nodded but kept her expression as solemn as his.

What had this boy seen; what had he lived through? Overcome with sorrow, she wished she could take him in her arms and hold him, if only for a moment. Life could be so unfair sometimes.

Tears unexpectedly filled her eyes, and she dashed them away. When she glanced up, Enzo was watching her.

"Perché sei triste?" he asked in his clear soprano voice.

Triste . . . That meant sad, so she guessed he was asking her why she was crying.

She gave him a small, watery smile. "I doubt you will understand me," she said softly so Marcie wouldn't overhear, "but I have a small boy of my own. *Un ragazzo,*" she added, remembering the word in Italian. "And I miss him."

He watched her silently for a moment more, then put down the button in his hand and crawled over to hug her. Stunned, she froze, hardly able to breathe. The heavenly smell of warm little boy filled her senses. She closed her eyes under the rush of emotions. For one sweet instant she imagined it was Jimmy's silky, soft cheek pressed against hers, his thin arms thrown around her neck. Jimmy. He was in her arms at last. Her love, her son.

"Enzo, *mimmo,*" the clerk called, her tone managing to be both stern and tender.

Enzo looked up, then posed a question that made the woman gasp. Startled by the woman's reaction, Vi glanced up. The clerk had gone pale, and her hand had risen to her throat as if wishing she could somehow silence or call back what her son had said.

"What did he say, Marcie?" Vi asked in a neutral voice, so as not to distress Enzo, who was still in her arms. If she had heard him correctly, he had plainly asked something about the *Stati Uniti d'America.* One didn't have to know Italian to guess he was talking about the good ol' USA.

Marcie gave Vi an odd look. "He asked his mother if you were the one who was taking them to the US."

Thrown by the question but not wanting to alarm the boy, Vi looked down into his now-troubled face and smiled. "No, Enzo. *Spiacente.*"

He nodded gravely, accepting her apology, and then scooted back to his button box.

Vi's thoughts raced as she stood. Something was off. Something about this whole situation, in fact. A mistake could've been made about the watch, or maybe the wrong address had been given in the note, and people were fleeing Europe all the time, with the war going on and all. Enzo might have confused her with a Red Cross worker, who were often in uniform. But none of that accounted for the woman's extreme alarm at a seemingly innocent question.

"We should probably get back," Vi said casually, as if nothing odd had occurred. "You've got a big night ahead of you, after all."

"True." Marcie smiled at the still-pale woman. *"Grazie, signora. Arrivederci."*

The woman managed a smile of her own and wished them both good evening as she unsubtly shepherded them to the door. Bells tinkled inside the shop as the door was shut firmly behind them. A scraping sound of a sign being turned on the other side of the glass window told Vi the woman had now closed the shop as well.

Marcie drew a deep breath. "Well, that was peculiar."

"No kidding." Vi hooked her arm through Marcie's. "But no time to worry about it now. We're going to be late if we don't get a move on."

"Why did Enzo's mother seem so upset by his question?" Marcie asked, resisting Vi's efforts to propel her toward the bridge. "And what happened to the watch?"

"Maybe wires got crossed and the note was supposed to go to a different actress, who already picked it up."

Marcie didn't respond. Instead, she bit her bottom lip and looked back at the shop.

Vi shook her head, knowing all too well the direction of her friend's thoughts. "No, Marce. We are not going to investigate. Not only is it none of our concern but you are going to ruin your Broadway future if you don't get back in time. Sue doesn't strike me as the type to forgive late entrances."

"But aren't you curious what's going on?"

"Nope." Vi pulled harder on Marcie's arm. Curious was the exact opposite of what she felt at the moment. If the deep itch at the base of her spine was right—and it usually was—she and Marce had stumbled into something potentially dangerous, which meant all she cared about now was getting Marce out of there.

"I suppose you could be right," Marcie said, finally letting herself be pulled forward. "If the army can misdeliver mail bags, I guess couriers could mix up notes."

"Just so," Vi said, unable to keep the relief out of her voice. "Now let's get you back—"

A familiar face at the end of the block stopped her cold. In disbelief she watched Luciana's eyes widen, and for the briefest of seconds their gazes locked.

"What's wrong?" Marcie asked.

"I—" Vi stopped as Luciana darted into a store and disappeared from view. She blinked in surprise and shock. "I thought . . ."

Then the implications of what she had seen snagged the rest of her words from her tongue. What would it do to Marcie if she told her that Luciana was back in town? An uninjured Luciana, at that, if the speed with which the actress had fled was any indicator, and within a few hours of Marcie's big debut.

It would knock her for a loop is what it would do.

More alarm bells went off with the realization that Wyatt had been right; Luciana had likely faked her injury in Nettuno. Or at least exaggerated it. Nor had the actress wanted to be seen today. And what were the chances that Vi would see her, of all places, close to the clock shop?

Did that mean Luciana had overridden Wyatt's objections and that Sergeant Danger no longer needed a replacement? A cautious hope flickered in her chest. Perhaps everything would be all right, after all. The possibility left her almost giddy.

"Well?" Marcie asked impatiently.

Get it together, Vi. Marcie's waiting for an answer.

"I—I thought I had dropped my wallet at the shop, but"—she gave a little laugh and pulled her wallet from her skirt pocket—"here it is! So, we can keep going."

Marcie rolled her eyes. "Is that all? I was hoping for something more exciting. I mean your eyes were so wide, I thought you had seen a ghost."

Vi drew a breath and smiled. "Nope. No ghost."

Just a living, breathing person who was someplace she shouldn't be. But that was Wyatt's problem, not Vi's.

Chapter 25

That night, as Ann uttered the final words of the performance, Vi barely heard the audience's cheers. Despite her relief over Luciana's reappearance this afternoon, she was still uneasy. She couldn't get the scene from the clock shop out of her head. She just couldn't shake the feeling that little Enzo and his mother might be involved in something dangerous. Nor could she shake the feeling that she and Marcie may have inadvertently made the danger worse by following up on the note.

If only she could corner Luciana or even Sergeant Danger, she could alleviate her fears. But neither had stopped by the theater before the performance. Now she could only hope one of them would swing by after, like Sergeant Danger had in Nettuno.

Sue cued the curtain and blackout. Vi reluctantly joined the cast as they reassembled in the dim backstage light for curtain call. From the corner of her eye, Vi saw Wyatt head toward the other side of the stage. What would he do if he knew Luciana was in Rome?

Sue beckoned the actors closer in preparation for the final bows. "Lights up . . . Dancers go."

Frances, Gertie, and Vi ran out onto the stage, and a cheer went up. For a brief moment Vi shoved aside her worries and let them float away like the dust motes swirling in the spotlights. This was her favorite part of any performance. It always had been. The clapping and cheers, along with the occasional whoop, fueled her like nothing else. Almost more than food or sleep.

Sharing an ecstatic look with Gertie, Vi backed up in step with the others. Then Marcie, Victor, and Charles ran out, and a fellow shouted from one of the boxes, "Lydia, marry me!"

Marcie blushed as laughter rippled across the house, along with more shouts of "No, marry me!"

Then Ann and Matt joined them. With great dignity, the entire cast acknowledged the thunderous applause from these rough men who had been to hell and back. Vi could hardly see for the tears in her eyes. Then she strode offstage with everyone else, her legs shaking with emotion.

"I don't think I've ever been so high," Ann announced, her eyes sparkling as everyone shared hugs backstage. "I may just spend the rest of my life doing USO tours. Did you hear them swoon when Matt kissed me at the end?"

"If you mean the shouts of 'Pass it around, sugar,' yes I did," Victor said wryly as Ann threw her arms around him and squeezed.

"You're just jealous because they didn't boo you this time," she teased.

"More important, they didn't shoot me!" Victor said, before turning to Marcie. "And you, my dear, made a marvelous dastardly diva, the marriage proposal notwithstanding."

Marcie hugged the older actor with abandon. "Thank you! I didn't even need your help to remember my lines."

"Of course not." He pressed a fond kiss on the top of her head. "You're getting better all the time."

"Here they come," Matt called out excitedly. "Incoming!"

Sure enough, soldiers were already streaming past the MPs. Pasting on a bright smile, Vi braced herself for another hour of performing, this time for much higher stakes.

"Have to say the show gets better every time I see it." Sergeant Danger's low voice in her ear made her jump.

"Hey, buddy," the sandy-haired soldier that she had been about to greet protested angrily. "Wait your turn like the rest of us."

"It's not like that," Vi said to the soldier as she seized Sergeant Danger's arm to keep him from leaving. She was afraid he might vanish again as quickly as he appeared. "The sergeant here has been helping me reach my family back home—it's an emergency situation—so I asked him to interrupt me when he had some news."

She hated lying to the fellow, but she had given her word she would put Marcie's interests first.

"You heard the lady." Sergeant Danger shot the soldier a hard look, an aura of command almost visibly radiating off him. "Move along."

The soldier held up his hands in mock surrender. "Fine. I'll go find another doll to talk to."

Sergeant Danger glanced down at her after the other man left. "So . . . what's the family emergency?"

Vi released him. "I needed to talk to you, but in private."

His eyebrows rose. "You made me pull rank for that? All you had to do was ask."

"Except that you have a way of appearing and disappearing on a girl," she said, a little exasperated. "And this is important."

He crossed his arms and settled into a wide-legged stance. "All right. Shoot."

"Well . . ." Vi glanced around and then leaned toward him. "I saw Luciana today, in the crowd near the Tiber river."

"Really?" His expression didn't even flicker. "And you're telling me this why?"

"Because you're the only one who seems to know what's really going on around here."

He huffed a soft laugh. "Glad one person thinks that."

"Oh, I do," Vi said, pouncing on that tiny crack in his tough-guy facade. "I also think you're smart, loyal, and one of the truly good guys. Which is why I'm coming to you with this information, and no one else. And believe me, that's a compliment, because I don't trust easily. I've been burned in the past. Badly."

Something flickered in his eyes. Something that made her think he might have been burned, too.

On impulse, she reached out and caught one of his hands. If Marcie's well-being meant throwing herself at this man, she would. Virginia's future be damned. Except she had underestimated the impact of having his rough, calloused fingers beneath hers as she brought them to her chest. His skin was surprisingly warm, almost hot. Her pulse fluttered unevenly. No longer sure what she was doing, she pressed his hand against her heart, seeking comfort from his innate strength as much as she wished to give it.

She hadn't realized until this moment how true her words had been. She did trust him. And admire him.

And want him.

"Virginia," he said in a low voice. Surprised by his use of her first name, she glanced up. And immediately fell into the mesmerizing beauty of his eyes. "What are you doing?"

The question jolted her out of her fog.

Jumping back, she released his hand. "Sorry. I guess I was still in character from tonight. Nothing to worry about."

"Worried wasn't part of the equation, exactly," he said slowly, his eyes not leaving hers. "More like, are you aware of our audience?"

Her pulse leaped again, but this time for an entirely different reason. Falling back on her hard-earned acting skills, she immediately smoothed her expression and adopted a more relaxed posture. "Thank you for that," she murmured with a slight smile. "You have a way of making a girl forget herself."

He hesitated and then said in a low voice, "I'd say the problem is mutual, Miss Heart."

The heat that flickered in his eyes nearly knocked her knees out from under her. Then his expression cooled. "For the record, Miss Rossi is still in Nettuno, recovering from a sprained ankle and wrist. When she's cleared to rejoin your unit, I'm sure Lieutenant Holland will let you know."

He turned and began striding away without so much as a backward glance.

"Wait!" she called after him.

If he'd heard her, he gave no sign. Vi ground her teeth in frustration. Drat the man! She had no more answers now than she had started with. Worse, he had neatly turned all her attempts at bamboozling him back on herself. And he had done it so easily. It pained her to even think about it.

Yet he wasn't immune to her. That much was clear. If she could just get him alone and not lose her head this time . . .

The idea, once sprung, refused to die.

She glanced around for Marcie. Spotting her, Vi hurried over, smiling apologetically at the soldiers who tried to catch her attention. It nagged at her conscience to push them away, but the other actors and actresses were still there to take up the slack. Solving the mystery around Luciana to protect Marcie took precedence at this point.

"Marcie," Vi hissed, taking her friend's arm. "I need your help."

"Just a moment, Lou," Marcie said with a bright smile for the soldier in front of her as she resisted Vi's tug. "I want to hear more about that puppy you found as soon as I can get rid of my friend here."

"What do you want?" Marcie asked irritably when Vi got her alone. "And before you bust my chops, I wasn't flirting with him."

"Sure. Look, are you fine going back to the hotel without me? I've got a killer migraine and want to go lie down."

Marcie's eyes widened with concern. "Oh, you poor thing! Do you want me to go with you?"

"No need," Vi said quickly. "I'll be fine. Besides, there are still a lot of men waiting to congratulate you."

Marcie bit her lip, her gaze flying back to the line of eager soldiers. "Well, if you're sure."

"I'm sure." Vi forced herself to smile despite her impatience. Sergeant Danger, having finished his conversation with Sue and Mr. Stuart, was heading for the exit leading to the auditorium. "I'll see you back at the room."

Praying that Marcie wouldn't follow her, Vi dived into the crowd again. She struggled to keep the sergeant in sight, jumping up on her toes every few strides. Then he disappeared through the door, and Vi abandoned caution. She bolted after him, barely having the presence of mind to snatch a coat off a chair on her way out—a necessity given she was still in her sparkly, rather revealing dance outfit.

Several more GIs attempted to stop her on her way up the house. She smiled and accepted their kind words as expeditiously as she could. She didn't want to be rude, after all. To her surprise, there seemed to be quite a few civilian well-wishers loitering about, too. She would have to remember to tell the troupe about that fact.

Finally she had worked her way up the aisle, through the curtained foyer, and out onto the street. It was eerily dark on the sidewalk, with the city under strict blackout orders.

Nervous perspiration dampened her costume as she waited for her eyes to adjust to the gloom. She didn't want to lose him, but charging blindly into the dark street wouldn't do her any good. It might get her killed, since the blackout applied to vehicles as well, requiring their headlights be switched off or painted to reveal only a thin beam of light. With only moonlight illuminating the narrow streets, drivers often didn't see pedestrians, or other traffic, until it was too late.

And was there ever a lot of traffic! With the war continuing in the North, military trucks of all sizes prowled the streets, delivering matériel and men even in the depths of the night. There were a fair number of taxis and carts and pedestrians on the streets as well, as the good citizens of Rome had refused to stop living their lives, which only made the nightscape that much more dangerous.

Tamping down panic as the seconds ticked by, she was soon able to sort out the shadows by size and distance. Her pulse leaped when she saw a soldier about the right height and build waiting at the corner for a mule-drawn cart to pass. Except he wasn't headed in the right direction. The hotel was the other way.

She bit her lip. Perhaps she should go back and wait to see if she could corner Danger later. Then the soldier stepped off the curb and strode away. The familiar loose-limbed stride sealed her decision, and she hurried after him.

"Sergeant Danger, wait!"

He didn't pause. If anything, he seemed to lengthen his stride as he disappeared down the dark sidewalk, taking her peace of mind with him.

Frustrated and desperate for answers, she started after him. If he wasn't going to tell her what was going on with Luciana directly, so be it. She would just find a different way to get the information she needed, because she was willing to bet her last sawbuck that he'd already known Luciana was in town. The louse hadn't even batted a damn eyelash when she had mentioned it. And if she were the sergeant, her first stop after leaving the theater would be at wherever Luciana was staying to give the actress a heads-up that she'd been seen. And likely a stern order not to let it happen again.

If she was right about all that, then the sergeant would lead her directly to Luciana and all the answers Vi needed to keep Marcie safe. Assuming she didn't lose sight of him. And that she didn't give herself away.

Keeping to the shadows, and staying as light on her dancer's shoes as she could, she followed him through an increasingly tangled path of medieval streets and dark alleyways. She flitted from shadow to shadow in his wake, trying not to let the twisting path alarm her too much.

Rome wasn't laid out in a tidy grid, like the cities back home, she knew. And given all the shops, she guessed they were still close to the city center. But between not being able to read the street names and all the storefronts being buttoned up by heavy shutters, she was perilously short on landmarks. If she lost him now, she would have a heck of a time finding her way back to the hotel before morning.

The sergeant abruptly slowed, and Vi jumped into the nearest alcove. Making herself as thin as possible, she pressed against the slick, painted wood of a door.

And that's when she heard what she had missed before: furtive footsteps not from in front of her, where the sergeant was, but behind her. Light, almost silent treads, as if someone didn't wish to be heard. A cold sweat broke out between her shoulder blades as the sounds stopped.

With no idea who this new person was, or how close, or if they represented a threat, Vi hardly dared breathe. Was someone following her, a woman alone on the streets at night, thinking to rob or rape her? Had the sergeant heard the footsteps, too? He hadn't let on that he knew he was being tailed, and if he hadn't heard her, he likely hadn't heard the person now tailing her, either.

Out on the sidewalk, the sergeant's boot steps resumed, the sound receding as he continued on his way. Vi waited to see what the fellow behind her would do. Seconds passed with no sound, no whisper of movement. Meanwhile, the sergeant and the safety he represented were getting farther away. Since being lost and alone on the streets of a foreign city was not at the top of her list of good ideas, she threw her lot in with the sergeant and bolted out onto the sidewalk.

The sergeant was gone. Worse, something scraped on the pavement behind her. Adrenaline streaked through her veins. She whirled around, and screamed as a man in a long coat rushed forward. She raised her hands to fend him off, only to have strong fingers close around her neck, cutting off her breath. Not about to give up, she went for his eyes even as her own vision started to tunnel. He jerked his head out of reach, his hold unbroken. Desperate, she grabbed his wrists. The need for air overpowered all other thought.

His family jewels, a voice whispered dimly in the back of her head. *Knee him! Come on!*

With the last of her strength, she raised her knee up as hard as she could. And missed.

With a soundless whimper, she clawed at his hands again, her world shrinking to black.

And then she was on the sidewalk, her knees bruising on impact. Her lungs sucked in sweet air with a painful rasp. Her second gasping breath brought her to full consciousness. Not ten feet away, two men grappled in silence except for the sound of their strained breathing and occasional grunt. It was the sergeant and her pursuer.

She shoved herself to her feet and then put her hand out to steady herself on the wall as her vision swam. *Come on, Vi. Get in there! Two on one is much better odds than one on one.*

Praying that her idea would work, she launched herself forward. Years of dance had taught her a person's center of gravity was right below the navel. One shove near the hips, and the person can't help but move. As luck would have it, the two men had rotated so that the assailant was closest to her. The collision drove the air from her lungs again, but the man staggered, his grip on the sergeant broken.

She landed on the pavement with an excruciating scrape of skin. Trembling from shock and pain, she pushed to her hands and knees, only to be flattened when someone tripped over her. Her head hit the ground. For a few terror-filled seconds, swirling pricks of light filled her vision. Then they slowly faded, and she saw the sergeant standing over her, his hand held out.

"Come on," he said urgently. "We've got to go."

She took his hand and then gasped as he immediately hauled her to her feet. Her body hurt all over. On the other hand, pain was nothing new to a dancer. "I'm ready."

"Stay with me and don't speak."

In the next instant, he turned and began to run. His grip on her hand was all that kept her from falling again, but she soon caught her balance. "What's going on?"

"Later." The hard edge in that one word silenced any further questions, but not her whirling thoughts. It didn't help that her head was pounding, a situation made worse with each jarring footfall. All that she could come up with was that her attacker must not have been a casual footpad—otherwise why not just raise the alarm and have someone call the police?

To her relief, they didn't go far. Maybe another two blocks. He slammed to a stop in front of a door between shop fronts and fished out a key. While she caught her breath, she looked around, half to see if anyone was following them and half to see if she could recognize where they were. The answer to both was no.

"I don't have time to explain," the sergeant said in a low voice as he unlocked the door. "I just need you to trust me. All right?"

"All right."

He opened the door and shoved her inside.

She was in a dimly lit passageway, with a stairwell to the right of her and what appeared to be a dark courtyard ahead. If it were day, she suspected she might see a small garden, or bicycles parked within the safety of the surrounding buildings. But now, with no illumination, it loomed ominous and threatening.

The sergeant gestured toward the stairwell. "Let's go. When we get to the top, I'll need to blindfold you, so be prepared."

A shiver went through her. "Why?"

He gave her a little push toward the stairs. "Because I'm meeting with partisans—resistance fighters—who wouldn't think twice about slitting your throat to keep their identities secret. And given the bad news I'm bringing, they're likely to be even more jumpy than usual."

"The man who attacked me," she said, not even making it a question.

"Was likely a Nazi agent, which is why I had to bring you with me. Where there's one, there's likely more. And given how the last safe house had a hand grenade chucked through the window, there's no time to lose getting everyone out of here."

She eyed all the apartments they were passing. "Shouldn't we be knocking on everyone's door?"

"Not yet." He stopped her on the landing of the third floor. "This is as far as you go. Turn around."

Her pulse leaped as she saw him unsheathing a knife from the belt at his waist. "What are you doing?"

"Keeping you safe," he said before she could speak again. "Now sit down. Near the wall."

The command to trust him was left unspoken. Her one comfort was that she still believed him to be a good man. But that didn't mean she was free of misgivings. Her life, after all, would literally be in his hands.

She sank to the tiled floor while he cut a strip of cloth from his trousers. His knife flashed with rapid, deadly precision. Then he knelt by her and tied the strip loosely around her neck.

"Sorry about this." He yanked the loop up, smooshing her chin and nose until it was past them and tight around her eyes. "Don't move. Don't speak."

She nodded, her mouth dry with fear now that her vision was cut off.

The soft rustling of clothing and the whisper of leather on tile were her only clue that he had moved away. A soft knock on wood focused her remaining senses.

A quiet squeak of metal on metal, like hinges on a door.

There was a heartbeat of silence. "Who is that?" a woman asked in a hushed voice, her English made almost musical by her Italian accent.

Vi's ears perked up. She had heard this woman somewhere before. Like many performers, she had a gift for recognizing voices.

"Never mind her. We've been discovered. I left a body in the street, so we don't have long."

"You will come in?" the woman asked softly. "We must talk, but without her."

"Did you not hear what I said?" he asked, frustration clear despite his quiet tone. "I was followed."

Even though he didn't say as much, Vi suspected she was the reason for that. She and her stupid impulsive streak. Utter and complete humiliation made her want to shrink into the floor.

The door scraped closed, and she was alone. With nothing to look at and nothing to do but wait anxiously for the sergeant's meeting to be over, she tried to focus her racing thoughts on something more productive than panic. A far better use of her time would be to assess the current situation and try to come up with a plan in case she had to make a quick exit.

First fact—she was unarmed and outside a partisan lair with bad guys about to storm the place any minute. Second fact—as much as she wanted to remove her blindfold, she had been warned it would get her throat slit. Third and most important fact—Sergeant Danger wasn't above using violence to secure his mission. The man they had left behind, given the sergeant's description of the situation, was probably dead.

The thought gave her the heebie-jeebies. On the other hand, if the sergeant hadn't intervened, that dead body likely would've been her. Her stomach twisted as the reality of that sank in, and she swallowed hard.

A muffled argument came through the door. She could pick out the sergeant's signature baritone, as well as the alto of the woman. There was another man as well, and whatever was being discussed wasn't going well.

A bead of nervous sweat trickled down her temple from under the blindfold. She swiped it away, her nausea increasing with every passing second. She would give him another minute or two. If he didn't come out by then, she was going to make a break for it. Better to be lost and on the streets all night than trapped and dead.

The sudden click of the door latch at the bottom of the stairs being opened froze her in place. Straining her ears, she waited on pins and needles to hear what she hoped would be the normal noises of a resident coming home late. And waited. Only silence filled the stairwell. Her heart raced.

A faint scuff of what might have been a leather sole on tile registered. Then the whisper of something brushing against plaster walls. Vi tensed. Someone was coming up the stairs. Someone who was making a real effort to be silent.

Praying the partisans would understand and forgive her, she silently slid the blindfold up just enough to see. A deep gloom shrouded the stairwell. Someone had shut off the one dim light. Rapidly blinking to adjust her vision to the dark, she scoured the shadows for any sign of movement.

A faint exhale lifted the fine hairs on her neck. The sergeant's warning about grenades blowing up safe houses echoed in her mind. As she waited for the next sound, a cold sweat gripped her.

Unarmed as she was, her only advantage would be surprise. No one could possibly expect a USO dancer to be just sitting outside the door of a partisan rendezvous.

Another swish of fabric against a wall, slightly louder. Whoever was coming was almost there.

Torn between terror and resolve, she took a deep breath, hoping it wouldn't be her last.

The shadows deepened on the stairwell. It was almost time.

One . . . two . . . three . . .

Knowing this might be the last thing she ever did, Vi opened her mouth and belted out the loudest shriek of her life. Her voice teacher would've been horrified. Her own ears hurt from it. And as hoped, the shadow flinched just as the door next to her flew open, spilling light onto the landing.

"What the——?" Sergeant Danger said.

Rapid, deafening cracks of gunfire exploded around her, along with the sparks of bullets ricocheting off walls and railings. Shards hit her from every direction, piercing her exposed skin. Terrified, she cowered into a small ball.

Abruptly, the shooting stopped. She waited—five seconds, ten—too scared to move, her ears still ringing painfully. Finally, she peeked to see if anyone was left and shrieked at the sight of a strange woman crouched next to her.

The woman reached out and Vi shrank back, her pulse leaping painfully. The woman's red hair shone like copper in the light coming from the apartment. The color seemed oddly familiar, as did the face, and that's when Vi realized she knew her. It was the woman from La Fiorentina. The one who had delivered the note.

And all the pieces of the puzzle started to fall together.

Chapter 26

Sergeant Danger thudded up the stairs at a dead run. "Virginia! Are you all right?"

"I think so," Vi said as the redheaded woman stood. Then Vi noticed the blood on his ripped trousers, and her eyes widened. "Are you?"

"I'm fine." He knelt and ran his gaze rapidly over her. "I don't see any major injuries. Think you can run?"

"Where is Ric?" the woman asked sharply, though in the same musical accent Vi had recognized earlier.

"Hiding the body." The sergeant held his hand out to Vi. "He said he'll meet you outside."

The woman grabbed his arm, her face pale in the light. "You will deliver our message."

"Yes." The sergeant pulled Vi to her feet as easily as if she were a child. "We'll be in contact."

"Grazie."

Not wasting another second, the sergeant started down the stairs, and Vi was hot on his heels. In any other situation, a man might have asked her to go first, but with unknown assailants popping up like dandelions, she was more than happy to have him clear the way for her. Outside the building, she could hear the faint two-tone wail of a police siren. Pushing aside her panic, she focused on the sergeant's broad back as they cleared the final landing and raced into the passage between the buildings.

Instinctively, Vi turned toward the front door. The sergeant seized her arm and pulled her toward the courtyard. She stumbled after him, nearly tripping over a fallen bicycle.

His grip tightened, catching her. Determined not to make an even bigger mess of things, she took a deep breath and concentrated on her footing. It was hard, though. Too much adrenaline jittered in her veins, and her brain couldn't let go of the two men who had died tonight within mere feet of her. Or the redheaded woman from the restaurant being a partisan. Or the possibility she might yet die tonight, and it would be all Luciana's fault. Luciana's and that dratted note's.

Questions burned on her tongue as they cut through another building corridor and then darted across the street. Finally, the tension left the sergeant's shoulders, and Vi allowed the words to slip free.

"That woman," she said quietly after they had ducked into an alley. "I've seen her before. She's the one who gave me the note I think was meant for Luciana."

"I know."

She flinched at his steely tone, but Marcie's safety was too important to let the subject drop.

"Well, there's more. Marcie and I went to the clock shop by the Tiber, the one mentioned in the note. A little boy there, Enzo, asked if we were the people who were going to help them get to America, and his mother panicked."

He cursed under his breath.

Vi pulled him to a stop when they reached the street again. For this next part, she needed to see his expression, though the light was little better than it had been in the alley. "I overheard you and Mr. Miller and Luciana arguing in Nettuno. I know there's something going on, something dangerous that involved at least you and Luciana, and the partisans. So I need you to be straight with me. Is Enzo in any kind of danger? Or Marcie, for that matter. Because if they are, even the tiniest bit, I want to know."

"You're worried about a little boy you've barely met and Miss May?" His tone was somewhere between exasperation and disbelief. "Not Luciana? Not you?"

"I asked you a question, Sergeant. And as I'm an officer in the USO, I command you to answer me."

He huffed a tired laugh, the hard edges of his cheekbones and jaw stark, almost frightening in the half light. "That rank is an honorary one, Virginia. It's not real, so I don't have to tell you a damn thing."

"Are they in danger?" she asked, refusing to be intimidated.

"There's a war going on, Miss Heart." His tone was sarcastic. "What do you think?"

"That you are being deliberately obtuse."

He drew in a long breath. "Fine. No, Miss May is not in any danger above the usual and customary for a USO performer in a war zone. And Enzo should be just fine. That said, stay away from that clock store, and"—he poked her in the chest for emphasis—"never follow me anywhere again. Got it?"

Vi rolled her eyes, exasperated. "You're the one who ran away before I could talk to you. And by the way, you could thank me. If I hadn't followed you, I wouldn't have been on the landing to scream, and you would be dead right now."

"If you hadn't made such a ruckus while following me, I likely wouldn't have picked up a tail."

"You don't know that," she said, even as the truth of that twisted in her chest.

"You endangered a lot of people tonight, Virginia. That no one died is a miracle."

"But what about the man—"

"He was an enemy agent. As was the man in the stairwell. So I don't count them."

"Oh." Her breathing constricted. Not because she regretted their deaths, per se. There was a war going on, after all, and both men had tried to kill the sergeant. But the matter-of-fact way the sergeant mentioned it, as if the men's deaths were of no significance, struck her as somehow wrong.

"Hey." He lifted her chin and looked directly into her eyes. "I couldn't let them live. You know that, right? If either agent had gotten away, a lot more people would have been killed later. Good people. People on our side."

"I . . . I know. It's just . . . well, it's hard knowing you were the one who did it."

"Should I not have?"

She hesitated, not sure. She had always hated Tony for being so cavalier about life and death, for killing people just because someone had deemed them a threat to the family. To be faced with the fact that the sergeant had likely killed so many more men, also deemed threats, only this time to the Allied cause . . . Did that make them the same?

No. Whatever the sergeant was, he wasn't Tony. Somehow she knew in her bones that Sergeant Danger was a good man caught in an awful situation.

She gently touched her fingers to his jaw, wishing she could have met him in a different time, in a different place, untouched by war. "You're right. You did what had to be done. And I'm sorry."

A beat passed, and then he exhaled. "Let's get you back. I think we've both had enough excitement for one day."

She huffed a soft laugh and reluctantly dropped her fingers from his face. "Roger that."

A companionable silence surrounded them as they started down the street. A curiously relaxed feeling settled over her, as if the dangers of the last hour hadn't happened. As if facing them down, with the help of the man by her side, had made her somehow invincible. With new eyes she took in the ancient buildings and narrow streets.

"How is it you're not lost?" she asked as he turned them onto another street. "Have you spent a lot of time in Rome?"

"No. But I'm good with maps, mental or otherwise. Before the war, I was a surveyor."

"Really?" She laughed. "And here I thought you were a bank president."

He slid her an amused look. "I'd have to work in a city for that, and I don't like cities."

"So, a surveyor, huh?" She followed him into a quiet plaza that looked vaguely familiar. "I bet the army was happy about that."

"The army? Nah, they didn't care. They put me in the infantry, where I could work on my hand-to-hand combat skills."

"But wait—if you're in the infantry, why are you in Rome?" she asked, surprised.

"Because I am." It was clear from his tone that he was done with questions, which was fine. Vi had her answer on whether Marcie was in danger. With that worry removed, anything else she learned merely iced the cake. Another turn, and she started recognizing stores and landmarks despite the dark.

"We're almost at the hotel," she exclaimed, relief lifting her spirits.

"We are." The sergeant's grim tone reminded her that his evening had been decidedly less successful.

"I'm sorry about tonight," she said, meaning it. "And I'm sorry you had to ruin your trousers. You won't get in trouble, will you?"

"No. Uniforms tend to get ruined when there's a war going on." He slid her a questioning look. "Speaking of which, where's yours?"

"My . . . ?" Her hands flew to the lapels of her borrowed coat as sudden dread washed over her. "Oh, Lord. My uniform is at the theater. I was in such a rush to follow you, I never changed."

"Guess you'll have to get it tomorrow."

She pulled him to a stop. "But I need to wash my blouse tonight."

He held up his hand to quiet her protest. "I'm not taking you back to the theater, period. It's already past your curfew."

"But—"

"I said no, Virginia."

The sudden steel in his voice brought her up short. All of a sudden, the emptiness of the streets, the darkness of them, struck her. If she never made it back to the hotel, there was no one to connect her disappearance with the sergeant. She hadn't told anyone what she was doing.

He would be free and clear, and she would be dead.

Swallowing her sudden fear, she took a step back, ready to bolt if she had to. Except the sergeant was in great shape. And certain to be faster than her, given her bruised knees.

He sighed. "That wasn't a threat, Miss Heart. I don't kill women or children, even if ordered to, unless they're armed and about to kill me or one of my men."

"Women and children have tried to kill you?" The very notion shocked her.

"Not everyone is fond of American soldiers," he said dryly, "particularly near the Austrian border."

"But Austria . . ."

"Is behind enemy lines. Yes, I know." He gave a humorless laugh. "Believe me, I was well aware of that."

"I'm glad they didn't succeed," she said quietly. She had never meant anything more. And she had never wanted anything more in her life than for this damn war to be over.

"Tell you what—seeing as I can't waltz into the hotel with you on my arm without causing a scandal—I'll head back to the theater and get your uniform. There's a good chance your friend Miss May might have brought it back to the hotel for you already, since you've been gone so long. But if not, I'll knock on your door when I return. Give me thirty minutes or so. I've got something else I need to do first."

Guilt washed over her again. Of course he had other things he needed to do tonight, things that were going to end up delayed because of her impulsiveness. "Thank you."

"And, Virginia, as far as you or anyone else knows, Luciana is still in Nettuno, recovering. Got it? Because if Mr. Miller hears otherwise, your friend will be back in the chorus faster than you can blink."

"Yes, sir." She saluted smartly.

"You don't salute sergeants, Vi," he said, sounding a little exasperated.

"Oh, sorry," she said, tucking the information away. "And I can get to the hotel by myself from here."

"You got a key? The front door is likely locked by now."

"Of course it is." She closed her eyes as unexpected tears of exhaustion and embarrassment welled up. "Criminy, but you must think I'm a big ninny!"

"No, I don't. Come on." He took her elbow. "I've got a key."

"You know, I'm not always this much trouble," she said once they were walking again.

"Is that right?" He stopped outside the front door of the hotel and pulled a key from his trouser pocket. "Good to know."

She wiped her eyes and looked up at him. "Will you ever forgive me?"

His hand lifted as if to touch her face, then dropped to his side again.

"I already have." He unlocked the door for her and then stepped back. "See you in thirty."

Chapter 27

Vi slipped inside the dark foyer of the hotel, her heart in her throat as she peeked around. It would be a cruel irony if she was tossed out of the USO now, over a curfew violation that had nothing to do with sexual impropriety, after being so careful to hide her past all these weeks. Not seeing anyone, she tiptoed across the tile floor. A small light in the stairwell illuminating her way. Even though it was after midnight, she knew not everyone in the place would be asleep yet. But if she stayed really, really quiet—

"Out kinda late, aren'tcha?" Frances's voice pierced the silence.

Vi jumped and then pressed a hand to her chest. "Good Lord, Frances. You just took five years off my life."

And of all the rotten luck . . . Of course it would be her archenemy to see her.

"Who were you out with?" Frances asked.

"No one." With no choice but to brazen it out and hope for the best, Vi peered into the gloom of the foyer, trying to locate the girl. She finally saw her lounging on an upholstered chair in the corner, her stockinged feet dangling over the edge of the arm. "What are you doing down here?"

Frances shrugged. "Couldn't sleep. Gertie snores, and I didn't feel like waking her."

"That's really . . . kind of you," Vi said, trying to hide her surprise.

"You know, I'm not as big a bitch as you think I am," Frances said dryly.

"I never thought you were," Vi said, edging toward the stairwell.

Frances scoffed. "Liar. But that's fine. I don't like you, either."

"Why is that?" Vi paused. The sheer injustice of the girl's animosity toward her demanded a reason, at least to Vi's mind. "I've never done anything to you."

"It's what you haven't done. Like scrapped for a living, trying to find a way out of the tenement slum you were born into, doing whatever was necessary." Frances laughed harshly. "I know all about your kind: born with a silver spoon in your mouth, never lacking for anything, taking what others have worked their buns off for, without a second thought."

Vi bristled. "Now hold on there! You don't know the first thing about me."

"Really? Are you saying your daddy wasn't rich? That you didn't have new shoes and dresses growing up? That you didn't always have enough to eat?"

Vi took a deep breath. "I'm sorry your life was hard. But that doesn't mean—"

"You know, Janet was a scrapper, too," Frances continued, as if Vi hadn't spoken. "Her daddy liked to beat the hell out of her just for fun, but she didn't let that hold her down. Like me, she worked her way up from nothing."

Ah, Vi thought, the root of the problem suddenly coming clear.

"Did you even stop to think about what might happen to her when you breezed in like the queen anointed?"

"Janet was your friend," Vi said with quiet conviction.

"And she's twice the person you are," Frances said, sitting up. The anger in her voice was sharp enough to draw blood. "And yet she was replaced by you. You! A two-bit corn princess with rich parents—and don't bother denying it, I can tell just from the way you talk—who was out late tonight, likely doing things far worse than Janet ever did."

"You're wrong about tonight," Vi said, reaching for a calm she didn't feel. "And about me not understanding what it's like to fight for a living."

"Oh really?"

Vi debated whether to have this out now or wait until they were both less exhausted and irritable. On the other hand, she remembered the power of confidences shared in the dark. It was about the only time her older sister would talk to Vi as an equal, when the rest of the world dropped away.

Keeping her coat close around her to hide her costume, Vi walked over to the chair across from Frances and sat.

"Look, I know you have no reason to believe me, but I'm not the pampered princess you think I am. I've slept on the floors of bus stations more times than I can count. I've had to choose between eating and buying new dance shoes because the ones I had had holes. And, believe it or not, I worked my ass off to become as good as I am.

"I'm really sorry your friend was canned. But it wasn't my call or even my suggestion. And, like it or not, there's nothing either of us can do at this point except make the best of a bad situation. And since the troupe needs us both to succeed, can we at least call a truce?"

Frances, wrapped in shadows, didn't reply.

Vi's hopes faded.

She started to get out of the chair. "Well, I should—"

"I'll have to think about it," Frances said at last.

A weight lifted off Vi's shoulders, one she hadn't even realized she was carrying.

"Will you think about calling a truce with Marcie, too?" she asked, her fingers crossed. "I know for a fact she had nothing to do with Janet losing her spot."

At least not knowingly, she silently amended.

"No." Frances's tone was flat.

Vi sat back, honestly perplexed. "Why not? She's apologized for insulting you and been on her best behavior recently."

"She's a wop."

Anger flashed through Vi's veins at the slur. "Stop! Don't ever say that word in my presence again. I'll put up with a lot of nonsense from you, but not that."

"Why not? Can't I call a spade a spade?" Frances asked mockingly.

"Not in front of me, you won't. And you do realize you're in Italy, which is filled with the very people you're insulting."

"Yes, and I hate every minute of it." Frances's voice cracked with emotion, throwing Vi off-balance yet again. She couldn't see the girl's face in the gloom, but she was pretty sure she was crying, or else very close to it. Frances, the unassailable . . . To witness her so vulnerable was unsettling.

"I didn't want to come here," Frances continued in a whisper. "I didn't even know it was a possibility. I wouldn't have signed on if I had known. I was thinking France, or the South Seas, or England. Anywhere else would've been okay . . ."

A fraught silence filled the dark, and Vi shifted uncomfortably in her chair. "Frances, why do you hate Italians so much?"

There was a small, choked sob from the other chair.

"I won't tell anyone else; I promise." Vi leaned forward, trying to see through the dark. "Please tell me. I want to understand."

"They killed my brother."

The fury and anguish in Frances's voice made Vi's heart catch. She closed her eyes in shared sorrow, the enormity of the loss stealing all the air from the room. "I'm so, so sorry, Frances. For you and for your family."

"He was in North Africa, in the tank corps, and the Italians shelled his position." Frances's voice broke. "They killed him!"

"It was the war that killed him. It could've been the Germans or the Japanese or anyone."

"I don't care." The coldness in Frances's tone declared the subject closed.

Vi drew a deep breath. "No, I suppose you don't. And I'm sorry."

Frances sniffed. "Why? You never met him."

"No, but I have a sister I love like life itself. And I can't imagine how I'd feel if Fern were killed, other than very, very angry at whoever did it." Her anger at herself for betraying her sister's trust was gut wrenching enough.

Aware of the minutes sliding by, Vi got to her feet. As awkward as it was to be caught by Frances coming in late, she at least hadn't been caught by Sue or Wyatt, though her chances of that happening were increasing with every second. Nor did she want to be in the lobby when Sergeant Danger returned with her uniform in his hand. By himself, the sergeant could likely dance around Frances's questions, disarming the girl's suspicious nature. Heaven knew he had handled Vi's attempts at interrogation easily enough. But she suspected he would have an easier time of it if she weren't standing right there, arms outstretched for her clothes.

"I'm heading up. You should probably get some sleep, too, since we have another performance tomorrow."

Frances waved her hand, and once again Vi wished she could see her expression in the dark. "You go ahead. Gertie's probably still snoring."

Exhaustion hit her like a brick wall as she climbed the stairs. Forcing herself to stay upright, she knocked softly on her room door. Like everything else, her room key was still at the theater.

"Marcie," she called softly through the door. "It's me. Can you let me in?"

The lock snicked, and the door opened an inch. Marcie peered out blearily and then opened the door farther when she saw Vi.

"Well, it's about time," Marcie said sourly.

"Shhh." Vi glanced up and down the hallway, hoping no one had heard her friend. She slipped inside past Marcie. Marcie closed and locked the door while Vi unbelted the coat she had borrowed.

"Where did you go tonight?" Marcie asked in a quieter voice, though her annoyance was still plain. "I thought you had a headache."

Vi felt around for her mattress. With the blackout curtains drawn, it was like a tomb in their room. "I do, but I was out of aspirin powder. Do you know how hard it is to find a drugstore open at this time of night?"

"You should've just waited for me to get home, because I have plenty. All you had to do was ask."

"I'll remember that for next time," Vi said, sinking onto her cot. She thought longingly of her pillow but knew she couldn't head off to dreamland yet. Sergeant Danger might knock any minute now, and she wanted to be the one to answer the door. Which reminded her . . . "Sergeant Danger may be knocking soon. He was out trying to find me some aspirin, too, but I think I got back first."

"Mmm-kay," Marcie said sleepily, and then her cot squeaked as she made herself comfortable.

Smothering her own yawn, Vi debated whether she had time to wash her face before he arrived. The bathroom was just three doors down, and it hadn't sounded like anyone was using it when she was in the hallway.

She could brush her teeth, too. Then all she would have to do was change into her pajamas and she would be ready for bed. Or maybe she should change first. As much as she loved her sparkly costume, it was also rather scratchy from all the sequins. And it had to last at least a score more performances.

Marcie's soft snores began to fill the room. Deciding to make a dash for it now and change later, Vi grabbed her toiletry kit. She was about to open the door when she heard voices in the stairwell. Male and female. Sergeant Danger and Frances.

Spirits sinking, Vi leaned her ear against the door to listen. She couldn't believe her bad luck tonight. Ever since she had left the theater, nothing had gone according to plan.

As she waited for Frances to realize whose uniform the sergeant was carrying, for the ax to fall, because she had no illusions that Frances wouldn't turn her in, despite their little chat tonight, she had to suffer through listening to the woman flirt with the man right outside her door. Worse, he was flirting back, which tied her stomach in a knot. She didn't want him to be attracted to Frances. She wanted him to fall for her.

The sudden realization stole her breath. She had believed her heart permanently hardened by Robert's betrayal. Love required trust, and she had lost that ability a long time ago. Hadn't she?

Frances giggled. Vi's fingers closed into a fist as she imagined the girl sliding her hand up Sergeant Danger's strong chest, her full lips parting for a kiss . . .

"I've got to turn in now," the sergeant said, his voice a low rumble through the door.

"See you tomorrow?" Frances asked breathlessly. Vi wanted to throw her hairbrush at the brunette, but the sergeant wasn't hers to defend. He could like whomever he wanted.

"Probably not. I'll be moving on tomorrow."

What? Vi stifled her gasp of dismay just in time. She didn't want to get caught eavesdropping.

"Aw, really?" Frances said, drowning out any sound Vi might have made.

"Really. So if you'll excuse me, I gotta get packed," Sergeant Danger said, his voice moving toward his room at the end of the hall. "Good night."

"Good night," Frances called after him.

Vi remained motionless until she heard two doors open and then close, one after the other. She released her breath and considered her new problem. Unless she had missed something, Sergeant Danger had just taken her uniform into his room with him.

What a night. What was it that soldiers called missions that went horribly awry? She leaned her head against the door. FUBAR, that was it. Fouled up beyond all recognition. What an apt description of her current situation.

If she weren't so tired, she might have laughed. Instead she tucked her toiletry bag under her arm and unlocked the door. After checking the hallway again for unwanted company and finding none, she sneaked out of her room and hurried down the hallway.

She rapped lightly on the sergeant's door and then waited, praying he would answer. Hesitant to spend too much time in the hallway, she glanced over her shoulder and then rapped again. This time the door opened to reveal Sergeant Danger. Her gaze fell to the misaligned buttons on his shirt. He must have thrown it on seconds before answering her knock. The tantalizing image of a partially undressed sergeant took form in her imagination, and her mouth went dry.

"Good, you're here." His low whisper brushed over her nerves like roughened velvet, and her skin tingled. He turned to reach behind him, likely for her uniform, when the sound of a door opening made her pulse leap.

He must have heard it, too, because the next thing she knew he was pulling her into his room. She stumbled as he released her to shut the door. It had barely closed when she heard footsteps in the hall. They both froze as they waited to see where the midnight prowler would go. If she had been seen, she was in an even worse pickle than she was before. She might be able to explain away leaving the theater in her dance outfit. But being in Sergeant Danger's room late at night, without a chaperone? Not likely.

The footsteps stopped, and then what sounded like the bathroom door closed.

Vi closed her eyes in relief.

"That was close," Sergeant Danger said softly. "If you're quick, you should make it back to your room in time."

Vi hesitated, considered the odds, and then whispered back, "Actually, I think it would be better if I wait until he or she is done. Some people don't spend much time in there."

He drew a deep breath and then exhaled tightly. "As you wish."

He turned back to his bed, where he had his clothes laid out in neat piles.

"You're packing," she said in surprise.

"I am."

It shouldn't have surprised her, since she had overheard him telling Frances he was leaving in the morning. Yet, from the conversation he'd had with the redheaded woman tonight, it was clear whatever business he had with the partisans wasn't concluded yet.

"Where are you going?"

He went to the bedside table and opened the drawer. "Elsewhere."

"Because of what happened tonight?"

"Because I don't want to endanger everyone in the hotel on the off chance that an SS agent is still on my tail."

"And I suppose Luciana needs you more than we do," she said glumly.

He shot her a hard look. "For the last time, Miss Rossi is still injured and in Nettuno."

"Right. Sorry." *Great, now he thought her an idiot, too.* Her spirits took another nosedive. She used to be good at keeping various stories straight. Apparently not anymore.

Returning to his packing, the sergeant removed an oddly shaped item from the drawer and laid it on the bed next to his clothes. Curious, Vi moved closer. She blinked and then blinked again, not quite believing what she saw. It was a small cloth doll with dark hair, a light-blue blouse, bright-yellow skirt, and a black apron elaborately embroidered in vibrant shades of reds and greens. A rose-and-lemon-embroidered shawl covering the doll's head completed the ensemble. As a costumer, Vi admired the bold mix of patterns and colors. It was very striking.

And quite the unusual item for a soldier to be carrying around.

"That's beautiful," she said, gently touching the smooth satin stitching of the lemons. "Where did you get it?"

She hadn't seen anything as fine in the stores near the hotel.

"From an old lady in the *Piemonte*. She used to make them for tourists before the war started." He gently moved the doll out of Vi's reach. "It's for my daughter."

"Daughter?" she echoed, stunned. And, oh, wasn't that just her luck to fall in love with a married man? He was completely off-limits now, of course. Her morals might not be as top notch as all that, but she drew the line at lusting after other women's husbands.

"Yeah. She's just a baby now, but I thought maybe when she's older, she could look at it and think of me."

A different emotion stole her breath. "You don't think you'll make it back?" *Alive*, she had almost said, but then stopped, unable to say the word.

He shrugged. "It's a possibility. I'd be a fool to think otherwise."

She sank onto the chair by the bed. "How can you bear it, the thought of never seeing your daughter again? I . . . well, I couldn't. I'd have to believe I'd see my baby again."

He paused in his packing and looked at her. "Maybe because there's no 'again' to it. She was born while I was in North Africa."

"I'm so sorry. I hope your wife sent you a photo of her, at least."

"My wife is deceased." He rolled the doll in one of his undershirts and placed it in the bag. "She died when Melinda was born."

"I . . . I'm sorry," she said, completely derailed by the news.

He straightened, his gaze remaining on the bag. "Yeah, well . . . considering I'd been overseas for almost two years by that point, little Melinda is something of a miracle baby, you might say."

"Your wife . . ." Vi wasn't sure how to continue, the dots not connecting in a pretty line.

"Was steppin' out on me," he confirmed, sounding tired. "I guess she got lonely waiting for me to come home, as if I have any control over this goddamned war. Anyway, Clarice couldn't even stick around long enough to clean up her own mess. My parents, thank God, did. They stepped in, told everyone some cockamamie story about how I'd come home briefly on leave—very briefly—and that Melinda was really mine."

"And you're all right with that?"

He glanced at her then, his face haggard in the light of the single lamp. "Yeah, I guess I am. I figure we've both been wronged by Clarice, which makes us kin of sorts, by circumstance if not by blood. And, to my mind, no bitty baby should be made to suffer for her mother's mistake. After all, it's not like I haven't made a few myself."

Vi couldn't speak. Her heart was in her throat.

He laughed sadly. "I know what you're thinking. What a chump for hoping a little girl will remember me fondly after I'm gone, even though I'm not really her dad."

"No." Moved by his confession, by what had to be the kindest act she had ever heard, she stood and went over to him. He watched her warily as she raised her hand. She laid it on his bronzed cheek, the unshaved beard hair prickling her palm. Patiently, she waited for his gorgeous blue eyes to meet hers. When they did, her heart skipped a beat at the naked vulnerability she saw there.

"You are not a chump, Sergeant. You are the bravest, kindest man I've ever met. A girl couldn't do better for a father." Tears blurred her vision, and her chest constricted. "So no more thinking that, you hear? I won't allow it."

He caught her hand and pulled it down, away from his face. But he didn't let go. "You won't, huh?" Faint amusement colored his voice.

"No," she said in a fierce whisper.

He wiped her tears from her cheeks. "Not many people cry over me."

"Well, maybe they should."

"And maybe they shouldn't." He released her hand and started to turn away. "You can go now. Whoever was in the bathroom is done. I heard a door close."

"I don't want to go." The words, which were truer than she wanted to admit, were out before she could stop them. "I want to stay."

His gaze flicked over his shoulder at her, his eyebrows gathered in confusion. "Pardon?"

She untied the bow of her top and slowly let the sides part. "I said I want to stay. I don't want to be alone after everything that's happened tonight. I don't want *you* to be alone."

Not after everything he had told her about his wife, or his little girl, or how he thought he would die soon. She wanted him to live and to feel joy, even if only for a night.

Frank consideration stole into his eyes, and then pure male desire. Her pulse leaped, her need to touch him taking on a life of its own.

Then, to her distress, he shook his head and backed away. "No. It's late, and you've got a busy day tomorrow."

"Are you sure?" Her pride hated her for asking, but she wanted him so badly.

"I am." Gentleman that he was, he came over to open the door for her.

"Will you at least let me mail the doll for you?" she asked suddenly. "It might get damaged if you keep carrying it around. And I've likely got more free time than you do."

He paused with his hand on the doorknob. "No thanks. I guess I'm still hoping I'll get to deliver it in person someday." His smile was a little crooked as he looked down at her.

Perhaps it was the late hour or the recent shared confidences that broke down her reserve, or the tantalizing smell of warm male skin filling her head. For the next thing she knew, she was on tiptoe, kissing him. He didn't react at first, but she didn't care. This was for her and her alone, because she wanted to never forget him.

Then he began to respond, and all thought vanished.

Pleasure, as heady as the finest bourbon, flowed through her veins. She melted against him, lost in the embrace. His heat, his strength, his taste—it was everything and not enough. A moan of longing escaped her as his strong arms pulled her closer, tighter against him.

Abruptly, he released her, and a sudden, unwanted space opened between them. Her body tingled in protest at being abandoned, and she fluttered her eyes open.

He was staring at her. His expression was . . . enigmatic.

Reality crashed back with a vengeance. She had just forced a kiss on a man. One who had only seconds before turned down having sex with her. What on earth was wrong with her? If anyone found out, she'd be kicked out of the USO in no time flat. And who would blame them?

She swallowed nervously and backed up. "I—I should be going."

Her back hit the door, and she whirled around, fumbling for the doorknob.

His hand got to it first. "Virginia—"

"No! No, don't say it. I'm sorry, and it won't happen again." Tears spilled down her cheeks as she fought to open the door.

"Virginia," he repeated more forcefully, holding the door shut. "Will you please hold still and listen?"

Obediently, she stilled, but she wouldn't look at him. She didn't dare. Instead, she kept her wet face against the door. Her breath came in soft gasps.

"You're not in trouble, and I'm not angry."

"Then what are you?" she asked, her tears welling up again. Oh, why wouldn't he let her escape?

He exhaled a long, slow breath. "I don't know. Surprised, maybe? That kiss caught me off guard."

"I'm sorry," she said again.

"Well, don't be. It was . . . nice. But it can't happen again."

"No, of course not." Her heart fractured under the finality of his words. "I understand."

He bent down and snatched a bundle off the floor. She wanted to kick herself when she saw what it was: her uniform. Lord above, her brain wasn't working tonight.

"You'll need this," he said, handing it to her.

"Thanks." She held it against her chest as he opened the door for her. Not daring to look at him for fear of falling apart, she scooted out of his room and down the hall.

She had almost made it back to safety when the door to the room across from hers cracked open. She didn't need to hear the soft snores emanating from the room to know which roommate had caught her. There was no mistaking those cold, green eyes.

Frances.

The door closed again before Vi could speak, but it didn't matter. The damage was done. Vi was officially in deep trouble.

Chapter 28

"And that's all I have for notes," Sue said the next morning. "First call is two o'clock this afternoon, for the matinee. Then we'll break for dinner and reassemble at seven. Any questions? No? Then I'll see you all at two. And good job last night."

Vi stayed in her seat while the other cast members stretched and got up to leave.

So far this morning she had managed to avoid Frances while simultaneously keeping an eye on her. The good news was that Gertie hadn't treated Vi any differently this morning, which certainly would've been the case if Frances had said anything about last night. Gertie was one of the most morally upright people Vi had ever met. She would never have been able to look Vi in the eye if she thought Vi was breaking USO fraternization rules.

On the other hand, Vi wasn't exactly reassured by Frances's silence. For all practical purposes, Vi had handed her a loaded gun that could, and likely would, be used against her in the coming weeks. The question was when.

Someone tapped her on the shoulder. Springing to her feet, she spun around and pressed a hand to her chest.

Marcie's eyes rounded. "Wow, are you ever jumpy this morning. Everything all right?"

"Fine." Vi relaxed her shoulders. "Just a little wound up, I guess. I didn't sleep well last night."

"I didn't, either. All I could think about was having two shows today." Marcie shuddered. "I'm not sure I'll be up for the challenge. Just one show takes so much out of me."

Vi threaded her arm through Marcie's. "Remember to pace yourself and you'll be fine."

"That's what Ann said. Oh, and she recommended a little time in the sun this morning to work on our tans. She says nothing soothes the soul like soaking up the rays."

"Did she have a place in mind?" she asked as they exited the theater.

Unlike Caserta, there were fewer places with swimming pools for the cast to lounge around. Most of the villas in Rome were still occupied by their owners and had yet to be taken over by Allied officers.

"She said there was a Count Somebody-or-other who is so enamored with American theater and music, he's given a standing invitation to all USO personnel to use his tennis courts and swimming pool whenever we want."

"Which would be terrific except I have neither a tennis racquet nor a swimsuit."

"I'm sure he has extras of both."

Vi shook her head. "No thanks. I learned my lesson when I borrowed Ann's swimsuit in Caserta and my bust nearly busted the seams."

"How about we go shopping to find one that fits better?" Marcie said, undeterred. "I bet we could find something. There were a lot of stores where we were yesterday, over by the clock store."

Vi tensed at the mention of the shop, the sergeant's warning from the night before ringing in her ears. "Oh, I don't think so."

"Hiya, Marcie, Vi!" Gertie ran up to them, her army cap nearly falling off in the process. She resettled it over her pinned-up hair. "I was looking all over for you two. Are you going swimming with us? Frances just told me about Count—"

"So-and-so's pool," Vi and Marcie said together.

Then Marcie continued, "I want to, but Vi doesn't have a suit."

"Oh." Gertie's face fell. "Ann was the closest to your size, wasn't she?"

"And we all remember how well that worked," Vi said dryly.

"I suggested we go shopping this morning and find her a new one, since it sounds like we might be in Rome for a while." Marcie sighed dramatically. "But, alas, Vi said no. Maybe if you worked on convincing her . . ."

"Convince who to do what?" Frances asked, coming up to join them.

Vi's hopes for a relaxing morning slid away. "Nothing."

"Vi to buy a swimsuit," Marcie said, contradicting her. "I thought I saw a store over on the west side of the Tiber. There's a whole neighborhood of shops there."

"Oh, let's go," Gertie said, excitedly. "Then we can all swim together whenever we like. I don't want you left out, Vi."

"There are no ready-made swimsuits in Rome, thanks to the war," Vi said.

Marcie waved her hand. "You don't know that if you don't look. And we could look for postcards, since we never got around to it yesterday."

"Ooh, yes, postcards!" Gertie clapped her hands. "That would be perfect. It's my little sister's birthday coming up."

"And I know just where to look," Marcie went on. "There are the cutest little stores over by the Janiculum. It's a bit of a walk, but I hear they aren't picked over yet."

Alarm shot through Vi at the intrigued expressions on the other dancers' faces. "We are not going all the way to the Janiculum."

"Don't be so hasty, Virginia." Frances gave her a speculative smile that made Vi's skin crawl. "I think going on a nice walk sounds keen. Or did you have an appointment closer to the hotel to keep?"

Vi looked Frances right in the eye, irritated but not surprised by the innuendo. "No, as a matter of fact, I don't."

"Then let's go. And we can look for postcards and a swimsuit, too." Gertie was practically dancing at this point.

Marcie gave Vi a smug look. "Looks like you're outvoted. And you know how Sue feels about us going anywhere without our travel buddies."

Not wanting to get anyone started on that subject, Vi sighed and gestured for Marce to take the lead. Gertie joined Marcie at the front of their little group, and soon the two were chatting up a storm. Frances silently dropped back beside Vi. Large, puffy clouds drifted over the sun, casting chilled shadows as they passed. Vi suspected the girl was waiting for her to broach the subject of last night. But Vi knew when to hold her cards close. Now was one of those times.

Frances could think whatever she wanted, but she had no actual proof of any wrongdoing . . . unless Vi opened her mouth and gave it to her.

Twenty minutes of self-imposed silence later, Vi crossed the same bridge she and Marcie had yesterday afternoon. Vi scanned the street cautiously, worried Luciana might be hanging around.

Marcie, with Gertie in tow, made a beeline for the clock store, likely to show off some treasure she had found yesterday while Vi had been preoccupied with Enzo. A terrible emptiness opened in her soul as she remembered the feel of his little body in her arms, and she found her convictions weakening. Surely it wouldn't be that awful if they all went inside for a quick look around, as long as there was no talk of notes and watches.

The bells tinkled over the door as they filed into the store. Vi's gaze immediately sought out the corner where Enzo had sat with his button box, but it was empty. Disappointment twisted in her chest.

The curtain to the back room rustled, and Enzo's mother appeared. When she saw the four USO dancers, she froze. Vi did likewise. The woman's face, so pretty and smooth yesterday, was a mask of swelling and bruises beneath a layer of thick makeup. Vi's disappointment shifted into horror. Violence against women wasn't unknown to her—it was a regular scourge among strippers and prostitutes—but it never failed to shock her.

Worse, if someone had been willing to abuse the clerk this way, who could say what that person might have done to Enzo?

The woman visibly paled despite her heavy makeup. She immediately made shooing motions with her hands. Vi didn't understand the clerk's rapid Italian, but her tone made it clear she wanted them gone. Marcie, her eyes wide, responded in the same language, but far more gently, as she gestured toward the woman's face, clearly asking what had happened. But the clerk was having none of it. In a flurry of movement and words, she slowly backed them toward the door.

Vi racked her brain for the Italian words she needed. She no longer cared if the sergeant disapproved of them being there. Not when it was clear something was very wrong.

"Enzo," she blurted, interrupting the woman's tirade. *"Dov'è Enzo?"*

Where is Enzo?

The change was instantaneous. Whereas her skin had been pale before, a flush spread up the woman's cheeks, and her face tightened. Her blue eyes turned glossy with tears as she turned on Vi. Without warning, she snatched up a small clock off the table and hurled it at Vi. With reflexes honed by years of dancing, Vi dodged the object.

It crashed into the wall behind her, ending any further discussion.

Subdued and silent, the girls hastily left the store. Gertie jumped as the door slammed shut behind them. The OPEN sign was flipped to CLOSED in the following instant.

"Well . . ." Marcie looked shaken as the group reconvened on the sidewalk. Vi felt the same way. Something had clearly happened between yesterday afternoon and this morning, and the clerk obviously blamed them for it.

"We can still look for postcards," Gertie said uncertainly. "And there's Vi's swimsuit."

Frances narrowed her eyes at the storefront they had just left. "What was she saying about us in there?"

"It wasn't anything about you, in particular," Vi said, newly sensitive to Frances's irrational dislike of Italians. "Right, Marce?"

Marcie blinked and then seemed to give herself a mental shake. "She thought we had ignored the closed sign and was upset that we had barged in. But it turned out she had forgotten to turn it."

"Seems to me she could've just politely asked us to leave," Frances said, her suspicions still in full force.

"You're right," Vi said soothingly. "But she didn't, and we're all okay, so let's go find those postcards."

The group turned away from the river and wandered farther into the neighborhood. This time Frances and Gertie led the way, while Marcie and Vi hung back.

"I heard you ask what happened," Vi said softly while Gertie stopped in front of a fabric shop to ooh and ah over some lace in the window. "What did she say?"

Marcie's expression became troubled. "That we needed to leave before anyone saw us, and to never come back."

"That much was clear when she chucked the clock at my head. Did she say anything else?"

"No." Then Marcie grimaced. "Did you see her face? Someone really socked it to her last night."

"I noticed that, too." Vi shuddered, the memory of the shock and pain following a blow from a man's fist still fresh, even though it had been years ago.

Once, not long after Jimmy was born, she had been hit like that by a coked-up john. It had taken almost ten days for the bruises to fade, and a lot, lot longer for the fear to. It was one of the reasons she had given up the trade, despite how lucrative it had been. A girl could take only so much abuse before it left a permanent scar.

"Do you think we were the cause, somehow?" Marcie's eyebrows gathered in a frown. "I mean, it would explain her anger, but I don't see how we could've been. We weren't the ones who wrote that note."

"Maybe it wasn't us in particular but Americans in general. There are a lot of us in the city right now. Being an occupying army and all. Maybe us being seen in her shop is bad for business?"

"Certainly bad for her face." Marcie was quiet a moment. "I hope nothing like that happened to the little boy. Did you see her expression when his name was mentioned? Good use of Italian, by the way."

"Thanks." But the compliment did little to ease the dread building beneath her skin. "And I did see it, which is why I almost missed the clock."

"Do you think we should report it to someone? I hate to think of her being roughed up on our account. Maybe if we told Lieutenant Holland?"

Oh, no, no, no. Vi was not going to let Marcie pursue that thought. She had already dropped the ball once today by not insisting Marcie stay out of the clock shop. The last thing she wanted was for Sergeant Danger to find out how cavalier she'd been with Enzo's and his mother's safety. Especially after the fiasco last night. She was in deep enough trouble with him.

Vi shook her head. "I doubt the lieutenant could, or would, do anything. Couples get in fights all the time, even in the States, and the authorities typically refuse to get involved. No, I think the best thing we can do is take her advice and stay away from here on out."

"It's not right," Marcie said, an angry glint in her eyes.

"I agree, but we have to trust she knows what's best for her."

Marcie gave her a pained look but didn't say anything more as Gertie dropped back to ask if they wanted to go inside the shop with her.

⁂

Enzo's absence and his mother's bruised face were still troubling Vi that afternoon, even though the matinee show went off without a hitch. While the rest of the cast joked and laughed backstage, flying high on postperformance excitement, Vi kept an eye on the door leading to the auditorium. She half hoped, half feared that Sergeant Danger would make an appearance. If anyone could find out if Enzo and his mother were all right, it would be him. On the other hand, asking him to investigate would be tantamount to an admission that she had ignored his warning.

As she wiped the stage makeup off her face, she tried to tell herself that her only responsibility was to keep Marcie safe, and no one else. The partisans could watch out for their own, assuming Enzo's mother was one of them. Or perhaps Luciana would step in, assuming Vi was right about the note having been meant for the actress instead of Marcie. And if Luciana needed help, Vi was certain the sergeant would come to her aid, just as he had rescued Vi last night.

And if Luciana wanted to show her appreciation to the sergeant the same way Vi had, with lingering kisses and offers of sex, and if the sergeant decided to accept Luciana's offer, unlike Vi's? Then that was their business, not hers. All that mattered was that Marcie was in the clear.

Wasn't it?

Disgusted with the jealous drift of her thoughts, Vi tossed the cloth aside and stood. With any luck, Marcie would opt for a nap this afternoon instead of dragging Vi around for more shopping. The last twenty-four hours had left Vi exhausted and wrung out emotionally.

Not that she worried it would affect her performance. Put her in front of an audience and that was all the fuel she needed. It was like a surge of electricity through her veins. To leap, to flex and spin with the music was a drug unto itself. Each move propelled the next. Like turning straw into gold, dance transformed physical exertion into pure release. Nowhere else did she find the same kind of freedom, the same kind of joy.

It was after the show, when the applause was nothing but a memory and a steady tide of well-wishers demanded her attention—that's when she was afraid her exhaustion would trip her up and she would say or do something wrong. Like last night, when she had chased after Sergeant Danger and unleashed a whole torrent of unintended consequences.

It was with that thought in mind that Vi greeted the new crowd of soldiers that night. She did her utmost to focus on the man in front of her rather than let her thoughts stray to whether the sergeant had disappeared from Rome, or if Enzo was badly injured, or if she would see either of them again. These men were the reason she was over here. She would give them her best.

She had almost made it through the entire line when a disturbance at the door quieted everyone's chatter. An older, well-dressed man in tails was being detained by the MP at the door, and it was clear from the man's cold demeanor that he was unused to being denied what he wanted. Sure enough, after another few seconds of being lectured, he raised his hand as if to silence the MP, said something, and then walked right past him.

Vi was about to excuse herself from the private she was talking to when she saw Sue hurry over to intercept the man. The two fell into a deep conversation, and then Sue, instead of escorting the fellow out as Vi had expected, gestured toward Marcie, who was chatting with several soldiers of her own. Vi frowned in surprise.

"What is it?" Vi's soldier asked her, turning to look over his shoulder. "Some fellow being rude?"

"No," she said soothingly. "Nothing like that. But will you excuse me for a moment? And be sure to write down your mother's address and leave it with one of the stagehands. I'll be happy to write and ask her to send one of her world-famous pecan rolls to you."

The fellow smiled. "Thanks, miss. You gals really are the best for coming over here."

"I wouldn't have missed this for the world," she told him honestly. Emotion filled her throat as she shook his rough, calloused hand. "God bless you and keep you safe."

After excusing herself from the next fellow in line, she made her way around the small groups of soldiers and actors on her way to Sue. Civilians weren't usually allowed backstage until all the GIs had had their turn first. That Sue had directed him over to Marcie had set off alarm bells in Vi.

"Sue." Vi took the stage manager's arm and drew her to the side. "Who is that man? I swear I've seen him before."

She hadn't, of course, but it made her question sound less suspicious.

"Maybe you have." Sue's attention strayed back to the soldiers waiting to talk to the directorial staff. "His name is Sr. Conti, and he said he owns several businesses in Rome, one being a jewelry store. He said Marcie had brought in a watch to be repaired, and as he was going to be here tonight, watching the show with friends, he decided to deliver it in person."

Vi barely hid her shock behind a bright smile. "That's right! I remember the clerk saying it would be ready today."

Sue waved the information away impatiently. "While it was kind of him to bring it tonight, tell Marcie to apologize later to the MPs, will you? Their noses are a bit out of joint over him barreling in here, even if he is a friend of the prime minister's."

"Will do," Vi said with a mock salute, earning a small smile from the stage manager.

Vi waited until Sue returned to her conversational group before practically sprinting toward Marcie. There was no watch. There had never been a watch. Whatever reason Sr. Conti had for hunting Marcie down, it couldn't be good.

To her dismay, the man noticed her almost immediately. His dark eyebrows rose toward his slicked-back, snow-white hair as she immediately slowed her approach to something she hoped would seem more casual, unplanned. Marcie eyed her curiously, picking up on Vi's disquiet but apparently not the source. Vi guessed that meant he hadn't mentioned the watch yet, though why not, she couldn't begin to fathom. If anything, it only made her more nervous.

"Hiya, Vi," Marcie said, her smile open and easy. "You should come meet Sr. Conti. He's a big fan of our production."

"How do you do?" Vi asked politely, even though she would much rather kick him out of the theater.

"I am much better, Signorina, having made your acquaintance." He bowed slightly and smiled. Vi knew better than to be charmed, though. Despite Sr. Conti being a handsome man, with his intelligent, dark eyes and a fashionably thin, well-groomed mustache, she had met his type before. A little too suave, too debonair to be trusted.

"I invited Signorina May to come to my apartment later, to have some wine with me. Maybe you will come, also? To celebrate your beautiful dancing."

The heat in his gaze as it ran over her dance costume made it clear he thought more than just her performance was beautiful. Oh yes, Vi had indeed met men like him before.

Smiling with just the right amount of regret, she shook her head. "I'm sorry, but we simply can't tonight."

"Vi," Marcie protested.

"With two shows tomorrow," Vi went on, "we girls need to get our beauty sleep. Right, Marcie?" She shot her friend a stern look.

Marcie sighed. "Maybe another time, Sr. Conti."

"Ahimè," he said, pressing his hand to his heart as if wounded. "My night will be less pleasant now, but I will survive." Then with a laugh, he recovered and gestured toward Gertie. "And yet another talented dancer! Introduce me, *per favore?"*

He asked the question of Marcie, but Vi took it upon herself to answer. "I can do it."

She smiled sweetly even as she thought of different ways to rouse the MPs into action. Even if he was the self-avowed friend of the Italian prime minister, he didn't need to be backstage looking for female companionship. He was a wolf in gentleman's clothing and a clear threat to innocents like Gertie and Marcie. That he might also be attached to a dangerous mission only added to the problem.

"Grazie, Signorina . . . ?" Sr. Conti prompted as she led him over toward Gertie, who was, thankfully, near an MP.

"Heart," Vi answered, trying to catch the MP's eye.

"Signorina Heart," he said, leaning close, his voice soft, "may I call on you later? I would like to know more about America, and about you. Would you like to have dinner?"

"I wish, signor," Vi said, barely controlling the urge to roll her eyes at the predictable pitch. Romeos apparently operated from the same playbook no matter what country they came from. "But our stage manager is very strict about us not going out with men at night."

"I am sorry to hear this," he murmured back, his gaze already running appreciatively over Gertie.

Over my dead body, Vi thought. Whether he knew it or not, Casanova here had met his match. She was already sorting through possible scenarios that would get him tossed out.

As they approached, Gertie looked over and smiled, her face positively glowing with postperformance excitement. "Hiya, Vi. Who you got with you?"

"Gertie, this is Sr. Conti."

"It is a pleasure." Sr. Conti executed a small bow over Gertie's hand, and Gertie blushed. Vi tried again to subtly catch the MP's attention, but the dratted man was too busy watching Ann.

Sr. Conti raised Gertie's hand and gazed at it. "Such a delicate wrist, Signorina. It must be difficult to find a watch that fits properly. But perhaps you know this?"

"Oh boy, do I ever," Gertie said with a rueful laugh. "I'm forever punching extra holes in the strap so it won't slip off."

He laughed, too, and then said, "Perhaps you are the one who ordered a watch from my shop, then? I received an order with no name—"

"That would be mine," Vi jumped in before she could think twice. There was no doubt in her mind that the watch order wasn't Gertie's. The girl had been with them today at the clock shop and had shown no interest in the wares. "I didn't mean for you to come all this way to deliver it, though." She fluttered her eyes coyly. "That was very nice of you."

"Think nothing of it." He turned a warm smile on her, though she noted it didn't quite reach his eyes.

She took his arm, determined to get him away from Gertie now that the watch conversation was in play. If she had been more ruthless, she might have let him go on thinking the other dancer was his target. After all, it would have kept him away from Marcie, whose safety was Vi's real goal. But she wasn't that callous, or that despicable.

Pulling the fangs of dangerous men was a survival skill she had learned from her years at the club. It was tricky and required experience—something neither Marcie nor Gertie had.

"If you would be so good as to come with me, signor." She dimpled at him as she ran her free hand along her collarbone. As she had hoped, his gaze dipped to her cleavage, so amply exposed by her costume. She leaned in to give him a better view and whispered, "That watch was meant to be a surprise for our stage director. Perhaps we could agree to meet later, so as not to give away the secret?"

She had no intention of following through on that agreement, but he didn't need to know that. With any luck, the troupe would finish their Rome run and be on the road again before he lost patience and forced the issue.

A slow, sensual smile curved his lips, and she barely repressed a shudder. "I think that would be . . . most agreeable, Signorina Heart." He reached into his evening coat and withdrew a slim silver case. "I give you my calling card. Come any night this week and my servants will let you in. Come any later, and I may have returned to my villa."

"Don't worry, Sr. Conti." She gazed up at him through her eyelashes as she took the card and then tucked it discreetly into the top of her dance costume. "I will come. Surprises are so delightful, after all."

"Good evening, signor. Miss Heart." Wyatt's calm voice made Vi start guiltily. The disapproval in his expression made her feel two inches tall, but there was no way she could defend herself with Sr. Conti standing right beside her. To do so would undo all her hard work. "I hear from Miss May that you enjoyed the show. May I introduce you to the director? He would be pleased to hear your opinion for himself."

Vi held her breath, hoping the fellow would go with Wyatt. With her objective of securing Marcie's safety having been achieved, she no longer wanted him anywhere near her. But there was only so much a twenty-one-year-old woman could do when it came to persuading older men to move along. It was a power imbalance incredibly difficult to overcome without help.

"Grazie, Signor . . . ?" Sr. Conti raised an imperious eyebrow.

"Miller." Wyatt held out his hand. "And you are?"

"Stefano Conti." The two men shook hands as Vi committed his first name to memory.

If . . . when she saw Sergeant Danger again, she needed to tell him about Sr. Conti's visit.

"What do you make of him?" Frances asked softly, having come up beside Vi. Her features were pinched with suspicion and dislike. In this case, Vi actually agreed with her.

"Nothing good. He was trying to get Gertie to meet him later at his place."

"Not gonna happen," Frances vowed.

"He was also after Marcie, but I was able to shut that down," Vi replied, her gaze on Sr. Conti as he chatted with Mr. Stuart. "Tell you what: you keep an eye on Gert, and I'll do the same for Marcie. Something about him seems fishy."

"He's a horny dog. That's what he is. I've dealt with men like that before."

Vi glanced at Frances in surprise. "You too?"

The brunette's green eyes were stormy as she watched the man. "Men with money always think women without are for sale. Particularly the pretty ones."

"Sometimes they are," Vi said, thinking of her own past. "And if a girl is hungry, would you blame her for wanting to eat?"

Surprise flickered in Frances's expression, and then it hardened. "If she gives in, she makes it harder for everyone else. Because success with one girl means those jackasses won't take no from another."

"I doubt a single instance of success would lead a man to that conclusion."

"If you let a dog eat off the table once, he'll forever think it's allowed," Frances said coldly.

"Men are not dogs," Vi said.

"No, you're right. Men are capable of viciousness inconceivable to a dog." Frances turned and strode away.

Vi chewed on her lip, the revival of her painful past dimming her joy from the evening's performance. She had done what she'd had to. It was easy to say one would never stoop so low when one wasn't starving. But was Frances right? Had she somehow endangered other young women by her acquiescence? She would like to think she hadn't. It had seemed her only choice at the time, but had it been, truly?

Life wasn't always black and white. She had learned that in more ways than one. Sal was a good man who worked for horrible masters. Some of the nicest people she had ever met were other burlesque dancers, who took off their clothes for a living. Some of the worst were ministers who seemed more concerned with condemning people than loving them. Young men were considered heroes if they killed and slaughtered the enemy. A dancer could wear the skimpiest costume imaginable, but as long as she was of "fine moral character," no one blinked an eye, whereas Gypsy Rose Lee was called a whore even when fully clothed.

What was one supposed to do in such a crazy world?

"Penny for your thoughts."

Vi jumped and spun around, relief spiraling through her. "Sergeant Danger, you came!"

He frowned in confusion. "Should I not have?"

"It's not that. It's just . . . wait." Grabbing his arm so he couldn't disappear on her, she turned to find Sr. Conti. He wasn't there. Panic squeezed her lungs as she searched the crowd but didn't see him. "Where did he go?"

"Who?" Sergeant Danger asked.

"Sr. Conti." She went up on tiptoe to see if that helped. "He was just here."

The muscles of his arm flexed and turned to steel under her fingers. Startled, she glanced up. The sergeant's gaze was sweeping the area, his jaw set.

"What did he look like?" he asked casually, but Vi wasn't fooled.

"White hair, dark eyebrows and mustache, polished manners, not very tall."

"And you say he was here? Backstage?"

"He waltzed right past the MP, saying he wanted to meet us because he loved the play."

Sergeant Danger's eyes dropped to meet hers. "If you see him again, you walk the other way."

"Gladly." She hesitated. "But it might be too late."

"Why?"

She took a deep breath and steeled herself for his reaction. "Because I think he'll be back, because he was here looking for Luciana."

Chapter 29

If Vi had ever doubted whether Sergeant Danger had it in him to be a cold-blooded killer, his expression in that moment rid her of the notion. She actually stepped back, even though she was fairly certain she wasn't the one in danger.

"What makes you say that?" His voice was calm, but she could sense the coiled violence lurking beneath the surface.

With no reason to prevaricate, Vi rapidly relayed everything she could remember, right down to her telling Sr. Conti the watch was for her, and his subsequent invitation to visit his apartments. If she had hoped disclosing her quick-witted actions to protect Marcie and Gertie would help diffuse his anger, she was wrong.

Instead, he wordlessly grabbed her arm and began hauling her toward Mr. Stuart and Mr. Miller.

The two men stopped their conversation, their eyes widening as he approached.

"Miss Heart will be leaving with me," Sergeant Danger told the two men, addressing both and neither in particular. "Now."

Vi stiffened. "Wait a minute. Don't I get a say?"

Mr. Stuart drew himself up and glared at the sergeant. "No one goes anywhere unless—"

"That wasn't a request," Sergeant Danger snapped.

"Excuse me!" Vi angrily tried to pry his fingers from her arm. "But I'm not leaving my travel buddy stranded."

"Fine, she comes, too."

"Like hell she will," she said through her teeth. "Marcie has played no part in any of this, knows nothing about it, and never will as long as I have breath in my body. Do you hear me?" On this she would not budge. No matter the sergeant's plans for her, she would keep Marcie clear of them, even if it cost Vi her life. Marcie's safety came first.

Sergeant Danger pinned her with a hard look. Refusing to be bullied, she glared right back.

"Fine." The sergeant turned back to the two men. "Don't let Miss May out of your sight until you hear back from me."

Wyatt's expression was stony. "Virginia, if you don't want to go, say so, and I'll have the sergeant tossed out."

She bit her lip, touched by his concern but not sure her refusal would be wise at this point, since the situation was far more complicated than Wyatt knew.

"I think I should do as the sergeant asks," she said, praying that she wasn't making a mistake. What if Mr. Stuart took exception to her leaving with the sergeant tonight and kicked her out of the production? It had to look darned irregular, perhaps even scandalous.

Sergeant Danger apparently had no such worries as he all but dragged her toward the women's dressing room. "You have two minutes to change or you go as you are."

"Go where?" she said testily. After all, she wasn't the one at fault here. She hadn't asked Sr. Conti to show up tonight. "I think I have a right to know."

"Two minutes, Virginia."

The use of her first name silenced further questions. It reassured her that he hadn't forgotten last night and the fragile connection that had formed between them.

She quickly changed, switching from chorus girl to USO officer in record time. As soon as she had her hat pinned on, she bolted toward the door, her last costume still swinging on its hanger behind her.

Sergeant Danger was leaning against the wall, his brow furrowed in thought.

"Ready," she said to catch his attention. He looked up, and to her surprise the anger had all but vanished from his eyes. What remained were shadows and sorrow.

Her steps slowed. "What's wrong?"

"Ever hear the word 'FUBAR'?"

"Sure. Fouled up beyond all recognition, right?"

"Yeah." His laugh was bitter. "Though I would have used a slightly different word than 'fouled.'" He straightened off the wall. "Anyway, that's about where things stand right now, and I've got to find a way to fix it."

She hesitated. "It wasn't my intention to cause trouble."

"I know. But intentional or not, you've landed smack dab in the middle of something extremely dangerous." He gestured toward the exit at the back of the theater. "So let's go. There's someone who needs to hear your story."

"Who?"

He opened the door to the alley and glanced both ways. "Someone who can hopefully help get you out of this mess."

Stopping her at the curb, he flagged down a military vehicle, held a hushed discussion with the driver, and then helped her in. Ten white-knuckled minutes later—the pitch-black streets were even more terrifying when trapped inside a hurtling car—they were let off in front of a wrought iron gate. Up the driveway beyond was what looked like a large mansion.

A uniformed guard stopped them.

"We're here to see Major Ricca," Sergeant Danger said quietly. "And no, he's not expecting us."

The guard radioed to someone inside with their names and their business. After a brief static-filled moment, a disembodied voice gave permission for them to enter.

After the guard opened the gate, Vi preceded the sergeant onto the drive.

"Where are we?" she asked, a bit intimidated by the size of the house and all the guards.

"Nowhere I want you to talk about later." He put his hand on the small of her back and guided her forward. The pressure of his palm against her body both reassured and unnerved her. It was an oddly intimate gesture.

"Is Major Ricca your boss?" she asked, nervously glancing up at the blacked-out windows. No light peeped out beneath the curtains. No sound, either.

"I can't answer that."

"Can I know anything?" she asked, her temper sparking. "How about your name, at least? Your first name. That seems fair since we kissed last night."

"Do *not* mention that in front of the major," he said sharply, and with a touch of panic, even.

The irony of that, given she was in the same boat with her bosses, almost made her say something. But she didn't, pretty sure he wouldn't appreciate the comparison.

"Ansel," he said quietly as they climbed the front steps. "My name is Ansel."

She turned the unusual name over in her mind as they stopped in front of the ornately framed front door. Oddly, it fit him.

Vi took a deep breath and wrapped the security of his trust—for names had power; she of all people knew that—around her like a blanket. "Thank you. And mine is Violet."

Ansel gazed silently at her for a moment, his expression lost in the shadows. "That's a pretty name. I take it Virginia is your stage name?"

"Yes." She squeezed her hands together to quiet her nerves, not sure why she had told him, except that it had seemed right to. He had trusted her with so much of his past, and she had done so little. "My real name is Violet Ernte of Chariton, Iowa, but I'd prefer to be called Vi."

"Vi it is, then." He turned and knocked on the door. It swung open to reveal a heavily armed and uniformed soldier.

Showtime! Vi squared her shoulders as the soldier gestured for them to enter.

The soldier shut the door firmly behind them. "Major Ricca is in the study."

Ansel nodded and began escorting Vi down the hall, his hand once again on her back.

Maybe it's to make sure I don't run away.

She could see the appeal of trying to make a break for it. The environs screamed power and privilege. She tried not to stare as she took in the crystal and gilt elegance of the light fixtures, the polished oak wainscoting and thick felted carpets.

She may have been raised a banker's daughter and may be well able to hold her own at a formal dinner party, but more recently she had been a lot of other less socially acceptable things. What if they had somehow marked her?

"Relax and follow my lead," Ansel murmured as they stopped outside two paneled doors.

Her knees felt like they were made of water.

His expression gentled as he gazed down at her. "I've got your back, Vi. Don't worry."

"Who says I'm worried?"

His lips curved beguilingly. Then he sobered and knocked on the door.

A man's muffled voice came through the thick wood. "Come in."

Ansel opened the door, and Vi took a deep breath. Curtain up.

"Sergeant Danger, I wasn't expecting to see you tonight." A dark-haired man, with a thin mustache and graying temples, stood behind an imposing desk that was covered with file folders and stacks of papers. Dressed simply in a nondescript white shirt and patterned tie, his jacket slung over the back of his chair behind him, he looked more like an office worker than an army major. A very well-paid office worker, though, given the quality of his cuff links.

He smiled pleasantly at her while he waited for Ansel to close the door. "And you must be Miss Heart. I caught your unit's show last night. It was quite entertaining."

"Thank you." She returned his smile with the ease of an actress, even as shock raced through her. Had he and Ansel watched the show together?

The major gestured toward the two chairs across the desk from him. "Please, sit."

Vi sat, wishing she had gotten a better night's sleep or at least had given one fewer performance today. She was hardly at her best, and she had the feeling this man didn't miss much. Despite telling Ansel her real name, there was still a lot about her past she wanted to keep buried. She had a friend to protect, a USO tour to finish, and possibly a Broadway spot to claim, all things that could be ripped away from her if she wasn't careful.

While Ansel seated himself, the major settled back and regarded her intently for a moment. Vi fought the urge to squirm under his inspection. Even though she had changed, she was still sweaty and disheveled from the performance.

"So to what do I owe the pleasure of this unexpected visit?"

Ansel took the lead, as promised. "Sorry to intrude so late at night, sir."

"Please, no worries on that account." Major Ricca gestured to the piles of paper on his desk. "As you can see, I was hardly asleep."

Ansel took a deep breath and tried again. "There's been an unfortunate development. One I think you need to be aware of, sir."

"Go on." The major's tone was pleasant, seemingly unconcerned.

"Stefano Conti showed up backstage of *One Fine Mess*, asking questions tonight."

Nothing flickered in the major's eyes at the mention of Sr. Conti, but that didn't mean anything. Even second-rate actors could portray indifference. "There's no law against civilians attending a USO show."

"No, sir. But Miss Heart and her friends also received a note several days ago asking them to claim a watch. From his store near the Tiber."

The major's expression shifted almost imperceptibly, but Vi caught it. Vindication sang in her blood. She had been right about Sr. Conti being tied to the note somehow.

Major Ricca smiled apologetically at Vi and started to get to his feet. "If you wouldn't mind stepping into the hall, Miss Heart. The sergeant and I need to speak privately for a moment."

"You should also know that after I got the note, I went to that clock shop," Vi said, wanting to get her version told first, one that didn't include Marcie. "Because I thought the watch was Luciana's and wanted to do her a favor. Only there was no watch. And then the little boy there asked if I was taking him to the US. Even more surprising, on my way out, I saw Luciana in the crowd, heading toward that store."

Major Ricca paused and then sat down. "I see."

"But I didn't tell anyone else in the troupe," Vi said in a rush. "Nor did I tell anyone about the note being tied to the partisans. And for the record, my knowing wasn't Sergeant Danger's fault. I shouldn't have followed him last night, but I didn't know he was going on a mission or that we were going to run into enemy agents or that Ansel would have to kill them."

"The *sergeant* will get a chance to speak for himself in a moment, Miss Heart," the major said coolly.

275

Ansel shot her an annoyed look. Belatedly, she realized she had used his first name in front of his boss and had probably revealed a lot more about the botched rendezvous than he had wanted her to.

Good job, Vi, she thought, wanting to kick herself.

The major's gaze switched to Ansel. "Why do I not remember Miss Heart being mentioned in your report?"

Ansel shifted uneasily in his chair. "Because she's not in there."

"I see." The major's face was like a mask. "May I ask why not?"

"He likely didn't want to get me in trouble," Vi said, trying to draw the major's ire away from Ansel. "I wasn't supposed to leave the theater without my travel buddy."

Major Ricca pinned her with a hard look. "Again, Miss Heart, I think the sergeant can speak for himself."

"Miss Heart is correct," Ansel said calmly. "I didn't want her to suffer any repercussions for her unwitting involvement in last night's mission."

"Despite her being a possible security leak."

Ansel met the major's stare without flinching. "I judged her not to be one, sir."

"Major Ricca, sir . . ." Vi hesitated, not sure if she dared ask but also desperately wanting to know. "Forgive me, but is the little boy from the clock shop, Enzo, all right? He wasn't there today, and his mother looked like she'd been beaten."

"I'm sure Sr. Conti won't let any harm befall his only son," Major Ricca said, flicking her an irritated glance.

Vi blinked in surprise. "Son? Sr. Conti is Enzo's father?"

"He is." This time only one eyebrow rose. "Are you shocked, Miss Heart?"

"Only by the fact that he would ask me out knowing I'd met his wife."

"But I doubt you have. Sra. Conti is currently at their very nice villa fifty miles to the north of here, unaware her husband is in Rome for anything but business."

"So Enzo is his illegitimate son." She chewed on this new piece of information for a moment, and more pieces of the puzzle fell into place. "Which is why Enzo's mother panicked when her son mentioned going to the US, because if Sr. Conti found out she was going to take his only son"—she glanced up at Major Ricca for confirmation and received a slight nod—"out of the country, he would likely react badly. Perhaps even put her in the hospital this time."

"An interesting conjecture, Miss Heart."

"Not much of a conjecture if you had seen what he'd done to her face!" Vi felt her temper spark. "Nor is it much of a stretch to think she might have told him about Luciana and the watch ruse and everything else that might have been going on. Did you think of that? Why else did he show up tonight, fishing around for the owner of the mythical watch? No, scratch that. I'll tell you why. To warn off anyone who might be trying to take his son from him."

"Interesting," Major Ricca said, sounding anything but. "Assuming all that actually happened, why didn't he just say his piece and leave once he found you?"

It was a valid point. Vi considered her response. "I guess, if it were me, I would be curious as to what my mistress and son were planning on trading for their safe passage. So I might not show my hand right away. Because she had to be offering something of importance. Something valuable enough to get the US Army involved."

The major gave her an indulgent smile. "You have quite the imagination, Miss Heart."

She straightened as something else clicked in her memory. She turned to Ansel. "You told me you'd just come from up north. Austria, I believe. And Luciana's family, the ones she learned were taken by the Nazis, were also from the North, as I remember. And her cousin was a partisan . . . as was the redheaded woman looking for her that night in La Fiorentina . . . the one I saw last night in the stairwell. It all ties together."

Ansel's lips quirked, his expression seeming to be caught between dismay and rueful amusement.

Major Ricca rubbed his temples as if he had a headache. "Sergeant?"

"Now you see why I brought her here. Though, the good news is, it appears I'm the only one she's told that theory to."

"So far," the major said dryly. He turned back to Vi. "*Is* there anyone else you've told this . . . tall tale to?"

Ignoring the question, which was clearly meant to make her doubt herself, which she didn't, she returned to her real concern. "Major, this evening Sr. Conti made a point of singling out me and my friends. If he's a threat to them, I need to know."

"To do what, exactly?" he said, unmoved.

"Whatever I have to." She leaned forward in her chair, her patience running out. "Look, I know something is up and that it involves the clock shop clerk, Luciana, the partisans, and Sr. Conti. That I'm here tells me that it's serious. And as I'm in charge of Miss May's safety, either tell me what's going on or I investigate it myself."

"She has his card, Major," Ansel added. "Sr. Conti's, that is. He told her to come by anytime."

"He did?" The major sat back, his eyebrows raised. "That's wonderful news. Why didn't you tell me sooner?"

Vi looked from the major to Ansel and then back. "Why's that good?"

Ansel kept his eyes on the major, his expression tightening. "She's a civilian, sir."

"She's part of the army, Sergeant." Major Ricca rubbed his jaw. "But you're right. Who was that other gal? Miss May, I think. In an earlier report, you mentioned she speaks Italian. And as I recall from Miss Heart's conversation, Sr. Conti was interested in her friends, too. Perhaps we should send Miss May instead, given her language abilities?"

Vi jumped to her feet, horrified. "No! You can't do that. Not Marcie!"

Major Ricca flicked a glance at her. "Sit down, Miss Heart."

"He'll eat her alive. She has no experience with men. She'd be raped before you could say 'jackrabbit.'"

"I said, sit *down*!" The major's voice was like a whip.

Vi inwardly flinched but held her ground. "If you need someone to go, send me. I may not speak Italian, but I'm fluent in German—"

"Except we're not in Germany, Miss Heart." The major's face was starting to flush with anger.

"For the record, Sr. Conti seemed perfectly fluent in English," Vi continued, undeterred. "And I know how to defend myself if Sr. Conti should turn violent."

Ansel snorted at that, no doubt thinking of her lack of success last night. But that fellow had gotten the drop on her, something she wouldn't allow with Sr. Conti.

The major was quiet for a moment, his color returning to normal. Then he laughed softly. "You certainly don't lack for courage. And you raise several good points."

Ansel stiffened in his chair. "Sir, you can't be thinking—"

"She already knows more than she should and has even secured an invitation to Sr. Conti's private apartments, something our other agents haven't been able to do."

"She's not been trained for this," Ansel said a little desperately.

"Oh, come now, Danger," the major said, admonishing him. "We've been using civilians in more dangerous operations than this for months now. All she need do is seduce Conti into telling her where the item is. How hard can that be?"

"She's an innocent," Ansel ground out.

"Then we can use one of the other dancers. I believe your report mentioned another girl—"

"No," Vi interrupted. "The person you want is me."

Ansel's hand grabbed her arm. "No, Vi—"

She shook his hand off as she turned to Major Ricca. "If you need someone to seduce Sr. Conti, I'm your gal."

"Vi!"

She drew a deep breath, her heart breaking as she prepared to fall on her own sword. But it had to be done; she had to protect Marcie. "Actually, seducing men is something I'm quite good at. Far better than Marcie could ever be. Better than anyone else in the cast. Because, you see . . ." She couldn't look at Ansel, couldn't bear to see his reaction, his look of disgust. "I used to do it for a living. I was a striptease artist in Chicago . . . and a prostitute. So you see, if anyone could handle a randy Italian nobleman, it would be me."

The silence that followed her confession was like a knife in her soul.

No more Broadway dreams. No more touring with the USO. No more Ansel, because who would stay with her after such an admission?

But Marcie would remain safe and out of Sr. Conti's clutches. Vi likely wouldn't be around to keep her friend out of future trouble, but maybe she could find someone else to take over that duty for her.

"How about we just knock him unconscious so we can strip-search him somewhere more convenient than his apartment?" Ansel asked, his voice flat.

"Actually, I could help with that, too," she said, squeezing her hands in her lap to keep from showing her distress. "All I would need is some chloral hydrate, some strong booze to mask the smell, and a little ice to kill the taste, and he'll never know what hit him."

The major stroked his chin thoughtfully, seemingly unfazed by her confession. "Interesting. In fact, that might solve a number of problems. It will shield our contact in his household from reprisal, deflect suspicion from the partisans, and introduce what could be a useful level of confusion on his part. Yes. I like it." He picked up his pen to make a note on one of his papers. "I believe it was Giulia who said she knew someone on the staff of a local hospital who could be trusted."

Ansel turned on her angrily. "You do know what Conti will do to you if he figures out you're trying to drug him? You saw what he did to his mistress!"

"Don't worry." Vi waved the possibility away, even as a little thrill that the sergeant might still care about her warmed her frozen hopes. "I've slipped Mickeys to more dangerous men than him and always gotten away with it."

"When?" Ansel demanded, his arms crossing over his chest as he continued to stare.

She had opened her mouth to tell him about Tony when the major interrupted.

"Now, now, Sergeant. Didn't your mother teach you it's impolite to doubt a lady's word?" The major finished his note, sat back, and smiled. "I'm so glad Sergeant Danger brought you here tonight."

"Me too." Vi tried to smile back but failed, too aware of the grim soldier next to her. *Come on, Vi, you wanted to secure Marcie's safety, and now you have.*

She just hadn't expected it to come at such a high price.

"We'll just need to check out your story, take a look at your passport." Major Ricca folded his hands on the desk and cocked an eyebrow. "That shouldn't be a problem, should it?"

Vi shifted nervously. "I—I don't have my passport with me."

"I see. But all the information on there is correct, yes?"

"Uh . . ."

"I suspect it has her stage name on it," Ansel said coldly, not looking at her. "She told me her real name is Violet Ernte of Chariton, Iowa. But seeing as she also said she was a stripper from Chicago, maybe that isn't her real name."

Oddly, the major's smile deepened. "Don't be disappointed, Sergeant. I'm sure she has a dozen or so names."

Vi stilled, aware of a curious shift in the room's atmosphere. "Is it a crime to have more than one stage name?"

"Stage name? No. But that's not what we're talking about here, is it, Miss Heart?" The major's gaze sharpened. "Or should I call you Fräulein Ernte?"

Alarm bells rang in her head, turning her stomach to ice. "Wait! What?"

"Not that it matters." The major stood. "Thank you, Sergeant, for bringing this young lady tonight. I'll take it from here."

"Sir, I don't think—" Ansel began, also getting to his feet.

"Wait, what's going on?" Vi asked, glancing uncertainly between the men.

The major started walking toward the door. "What's going on, Miss Heart, is you're under arrest."

Chapter 30

"What? No! Why?" Vi's whole universe shrank to just those two questions. Her ears buzzed. This couldn't be happening. Maybe she had fallen asleep backstage and this was just some weird dream . . .

"Oh, come now, Miss Heart." Major Ricca gave her a disappointed look, as if he'd expected better of her. "A German-speaking American who just happens to intercept a partisan message, then shows up at the store and attempts to interrogate one of our contacts. When that fails, she then tails Sergeant Danger to a partisan rendezvous—"

"But that's not how it happened," she said desperately.

"A rendezvous," he continued over the top of her, "which was conveniently visited by not one but two SS agents, ultimately allowing her to save the day and gain the trust of the partisans—as well as Sergeant Danger here. And now that same young woman is more than happy to take on the task of seducing a dangerous man—one that is, perhaps not coincidentally, also of interest to the Nazis because he stole something from them—because, as she so readily admits, she has experience drugging men."

"I'm not a spy," she said, her voice shaking.

"Really?" The major cocked an eyebrow at Ansel. "Sergeant, what do you have to say in the matter?"

He sighed. "I was told the circumstances surrounding Miss Ernte joining the show were a bit irregular. An anonymous tip had a dancer fired right before the troupe left New York, and Miss Ernte was hired by the director shortly afterward. Sight unseen, as near as anyone could tell."

"I can explain that," Vi said, her heart beating wildly in a panic. "I know it looks bad, but it's not what you think."

"I'm sure it isn't, but I'll leave that to the interrogators to sort out." Major Ricca started walking toward the door.

"Wait," Vi said, desperate now. "Yes, I took Janet's spot. And yes, I'm here under an assumed name, but I can explain. It's not because I'm a spy. It's because I'm hiding from the police."

"As alibis go, that's a rather weak one," the major said as he put his hand on the doorknob.

"I'm not working for the Nazis. I'm . . . I'm working for the Mob."

A look passed between the major and Sergeant Danger, and the major returned to his chair and sat down.

"Tell me more."

Vi's breath released. The dam broken, she poured out her story about Tony's death, and Sal finding her this position, and her orders to keep Marcie safe from oversexed soldiers and the girl's own impulsivity, and how the whole reason she had followed Ansel the night before was to keep Marcie out of trouble.

Exhausted and finally out of words, she braced herself for the major's verdict. She couldn't even look at Ansel, too afraid of what she might see in his rugged face after this new revelation.

Someday she would learn her lesson and never again dream of redemption. Her bad choices in life had forever ruined her. She needed to just accept that.

"We'll need to verify your story, of course," the major said, finally. "Given the sensitivity of the situation, I'm afraid you'll have to stay under guard until we do."

"What is the Mob's real hold on you, Vi?" Ansel asked, startling her.

"Isn't avoiding arrest reason enough?" she asked with a careless wave of her hand, hoping he'd let it go. She'd shared enough secrets tonight.

"No." Ansel pinned her with a hard look. "I don't think so. If that were it, you could've skipped town, given yourself a new name, and started over somewhere else. The police would've had no real reason to pursue you. Not over a mobster's death."

"But the Mafia would have," Major Ricca pointed out.

"The Mafia thinks she's innocent," Ansel said, his gaze never wavering from hers. "Otherwise why employ her to guard Miss May? So, what is it, Vi? What are you hiding?"

"It's personal," she said almost reflexively.

"You're about to be executed for treason," he said coldly. "Is that really your final word on the subject?"

Executed? Vi's breath seized. She knew the major had drawn some wrong conclusions about her, but she hadn't realized how wrong. "I'm not a traitor. I love my country!"

"Then what is it, Violet?" The steely edge in his voice slashed what remained of her defenses. She didn't want to lose his good opinion, but she didn't want to die, either. "We can't trust you if you won't come clean."

She twisted her hands in her lap. "I . . . I can't just leave and start over. I have a son. Jimmy. He's five, and if I don't go back to Chicago, I'll never get to see him again."

"Well, shit." Ansel leaned back. He looked as if he'd been punched, and Vi felt her world crumble a bit more. "You have a son?"

"We'll need to verify that, too," the major said much more matter-of-factly. "Who's he staying with?"

She was torn as to which question to answer first. Her heart said Ansel; her brain told her to focus on the major.

"I do," she said, keeping her gaze on Ansel. "And before you ask, no, I'm not married. Never was. Jimmy was an accident."

Drawing a deep breath, she turned her gaze to the major. "If you need to verify that, too, I can give you the name of the adoption agency I used. I can also give you the name of his new family if you need it, but they don't know anything about me. And I'd like to keep it that way if I can."

"We can be discreet," the major assured her.

"All right."

The major handed her a pen and note card.

She jotted down the information needed and handed it back. "Now that I've told you everything, may I please go back to the hotel?"

"I'm sorry, but no." The major opened the door and gestured to someone outside.

Vi stiffened. "Major, wait! If you don't let me go back, who will watch over Marcie? I can't just leave her to her own devices. She'll probably be frantic and go looking for me."

"I'll take care of Miss May," Ansel said. "I'll talk to her when I pick up your belongings."

"But what are you going to tell her?" she asked, eyes wide. Somewhere over the past six weeks, Marcie's friendship had become dear to her. She didn't want to lose it over this.

He exhaled tiredly. "That you unexpectedly fell ill and I took you to the infirmary. Since the doctor doesn't know how long you'll be there, I was ordered to fetch your things. Is that acceptable?"

"Yes," she said, nearly overwhelmed with gratitude. He was under no obligation to lie for her. That he would gave her hope that he didn't hate her. "Thank you."

A soldier appeared in the door, and the major gave him instructions in a low voice. After the soldier nodded, the major returned his attention to her. "If you'll excuse me, I still have work to do tonight. Corporal Merritt will take you to your room."

Having been dismissed, she got to her feet. And then almost collapsed, her legs not wanting to hold her.

Ansel was beside her in an instant, his hand under her elbow. "I've got you."

The calm strength in his whiskey-rough voice made her want to cry. If only she were someone else, someone with no past, someone he could love.

Then her mind clicked on to something Ansel had said. What if it did take more than a single night to clear her name? Worse, what if it was never cleared? Someone needed to watch over Marcie, or Vi would be as good as dead herself.

Frantically, she sorted through cast and crew members, assessing dependability against the risk of asking such a favor. If all went well, she would be returning to the troupe, which meant she had to be careful what she said and to whom.

Then it occurred to her who would be perfect for the job: Frances.

The dancer was familiar with the darker side of men. She had a protective streak, which at the moment extended to only Gertie. And the gal was tough as nails and naturally suspicious of everyone. A perfect bodyguard.

The problem was Frances hated all things Italian, including Marcie, even though Marcie would insist Sicily wasn't part of Italy.

"Is there a problem?" Major Ricca asked, but Vi barely heard him.

Getting Frances to like Marcie might be like asking a leopard to change its spots. But what if she attacked the problem from the other direction?

"Vi?" Ansel's voice made her look up.

"I remembered something I need to tell Marcie. It has to do with the play and changes to the dance choreography. May I write her a quick note, in case I don't see her right away, and before I forget?"

"I don't see why not," the major said when Ansel glanced at him.

After she was given a pen and paper, Vi quickly wrote what she needed to, basically asking Marcie to warn Frances she might have to redo all the choreography if Vi was slow to recover, and suggesting that maybe she should also teach Frances Lydia's lines in case she came down with the "same thing" as Vi had.

Satisfied that the prospect of learning Lydia's lines would be enough to encourage Frances to keep Marcie alive for a few days at least, she handed the note to Ansel.

Ansel immediately gave it to the major, which came as no surprise—good thing she hadn't said anything personal, though what secrets had she left? After the major read it, he handed it back to Ansel, who folded it and tucked it into his shirt pocket.

"I'll have your gear here in the morning," Ansel told her. "Will Marcie know what all you'll need?"

"She should." Vi frowned. "Can't I have my things tonight? I don't want to sleep in my uniform."

He glanced at the major before replying. "I'm sorry, but no."

Understanding slowly dawned. "You're going to go through everything first because you still think I'm a spy."

"We take our job seriously, Miss Heart," the major said, making no apologies.

Ansel wouldn't meet her eyes.

Recognizing she had no choice in the matter, she nodded her permission anyway. "That's fine. Be as thorough as you like; I've got nothing to hide."

"Of course not." Major Ricca then turned to Corporal Merritt. "Miss Heart is ready to see her room now."

Her room turned out to be what likely had been a servant's room on the top floor. The armed guard by her door nodded to her politely, his expression as blank as the walls. He was a private, if she read his sleeve correctly. Likely the lowest man on the totem pole. Still, he had a gun, and she didn't, so the odds were in his favor, no matter his rank.

The corporal showed her in and then left her alone, locked in for the night. She looked around. As prison cells went, she supposed she should be grateful. Even though the room had been stripped of everything but the bed, the walls had nice wallpaper with darker patches where pictures had once hung, and there were blackout curtains on the windows instead of bars.

She switched off the overhead light, and the room plunged into darkness. Almost instantly, a queer claustrophobic feeling swept over her. It was as if all the air in the room were vanishing, taking her ability to breathe with it. A wave of despair and panic rapidly built within her. She groped her way over to the windows. Yes, there was a blackout order, but surely it would be all right to move the curtains aside if she kept the light off. She couldn't bear to be alone in all this blackness.

Pulling back the curtain, she immediately inhaled a deep breath and looked up. It took a moment, but then the familiarity of the night sky began to anchor her. Pinpricks of hope started to pierce her loneliness like tiny stars. She could tell from the shadows that the moon was on the other side of the building. But it didn't matter. Its gentle light was a constant in the universe, and would be the same whether it shone down on the soldiers in the North, or her family back home, or Jimmy asleep in his bed.

Her pulse calmed. She was still in a terrible fix, but she had talked her way out of being shot, at least for the moment. She had fought her way back from the brink before. She would just have to do it again.

Her resolve restored, she left the window. Tired beyond anything she could remember, she let herself collapse on the bed, uniform and all, and slept.

Chapter 31

"What do you mean, I'm free to go?" She stared at Lieutenant Holland, the unit's Rome liaison officer, in utter incomprehension. "Did Major Ricca agree to this?"

As much as she would love to rejoin the production, last night's fiasco was still fresh in her mind. The last thing she wanted was to be shot while "trying to escape."

Morning sunlight streamed through the window she had uncovered last night. She had been sitting on the bed, contemplating whether she should ask the guard to let her use the bathroom, when the door had opened and Lieutenant Holland had poked his cheerful mug in.

The lieutenant shrugged. "He didn't seem opposed. He said it was all a miscommunication and that you should get back to your unit ASAP."

"Really?" She couldn't quite keep the suspicion out of her voice. Something about the situation didn't smell quite right. On the other hand, did she want to stick around if she didn't have to? The answer to that was a resounding no. She needed to get back to Marcie.

But first things first.

She dragged her fingers through her snarled hair. "Let me ask the guard where the bathroom is, and then give me five minutes to freshen up."

The lieutenant looked puzzled. "What guard?"

"The . . ." She stopped and quickly reevaluated what she had been about to say. Had the major removed the guard before sending Holland up? If he did, then . . . "What exactly did Major Ricca say transpired last night?"

"That you were found wandering the streets alone, lost, and were brought here for assistance. While talking to the major, you began slurring and confusing your words, which made him think you were drunk. Then he found out from Miss May that you hadn't been drinking and were likely exhausted from the double performances, so he dropped all charges of drunk and disorderly and said to convey his apologies for any inconvenience."

"Swell." Vi rubbed her eyes, which still felt gritty from a poor night's sleep. "Well, I'll still need a minute or two."

"Of course," Lieutenant Holland said cheerfully. He politely got out of her way as she headed toward the door, his gaze roaming around the room. "Not much of a guest room, is it?"

Vi almost laughed but decided her energy was better spent getting herself ready. Less than ten minutes later, she rejoined Lieutenant Holland, looking far more respectable than she had. To her relief, no one stopped them on their way out. On the other hand, she didn't see Major Ricca or Sergeant Danger, either. Or her belongings.

Lieutenant Holland had a taxicab waiting for them outside the gate. Again, she half expected to be stopped by the guard as she passed, but he merely waved them through.

She couldn't imagine they had verified her story that quickly. Yes, there was a time difference between Rome and Chicago, but it went in the wrong direction. One in the morning here had been six in the evening there. Everyone would be home with their families then. Though, with the war on, maybe intelligence gatherers didn't get time off.

"Where on earth did you go?" Marcie whispered the moment Vi sank into the auditorium seat next to her. Sue was just getting everyone gathered for notes on last night's performance. "And why did Sergeant Danger stop by last night to get your things, only to return them this morning?"

"There was a snafu with communications," Vi said, deciding to use Major Ricca's latest story. "The MPs thought I was drunk and were going to throw me in the stockade but then decided I was merely exhausted, and here I am."

"Meaning they let you sleep it off," Marcie teased.

Frances leaned forward over the seat back, having sat in the row behind them. "The person you should apologize to is Gertie. She was beside herself this morning when you didn't show for breakfast, sure we'd have to change all the formations again."

"Shoot." Vi looked over her shoulder. "Sorry, Gertie! I didn't mean to spook you."

"That's all right." Gertie smiled, but it didn't quite reach her eyes.

Vi wanted to kick herself. She hadn't even thought of Gertie last night. Marcie, yes. Frances, yes. But not the one dancer who had apparently taken her absence the hardest.

Matt strolled up, a cigarette in his hand. Vi's nerves were so jittery at the moment, she almost wished she had one, too. "So you decided to rejoin us! Charlie was convinced you and Sergeant Danger had eloped after you two vanished last night."

"Oh, ha ha," Vi said sarcastically, even as she inwardly cringed. "Not even close."

Frances leaned forward again. "Didn't you hear? Vi got picked up by the MPs for drunk and disorderly."

"I did not!" Vi protested sharply.

Frances rolled her eyes. "Oh, that's right. You were just *really* tired, which is why you were slurring your words. Personally, I don't believe a word of it."

"Hey, it can happen," Matt said. "I was pretty all in myself."

"Yeah, Frances. Be nice," Marcie added. "Remember we're all in this together."

"If you'd give me a chance to finish," Frances said acidly, "what I was going to say was that, rather than being drunk, she probably got herself locked out of the hotel by coming home too late, and that's why she was picked up."

Which, despite coming from Frances, was a perfectly rational, much more innocent explanation than Major Ricca's.

"There was that, too," Vi allowed. "I'm forever without my key."

"That's the truth," Marcie agreed, and to Vi's relief, everyone laughed.

"All right, everyone," Sue said, taking her place next to the stage. "Time for notes."

While Sue began talking to the actors, Frances leaned forward a third time. "I told Gertie to stay away from that snake last night," she said close to Vi's ear. "And I told the front desk not to send any calls through to either our room or yours, so he couldn't renew his offer."

Vi briefly closed her eyes in thanksgiving. "Thanks, Fran."

"You're welcome. And you know, you're not the only one who cares about this show."

"I know, and I'm sorry I ever doubted you," Vi whispered back, surprised to find it was true.

"Dancers," Sue called out, and Frances sat back as Vi straightened in her chair. "I saw a couple of late kicks in the last number. Let's tighten things up. Otherwise, I think that's it," she said, glancing at her notes.

"No one leave," Mr. Stuart spoke up, startling everyone into silence. "I've been informed by the USO that we're to receive additional training in self-protection this morning. Apparently our unit will be moving closer to the front, and they want us prepared."

Sue turned to stare at her boss in surprise. "When was this announced?"

"Just now," Mr. Stuart said smoothly. "Instruction will begin back-stage as soon as notes are finished."

Ann and Matt looked at each other. Charlie raised his hand. "Should we change first?"

"Not necessary. The instructors wanted it to be as true to life as possible. So if everyone would please follow Mr. Miller." Mr. Stuart gestured toward Wyatt, who had taken up a spot by the edge of the auditorium, next to the stage door.

"Well, troops," Victor exclaimed, getting to his feet. "Let's go. Hup, hup!"

Marcie dropped back to Vi's side as the actors and Ann led the way. "Should we be concerned? I haven't heard of any other units being given extra instruction."

Vi shrugged, just as confused as the rest. "Maybe we're particularly hopeless?"

"I hope it doesn't mean our tour is going to be more dangerous than most." Gertie shuddered.

"If it does, we'll just be that much more prepared," Frances said, giving her a playful punch in the arm. "And think how useful all this training will be when we get back to New York!"

Consoling herself with that thought, Vi filed backstage with the others. What she would much rather be doing was taking a nap after last night. She still had a lot she needed to sort out, and she could think of no better place to do it than stretched out on her bed at the hotel.

"Well, well," Frances said under her breath. "If it isn't Sergeant Danger and a drool-worthy friend."

Jerked from her thoughts, Vi looked over toward where their instructors stood. Sure enough, Ansel stood talking to Wyatt, his arms crossed over his chest and his legs slightly apart. Electricity began to hum through her veins the instant his pale blue eyes met hers.

Oh yes. Drool-worthy, indeed, she thought. And likely mad as a wet hen at her.

"He certainly looks a lot nicer than Sergeant Danger," Gertie agreed, and Vi blinked. She had altogether missed the fellow standing to Ansel's left. Her stomach sank. It was the corporal from last night, the one who had escorted her to the "guest room." She really, really hoped he wouldn't say anything about that in front of the others.

Dread pooling in her gut, she hung back as the others moved ahead.

"We're going to divide into two groups," Sergeant Danger announced, his voice assuming a tone of natural command. As one, the unit fell silent to listen. "I want the following people to go with Corporal Merritt: Charles Cooper, Matthew Clark, Marcie May, Virginia Heart, and Sue Daldakis. The rest of you will be with me."

"At least we get to be together," Marcie whispered to Vi. "And I wouldn't mind practicing on Matt. He's such an ass some days."

"Ann doesn't think so," Vi pointed out.

Marcie sniffed. "Ann also admits to having bad taste in men."

Sergeant Danger's voice rang out again, quieting the chatter. "In deference to your performances later today, please take it easy. We'll be showing you various moves, but take care not to injure yourselves."

"What about us injuring you?" Matt asked.

Ansel smiled coolly. "Don't worry about us. Hand-to-hand combat is something both Merritt and I excel at, or we wouldn't be here to teach you."

With that sobering thought, the group split up.

Vi couldn't decide if she was relieved or crushed Ansel didn't put her in his group. Despite his betrayal last night—what had he been thinking, taking her to see the major like that and almost getting her arrested?—she still was drawn to him like a moth to a flame. Oh, why couldn't her body remember the horror in his eyes when she had revealed Jimmy's existence instead of his deep, soulful kiss?

The fact he had put her in the corporal's group should have been reminder enough. Except her gaze kept drifting back to him. She loved the confident way he stood, the quiet attentiveness he showed her friends when they asked questions, the beauty of his fleeting smiles.

"Miss Heart." Corporal Merritt's voice pulled her attention back to her group. "I'd like you to participate in my next demonstration."

For the next two hours, Corporal Merritt showed them all just how badly they were prepared for a one-on-one attack. Dread slowly suffused her as she realized how much she had overestimated her abilities. Even after he taught them how to disarm a person who had a knife, and one with a gun, and one who was bent on strangling them, her confidence in actually being able to do any of this against an infuriated Sr. Conti was close to zero.

She felt better when the corporal switched to more personal ways to disarm an opponent, particularly one bent on rape. This was right up her alley, though he did correct her knee-to-crotch positioning.

"As soon as you make contact, be ready to push, or he'll fall on top of you as he crumples," the corporal said.

He grabbed her and let his weight shift forward, to show what he meant. What happened next was pure reflex. The second she had felt his body starting to trap her, blind panic overcame her, and she fought back with an ear-piercing shriek. Next thing she knew, the corporal was on the floor, and her foot was raised to stomp on his family jewels.

Embarrassed, she stopped herself in the nick of time.

"Having some trouble over there, Merritt?" Ansel called from his group.

To Vi's relief, the corporal laughed as he picked himself up off the floor. "Nope. Just got caught off guard by a doll. Nice throw, by the way," he added, as he stretched to realign his back.

"Thanks," she said with a shaky laugh.

Matt put his arm around her shoulders. "I think if I go out from now on, I'm taking Virginia along to protect me."

The troupe laughed, and the exercises continued. Another twenty minutes, and they were done.

"Thank God," Sue said, looking uncharacteristically sweaty and rumpled. "I'm all for staying alive, but I was wearing far too much wool for this."

Wyatt raised his hand to get people's attention. "Everyone, go get some lunch and then report back here at one to get ready for first call. Curtain is at two."

"Ugh." Marcie fanned herself with a piece of paper she had found on the floor. "I don't know if I have two shows in me after that."

"Of course you do," Vi said, positioning herself to catch some of Marcie's breeze. "Soon as you get some food in you, you'll be ready and raring to go again."

"Miss Heart." Ansel's voice made Vi jump. "If I could speak with you for a moment."

Marcie slid her a speculative look, one Vi did her best to ignore.

She gave her friend a tight smile. "You go ahead, Marce. I'll be right out."

"Okay. Just don't disappear on me like you did last night."

"Not a chance," she said firmly. "You can trust me on that."

After everyone had left, including the directors, Vi turned to find Ansel and Corporal Merritt waiting for her.

She drew a deep breath. "Am I in trouble?"

"No," Ansel said. "It's about tonight. I need to brief you."

"So I guess my story checked out?"

"It did, and a note was sent to Sr. Conti indicating you would be meeting him tonight, after the show."

"Hence all the extra instruction this morning?"

Ansel hesitated. "Major Ricca doesn't like to send citizens into danger unprepared."

"And what about you?" she asked. What she really wanted to know was how he felt about her in general, but she was too afraid of the answer.

A small muscle flexed in his cheek. "I brought Merritt along this morning for an independent assessment of your abilities," he said, avoiding her question as usual. Her spirits sank.

"And . . . ," she prompted, her attention sliding to the corporal.

Merritt winked at her. "You passed with flying colors. Just remember what I told you about pushing away. And try not to scream. While that normally makes sense, in this case, you'll want to attract as little attention as possible."

"But what if I could use some help?" she asked, still not convinced she could handle Conti by herself, despite the corporal's confidence in her.

Ansel answered her this time. "You'll be out of luck. Which is why I'm giving you a chance to back out. You weren't trained or brought over for this."

"Was Luciana?"

He hesitated again, which was an answer in itself.

She exhaled. "So, yes."

"And no," Merritt said. "Miss Rossi is a special case. You have to understand we've a real dearth of people who speak Italian fluently and can be counted on to be loyal to the Allies. We tried using Italian citizens but had bad luck with people switching sides depending on who was paying more. Not that I blame them. When an armed force is razing your country, you don't really care if they are good or bad. You just want them gone."

Vi considered that for a moment. "And with Luciana having family rounded up by the Nazis, I bet she was eager to help the Allies out with more than acting."

"Actually, acting isn't far off the mark in intelligence work," Merritt said with a laugh. "One of our best recruits was a pro baseball player who spoke Italian like a native. His career on the baseball diamond had taught him to be cool as a cucumber under pressure, a skill that came in handy when he went behind the lines to interview Italian scientists on the state of Nazi weapon design."

"How wonderful!" Vi said, intrigued in spite of herself.

"What he's not telling you is the fellow also almost died," Ansel said darkly. "He was betrayed by an Italian businessman that we thought we could trust."

Merritt shrugged. "As I said, we've had some bad luck."

"You can still back out," Ansel reminded her.

She could, but . . . "I appreciate the warning, but I agreed to do this for a reason."

"Miss May can be kept in the clear without sacrificing yourself," Ansel said, his jaw tight.

"But what about the greater good? I heard you telling Mr. Miller that you were working on shortening the war."

Corporal Merritt hesitated and then spoke up. "Well, actually, not shortening it, per se. Not prolonging it would be more accurate."

"I don't understand." She looked at Ansel, hoping he would fill her in.

He sighed. "It's complicated. In a nutshell, Sr. Conti stole a map that shows the location of nearly a ton of gold."

"Which itself was stolen from the Bank of Italy right before the Germans pulled out of Rome," Corporal Merritt added. "As far as we can tell, the gold is still in Italy, and we'd like it to stay that way."

"As would the partisans, I'm assuming." Vi rubbed her neck, finding the whole thing hard to believe. "And I'm also guessing the Germans know about the map, hence the two SS agents trying to track you and the partisans down the other night?"

"The Third Reich is running out of money, which is reducing their ability to wage war," Ansel said by way of an answer. "But if they get their hands on that gold . . ."

He didn't have to finish. She got the picture.

She drew a deep breath. "Okay. So I'm to go in, knock Conti out, and find the map. Fine. Do you have anything else I can work with, like a description of the map or a possible hiding place?"

"The partisans have already searched his apartments from top to bottom. They also mugged him one night, but no joy. We're assuming he still has it, though, because he's been in contact with a banker in Switzerland."

"But it might only exist in his head," Vi pointed out.

Ansel hesitated. "Perhaps, but we've reason to believe he wears it on him somehow. Apparently not in his wallet or in his pockets, so perhaps somewhere more . . . intimate."

"Which is why you mentioned a strip search last night." She thought about that for a moment. "Has anyone actually set eyes on this map?"

"Only once," Ansel said, sounding frustrated. "While my unit did intercept a courier sent from Generalfeldmarschall Kesselring to his private banker in Switzerland, the fellow escaped when a German patrol ambushed us, taking his pouch with him. When we came across him again, several days later, he was dead, and the map was gone."

"So how do you know Sr. Conti has it?"

"We don't. But he did recently hire twenty-some laborers in the area of Monte Soratte, which—perhaps not coincidentally—is the rumored burial place of the gold. There's a bunker built into the top of the mountain, one that Kesselring used as a German command post for several months before pulling out. Locals said they saw cartloads of gold bars go in but never out. In addition, Kesselring ordered several sections of the bunker destroyed before leaving."

"And where's this *monte*?" Vi asked, still not sure she was following Ansel's logic.

"Thirty miles north of here." Ansel paused. "We also know a good friend of Conti's was recently killed under suspicious circumstances and that this good friend was friends with Kesselring's banker."

"And where there's smoke, there's fire," Vi said, the connection starting to become clear. "So why not skip the map and search the bunker?"

"Because, while we think that's where the gold is, we don't know for sure. Nor can we wait Conti out, since the Nazis are getting desperate. The only thing saving him from being kidnapped is his connection to the prime minister."

"Which won't protect him much longer if the survival of the Third Reich is at stake," Vi said.

"We're running out of time," Ansel agreed. "But that still doesn't mean you need to do this. We can find other ways to get the map off Conti."

Vi looked away so he wouldn't see the sudden rush of tears in her eyes. That he was willing to risk letting it fail rather than see her get hurt gave her hope. Perhaps he didn't hate her after all.

"You say you'll keep Marcie safe," she said, needing one last piece of information before she threw her life away. "But what of Luciana? It occurs to me that she could take my place, though I wouldn't wish this role on anyone."

"Miss Rossi already tried to befriend Conti," Corporal Merritt said. "And failed."

"So there really is no one else but me," she said, her hopes fading.

"Violet." Ansel's voice was a low, husky plea. "Don't go tonight. Walk away. No one will blame you."

Vi's heart squeezed with regret and longing. She glanced up at Corporal Merritt. "May I talk to Sergeant Danger alone, please?"

Merritt checked his watch. "How long do you need? We've got to get back to HQ."

"Five minutes, tops."

"Okeydokey." Merritt gave her a brief two-fingered salute. "I'll wait outside."

He winked at Ansel and then strolled off, whistling "I'll Be Around."

"Corporal Merritt has a funny sense of humor," Vi said as she watched him disappear through the door.

Ansel touched her arm. "Vi, I'm serious. Walk away."

She barely repressed a shiver, her whole body responding to his proximity. "If I do, will the gold fall into Nazi hands?"

"Maybe. Maybe not. The whole thing could be a wild-goose chase."

"Or the map could be in Conti's underwear. It's a possibility we can't ignore. I want this war over."

"As do we all. But did you ever stop to think there might be people better trained to handle this kind of situation? Or do you think you're somehow expendable, so it's okay to run in and get killed?"

"Well, I . . ." She blinked, the accusation catching her off-balance.

"Dammit, Vi." He took her by the shoulders and gave her a gentle shake. "You are *not* expendable. Get that out of your head, you hear? People care about you."

She shoved him away, anger and confusion sparking within her. "Well of course they do. But that doesn't mean my life is more important than anyone else's."

"No, but it also doesn't mean you have to jump in front of a bullet if you don't have to. Committing suicide is not a path to redemption."

She searched his face. "What are you talking about?"

"I watched you tear yourself apart last night, and for no good reason." He gripped her shoulders again when she started to shake her head in disagreement, and forced her to look at him. "Do you honestly think you're the only person who's made a mistake in his life? Or has let his parents down or done something he regretted the next day?"

She scoffed. "I slept with my sister's future fiancé and got pregnant. Tell me how I could've done anything worse!"

"I can think of a lot of things, actually. But let's focus on your son. What did you do?"

She looked away as a wave of pain and longing washed over her. "I gave him up after he was born. I—I couldn't give him the life he deserved."

"That sounds like the decision of a good person to me. And what about your sister?" he asked gently.

"I—I don't know. I left home and never went back. I write to my parents every few months so they won't worry. And I wrote an apology to Fern. But since I claimed to be on the road performing all the time, I never gave them a return address."

Yet, according to Sal, her father had tracked her down anyway. But how?

"So you have no idea if she forgave you or not?"

Her stomach twisted in horror at the thought. "I never told her the whole story! What kind of monster do you think I am? I didn't want her to hate Robert. I just wrote that I hoped she would forgive me for leaving without saying goodbye and that I wished her a wonderful life."

"Meaning she has no idea what kind of man she married," he said flatly.

"What? No. I was the one at fault. I was the one who seduced him. I thought Fern was through with him, and he was older and good looking, and I was tired of being overlooked—"

"And you were how old?"

She paused, a little alarmed by the set to his jaw. "Fifteen."

He cursed under his breath. "And how old was what's his name?"

"Robert," she said in a small voice. "Twenty-two."

"Jesus, Vi. You were a baby! He had no business romancing you. I don't care if you threw yourself naked at him—he should've walked away."

She straightened her spine, back on more familiar ground. "I was not a baby. Clearly not, since I was able to get pregnant."

With a frustrated sound, he tightened his fingers on her upper arms. "Stop blaming yourself for something that wasn't your fault."

"But I was there. I should've said no," she cried, tears blurring her vision. "Why are you defending me?"

"Because you need defending. And I can see you gearing up to remind me you were a stripper—"

"*Am* a stripper. I didn't quit the profession; my show was closing."

"Will you be quiet?"

"And don't forget I was also a prostitute." Her tears began falling in earnest. "Did I leave that sin out last night? Because I shouldn't have."

"Violet—"

"And I just turned twenty-one! How am I ever going to top myself?"

He kissed her, hard and without warning, silencing her.

Startled, she went still. Then the wondrous reality soaked in, and she closed her eyes. Oh, Lord, how she loved the feel of his mouth on hers. She loved his smell, his heat, the strength of his fingers digging into her arms.

Abruptly his kiss gentled and turned more coaxing. Teasing. And she decided she liked this version even better. She let her lips part, let her tongue touch his, and then lost herself as he pulled her tight against him, his mouth utterly bewitching her.

It was wrong, she knew. She shouldn't let him kiss her like this. Not in public. Not when anyone could walk in on them. He would be severely reprimanded; she would be sent home in disgrace. But, oh—to pretend she was loved by one such as Ansel. Desired, even, despite her past, in all its horridness, having been exposed to him.

Too soon, he broke the kiss and pulled back. She moaned in frustrated dismay. He leaned his forehead against hers and inhaled shakily. She understood, having been just as shaken by the kiss.

"Vi—" His breath was warm on her skin. "Please. I can't let you go to Sr. Conti's tonight."

It took a second to pull her wits around her. For his words to make sense. She backed out of his arms, needing space to think. Otherwise she wouldn't be able to get beyond wanting to kiss him again.

"No, Ansel." Vi squared her shoulders and inhaled deeply. Exhaled. "This is my chance to do something bigger than myself. To make a real difference in this war. If I don't go tonight, I will never forgive myself."

"You don't forgive yourself as it is, so what would be the difference?" he said, frustration turning his tone rough.

He was right, of course, but also so wrong. There was a difference. Wasn't there?

Suddenly exhausted, she closed her eyes. It was all too much, this emotional whipsawing of the last twenty-four hours. And it all began and ended with this man in front of her. "Go away."

"Vi . . ."

The desperation in that one word tore at her.

"Please." Her voice broke, her endurance at its limit. "Just go away."

There was a taut silence. "All right, I'll go. And I'll tell Major Ricca it's a green light."

Her eyes flew open at the tone of finality in his voice. "Will I see you again?"

He shook his head. "My role in the mission is over. I was supposed to head out this afternoon to rejoin my unit."

"But you're still here?"

"I asked to stay, hoping to talk you out of tonight." His gaze touched on her face and then stayed as if memorizing it. "But having failed that, I guess I also wanted to say goodbye."

Her heart squeezed, the pain making it hard to breathe. "Goodbye, then."

He nodded, hesitated, and then turned away.

You don't forgive yourself . . .

His accusation had hurt. But it was true, if she was honest with herself.

And she also wasn't the only one with that failing, she realized.

"Ansel, what was your wife's name again?"

He stopped but didn't turn around. "Clarice. Why?"

"You can't keep blaming yourself for Clarice's actions," she blurted out before she could think better of it. "You know that, right? She was the one at fault. No one else."

He was silent a moment and then glanced over his shoulder at her. "And I would say the same to you. That Robert fellow? He was a grown man, Violet. I wish you could get that through your head. He knew better than to touch you, but he did anyway. *He* was the one who failed, not you. He and he alone."

He was the one who failed . . .

She blinked as the words sank in. Something shifted in her soul, and it was as if a strap had been cut, and a weight on her conscience dropped away. Not all, but enough she felt dizzy from it. All these years she had shouldered the blame alone, thinking she had orchestrated her own seduction. Not once had she questioned Robert's culpability. Nor had anyone else. Not even Sal.

Why was that?

Ansel drew a deep breath. "I gotta go. Be safe, you hear?"

At a loss for words and unable to do the one thing he wanted, she bit her lip as he turned and walked out of the theater . . . and out of her life.

Chapter 32

"Are you feeling all right?" Gertie asked Vi as they came off the stage, the applause still in full force behind them. "You look really pale. Maybe you should skip greeting the soldiers tonight."

"No, I'm fine." Vi called on the last of her acting reserves to fake a smile. "I didn't get much sleep last night, and I'm starting to feel it is all."

Gertie's brow remained furrowed with worry. "Okay. But if you're getting ill, you really should go back to the hotel."

Guilt tugged at Vi's already-frayed nerves. Gertie's concern for her was so sweet and yet so misplaced. "I'm fine. Truly."

Just worried about tonight's mission, she thought.

No matter how blasé she tried to be on the outside, inside she worried that the mission wouldn't go well. That she would never again play in this theater, or in Rome, or even in a USO show.

A sense of nostalgia descended over her as the unit gathered backstage, readying themselves to meet well-wishers. She found herself trying to absorb every detail of the theater as she waited. The people, the sights, the sounds, the smells—even the bad ones like stale sweat—all seemed suddenly precious. This next half hour among these dear people might well be her last. That knowledge bade her to cry even as she prepared herself to smile.

Because the soldiers filing backstage deserved it.

A gentle tap on her shoulder startled her.

"Signorina," a woman said softly. It was the redheaded partisan from the other night. She was dressed in a uniform similar to the one Vi usually wore, only without any patches or pins, her hair pulled into a smooth twist. "It is time."

Vi glanced anxiously toward Sue and then Mr. Stuart. They were already meeting the first of the soldiers and paying her no attention. In fact, in a stroke of good fortune, the entire cast was similarly engaged.

As unobtrusively as possible, she eased back toward the dressing rooms. The partisan stuck close, and once they were beyond prying eyes, she handed Vi a satchel. "I hope this will fit. I had to guess your size."

Vi hurriedly opened the satchel, and a gorgeous, sleek sheath of a dress in rich gold silk fell out. She held it up and all but purred at the deep vee in the back and the single chain of rhinestones at the top to hold the shoulders together.

Sr. Conti would never know what hit him.

"It was my sister's," the redhead said. "She sang at Riccardo's nightclub before the war. She was very good."

Vi paused, catching the use of past tense. "Your sister is . . . ?"

"Not dead." A deep sadness shadowed the partisan's light-brown eyes. "But not alive, either. She was raped by German soldiers. Many times. So she lives, but doesn't. She used to sing but now doesn't even talk."

"I'm so sorry!"

The partisan shrugged. "It's the way of war, yes? Before I had no politics. Now I live only to see the Nazis driven from Italy."

"I can't even imagine . . ." If Fern had been brutally raped to the point of no longer speaking, Vi would be consumed with thoughts of revenge. No, not just thoughts . . . acts of revenge.

Vi reached out to the partisan and hesitantly took the woman's hand. "Thank you for loaning me her dress. I won't fail you, or her. I promise."

The woman took a deep breath. "Grazie, but you must hurry. Sr. Conti is waiting for you, and he is not a patient man."

Catching the hint, Vi quickly peeled out of her dance outfit and hung it up with care, on the off chance she would be back. No, that was defeatist talk. She would be back. To think otherwise would have her sobbing, and she couldn't afford the waste of time or energy. Not now.

Sternly telling herself to stay on task, she slipped the cool silk dress over her head.

Thankfully, Vi and the partisan's sister were not far off in size. It was a tad snug over her bust and hips but not as bad as it could've been.

Appreciation lit the redhead's eyes when Vi turned around. "Very nice. Sora would approve. You look like what Americans say, 'a hundred bucks.'"

Vi smoothed the fabric over her hips and felt another twinge of nerves. "While a hundred bucks is swell, I'd rather look like that ton of gold."

"Or at least a map leading to it." The partisan handed Vi a pair of earrings, the paste emeralds set off by diamond rhinestones.

Putting the earrings on, Vi eyed the rest of her ensemble in the mirror. It wasn't perfect—her dance shoes weren't nearly fancy enough—but it would do. As long as Sr. Conti had a pulse, she would succeed.

Together they sneaked out of the dressing room and through the door leading to the alley behind the theater.

"Riccardo will drop you off at Sr. Conti's. There, Minta, who is also one of us, will take you upstairs," the woman said as they picked their way past puddles and trash. "After Sr. Conti greets you, please ask for dinner. He may be reluctant, so please insist."

They had reached the end of the alley, and the partisan peered down the dark street. "When Minta brings the food, Sr. Conti will be distracted, and that will be your chance to fix his drink. You will have forty-five minutes, complete, to find the map. Then Riccardo will take you back to the hotel."

"Why only forty-five minutes?" Vi asked, inwardly calculating how much time would be eaten up waiting for the drops to take effect. "I might need more if the map isn't on him."

The woman glanced at Vi, her expression unreadable in the dark. "We were asked not to keep you out past midnight. Signorina Rossi will distract your superiors until then, but longer than that, she could not promise."

"Luciana is back?" Vi stared at the woman.

"*Sì*. She could not get Sr. Conti to see her, so she returns to your unit tonight. Sergeant Danger did not wish you to get in trouble, so she is helping to blind the USO to your disappearance."

Vi hadn't even thought to cover her tracks tonight, she had been so worried about the particulars of the mission. Thank goodness for Ansel! And Luciana, too. That two people she greatly admired would go out of their way to protect her did her spirits a world of good. She wouldn't let them down, even if she had to rip open every seam of Sr. Conti's underwear.

A delivery truck appeared out of the shadows, the engine growl echoing off the surrounding buildings. Vi's heart leaped with excitement and nerves.

"Ah, here is Riccardo. Quick, you get into the front. I will see you later."

The truck stopped at the curb in front of them. The idling engine seemed impossibly loud in the dark silence.

"Signorina Heart," a man called softly after popping the door open for her. "*Buonasera*. Get in, please. I am Riccardo."

Vi took a deep breath and then hopped in as best she could in the tight sheath. "Buonasera, Riccardo."

He watched her with pale eyes that seemed older than the rest of his angular face. His smile, though, was genuine and warm as he nodded in greeting.

The woman closed the door behind Vi. "Good luck, Signorina Heart. *In bocca al lupo!* 'Into the wolf's mouth,' as we say."

"May it die," Vi said back, giving the correct response to the Italian good luck saying. Thank goodness for Marcie, or she would've been at a complete loss.

Riccardo pulled away from the curb, and soon the theater was lost in the shadows that shrouded the streets each night. Vi wondered if she would ever see it again.

"How are you feeling tonight?" Riccardo asked her in surprisingly clear English as he turned onto the wide avenue leading to the outskirts of town. "Nervous?"

"A little." Actually more than a little, which meant it was time for a distraction. "Do all the Roman partisans speak English?"

"No." Riccardo shifted gears to get a bit more speed. Not that Vi thought it advisable. But the partisan drove with complete confidence despite the lack of light, celestial or otherwise. She decided he must have nerves of steel. "Only some. For instance, I owned a nightclub in Rome before the war. We had visitors from all over the world, so I thought it a good idea to learn many languages.

"Alessandra, the woman who helped you tonight, she was a nanny for diplomats. So she has knowledge of English too."

"She said her sister used to perform at your club."

"Yes, Sora. She was *magnifica*. A wonder. When she was injured, Allie and I swore revenge. And Allie, she is magnifica as well."

"She is," Vi agreed, wondering if there was more than a working relationship between the two. She hoped they would both survive the war.

Riccardo slowed as they went through an old stone arch. They were leaving ancient Rome. "Did Allie tell you that you have less than an hour?"

"She did. Do you have any idea what the map looks like? How big is it? What is it printed on?"

"I cannot help you with that. The person to ask would've been your Sergeant Danger. He is the one who has been chasing it all across Italy."

"So I heard."

"We know it was being carried by a German courier through the Alps, so perhaps not so big. And the general location is not a secret, so it needn't carry a lot of information."

"Ansel mentioned as much. What he didn't explain is why the partisans don't just search the bunker now that it's in Allied hands?"

"Because it is not small, this bunker. The tunnels run for many kilometers, and Kesselring destroyed many rooms before leaving. We can dig them out, to be sure. But to do so without a map, we might as well tear down the whole mountain, which would take years."

"I see." She imagined all the ways such information could be conveyed and tried not to be dismayed. Then she frowned. "What was Kesselring hoping this map would accomplish if the bunker is in Allied hands?"

"He was sending his friend, a Swiss banker, to recover it, under a false name, no doubt. Sergeant Danger said Kesselring is one of many who think the Third Reich will lose. Perhaps he hopes to retire in South America as a wealthy man."

"But wouldn't moving gold on Kesselring's behalf violate Switzerland's neutrality?"

"Who is to decide?" Riccardo stopped the truck and cut the engine. "Swiss banks are open to everyone, and in truth, many Swiss are sympathetic to their German cousins' plight. And then there is greed, which makes men do strange things."

He reached into his jacket and removed something. In the shadowy darkness it was difficult to tell what, other than that it was small. He held it out. Hesitantly, she took it from him. It was a glass vial. "The liquid you requested. We were not able to get much. The hospital is very careful with its chemicals, given the war."

"I don't need much." Vi slipped the vial into her handbag next to her passport. "Thank you."

"No, thank *you*. If you retrieve the map, all of Italy will be in your debt."

A door opened in the building next to them, the dim light spilling into the street.

"Ah, there is Minta. She will take you upstairs. I will be back when you are through."

The slight woman, outlined by the light, made a hurry-up gesture. Not wanting to start off on the wrong foot, Vi climbed out of the truck as gracefully as she could, given her dress, and hurried toward the light.

There was no more time to worry about the war, or Ansel, or anyone else. All that mattered now was the next half hour's performance. She was as prepared as she could be for a role she had asked for. A role she had spent the last few years honing the skills for without knowing it.

And now it was showtime.

Chapter 33

"Forgive me for not sending my driver to pick you up," Sr. Conti said as he escorted Vi into his living room. "But your note said you needed to be discreet."

"I do, so there's nothing to forgive." She gave him a dazzling smile, wanting to stop any further discussion of how she had gotten there. Then, to further distract him, she turned her attention to the lavish decorations of the room. People, wealthy or poor, always enjoyed having their belongings remarked upon, at least in her experience. "Your apartments are lovely!"

It wasn't a lie. Minta had led her past several rooms, all with high ceilings and tile floors, on her way here. More oil paintings than she could count hung on the walls. The crystal light fixtures sparkled as if all dust had been banned from the place. The garnet-red carpet that ran the length of the hall, likely the cheapest thing in the apartment, was as plush as a mink coat.

"I'm glad you like it," Sr. Conti said, clearly charmed by both her smile and her appreciation of his taste. "But none of its beauty can compare to you, Signorina Heart. Or may I call you Virginia?"

"I prefer Vi."

"And I prefer Stefano." He captured her hand and brought it to his lips. She shivered slightly as his mustache tickled the back of her knuckles, but at least the kiss itself was dry, polite.

He let her hand go and smiled. "I'm so glad you decided to come tonight. Would you like a drink?"

"That would be lovely." Then she remembered her instructions. "What I would really like, if it wouldn't be too much trouble, is dinner. I'm always too nervous to eat before the show, which leaves me starving afterward."

"But of course! It would be my pleasure. Let me ring the cook."

"It doesn't have to be fancy," she said quickly, not wanting to use up too much of her time. "Perhaps some bread and cheese?"

"No, no. For a special guest, I provide much better." He walked over to the door and pressed a small button on the wall. Someone knocked lightly and then opened the door. It was Minta. Sr. Conti told her something in rapid Italian, to which she nodded and then left, closing the door behind her.

"There, it is done." He gestured toward the sofa. "Please, sit. I will make you a drink. I have gin or perhaps some wine . . . ?"

"Gin is fine." She perched on the edge of the sofa and set her clutch down beside her. Actually, gin would be better than fine. It would be perfect. The bitter spirit would cover the taste of the knockout drops splendidly. "And ice if you have it."

"That is not possible, I am sorry." He poured a splash of clear liquid into each glass. "Has anyone ever said you look like the actress in *Gone with the Wind*?"

"Vivien Leigh?" She couldn't help but be flattered, in spite of herself.

"Sì, that one. I thought so the moment I saw you." He added a few drops of what she guessed to be quinine to the drinks, which given the prevalence of malaria in Italy wasn't an awful idea. He swirled the glasses to mix it and then brought them over to the sofa. "For you."

"Thank you." She took a tiny sip and barely repressed a grimace. To say it was raw would be an understatement. To be polite, she took a second sip, and then lowered the glass to her lap. "Signor—"

"Stefano, please."

"Stefano . . ." She licked her lips and was rewarded by a sudden gleam in his eyes. It was all the opening she needed. While a seduction wasn't strictly needed for tonight's performance, lust could blind him to a lot and make him less suspicious of her actions.

Sorting through various stage personas with an unerring feel for her audience, Vi tried to decide which one would get the best results. Given the attention he paid to his grooming and the blatant masculinity of his posture, she picked cultured and feminine.

Letting her posture relax into something more curved and sinuous, she leaned back on the sofa. Her hope was to undermine his ability to think by provoking his baser nature. Loose lips weren't always female ones. With a little coaxing, men could turn just as chatty as a teenage girl.

"Stefano," she said again, running her fingertip along the hem of her neckline, drawing his gaze to the swell of her breasts. "I hope you don't think I'm old fashioned, but I like to get to know a fellow before I . . . well, before we become close friends."

"Would you like that, for me to become a close friend of yours?" he asked with lazy interest.

She looked up through her eyelashes at him. "Maybe. Would you?"

A purely masculine smile curved his lips. "Very much so."

"Then tell me a little about yourself." She brought the gin drink to her lips again and paused. "You seem very rich."

He laughed. "I am. And about to be even more so. Does that interest you?"

"Very much so," she said, echoing his syntax with a teasing smile. "What actress isn't thrilled by stories of success?"

He cocked a dark eyebrow. "Then perhaps you would be pleased to learn I own a villa near Tivoli, a famous vineyard, and two businesses here in Rome."

"My, my," she cooed. "You must be important."

His expression became smug. "The prime minister himself has come to dinner several times. And my family was a good friend to Victor Emmanuel II. My father and the king used to hunt together."

"My goodness! Your father was really the king's friend?"

He puffed up in indignation. "I do not lie, signorina."

"Of course not!" she said soothingly. Then she leaned forward and rounded her eyes. "But what of the fascists and the Nazis? How did you avoid being imprisoned if you are a royalist?"

He snorted. "Those fools. They are just as in awe of titles as Americans." Then he stiffened as if realizing what he'd said. "No offense, of course, signorina."

"Vi," she reminded him, and then waved away his worry with a small laugh. "And how can I be offended by what is true? I do love everything royal, which is funny given how our country fought to be rid of kings."

"Indeed." He smiled indulgently at her. "What else may I tell you about myself?"

"Well, are you married? Do you have children?" she asked, despite knowing the answers. Might as well find out how truthful the man was.

His dark eyebrows rose. "Would it matter? I should imagine even if we become close friends, we might have others as well?"

Tapping her lips, she pretended to consider the idea, though really she wanted him looking at her mouth and thinking of kisses. "I suppose, as long as I don't need to worry about an angry Sra. Conti barging in on us."

He frowned slightly. "I don't know that word 'barging,' but if you mean will she disapprove, I doubt it, since she is far away in our villa, doing what she likes."

"So you are married!" Vi said, acting surprised. "Do you have children as well?"

Pride seemed to swell his chest. "I do. A son, who is my life."

317

"How wonderful!" Vi said with fake cheerfulness, even as her stomach twisted. She had been right. Given his statement, there was little chance that Stefano would ever let the child leave Italy.

"It is one of the reasons I come to Rome as often as I do, so that I may see him."

"He doesn't live with you and your wife?" she asked, remembering the role she was playing.

Sorrow entered his dark eyes. "Alas, no. Though my wife and I have no children of our own, she refuses to let my Enzo live with us."

Anger built within her. It was only the years of acting experience that saved her, that kept her expression neutral. Inside she was seething on behalf of Enzo, who deserved to be more than a pawn in his parents' lives. How dared Sr. Conti think he could blithely replace the boy's real mother with his wife? That Enzo wouldn't notice or care, or that he would thrive under a woman who didn't want him?

And what of the wound he sought to inflict on Sra. Conti, a woman who likely had been heartbroken to find herself incapable of having children? It was one thing to seek out an adoption as a couple, quite another to have a husband's bastard foisted on you.

Though that's exactly what had happened to Ansel, and he had accepted the responsibility with open arms . . .

A soft knock on the door distracted Stefano's attention and refocused Vi's. She carefully exhaled her emotions while a maid slipped in to whisper something in Stefano's ear. His mouth flattened into a firm line, and he waved the woman away impatiently.

"I'm sorry for the intrusion, my dear Vi. Now, where were we?"

"Is something the matter?" she asked casually despite the spike of adrenaline. If something had happened to Minta or the woman had changed her mind about helping Vi, she would have no backup. Ansel had made that fact crystal clear.

"No, no. No trouble. Merely my son—who we were just discussing—having trouble falling asleep."

Her heart stuttered. "He is here, with you?"

"Only for a visit while his mother recovers. She wasn't feeling well yesterday."

I bet, she thought, her anger resurfacing. And no wonder the poor thing couldn't sleep. Who could after being torn away from the safety of his mother's arms, especially after watching her be abused?

"That is so kind of you!" she said, all wide-eyed admiration despite the black fury boiling in her blood. That Stefano all but preened told her that her performance was dead on. Too bad Sue wasn't around to see it. "I know when I couldn't sleep, a kiss from my papa was just the thing to settle me down. Perhaps you should go and reassure him all is well?"

And give me a chance to doctor your drink? she added silently.

Stefano hesitated. "You wouldn't mind?"

"Not at all," she said honestly. It would be so much easier to add the drug now than during dinner.

To add a little push to her suggestion, she leaned back again and gave him her most seductive smile. "Actually, I find men who love their children charming."

Stefano's dark eyes became almost black as his gaze dropped lower to her breasts and then lower again. "In that case . . ." He called the maid back, gave her instructions in Italian, and then stood. "Let me introduce you to him so you can see how great my love is."

Alarmed at his suggestion, she straightened. "Is that wise? How will I explain my presence?"

And how will I ever doctor Stefano's drink with two pairs of eyes following my every move?

"Relax, my Virginia. He will think you a friend, a very beautiful one, but he is too young to think more than that."

Her stomach twisted painfully as the maid disappeared, the door closing behind her.

To steady her nerves, she took a larger swallow of her drink. It still tasted terrible, but her experience at tossing back shots of bourbon kept her from choking.

"While we wait," Stefano said, sitting back down, "I should like to know more about you, as well."

"Oh." She paused to gather her wits more tightly. "I'm a nobody. Just a girl from Iowa who likes to dance."

"I also like to dance," he said with a smile. Then he winked. "But only with a partner."

She lowered her lashes. Back in the game at hand, she gave a sultry laugh, acknowledging the innuendo. "Partners do add something to the dance, don't they?"

"Indeed, they do. Particularly if one can find two partners to form a trio. I find the pleasure is much greater . . ."

Her eyebrows rose slightly at the baldness of his suggestion, but not in shock. She had met men before who enjoyed threesomes. "Oh, not me. I much prefer duets."

He shrugged slightly and then raised his glass to her in a silent toast. "You are right, of course. I should enjoy my time with you without distraction."

"Just so." She let her lips curve into a smile of encouragement as he took a polite sip. With any luck the alcohol would start to numb his tongue, making any changes in taste less noticeable.

Minta opened the door, pushing a cart.

"Ah, dinner. Excellent." He held out his hand to her. It took everything she had to take it and let him pull her to her feet. After the callousness he had demonstrated toward his wife and mistress, she could barely tolerate being in the same room with him.

Still, she had a role to play. "Thank you."

"My pleasure." He held her hand a beat longer than necessary.

Hiding her disgust with a smile, she gently freed her fingers.

"I hope you don't mind if we eat here. It is informal but convenient. My personal rooms are through the door there." He gestured toward a closed door at the end of the room. "So not so far away."

Minta, who was laying the place settings quickly and efficiently on a beautifully inlaid parquet card table, didn't look up as they approached. Vi bit her lip, wondering how long it would take for the maid to bring Enzo in for his good night kiss. She was on a tight schedule and would rather not knock Stefano out while his son was standing there. No reason to traumatize the boy any more than he already had been.

On the other hand, she might not get a choice.

"Please sit, signorina," Stefano said, pulling a chair out for her.

She sat and then inwardly cursed as he took the seat next to her. She would have preferred him across the table, where it would be harder for him to paw her. Worse, the vial with the knockout drops was still in her handbag on the sofa, ten feet away, meaning she would have to find a way to excuse herself without raising Stefano's suspicions.

As Minta began to serve them, Vi glanced at the beautifully intricate silver clock on the wall. Delicately cast vines and leaves surrounded the face, creating a sense of false peace. The truth was she had only thirty-five more minutes to achieve her objective. Her stomach tightened.

Did she wait for Enzo to appear? It would make a good distraction, allowing her to fetch the vial. But what if the wait used up all her allotted time?

Stefano settled his larger hand over hers, causing her to jump. "You seem nervous, Vi."

"I—I've never been with an older man before," she said, and then blushed at the lie. "I'm afraid I'll disappoint you."

His smile was indulgent. "Don't worry, *mia cara*." He ran the back of his hand up her arm, raising gooseflesh as he did so. He leaned toward her, his breath tickling her bare neck. "You will not disappoint."

Thirty minutes. That was all she had to endure. She could do this. It was no worse than having drinks with Tony.

Minta finished serving and then returned to the hall with her cart. The door closed with a soft click. Vi flinched, the sound as loud as a gunshot in her keyed-up state.

"Shall we eat?" Stefano asked in a low purr. "Or shall we move on to different appetites?"

"Eat," Vi said quickly, and then dimpled to take the sting out of her reply. "I have a feeling I'll need all the energy I can get to keep up with a man like you."

He smiled in pleasure. "Then by all means, please eat."

The clock ticked quietly on the wall, counting off the passing seconds.

Think, Vi, think. She had no way of knowing how pure the drug would be, which could throw off how fast it took effect. Nor did she want to put too much in and accidentally kill Stefano, vile as he might be. He had a wife and child who depended on him for money and protection.

She knew what life was like without both of those advantages and wouldn't wish it on anyone.

Aware of Stefano's gaze, she took a spoonful of the soup in front of her. It might as well have been water for all she tasted. Her brain was too focused on how to retrieve the vial without arousing suspicion, particularly if Enzo didn't make an appearance in the next few minutes.

Perhaps if she spilled something . . . The idea took hold, and a series of steps unfolded in her mind. Mentally apologizing to Allie, she took another spoonful of soup. She lifted the spoon to her mouth, glanced at Sr. Conti, and then tilted the spoon as if distracted by him, spilling the hot liquid onto her chest.

"Oh!" She jumped up, not needing to fake her reaction.

Stefano leaped to his feet as well and began blotting her dress with his napkin. "Here! Are you hurt?"

"No," she gasped. "But my dress."

"Do you need water?"

"Stop, let me see." She batted away his hands. "Oh no!"

"Is there anything I can do?"

"Let me get my handbag. I've got a spot remover in there I can try." She sprinted over to the sofa before he could offer to get the bag himself. Hoping there was enough liquid to carry off the deception, she put a few drops on the damp silk. Then carried the bottle back to the table with her. "I think that should be enough."

She took her napkin and dabbed at the stain.

"Perhaps if you removed the dress, it would make the spot easier to clean?" Stefano suggested with an innocent air.

Vi wasn't fooled. She arched an eyebrow at him. "And if your son should come in and find me half-naked? That would be difficult to explain, even to a young child."

"Perhaps I should go see where he's at," Stefano said, frustration beginning to show in his tone. "Then we will have no more worries."

"Good idea." Vi opened the vial as if to place another drop on her dress.

Stefano hesitated and then left her to go to the door.

Seizing the moment, Vi quickly dumped the vial into Stefano's drink. To hell with dosage. She'd never heard of anyone actually dying from being slipped a Mickey. Dying from being shot at point-blank range afterward, sure, but not from the drug.

In any case she wanted him unconscious as quickly as possible. She had less than thirty minutes left before she had to get out, map or no map.

"Ah, here he is," Stefano said from the door. *Vita mia.*

In the next moment, Enzo appeared with the maid holding his hand, and Vi's heart broke. Hair tousled and dressed in puppy-print pajamas, he looked so impossibly small and vulnerable.

He rubbed his eyes, which were red and puffy, as if he'd been crying. "Mama?"

Sighing deeply, Stefano dropped to one knee and kissed his son on the forehead and then said something to him in Italian. Then he stood and, taking his son's shoulders, turned the boy toward Vi. "Signorina Heart, may I present my son, Enzo Ludovico Paolo Conti."

"Piacere," Vi said with a smile, forcing herself to stay where she was, even though all she wanted to do was scoop him up and comfort him.

The boy's eyes widened. Looking up at Stefano, he tugged on his father's trousers to get his attention. Once he had it, he asked a rapid set of questions, which made Stefano frown and then glance up at her.

"Forgive me, but my son has decided you are an angel and asks if he could come closer? He wants to ask a favor of you."

Her heart skipped a beat. She should refuse, given how little time she had left. And yet . . .

"I can send him away if you would rather," Sr. Conti said.

"No, don't." She set the glass vial on the table and then crouched, holding out her arms. *"Vieni qui,"* she said in her best Italian. *Come here.*

The boy hesitated for an instant, then glanced at his father, who encouraged him with a gesture of his hand. Shyly, his bottom lip caught in his teeth, Enzo shuffled toward her. Then he abandoned restraint and threw himself into her arms. Tucking himself firmly within her embrace, he began to sob.

Vi buried her face in his silky hair, her heart breaking. The urge to pick him up and flee this place nearly overwhelmed her. She could do it, the war and mission be damned. Everything she had ever wanted was literally in her arms. A precious small being who needed her. Wanted her. Could maybe even love her. Make her whole.

No, stop! Focus. This isn't Jimmy, a small voice in her head screamed. *Stay in the game, or you'll never see your son again.*

But was Jimmy really hers, or was she no different from Stefano, clinging to a child who didn't want or need her . . . ? Enzo pushed back, his tear-streaked face somber as he asked her something in Italian, something that included the word "mamma."

Vi's stomach twisted, pretty sure she was done for, given Stefano's perplexed expression. "What did he say?"

"He asked if his mother had already left with you."

"To heaven?" she said with a nervous laugh. "Does he think his mother is dead?"

"I don't think so," Stefano said, his gaze never leaving her face. He asked his son something in Italian, to which Enzo shook his head.

"Lei è in America."

Vi's breath caught as she translated the simple phrase. She's in America.

Chapter 34

Vi gently disentangled herself from Enzo and stood. "Enzo's mother is in America?"

"Not that I know," Stefano said crisply. "Though perhaps you know more?"

Vi puckered her brow as if confused. "Why would you say that?"

"Enzo, *mimmo*." Stefano held out his hand, and the boy obediently returned to him. Vi's chest ached with the void left behind as if she had lost part of herself. "We talk more in a minute, signorina. But first, I bring Enzo to bed."

It took all her willpower not to bolt the second he left. She hadn't missed how his English had deteriorated with his mood. Surely Minta would help hide her until Riccardo arrived in—she checked the clock—twenty-two minutes.

She would tell him she couldn't find the map. He would be disappointed, but he'd still take her back to her unit, and then she could go on with her life. Marcie would make it back to her father. A grateful Mob would clear her name with the police. She would be free to take a part in Sue's Broadway production. And then she could go home to Chicago as a legitimate dancer—someone Jimmy might someday be proud to call mother, should they ever meet.

Ansel was already on his way back to his unit in the Alps. Stefano would get his gold. It would be as if she had never been involved.

And she would be alive.

Yes, she believed in this mission, but she also wanted to survive. She was only twenty-one and too young to die.

But what if the map fell back into Nazi hands, as Ansel feared? Even if it wasn't used to prolong the war, the gold would certainly go to someone other than the Italian people, who were the rightful owners. Whether it was Sr. Conti or a fugitive German general, the wrong person would end up with all that wealth if she bailed out now. Could she live with that on her conscience?

Her whole life had been focused on what she wanted, and how had that turned out?

Besides, she wasn't that young. She'd already been a mother. Already held a job. Already traveled halfway around the world to perform. Already experienced more in life than many of the soldiers she performed for. Soldiers who would die at eighteen and nineteen.

And she had already lost Ansel in order to take this mission. It would be a cruel irony if she had done it for nothing because she was too cowardly and selfish to see it through.

The ticking of the clock mocked her. Time was passing. What was she going to do?

She heard footsteps in the hall. Stefano was on his way back, and with him came a return of her resolve.

Drawing a deep breath, she unfastened the rhinestone chain on the back of her dress. She had one chance to save the whole mission, and perhaps herself. Her innate sexuality had always been both a boon and a bane. She had fought it, embraced it, and been ashamed. Tonight, she would recognize her sexuality for what it was: a side of her that was neither good nor evil in and of itself.

What mattered was how she used it.

Stefano appeared in the door, his face like a thundercloud.

One thing she had learned from burlesque was that timing was everything. So she waited until his eyes were locked on her, smiled, and then let the front of her dress fall to her waist.

His stunned reaction was exactly as expected, given she wasn't wearing a brassiere. Keeping his attention right where she wanted it, she ran her fingertips around her nipples, prompting them to tighten into small buds. Stefano slowly walked farther into the room, his gaze fastened on her breasts like a man starved. He didn't even look away as he closed the door.

"Now that Enzo is in bed," she said in a low, suggestive voice, "maybe you can show me where yours is?"

He blinked, and awareness filtered back into his eyes. "My son says you know his mother."

She shrugged and slunk toward him, the fingers of her left hand making lazy tracings between her breasts. "Perhaps he saw me when I stopped by the clock shop asking about the watch."

"Ah yes, the watch." Suspicion darkened his tone. "I would like to know more about this watch."

She stopped in front of him and pouted, knowing it would plump her lips provocatively. "You would rather hear about the gift to our stage director than kiss me? Perhaps I should go . . ."

She reached for the front of her dress as if to pull it up.

He stopped her. "No. Stay. You are right. We can talk later."

"As you wish." She swayed forward, arching her back until his hand grazed her body. His sharp intake of breath told her everything she needed to know. He wanted her. Badly. All she had to do was turn that want into blind desire and the mission was as good as finished.

She captured his hand and held it to her bare breast. "Feel how my heart beats for you?"

His answer was a soft growl.

She stepped back but didn't release his hand. "Let's finish our drinks, and then we can find a more comfortable place to . . . talk."

He hesitated, and for a breathless second she thought he would refuse. Then he let her pull him back to the table. With a flirtatious smile, she picked up his glass and handed it to him. Then she picked up hers and poured as much lust and sexual promise as she could into her gaze as she raised her glass.

"*Alla nostra,*" she said, remembering a toast Marcie had taught her.

Stefano's smile turned predatory as he raised his glass and tapped hers. "*Sì,* 'to us.'"

Together they tossed back the contents of their glasses and then laughed.

The clock showed just over fifteen minutes left.

Vi's fingers trembled as she put the glass back on the table. If the knockout drops didn't work, she was in real trouble. Stefano might be close to forty or even fifty, but that didn't mean he was harmless. He looked to be a fit man and one who likely had experience in overpowering young women.

Stefano reached out to run his finger down her spine in a long caress. She shuddered and then stiffened as his fingertip hooked on the loose fabric of her dress and began pulling it lower. "You are very beautiful, my little Vi. I would see more of you."

She swallowed her fear and turned into his arms. "I would like that, too. But not here. Where is your room?"

"Not far." He brushed her hair aside and kissed her neck. "Come, my little love."

He placed his hand on the small of her back and guided her toward the door he had previously pointed out as the one leading to his private rooms.

On the way, Vi noted a pair of silver candlesticks. Would it be out of line to grab one and give him the kibosh? True, it would leave a dent in his head, but it would certainly get the job done. And a lot more quickly than those damn drops . . .

Stefano mumbled something in Italian, and his steps slowed, then faltered. Relief rushed through her veins as he swayed on his feet. Then his eyes rolled up in his head, and he dropped to the floor in a slow spiral.

Not bothering with modesty, Vi knelt beside him, her dress pooling around her waist, and began strip-searching the man. Tie, shirt, suspenders, pants, undershirt, underwear, socks . . . nothing was sacred. The sound of the clock echoed through the room, moving her ever closer to failure. Mounting frustration made her fingers clumsy, and she began to curse at herself, the stupid mission, Ansel, Stefano, anyone and anything.

Finally, she sat back on her heels, failure burning in her stomach like acid. She had found nothing that even remotely looked like a map, not even a scribbled note. Damn it all to heck and back. Major Ricca said they thought Stefano had it on him, because it wasn't in the apartment and it wasn't in his wallet. But what if the major was wrong?

She squeezed her eyes shut to concentrate. The courier had a map. It was taken from him. Then activity around the bunker had indicated the map was back in Italy, but by this point the information could have become verbal. But even verbal maps were likely noted somewhere. *If I heard something I wanted to remember, where would I write it down?*

Partisans had checked his pockets. They had checked his apartment. If it existed, it had to be on Sr. Conti's person.

Come on, Vi, you're running out of time.

She flipped the body and ran her gaze over his now-bare skin, looking for tattoos or any other marks. Nothing. Tucking a strand of loose hair behind her ear, she glanced back at his clothes. Her gaze landed on Stefano's tie. It was a beautiful silk one, but the blue-and-red diamond pattern was slightly frayed along the middle edge, where it would have rubbed on a collar, meaning it had been worn often. Which would be odd, given how wealthy Sr. Conti was. He should have dozens of beautiful ties to wear. Why continue wearing this one?

Curiosity piqued, she flipped it over to look at the tag on the back. There, beneath the manufacturer's name, were three numbers inked in, separated by letters and dashes: 2-R5-C27.

It could be nothing. It could be some kind of code. After all, Riccardo had said the gold was thought to be in a bunker with numerous tunnels and rooms. Maybe this would mean more to someone familiar with the bunker? In any case, it was all she had.

2-R5-C27.

She repeated the sequence several times aloud to embed them in her memory. Just in case.

Someone knocked on the door. Recognizing her cue, Vi pulled up her dress.

"Come in," she called as she struggled to fasten the rhinestone chain behind her neck.

Minta came in and then closed the door behind her. "Did you find it?"

"I think so." Vi grabbed the tie and got to her feet. "Will you take care of Sr. Conti? He needs his clothes returned."

"Certainly. May I see?" Minta held out her hand.

Vi shook her head and started toward the door. "Stefano will wake soon, and I can't be here when he does."

Minta moved to block Vi's steps, her hand still outstretched. "Please. Riccardo will wait. He wants the map perhaps even more than I do."

Alarm bells went off in Vi's head. Minta seemed nervous and was holding something behind her. "I'm not giving the map to him. It's going to Major Ricca."

Minta pulled a gun from behind her back and leveled it at Vi. "No, I don't believe so."

Outrage at realizing she had been double-crossed briefly overwhelmed her terror. Of all the rotten, low-down, dirty . . . "I thought we were all on the same team! How can you do this to your friends, who have sacrificed so much already?"

"Riccardo will give the money to the partisans in the North, who live like kings compared to the people in the South." Minta's expression hardened as her aim steadied. Vi's heart skipped a beat. There was no doubt in her mind that the woman meant to kill her if she didn't cooperate.

But damn it all, she was so close to success. So close to making all her sacrifices worth it. "But the partisans in the North are the ones fighting the Nazis," she said, hoping to reason with the woman.

"The Nazis are already defeated." A fanatical fire glinted in Minta's eyes. "Why use the gold for what is already decided by God? Better it is used to build schools and homes."

Vi edged toward the door, an icy sweat starting to trickle down her back. Letting God decide was all well and good, but she wasn't above wanting to give fate a little push. "Schools and homes are wonderful, but wouldn't it be better to save lives? If the Nazis are truly defeated, there should be plenty left over."

Her fingers tightened around the tie. She was almost close enough to make a break for it.

"Stop moving." But the gun wavered in Minta's hand, and Vi began to hope she was making headway.

"Let me go, Minta." Vi took another small sideways step. "You know it's better to work together than apart."

The pain hit before she heard the explosion. It raced up her side and across her middle, like fire. Startled, Vi looked down to where a hole had been torn in the purple silk, just to the right of her stomach. Blood slowly seeped into the fabric, spreading from the wound.

Her vision began to gray as the pain intensified. Minta had actually shot her. And it hurt a lot more than she had expected.

With her only thought of getting to Riccardo, she pressed her hand against the hole to stanch the bleeding and staggered toward the door. Riccardo would help her. She wasn't going to die.

I will survive. The thought bounced around in her brain, like an unending echo.

Her left leg collapsed under her. Another gunshot exploded. A shriek pierced the ringing in her ears as she dropped to the ground. It was as if someone had cut her leg in half with an ax.

When the shriek became sobbing, she realized the sound was coming from her. Aware she needed to conserve energy, she stopped and focused on breathing, the sound of her heart. Nausea threatened to overwhelm her. *Please, God, please let Riccardo have heard the gunshots . . .*

"Where is the map?" Minta shouted at her, but she sounded far away.

Vi closed her eyes, trying to focus her strength. Someone kicked her in the ribs, and the slash of pain tore a scream from her throat.

"*Porca miseria!* Give me the map."

Vi tried to focus. Where was the tie? Had she dropped it? Then, with a wheezing laugh that faded into a sob, she lifted her hand and held up a blood-soaked rag. She had used the tie to stanch her wound, without thinking, and had utterly ruined it. What had been written on the tag was likely gone forever.

The room began to tilt sickeningly as the pain in her side spiked. She gasped, her thoughts turning fuzzy as the room darkened.

The tie was torn from her fingers. A heartbeat pulsed in her ears. Was that a child weeping? Her eyelids felt too heavy to lift. Another dull pulse, and she thought she heard Ansel calling to her, telling her to hang on. But that couldn't be right.

Because Ansel was gone, and she was . . . well, dead.

Chapter 35

The tie. Vi awoke with a start, her fingers clutching air. She blinked as a hint of a breeze teased her exposed skin. Yellow leaves from an enormous tree drifted down around her. A dream, then. She had been dreaming again.

Except, as was frequently the case of late, it had been more of a nightmare.

She drew a deep breath and felt her heart slow. The crisp, clean taste of the late fall air lingered on her tongue. She closed her eyes as the awful stench of burned gunpowder and the coppery smell of blood faded back into mere memory. Gone, too, was the harsh tang of carbolic soap and medicinal alcohol that had encased her world for the last month. Maybe longer. Time meant little to her these days. To keep count would mean remembering the day she had lost everything but her life.

No, not everything. She hadn't lost her integrity. Her reputation was gone, yes, along with her spot in the USO, and her dreams of Broadway. But those things, when weighed against honor, patriotism, friendship, and love, were truly inconsequential. If given the chance to help Ansel and Major Ricca again, even knowing what the cost would be, she knew she would make the same choice.

Some things were just worth it.

A nurse leaned over Vi's wheeled chair to adjust the blanket over her leg cast and exposed toes. Vi appreciated the gesture and hoped that meant she could stay out here in the courtyard longer, dozing . . . able to pretend she wasn't still a patient in a hospital in Rome.

Tentatively, she wiggled her toes beneath the blanket, or tried to. There was a slight twitch of her big toe, but otherwise the fabric didn't move. A familiar despair stole over her. When she had first awakened from the anesthesia, the surgeon had warned her not to expect a fast recovery. The bullet in her side hadn't hit anything vital, but the one in her leg? He'd shaken his head sadly. Her left femur had been shattered, the bone fragments nearly severing the femoral nerve. He had pinned everything back together, but there were no guarantees.

She gritted her teeth. The surgeon was wrong. Her leg would get better, and she would not only walk but dance again. To think otherwise would be too much.

She already had enough tragedy weighing her down.

Chin up! You'll survive . . .

But would Marcie and the rest of her friends? The not knowing was driving her mad. That she was unable to finish the tour at Marce's side was one of her biggest regrets. But what could she do? Her damaged leg and being kicked out of the USO for "behavioral misconduct" had taken that decision right out of her hands. Not even Papa Maggio could expect her to overcome those hurdles.

No, it was the loss of Marcie's company that dimmed her spirits. She missed her travel buddy. Somewhere along the line the girl had become dear to Vi, and her safety had become personal, not just a means to return to Chicago.

All she could do was hope that Marcie had grown up enough to keep herself out of trouble from now on. Still, if only Vi could get some news, some reassurance that her friends were all okay. But there had been no visits, no calls, no letters. She didn't even know if Ansel had returned to his unit all right.

It was as if her disgrace had rendered her forgotten, and it hurt. A lot.

The nurse patted Vi's hand. "You have a visitor, Miss Heart."

Vi didn't bother opening her eyes. Likely it was another Red Cross volunteer, hoping to cheer her up.

"Hello, Miss Heart." A cultured, feminine voice broke into Vi's thoughts. "Though perhaps I should use your real name?"

Startled, Vi opened her eyes.

A woman in her midthirties, with shrewd, dark eyes and glossy, black hair styled in waves around her face, surveyed her with a detached air. She extended her hand and smiled slightly. "I'm Darla. I've come to discuss your recent adventure, if you won't find it too taxing."

"Are you with the USO?" Vi reached out and shook the woman's slender, fine-boned hand. The woman's grip was firm, professional. "If so, there's nothing more to discuss. I've already been told that I'm to be kicked out due to misconduct."

The words made her flinch every time she uttered them. Another unfortunate result of the mission she needed to get used to.

"Yes, I know." Darla turned to the nurse. "I'll take over from here. And I promise we'll only go for a short spin around the gardens. Nothing too exuberant."

The nurse's brow furrowed. "I'm not supposed to leave patients alone when they're outside."

"I'll take care of her as if she were my own sister," Darla assured the woman, gently edging the nurse away and taking hold of the wheelchair handles. "If it makes you feel better, you may remain here and watch."

Vi stiffened as Darla started to wheel her away. "Wait. What if I don't want to go with you?"

It was one thing to be around strangers while helpless in her wheelchair as long as the nurse was present. It was quite another to be whisked away by someone she'd never met, unable to even sit properly because of the rigid cast around her pelvis and leg.

"Don't be a baby," Darla said as the chair began to move. "You'll be fine. And besides," she continued in a low voice when the nurse was left behind, fidgeting like a nervous hen, "Major Ricca gave his word to Miss Daldakis that we would take good care of you. She was quite adamant on that point."

Vi's heart skipped a beat. "Sue doesn't hate me?"

"No. We had to explain your involvement to her, to keep her from contacting the police. Seems she had something of a riot on her hands when the cast learned you were shot inside Sr. Conti's apartment and that no one was investigating the crime. I believe the words 'kidnapped' and 'conspiracy' were being tossed around. Major Ricca, naturally, became alarmed by the stink your friends were raising, especially as Sr. Conti was threatening to retaliate by formally complaining to the Allied commanders about the blood you got on his expensive carpet."

"You're kidding me." Vi laughed bitterly. "I nearly lose my leg, thanks to his duplicity, and he's upset because I stained his rug?"

"Are you surprised?" Darla asked dryly.

"No." But Darla's report of the cast's reaction was another matter. That they hadn't automatically assumed the worst of her both astonished and thrilled her like nothing else could. Her injuries would prevent her from rejoining the troupe, in any case. But to know that people still cared about her, despite such damning evidence, released something deep inside her soul. For the first time in weeks, she felt real hope that everything would be all right.

"Since Sue now knows the truth, any chance Major Ricca could also clear my name with the USO?" she asked, her heart beginning to race. "I know I'm still guilty of being AWOL, but to have the indecency charges removed would mean everything to me."

Darla gave her an amused look. "Of all the things you're accused of, that's the one that bothers you?"

The woman had a point. Lily Lamour had been brought up on similar charges more than a dozen times in Chicago. But Vi wasn't Lily anymore. And the charges in Chicago were deserved. To be accused of something she hadn't done stung.

Well, actually, she had bared her breasts with the intent of inciting lust, but not for monetary gain. Well, not for *her* monetary gain, in any case. She had done it for patriotic reasons, and that should count for something. Shouldn't it?

For heaven's sake, she had been all but ordered to seduce the man.

"Violet, pay attention! I asked you a question: the map. Did you find it?"

Vi's brain snapped back to the present. "Maybe? Minta would know more than me, if you can find her."

"Yes, well . . . finding her isn't the problem. Minta's dead, which is why I need to know what actually happened in Sr. Conti's apartment."

"Dead?" Vi stared at the woman in utter shock. "Who killed her? She was alive when I passed out."

"We don't know. She was found later that night in the alley behind the building with her throat cut," Darla said, her gaze shrewd as Vi swallowed, the horrible image upsetting her stomach. Minta might have double-crossed the major and everyone else, but she hadn't deserved to die. She had only wanted to help her friends back home, and honestly Vi couldn't blame her for that.

"Do you remember who found you or anything about the trip to the hospital?"

"No, nothing." She decided against mentioning the crying child or her imagining of Ansel's voice. Neither party would have killed Minta, she was sure.

"What about the map?"

Vi glanced up to find Darla checking her watch.

That's right. No time to waste with a war going on . . .

With an effort, she took herself back to that awful night. "First, it wasn't so much a map that I found but what seemed like directions given in a series of numbers."

"Do you remember the numbers?"

Vi cast her brain back to the dream she'd just had. As always, it had ended with her trying to wipe the blood off the tag, but it kept being replaced. She shook her head. "No. I keep trying, but all I remember is it started with—" Vi's mouth snapped shut as a sudden thought hit her. Darla, for all her officiousness, hadn't actually identified herself. Was she being played for a rube? Her pulse spiked.

"With?" Darla prompted.

Vi gripped the handles of her wheelchair and drew a deep breath. "With a promise to keep my mouth shut. Loose lips sink ships, and all that."

Darla blinked and then laughed. "Just so. Ansel did warn me you were too smart for your own good."

"How like him. The king of backhanded compliments," she said, irritated that Darla was apparently on a first-name basis with the sergeant. "How is he?" Vi asked before she could stop herself. Inwardly she cringed at the wistful note that had crept into her voice.

"You've seen him more recently than I," Darla said a bit acidly.

Could it be the woman was jealous? Vi almost laughed, having just experienced the same emotion. What saps they both were! "I haven't seen him since right before the Conti disaster."

Darla hesitated. "You don't remember him coming to the hospital? He said he talked to you right after your surgery."

Vi sat up so fast, she almost fell out of her wheelchair. An immediate stab of pain in her side stole her breath, but it was nothing compared to finding out he had visited her and she couldn't remember a second of it. "You're kidding me," she finally managed.

"No." The woman sounded almost apologetic. "He did say you were pretty out of it, which is why—on his recommendation—the surgeon kept everyone away from you, lest you say something you weren't supposed to. Including your friend Miss May, who tried to storm your room and had to be escorted out by an armed guard. Luckily Ansel was able to calm her down before she called the police and outed your location."

Vi could easily picture Marcie taking on the hospital staff, her passionate loyalty on full display. Her lips curved. Her friend would have been, as Riccardo might say, magnifica.

And then her amusement vanished, fear taking its place. If Minta was dead and no one knew where the map was or what it looked like, might the murderer come looking for her next?

"Where are they now, my unit?" Vi asked as worry squeezed her chest. That she might have accidentally endangered them weighed on her more now than the possibility of never walking again. "Are they still in Rome?"

"No. They were transferred within a week of your being injured. We thought it best under the circumstances to get them out of Rome."

"Because whoever came after Minta might come after me." She released a tight breath. "So maybe it's a good thing I can't rejoin them."

Darla hesitated. "About that. Major Ricca and I were talking."

"Sure you were," Vi said, her suspicions back.

"Violet, I need you to trust me. If you want, I can show you my diplomatic passport, or, if you insist, I could take you inside to telephone Major Ricca. He'll vouch for me as being on the same side as you."

"What I want is the cast to have extra protection," Vi said firmly, thinking of Gertie and Victor and the other gentler, more trusting members of her troupe. Frances and Wyatt might be able to take care of themselves, but the rest? "I know we got extra training from Ansel and Corporal Merritt, but it's not enough. We're not soldiers."

"Miss Rossi will be monitoring the situation for us." Darla patted Vi's arm. "Try not to worry. If we do more, it would only call more attention to them."

"Speaking of Luciana, did she fake her injury?" It was one of the things Vi had been trying to figure out while cooped up in her hospital bed.

"She made a full recovery before rejoining your unit. More than that, I have no comment."

"And she's not being recruited for any more 'injuries'?" Vi pressed.

"No. She is one hundred percent committed to finishing the tour."

Vi collapsed back as relief swept through her. Marcie would hate giving up her new role. But the girl's safety was much more important to Vi at this point. With the actress back in place, any further communication with the partisans—if there were any, which Darla had made sound unlikely—would hopefully reach the correct person, leaving Marcie in the clear.

"Miss Heart. Violet," Darla said sharply, regaining Vi's attention. "I need you to concentrate, please. That night at Sr. Conti's—what did you find, and why did Minta shoot you?"

Vi shivered as she recalled the surreal scene: the pale, clammy skin of a naked Sr. Conti; the pungent smell of chloral hydrate on her dress; Minta standing at the door, the gun in her hand. "Fine. I'll tell you. But first, if you wouldn't mind, I'd like to see your passport."

Chapter 36

Twenty minutes later, after Vi was satisfied Darla was indeed who she said she was, and then had subsequently recounted everything she could remember about her visit to Sr. Conti's apartment and Minta's treachery, Darla exhaled a frustrated breath. "And that's it? No proof that those numbers were something other than a cleaner's mark?"

"No," Vi said tiredly. It had taken more out of her than she had expected, because to recall that night in its entirety also meant remembering Ansel and how he had begged her not to go. And how he had walked away when she had refused. "But I searched him everywhere: his clothes, his skin, everything, and the frayed edge on his tie was the only thing that seemed off."

"All right." Darla rubbed her temples with her perfectly manicured fingers. Vi hid her own chipped fingernails in her lap. "There's a chance the police found the tie on Minta and kept it as evidence. If so, we should be able to retrieve it."

"And if you do?" Vi asked.

"We'll likely destroy it. Better the gold stays where it is than wind up in the wrong hands."

Vi couldn't disagree with that. Better no change to the war than having it prolonged unnecessarily.

"One last question, Miss Heart. Does anyone other than Ansel know your real name?"

Vi frowned slightly. "Well, there's you and Major Ricca. But otherwise, no."

"Good. Then we think it best if Miss Heart died."

Vi sat up, appalled. "But what of my castmates? They'll be devastated by such news."

"Better devastated than endangered, don't you think? If Miss Heart dies before she can talk to anyone in her old unit, there would be no reason for anyone, partisan or not, to bother them."

The woman had a good point, and hadn't she just been worried about her friends' safety?

"All right, but what do you expect me to do if Virginia dies? I can't become Lily again, because she may have an arrest warrant waiting for her. And I can't be Violet."

Darla held up her hand. "Wait. Why not? You'd be safe as Violet, with a home to go to while you complete your recovery. Or are you afraid Lily's troubles might follow you there?"

"Well, no. There's nothing in Chicago to connect me with Chariton, except Sal, but he won't give me away."

"Then what's the problem?"

Not being sure of her reception in Iowa, for one. But not wanting to air her dirty laundry in front of a stranger, she asked instead, "Say I agree to this. What, then, should I do if I run into my USO friends later on Broadway?" Assuming her leg healed and she returned to the stage. But even if it didn't, the thought of not knowing Marcie's fate would drive her to contact Sue at the very least, if not Marcie herself.

Darla hesitated. "I suppose, once you are safely stateside *and* your unit's USO tour is finished, you could ask that certain clerical errors in the army paperwork be cleared up. War leads to a certain amount of chaos, after all. But I'd think twice before using the Heart stage name again. Even after the war, unless you hear from us saying the gold was found."

"That's fine. But how should I explain my injuries? I'm assuming the truth won't do."

"The official story is that you were shot trying to protect Sr. Conti from an assassin, which was quite valiant of you, by the way."

"Especially since it apparently killed me," Vi said dryly, and Darla chuckled. "I don't suppose my death would be enough to also clear my name?"

"Unfortunately, the Italian police have already recorded where you were found. I could ask Major Ricca to have a sworn statement attached to your death record saying that you were there at his behest, on a diplomatic errand, which should restore your reputation with the USO, at least a bit. However, being alone at Sr. Conti's apartment still violates their code of conduct."

"I see." Anger at the unfairness of it all flared in Vi's veins, only to be replaced right after by the ashes of resignation. And then a deep sorrow, since the partisan plot had probably put Enzo's mother in an even more precarious position. If Vi hadn't failed so badly, perhaps Sr. Conti would have been arrested, freeing Enzo and his mother to immigrate to wherever they pleased. Now she could depend only on the tenderness she had seen in Sr. Conti's expression as he hugged his son to keep them both safe.

Darla stood and pulled two envelopes from her pocket. "I should go. I'll be in touch later this week to see where you would like us to send you once you're discharged. Though it may be a couple of months yet. Meanwhile, these came for you." She held the envelopes out, then hesitated. "I should probably tell you that we've been in contact with your friend in Chicago, Mr. Fleischmann. First when we were checking out your story and then after you were injured. He was quite adamant that someone needed to contact your parents to let them know where you were and that you were badly hurt. For reasons I won't go into, Major Ricca conceded to his demands. I hope you won't be too upset."

"No, not upset." Vi took the envelopes. Stunned was more like it. And furious, as well as horrified, and even a little sad. Too many emotions to process all at once. Why had Sal betrayed her trust like that?

Hardly aware of what she was doing, she turned the larger envelope over while Darla went to summon the nurse. It was addressed to Miss Virginia Heart. Then she noticed it bore no return address, and her skin prickled with unease.

Hoping it was from either Sal or someone with the USO and not from Minta's murderer, she tore it open. A lone newspaper clipping fell out, and a rather small one at that. Frowning, she double-checked the inside of the envelope, but there was nothing else. No explanation. Confused, she read the article headline. And then read it again, her pulse kicking into a higher gear. **Arrest made in gangland slaying: Police Say Revenge Was the Motive.**

She skimmed the rest of the very brief text. No details were given, except to say the killer had been found and the public was not in danger. She read the name Antonio Vecchione twice to assure herself this was the correct case. For a moment she just sat there, letting the news sink in. She was free. She could go home to Chicago.

Except . . . did she want to? Even though there was no more arrest warrant, she still had no job, no money for rent, not even two good legs to stand on. And there was still Papa Maggio, and her broken promise. Though he might understand her predicament, he also might not. And did she want to risk her life finding out?

Maybe she should think about killing off Lily, too.

Doing so would mean throwing away five years of her life and likely never seeing Sal again, let alone Jimmy. But would that be a bad thing? She tucked the article away and took up the V-mail, surprised by the direction of her thoughts. It was as if holding Enzo had filled some hole in her life. And there was Ansel's commitment to a little girl not even his own. Maybe it was less who loved a child and more that the child was loved.

And she knew Jimmy was loved. She had seen it in his carefree smiles and doting nanny. She had seen it in the way he had grown and filled out. She could let go, and he would be just fine without her.

Blinking back tears, she turned the second envelope, made of thin parchment, over and checked for a return address. All the blood drained from her head as she recognized her mother's handwriting. Shock, pain, and grief—they stole her breath.

No wonder Darla had chosen to come clean about Sal and her parents. She had been trying to prepare Vi for this moment, but it hadn't worked. There was no way it could.

Closing her eyes, she fell back in time to her parents' kitchen. It was her fifteenth birthday, and her mother had handed her a letter. It had been filled with all the wisdom she had wanted to give Vi, her youngest daughter, on the cusp of adulthood. Vi had skimmed it, more interested in getting to the presents than worldly advice.

How much different her life might have been if she had actually heeded her mother's words to "think things through," "to take her time with life," "for there was always tomorrow for what you don't get to today."

But she hadn't, and had paid the price . . .

Remembering that the nurse would be with her shortly, Vi took a deep breath and opened her eyes. If she was going to break down and start sobbing from her mother's letter, which was likely, she would rather do it alone.

Opening the envelope, Vi forced herself to read the familiar script.

Dear Violet,

I pray to the good Lord this reaches you and that you won't throw it away before reading it. I don't know what we did to drive you away, but please know that we are so, so sorry. And that we are offering our sincerest hope that you will recover quickly and completely.

The gentleman who came to see us said you were badly injured while performing with the USO in Rome. I think both your father and I lost a good ten years off our lives with the news. To learn in the same breath that you were not only overseas but injured—well, it was quite a shock. Your father became terribly angry at the man and said the government should take better care of their performers! He only agreed not to press charges after the gentleman gave us your address at the hospital and promised you were getting the best of care.

And Vi—your father misses you terribly, as do I, and Fern. Please come home, if only to visit for a day or even an hour. Italy seems so far away.

We will pray daily for your safe return and that we may hold you once again in our arms . . .

Choking on a sob, Vi read the signature and then refolded the letter. Her heart broken all over again, she held the letter to her chest.

How could she have been so cruel? The answer was easy: she had panicked. She hadn't trusted her parents to love her and to stand by her like Ansel's parents had done for their daughter-in-law's baby. Nor had she given a single thought to whether Fern might have wanted to know what kind of man she was marrying. She had been so caught up in her own troubles, she hadn't considered the impact of her actions on others. In that, her behavior had been no different from Robert's. Selfish and cruel.

Forgive yourself . . . Ansel's parting words crept, unwanted, through her self-recrimination, angering her. She crumpled her mother's letter in her fist. He was wrong. She didn't deserve forgiveness.

And yet . . .

Her gaze dropped to the paper balled in her lap. Her parents wanted her home. They missed her.

Of course, they didn't know the worst of her sins.

But Ansel did. He had heard them all. And had kissed her anyway. *Forgive yourself . . .*

Could she? All the mistakes she had made, all the disasters in her life had come from trusting Robert. And Fern. But her sister had never meant to hurt her. She had thought Vi too young to fall in love.

But Robert. *He was a grown man, Violet. He was the one who failed.*

Once again, Ansel had seen what she had not. Robert was one person, and yet she had allowed him to alter her life like a cancer. Her sense of worth had been destroyed because she hadn't seen the situation clearly. She had seen it through the eyes of a child.

But she wasn't fifteen anymore. She was older, smarter, wiser. Yes, she had made a mistake and trusted the wrong person. But there were good people in the world, too. People she could trust. People who had been there all along had she only turned to them for help. People like Sal, Sue, Marcie, Ansel, Major Ricca . . . even Frances.

She didn't have to be a solo act anymore. It was okay to be part of an ensemble.

"Miss Heart, are you ready to go back in?" the nurse asked, genuine concern in her voice.

Vi wiped her cheeks, her sorrow gone. "Yes."

She was ready for a lot of things now, and highest on her list was apologizing to the cast members she loved most: her family.

Because Darla had been right. It was time to let Virginia and Lily go and try being Violet again.

Chapter 37

As the taxi driver turned onto the familiar tree-lined street, Vi pressed her gloved palm to her chest. Her heart raced as her emotions bounced between joy and terror. It had taken a month, but she was here, finally back in Chariton. She took a deep breath and shivered inside her wool coat, not from the early morning chill but from nerves over the upcoming meeting.

Breathing out, she turned her attention to the view, trying to distract herself as the taxi drove closer to her parents' home. The trees were bigger than she remembered, but the houses all looked the same. The lawns where she had played as a child were beginning to peek out from the snow. In another month, once April rolled around, the lawns would become green again.

She shivered again, wondering if she was calling too early. Pink and gold sunlight barely suffused the horizon, the day was so new. It still felt odd, after her time in Italy, not to see hills or mountains looming in the background. But it also reaffirmed that she wasn't dreaming this. She was here. She was home . . .

The taxi slowed, and Vi could scarcely catch her breath as the familiar two-story brick home loomed in front of her. Tears gathered in her eyes, but she wouldn't let them fall. Now was the time for strength.

She had written her parents and Fern that day in Italy, after Darla left. She had poured out her heart, her sorrow and regret over running away. She had apologized profusely for her selfishness and begged their forgiveness. She had closed with the sincere desire to come visit when she was back in the States.

She hadn't told them why she had left, though. Some things were best said in person.

The taxi driver looked back over his shoulder at her, his wrinkled, square face tired and a little impatient. She wasn't surprised. She was just another ride to him. If people had looked for the runaway Violet five years ago, they had likely long since stopped. A war had started, and bigger tragedies had struck the town as white-star flags turned into gold ones, indicating the death of a loved one.

Would her parents even recognize her? Five years was a long time.

"Do you need some help with your luggage, miss?" the driver asked.

"Yes, maybe." She took a deep breath. "Actually, can you wait while I make sure I have a place to stay? If not, I'll need you to take me to a hotel."

A frown of concern deepened the wrinkles. "Do you want me to come with you?"

"No. It'll be fine. I hope." She opened her door and swung her cane out. Her muscles protested the change in movement as she stood, but it also felt good. She would never take standing on her own for granted again. In fact, there was a lot she would never again take for granted, like food, and window glass, and the earthy smell of manure in the fields, which was far better than rotting hemp and charred earth.

She slowly made her way up the concrete path to the front door. Her stomach cramped with nervousness. Pain and memories had kept her awake on the train from Chicago. She hadn't taken any time to see Sal when she had changed trains, the chapter on that part of her life closed.

On the long voyage home aboard the hospital ship, she had written him a multipage letter.

She admitted to being furious with him for a while for forcing her hand. Because it had become clear to her, after rereading his first telegram, that his meddling had started long before the OSS had contacted him. He had been very careful with his wording in that missive. He never actually said her father had found him, only that her father wanted her address. Which of course he probably did.

What Sal had really been looking for was permission to reach out to her parents. Because he wanted something better for her than a life spent working at the Palace. He had wanted her to forget her "unhealthy obsession" with Jimmy. He had wanted her to go home and be who she was supposed to be.

Because Sal loved her, which is why she had completely forgiven him. And why she wouldn't be going back to Chicago, at least not right away. Maybe not ever. Because she was done living a lie. Even if her parents kicked her back out, she owed them and Fern the truth.

She was done running away.

Realizing she had been staring blindly at the doorbell button for over a minute, she squared her shoulders and pushed it.

Time to face the music.

Inside the house, she heard the familiar chimes. Goose pimples rose on her arms as memories, good and bad, assailed her. Would the house smell the same when the door opened? Would the furniture be the same? The wallpaper, the light fixtures?

"Coming." Her mother's muffled voice came through the door.

Vi smoothed her skirt with one hand but had lost the ability to breathe. Her heart pounded so hard she could barely hear the birds twittering in the neighbors' trees.

The door opened, revealing her mother's beloved face, and time stopped for Vi. For several unbearably long seconds, her mother stared at her, unmoving. Shock, wonderment, fear all crossed her mother's face, and then her eyes filled with tears, her face crumpling. Vi couldn't stand it, and tears streamed down her cheeks as she took the first tentative steps toward her mother. "Mom?"

Suddenly Vi was engulfed in her mother's arms. "Oh, my Lord," her mother said, her voice choked, as she squeezed Vi tight. "Oh, my dear sweet Lord. Thank you, thank you. Thank you!"

Overcome by the love in her mother's welcome, Vi closed her eyes against the flood of rioting emotions. Relief, hope, love, joy . . . she couldn't breathe for it. She leaned into her mother's embrace and hugged her back. All her carefully planned speeches were forgotten. It was all she could do to not start sobbing against her mother's chest.

"Frank!" her mother called over her shoulder for Vi's father. "Frank, you've got to come in here. Violet's home! Vi—" Her voice broke. "Vi's come home."

A chair scraped on the floor in the dining room. And then she found herself being passed into her father's embrace. The familiar scents of pipe tobacco and coffee, her father in a single whiff, engulfed her. More emotions came unleashed, guilt and remorse at the top of the list.

"I'm so sorry, Daddy," she said, her voice muffled as she burrowed her face into his soft woolen sweater-vest. "So, so sorry!"

"It's all right, honey. You're home. That's all that matters." Her father's deep bass voice rumbled under her ear, just like when she had been younger. Her hero. Her protector. "Do I need to pay your taxi?"

Appalled that she had forgotten all about the poor taxi driver, she sniffed and pushed back. "I can do it. Give me a sec."

Her mother threaded her arm through Vi's free one. "Frank, pay her fare while I get her seated in the parlor. She's practically swaying on her feet with exhaustion."

With a rush of gratitude, Vi let her mother pull her into the parlor. Her knees weakened as she looked around, the rush of memories provoked by the familiar details almost too much to withstand. The upright piano she and Fern had practiced on every day after school. Tante Elke's tatted doilies on the back of the couch. The framed, yellowed photographs of Opa and Oma Ernte on the end table.

To her chagrin, her mother wouldn't let Vi sit on the couch and insisted she take her favorite chair by the window. Not having the energy to protest, she eased herself down. The polished chintz cushions released a soft sigh of her mother's favorite perfume. An unshakable sense of unworthiness tightened her chest. She had hurt these two people who loved her so deeply. Hurt them badly. Why was her father paying her driver and her mother giving her the best chair? They should be yelling at her. Making her pay for all those years of pain.

They don't know the worst of it. That's why.

She bit her lip. It would take all her courage to get through these next few minutes, but she would do it. She would finally say what she should have five years ago and let the chips fall as they may. If she had to make a quick phone call to fetch back the taxi, so be it.

Her mother sat across from Vi on the couch, which was still upholstered in the worn navy-and-white striped fabric she remembered. Vi nervously repositioned her cane against the chair's arm so it wouldn't fall. Too soon for comfort, she heard the front door close, and then her father came down and sat next to his wife. An awkward silence broken only by the ticking of the mantel clock settled over the room as she and her parents drank the sight of each other in.

Her parents had aged, which shouldn't have been a surprise. Her mother's brown hair had become streaked with white, her warm brown eyes flanked by deeper creases, but in Vi's opinion she was as beautiful as ever. Her father, likewise, had a bit more silver at the temples, and he had traded his wire rims for dark horn-rims—they looked nice on him. Vi wondered if Fern might have had something to do with it, since her sister had always been after their father to look less stodgy.

Thinking of Fern brought her back to what she needed to say. She took a deep breath and sorted through all the possible ways she could start. Her father beat her to the punch.

"How long are you home for? A while, I hope. Your mother wanted a chance to get the whole family together to see you." The hesitation in his voice was like a dagger to Vi's heart. She hadn't considered that her parents might be just as anxious about this reunion as she was.

She sat forward, the need to reassure them erasing her own fears. "Oh, Daddy. Mom. I didn't stay away because of anything you did. And I'll gladly stay as long as you'll have me. To be honest, I'm a little lost as to what I want to do with my life."

"Because of your leg," her father said, gesturing toward her cane. "How long until you're fully healed?"

Her chest contracted with pain. "Maybe never."

Her mother half rose off the couch, her face pale. "Oh, Vi! You must be devastated. All you ever wanted to do was dance."

"But she can still walk a stage," her father pointed out quickly, his expression wary as he glanced at her.

"Maybe," Vi said, even though she had her doubts whether anyone would hire a crippled actress. "But I didn't come home to talk about my injuries. Or my time in Italy, though I'll be glad to tell you all about it later." She took a deep breath. "But first: How is Fern?"

Her mother and father shared a startled glance. Then her mother said, "Fern is fine. Why?"

"How is your relationship with Robert?"

This time her father answered. "Well, I'm not sure how to answer that, since Robert is dead."

"Dead?" Vi's brain struggled to absorb this news. "When? How?"

"In a car accident not long after you . . . well, that winter. His truck skidded off the road out by Gratz's bar. Drunk as a skunk, as usual. Anyway, he must have passed out, and it was bitter cold that night. By the time he was found the next morning, he was dead, frozen solid."

"Well, frozen as much as anyone could be, considering how much alcohol was in his system," her mother added dryly.

Vi blinked, still reeling from the news that Jimmy's father was dead. Not that she would miss him, but it was still unsettling to think the man with whom she had shared something so important as a baby was no more. "Poor Fern."

Her father sighed and looked down at his steepled hands. "Yes and no. Their marriage wasn't going well. If he hadn't ended up in that ditch, I'm pretty sure she would've moved out on him."

"Fern wasn't happy?"

Her mother traded a guilty look with her husband. "I hate to speak badly of the deceased, but that man was bad news. I just wished we had all realized it sooner."

Guilt swamped Vi. All this time she had been afraid of spoiling Fern's happiness when she could've saved her sister heartbreak. How different would all their lives have been if she had been brave enough to face Fern's anger all those years ago? Fern would have forgiven her, eventually. Instead Vi had allowed Robert to ruin both their lives.

"Is there a reason you're asking?" her father asked.

Vi couldn't meet his eyes. She wouldn't survive seeing the love that was there now turn to disgust once she told them the truth.

"Violet?" he prodded gently.

She chickened out and asked a question instead. "Did she remarry? Fern, I mean. Is she happy now?"

"She did," her father said slowly. "To Joe Rydahl. A real good man, solid, steady, well liked. He moved into town not long after you left and took on the position of assistant postmaster. After Robert's death, he asked Fern out. They got married . . . well, it'll be three years in May."

Vi smiled then, truly happy for her sister. "I'm glad."

"You've got a little niece, Vi," her mother added, a sparkle in her eyes. "Claire. She'll be two next month, and the sweetest little thing. She reminds me of you."

"Poor Fern," Vi said with a regretful laugh. "I was a hellion growing up."

355

"No, you weren't," her mother said firmly, giving her the look Vi remembered so well. Half-fond, half-exasperated. "You and your sister were different, to be sure, like the sun and the moon. One calm and gentle and the other all fire and light. But you were my little sunbeam growing up, and I never regretted having you."

Vi's eyes filled. "I'm glad. But I'll forever regret all the pain I must have caused you."

"It wasn't easy, not knowing if you were okay or just pretending," her father said, putting his arm around Vi's mother, who had started crying like Vi. "What would make it a whole lot easier to understand is if you told us why you left. Was it something we said or did or—"

"No! It wasn't anything like that." She took a deep breath and blurted out the words she should have said five years ago. "I was pregnant. And Robert was the baby's father."

Her parents froze, stunned, by the looks on their faces.

Tears blurred her vision again. "I'm so sorry I didn't tell you sooner. I was . . . terrified."

Her father recovered first. "Did he . . . were you . . . Damn, but I wish I had known while he was still here. I'd have killed the bastard with my bare hands."

Her fingers balled into fists in her lap. How easy it would be to let him think the worst, and how wrong it would be.

No more lies, Vi. "It wasn't rape, Dad. I . . . I didn't . . . that is, I was a willing participant at the time."

"Oh, Vi." Her mother sighed and closed her eyes.

"I know, I'm an awful person. And I'm so, so sorry. But I didn't think Fern and he would get married! She told me she was through with him."

Her mother's eyes were filled with disappointment when she looked at Vi again. "I wish you had told us. It would've saved everyone a lot of heartache."

"Your sister would've been shocked but all right in the end," her father added.

"We all would've stood beside you, Vi. But you never even gave us a chance," her mother said, sounding sad now.

"Would you have made me marry him?" The thought had haunted her all these years and still made her feel ill.

"At fifteen? Absolutely not," her father said, aghast. "You were a child. What he did was criminal. He manipulated you, Vi. It was not your fault. None of it was."

"But why would he sleep with me if he loved Fern?" The fifteen-year-old part of her couldn't understand that part. It didn't make sense.

"Because the lazy bastard wanted to live on easy street. So he courted Fern, and when she said she wouldn't have him, you were his fallback plan."

Vi must have looked horrified, because her mother was up and off the couch in a flash. "It's all right, sweetheart. There's no way you could've known he was after our family's money. You were so young."

"And stupid." Her parents might be willing to let her off the hook, but she wasn't. "If I hadn't been so competitive, so jealous of Fern, I would've seen that there was no way he could prefer me to her."

"Violet Louise, that's enough!"

Vi's gaze jerked up to meet her father's. The love she saw there stole her breath.

"You were fifteen," he said firmly. "Of course you were jealous of Fern. All younger siblings are at some point, because the older sibling has what the younger one wants: greater freedom. If anyone is at fault, it's your mother and me, for not noticing that Robert was seducing you."

"He told me not to tell anyone." Her lips felt numb.

Her father's jaw tightened. "Of course he did. Because he knew what he was doing was wrong."

Vi's view of her past shifted, and then reassembled, and then shifted again.

"Did you have the baby, Vi?" The mix of emotions in her mother's voice twisted through Vi's aching heart.

"I did. But I gave him up for adoption. He lives in Chicago with his new family, and—oh, Mama—he's healthy and gorgeous and has the sweetest smile."

Her mother bit her lip and was silent a moment, moisture gathering in her eyes. Then she gave a watery smile. "Well, I'm glad my grandbaby is safe. You did all right. And you'll have more, someday, that I'll be able to spoil."

Vi winced under a fresh stab of pain. "Actually, I won't. The doctor said I can't have any more children."

Might as well put that truth out there, too.

Both her parents stared at her.

Vi tried to laugh so they wouldn't look so stricken. "It's all right. I've gotten used to the idea. And I've got a niece to spoil, right?"

"I'm so sorry," her mother said finally. "I didn't mean to bring up—"

"It's fine." This time her smile was more genuine. "I'm glad to have the truth out between us. It feels . . . good."

"You'll still need to talk to Fern," her father said. "She's got a right to know, and she'll take it better from you. She blamed herself for your disappearance."

Vi's stomach dropped at the thought of that challenging conversation. But she was committed to making things right between her and Fern. "I definitely want to talk to her. But perhaps I could rest first? The chair here is fine. It was a long train trip."

Her mother's eyebrows rose. "Wouldn't you rather lie down? The bed in your old room is all made up."

Vi's heart thumped unevenly. "I don't want to be any bother."

"Violet Louise, this is your home until you don't need it anymore. You've been gone five years, child. It'll take a month of Sundays, at least, until I get caught up on your life! Until then, don't even think you might be a bother."

Five years of guilt and grief shifted on her shoulders, crushing the breath out of her. "But—"

"No buts. You're home, Vi." Her mother pulled her into a fierce hug, and Vi lost the battle with her emotions. She sobbed onto her mother's shoulder as the trials and fears of the intervening years slid free.

It had been a long, difficult journey, but her mother was right: she was finally home.

And it was wonderful.

Chapter 38

Telling Fern the truth about Robert was the hardest thing Vi had ever done. She had fully expected her sister to spit in her eye and tell her to never speak to her again.

Fern surprised her, though.

Her sister, having gone through a pregnancy herself, understood how scary and overwhelming it must have been. She had cried and hugged Vi tight when Vi explained why she couldn't have any more children. Yes, she wished she had known what a rat Robert was before she married him. But if she hadn't been through that awful experience, she likely wouldn't have appreciated what a stand-up guy her Joe was.

Fern had even suspected Vi had a crush on Robert, which was why she had always blamed herself for Vi's disappearance. She had thought Vi's heart had been broken by the engagement announcement, and that's why Vi had run away. It came as almost a relief, then, to know Robert had been the villain.

Then Fern had made a confession of her own. She had taken advantage of Vi's absence to become a renowned actress in her own right. Or had once Robert had died, freeing her to try out for local productions. While she would understand if Vi wanted to return to the Chariton stage, perhaps she could let Fern have the occasional choice role? Vi had been shocked to learn of her sister's jealousy. If only she had known how Fern had felt about always being passed over, Vi might have bowed out once in a while.

Oh, who was she kidding? Not at fifteen she wouldn't have.

Vi made a face at herself in the mirror over the parlor piano as she remembered that conversation. No matter how much Vi might have wished otherwise, she had been far too selfish and spoiled all those years ago. But not anymore.

Fern clattered down the stairs and burst into the parlor.

"Violet, can you help zip me? Joe is swinging by in fifteen minutes to pick me up after he drops Claire off at the neighbor's."

Vi turned away from the mirror and smiled. "Sure, come here."

Her sister, a thinner, more angular version of Vi, hurried over and turned around. Her costume glittered like a waterfall with its hundreds of blue and green sequins, all sewn on by Vi at her own insistence.

That her sister had even considered going onstage for tonight's musicale in a plain sheath dress had actually caused Vi pain.

Fern lifted her curled and waved hair off her back. "Are you sure you don't want to come with us tonight? Joe said he could still get you a front-row ticket if you wanted."

"I'm sure he could, but seeing as the performance is sold out, I don't want to be responsible for what he might have to do to get me one." Vi smiled at the not-so-far-fetched scenario of her new, very sweet brother-in-law shaking down some poor soul to make sure his wife's sister could attend the Chariton Spring Revue. He would do anything to make Fern happy, which Vi found endearing.

Vi fastened the small hook at the top of the zipper. "All done, and you look fantastic."

Fern took a deep breath and turned around, her face pinched with worry. There were new lines around her sister's eyes that Vi hadn't gotten used to, ones Robert had likely put there in that one awful year of marriage. "You sure you won't come?"

Vi smiled reassuringly. "Don't worry. It's Mother and Daddy's turn tonight. Tomorrow night is your chance to knock my socks off."

"Darn Mrs. Schmidt for grabbing the last ticket."

"She's got just as much right as I do to see your opening night triumph," Vi said with a laugh. "Besides, I already told you, I've got a voice lesson tonight. If I'm going to go visit Marcie in New York, I've only got until June to get my voice in shape. I promised her that I'd be able to hold my own while singing at her cast parties."

Fern made a face. "Fine. You go get ready to visit your friend. I was just making it all about me again. Older-sister prerogative."

Vi's heart squeezed, pricked by the old ghosts of sibling rivalry. They both knew that when she was younger, she might have missed her sister's opening night for far different reasons than not wanting her brother-in-law to ruffle town feathers. And the memory shamed her.

She straightened a twisted sequin on Fern's gown. "As your fond little sister, I want you to know I am nothing but happy for you. If my leg would tolerate it, I'd gladly stand in the wings and cheer you on from there. But there's always tomorrow! So go break a leg." Then she laughed. "But not literally. I can tell you from experience, it's no fun."

Fern laughed, too. Then the sisters spontaneously hugged.

The doorbell rang, and Fern jumped. "Oh, that'll be Joe."

Vi rubbed the ache in her thigh as Fern ran to answer the door. The pain was less now, thank the Lord, but she still limped like the devil. She doubted anyone from the Palace in Chicago or from the USO unit would believe it if they saw her now. The graceful dancer she had been was nothing but a memory.

Someday, though, she would find her way back onto a stage. Of that she was sure. Performing was too much a part of her blood for her to abandon it. And the joy in letting herself sing again almost balanced her sorrow at no longer being able to dance.

Though she did have this idea of tap-dancing with a cane . . .

Fern hurried back in, her coat only half-on. "Here. Joe said to give this to you." She held an envelope in her hand. "He said it was marked general delivery, which is why it didn't get delivered earlier, and that he's sorry."

Vi took the envelope, surprised. "Thanks."

"Oh, also"—Fern's face pinkened prettily under her stage makeup—"Joe says I look like a million bucks, so thank you. For everything."

Vi gave her sister a fond if distracted smile. "You're welcome. Now shoo! You don't want to be late on opening night, it's bad luck."

"Fine! I'll go." Her sister blew her a kiss and then turned to leave. She stopped at the door and looked back. "By the way, thank Mrs. Housley for me, will you?"

"Why?" Mrs. Housley was Vi's voice teacher.

"Because your singing is better than ever! The house was so silent after you left. You'll never know how much Mom and Pop missed you. Me, too."

A pang of guilt tugged at her heart. "I missed you, too."

The front door thudded behind Fern and Joe. Finally alone in the parlor, Vi wondered who the letter was from. Not many people knew she was here. Marcie did, of course. She had been the first person Vi had written to after coming home six weeks ago. The exchanges had been terse at first. Marcie had been put out when Vi had told her the real reason for joining the troupe, but it had quickly faded under concern. And then she had blamed herself for not being with Vi when the "assassination attempt" had happened, blame Vi quickly absolved her of.

On the other hand, Vi still hadn't quite forgiven her father for the somewhat inaccurate article that ran in the local papers, touting her as a star of the USO who had been injured in the line of duty. It had not only caused a minor stir but had also made her a war hero of sorts.

He had pushed the altered narrative with the best of intentions, and the article had made it easier for her to reenter Chariton society. Unfortunately, it was also the real reason why she was going to miss

Fern's opening night, despite wanting to go. She had realized her presence might steal some of the spotlight from her sister, and that just wouldn't do.

Vi turned the envelope over. She hoped it was from Marcie with all the details of her friend's upcoming Broadway debut. Something Vi couldn't wait to witness. She was supposed to sit with Marcie's parents.

Except the return address wasn't Marcie's New York one. She frowned in puzzlement. It was from somewhere in Wyoming, and the envelope was addressed simply to Miss Violet Erndt—a common enough misspelling of her last name—via general delivery, Chariton, Iowa. It was from Mr. and Mrs. Joseph Danger.

Confusion and no little worry pricked her as she guessed that these were Ansel's parents. Were they writing to tell her of his death? Or that he was MIA? The war was drawing to a close in Europe. There was a cautious optimism in the country that Hitler might finally be licked, but that didn't mean soldiers weren't still dying. The fighting continued. She had just read this morning in the *Des Moines Register* about the liberation of Bologna, as well as the continuing guerrilla warfare in Italy. It had brought back such vivid memories of Rome and her encounters with Allie and Riccardo, with Enzo and his mother, and that final night with Minta and Sr. Conti. And most of all, it reminded her of Ansel.

The details of his face were so clear, she could almost feel the prickly texture of his five-o'clock shadow under her fingertips. The otherworldly blue of his eyes haunted her, and she had woken up more nights than she cared to recall with her lips tingling from his kiss. Sometimes in town she would spin around, searching for him, sure she had caught a whiff of his aftershave.

And yet she had thrown away whatever chance she had with him. All in the name of doing the right thing, sure. But it was still a regret that tugged at her when she was alone. A regret that would grow a thousandfold should she learn he was gone forever.

Exhaling, she summoned her courage and opened the envelope. No way to know what news it contained without reading it. To her surprise the one-page letter was wrapped around a folded, thinner letter.

Dear Miss Erndt,

The enclosed letter was delivered to us at the same time ours arrived. Somehow they got attached, but rest assured we didn't read very far before we realized the mistake. Hope this reaches you all right. Our son spoke very highly of you in his letter to us.

Sincerely,

Carol and Joseph Danger

Vi's fingers shook slightly as she unfolded the other letter, the one addressed to her.

If only she could remember Ansel's visit to the hospital. If not for Darla, she wouldn't have even known he was there. Her secret hope had been that he'd bared his soul to her and told her he'd fallen in love with her. Her heart had even skipped a beat every time a Red Cross volunteer had come through the ward with mail. Then her hopes had died, bowing to the reality. She had been a fool then, but no more.

And yet he had spoken highly of her to his parents . . .

The letter was written in a scrawling, masculine script.

Dear Violet,

I'm sorry I didn't write before now. There wasn't a whole lot of mail service up . . . well, I can't say where, but you can probably guess. But that didn't mean I wasn't thinking about you or regretting that I never told you how much I've always liked violets, even before I met you. They're tough as nails and yet pretty as a moonlit night in the mountains. So a lot like you.

I came to see you in the hospital, but I don't know if you remember. You were doped up so high on account of the pain, I think you thought I was a ghost. I thought you looked small and fragile, all bandaged up in that bed. I still blame myself that you wound up that way, though I can hear you saying I should forgive myself. And I will, just like I forgave you for not telling me about your life sooner. I won't lie, I was angry, even a bit hurt by that. But none of that matters in the face of you being alive. I thank God every day for that.

Anyway, the good news is that we've got the Germans on the run now. With any luck, they'll throw in the towel before too long. If that turns out to be true, I'd like to stop by and see you on my way home. Would that be okay? A lot of the guys in my unit are from Iowa and told me Chariton isn't that hard to get to. Would that be okay?

I hope you are well.

Sincerely,

Ansel

P.S. I got a field commission, so I'm a lieutenant now, if you can imagine such a thing. Also, if you want to write back, use the address above. It may not find me right away, but eventually the army gets things sorted out.

Vi's eyes filled with tears as she touched the photocopied paper, wishing she held the real McCoy. She could only imagine the ink would have contained some lingering essence of him.

I'd like to stop by and see you . . . She could hardly wrap her head around those incredible words. That he would want to do that, despite knowing all about her past, made her heart ache. There was always the chance they might not feel the same spark as they had in Italy, but she was more than willing to find out.

"Violet, was that Fern who just left?" her mother called from the stairs.

"Yes, and I'm about to take off, too." Vi limped her way to the front hall to fetch her coat.

"Vi," her mother said, appearing in the doorway, an earring in her hands. "It was sweet of you not to take Joe up on his offer tonight. I understand why you're skipping opening night, even if Fern doesn't."

Vi paused and debated whether to play ignorant.

"Once upon a time," her mother continued, not unkindly, "you wouldn't have thought twice about upstaging your sister. You two were always so competitive."

Vi winced, thinking of Robert and how that had turned out. "Yes, well. That little girl grew up. I've learned to share the spotlight."

Her mother smiled a little sadly. "They say war makes men out of boys. I guess it's no surprise it can make women out of girls."

Vi hesitated. "It wasn't just the war, Mom. I met someone." Her fingers gripped the cane as her chest tightened. "Someone wonderful."

"I'm so glad." Her mother stepped forward and cupped Vi's cheek. "It's time you had something good happen in your life."

"I'm sorry I didn't trust you and Daddy. I should've. It was thoughtless, and cruel, and—"

"Shh." Her mother's face softened. "You've done nothing but apologize since you've come home. Enough. Yes, you should have told us. But we have long since forgiven you. As has Fern. As has everyone. All that's left is for you to forgive yourself."

Vi reached up to give her mother's hand a fond squeeze. "Funny, that's the same thing this fellow told me while I was in Italy."

"And I hope you listened to him! He sounds like a very wise person."

"I'm working on it. And he is." Vi bit her lip, sudden emotion welling up inside her.

Her mother smiled. "I hope we get to meet him then."

Vi impulsively hugged her mother. "I love you, Mom."

"I love you, too, my not-so-shy Violet." Her mother's eyes were glossy with tears as she released her. "Now get on out of here before you make my mascara run."

Not one to disobey an order, Vi kissed her mother on the cheek and then quickly let herself out.

As the door closed behind her, she pulled her coat closer to her neck and gazed up into the fading twilight. Stars were starting to glow in the rose-and-purple-streaked sky, and the moon would be rising soon. The same moon that was gazing down on Ansel somewhere tonight. A smile curved her lips. Would she write him? Oh heavens. She would write him pages and pages. He would have no doubt in his mind that she wanted to see him again. She would see to that.

Hope slid through her veins as she limped down the sidewalk, cane clicking on the concrete path. This day might be ending, but a new season was starting. She could feel it in the air.

A hum built in her throat as her cane tapped a rhythm on the sidewalk.

Like spring following winter, it was a time for new beginnings. And oh, was she ready for it.

With Ansel. With her family. With herself.

It was time to let herself sing.

Acknowledgments

As always, thank you to my wonderful editors at Lake Union, Chris and Tiffany, for helping bring out the best in this story. It truly does take a village to raise a book, and I'm so glad you two were there for me. I would also like to thank Tami Richey, beta reader and friend extraordinaire. Without you, I probably would have burned this manuscript long ago—literally, computer and all. For encouraging restraint, my fireplace also thanks you.

A huge shout-out belongs to my critique partner, Lizbeth Selvig, for her last-minute help with revisions. Your advice is always spot-on, and your friendship means the world to me.

Thank you, as well, to my friends in Rome, Alessandra and Riccardo, for fueling my imagination with bottles of wine and tales of missing gold. A humongous thank-you to Deeva Rose, my burlesque instructor. Having the chance to perform burlesque in front of a packed house gave me wonderful insight into Vi's love of the art. It was also a lot of fun!

Finally, I want to thank my children for loving their distracted, disorganized mother. I know my texts didn't always make sense, but you replied anyway. I love you both to the moon and back! And to my beloved husband—what can I say? There are simply no words to describe my love and appreciation of you. Completing this book has been an adventure, but you stayed right by my side, every step of the way. I know I've said it before, but I'll say it again: you are simply the best.

General Book Club
Discussion Questions

1. What was Vi's greatest strength? Her biggest weakness?
2. Which character (or characters) did the most to help Vi become the person she is at the end?
3. Vi gives many reasons for why she ran away from home all those years ago. What do you think was the main one? How does she come to terms with it?
4. The topic of unplanned pregnancies comes up several times in the story, with each of the women taking different paths. How have times changed for women since the 1940s? How have they not?
5. Which characters were the most challenging to like? Did your view of them change by the end of the book?
6. Which character in the book would you most like to meet?
7. What do you think of the book's title? How does it relate to the book's contents? What other title might you choose?
8. What do you think the author's purpose was in writing this book? What ideas was she trying to get across?

9. If you could hear this same story from another character's point of view, who would you choose?
10. Of all the different subjects covered in the book (e.g., WWII, Italy, the USO, burlesque), which ones were familiar to you? What new things did you learn?
11. What aspects of the story could you most relate to?

About the Author

Ellen Lindseth is a graduate of University of Colorado, Boulder, and the Carlson School of Management. She has also studied at the Loft Literary Center (Minneapolis, MN) and is a member of the Women's Fiction Writers Association and the Romance Writers of America (RWA). She is the author of the novel *A Girl Divided*, a 2019 finalist for the RWA's prestigious RITA Award, and "As Time Goes By," a short story chosen for publication in the Midwest Fiction Writers' anthology *Festivals of Love*.

When not writing about resourceful women of the 1940s, she feeds her passion for adventure by flying as a private pilot, researching new experiences (such as performing burlesque onstage for a local fundraiser), and traveling the world with her husband (also a pilot) in search of plot ideas. Currently she calls Minnesota home, where she resides with her husband, two rescued cats, an elderly bearded dragon, and a handful of fish. For more information, visit www.ellenlindseth.com.